THEIR HEARTS BEAT FASTER...

Their gazes met and held. Katherine drew in a breath that was almost a sob. Pressing a trembling hand to her breast, she stood.

"You're here..." Her words trailed off, a mere whisper.

Iain crossed the room, his eyes never breaking contact with hers. She moved toward him as well, slowly, like a sleepwalker. She licked her lips nervously, her hands mindlessly clenching and unclenching. Time seemed to stop. She was drawn to the green of his eyes, the only color in all his darkness.

They met in the center of the room. She reached with trembling hands to touch him. His chest felt solid beneath her fingers. She let out the breath she had been holding. He was real.

He moved, his mouth covering hers, hard and demanding. His arms closed around her. She was soft and yielding. He pulled her tighter into his embrace. Even with the passing of years, she felt right there, as though he had held her through countless nights instead of just one...

EVERYTHING in Its TIME

Dee Davis

JOVE BOOKS, NEW YORK

This is a work of fiction. Names, characters, places, and incidents are
either the product of the author's imagination or are used fictitiously,
and any resemblance to actual persons, living or dead, business
establishments, events, or locales is entirely coincidental.

TIME PASSAGES is a registered trademark of Penguin Putnam Inc.

EVERYTHING IN ITS TIME

A Jove Book / published by arrangement with
the author

PRINTING HISTORY
Jove edition / July 2000

All rights reserved.
Copyright © 2000 by Dee Davis Oberwetter.
This book may not be reproduced in whole or in part,
by mimeograph or any other means, without permission.
For information address: The Berkley Publishing Group,
a division of Penguin Putnam Inc.,
375 Hudson Street, New York, New York 10014.

The Penguin Putnam Inc. World Wide Web site address is
http://www.penguinputnam.com

ISBN: 0-515-12874-0

A JOVE BOOK®
Jove Books are published by The Berkley Publishing Group,
a division of Penguin Putnam Inc.,
375 Hudson Street, New York, New York 10014.
JOVE and the "J" design
are trademarks belonging to Penguin Putnam Inc.

PRINTED IN THE UNITED STATES OF AMERICA

10 9 8 7 6 5 4 3 2 1

To Martha for giving me a chance,
to Barbara for believing in me,
to Julia and Kathleen for listening to me,
to Jim and Paula for reading my manuscripts,
to Lexie and Robert for loving me,
and to my Mevlyn—dreams can come true.

Prologue

KATHERINE STRUGGLED TO consciousness with a sigh. The room was dark except for a soft orange glow emanating from the fireplace. Coals, she thought sleepily. Stretching, she listened for a noise, something that might have awakened her. The room was quiet.

As her eyes adjusted to the darkness, she surveyed her hotel room. It was fairly large, nice in an antiquated sort of way. It had been late when she'd arrived. So late, in fact, that she had hardly noticed her surroundings. Bed had been her first priority. Now awake, she sat up, pulling the covers with her.

Pale moonlight spilled in through the window's archway, making its small diamond panes glitter. The room was certainly charming by moonlight. It danced along the walls creating intricate patterns of light and dark, complimented by the glow coming from the fireplace. She frowned. Surely there hadn't been a fireplace? Instead, she remembered there being a rusty-looking radiator in the corner. Of course, she *had* been exhausted when she'd arrived. Maybe she'd just imagined it.

What she needed right now was a glass of water. Cautiously, she stuck a foot out of the pile of blankets. The room was cold. She glanced at the fireplace and wondered if poking it would revive the dying fire. She'd been a Girl Scout, but that was years ago and besides, she had never really mastered the art of fire making.

With a groan, she left the warm comfort of the bed. The stone floor felt icy under her bare feet. Odd—she would have sworn there was carpeting. Padding over to the fireplace, she grabbed what looked to be a poker and prodded randomly at the glowing coals. They scattered and dimmed slightly. Okay, so she wasn't a fire builder. Giving up, she dropped the poker with a clatter. Where was the bathroom?

There was a large ornately carved door on the adjacent wall that obviously served as the entrance. Rejecting it, Katherine spotted a second door next to the fireplace. It was set into the wall under a stone archway that echoed the style of the larger arch over the window.

With a sleepy yawn, she stepped into the recess, waiting a minute for her eyes to adjust to the deeper shadows of the alcove. She squinted at the door. It was made of heavy wooden planks with iron hinges, a hammered metal ring serving as a doorknob. All in all, it was a heck of a door, especially for a bathroom.

Katherine's sleep-clouded mind struggled again with the vague sense that the room was different from what she remembered. She certainly hadn't noticed this door or its accompanying stone archway. In fact, now that she thought about it, she wasn't sure she remembered the window's being set into an arch either. She frowned. Obviously her exhaustion had dimmed her powers of perception. With a mental shrug, she pushed the heavy door open.

The room beyond was darker than her room. Moonlight seeped around the corners of some sort of drapery hanging from a window. The dim light kept the room

from being pitch black, but still relegated its contents to
deep shadow. She took a hesitant step into the room.
There was carpeting here, at least. Her toes curled into
the warmth. She tried to figure out where she was. She
wasn't in the hallway or the bathroom. Biting her lower
lip, she ran her fingers through her long hair, absently
combing out the tangles. Confused and uncertain, she
wondered if she was dreaming.

Slowly, cautiously, she stepped farther into the room.
If this was indeed a dream, she was safe from harm;
and, dream or not, her curiosity was aroused. She made
out the shape of a bed within the shadows. A bedroom.
In her hurry to sleep, she must have overlooked the connecting door last night. With cautious steps, she crossed
to the foot of the big bed. She reached out to touch a
bedpost, stopping in mid-motion when she heard a noise.
Heart pounding, she looked into the blackness of the bed
itself. Was someone there? It was simply too dark to
see. She strained into the darkness, listening intently.
Silence surrounded her. She let out her breath with a
whoosh and laughed at herself. Of course there was nobody in here. This room must be a part of her own, the
second room in a suite. If not, the adjoining door would
have been locked, wouldn't it? Calmed by the fact, she
moved around to the side of the bed.

"If you're going to invade my chamber, why no' join
me in the bed?"

Katherine froze. The dark voice was warm, like
brandy or whisky. It filled her, caressing her with its
smoky resonance. She peered into the shadows, trying
to find its source. Faltering, she took a step back, her
eyes locking on the dark shape moving within the con-
fines of the bed. Her heart was pounding again.

"Excuse me, I—"

The sound of her voice sent a shiver chasing down
Iain's spine. What manner of bewitchment was this?
He'd seen her for only a moment, illuminated by the
moonlight filtering in from the adjoining room. It had

silvered her long hair and caressed the soft curves of her body. But then she had moved, disappearing into the shadows. He'd thought her a figment of his imagination. The last vestiges of a fantasy. But now she stood by his bed. A living, breathing thing. His body tightened, responding to her nearness, to the sound of her voice. He needed to touch her. To assure himself that this wasn't a dream.

Katherine swallowed and took another step backward, but before she could retreat, he was standing in front of her, his strong arms encircling her waist. She sucked in a breath, inhaling the spicy scent of male. With a start, she realized she was pressed against hard muscle and velvet skin. Even as she thought to be afraid, she felt a curious warmth spreading through her body, an aching, tingling feeling. She looked up, trying to see his face. It was shadowed in darkness, but she could feel the warmth of his breath on her cheek, see the white of his teeth as he smiled. She opened her mouth to speak, but her words died as his mouth found hers. He brushed her lips with his and then tugged softly at her lower lip. She tensed, thinking to push him away, but her body rebelled at the thought, and of their own volition, her lips opened to his kiss. It began as a curious exploration, slow and invading, but as their tongues met, sparks ignited and the kiss deepened.

Iain's arms tightened around her. She was so soft. Her hair felt like silk where it brushed against his skin. Iain had only meant to touch her, to see if she was real. He had wanted to stop her retreat. But the feel of her breasts against his chest had stirred a longing deep within him, a hunger that increased in magnitude as the kiss they shared deepened. His hands, with a will of their own, traced the line of her shoulders and back, reaching down to cup her buttocks and pull her closer against the hardness of his groin. He felt her hands on his face. Then they moved to tangle in his hair.

Katherine pressed even closer to him, a whimper es-

caping from deep in her throat. She felt the hard muscles
of his chest and arms and the harder bulge that pulsed
against her thigh. This was crazy. She should be afraid,
or incensed, or something. Instead she was on fire. She
couldn't get enough of him. Dream lover. The thought
ran through her mind even as she pushed it away.

Iain wanted more. Still kissing her, his hand found the
soft swelling of her breast. He cupped it gently, feeling
it react to his touch. She arched against him. He growled
low in his throat and bent to touch her with his tongue.
He circled the rosy crest through the fabric of her night
shift, feeling the nipple harden into a tiny taut bud. She
moaned, trying to push her breast into his mouth. He
smiled slightly and greedily began to suck, drawing in
more of it. He felt the ache in his groin grow deeper,
hot fire singing through his veins. God's blood, he
needed her—wanted her. Without moving his mouth, he
swung her into his arms and carried her to the bed.

Katherine knew she should move, say something, but
the fire inside her was spreading too fast and the bed
was so cool and soft. In contrast, he was all hardness
and heat. He moved against her, his body touching hers.
She ran her hands down his back, massaging, pressing.
Her heart slammed in her chest. She felt him kissing the
pulse at her throat. Again she wondered what madness
had overtaken her. She felt his hand on the inside of her
thigh, warm and strong. Where was her nightgown? She
struggled to remember. Suddenly, his fingers found her.
All rational thought fled as she rocked with sensation.
Never had she felt like this. She moved against his hand.
He stroked her slowly. She wanted more, but wasn't sure
exactly what it was that she wanted. She felt a long
finger slide deep inside her, moving in and out, in and
out. His mouth again found her breast. She felt wild as
the fire continued to spread and an inner throbbing
seemed to overwhelm all her senses.

Iain struggled to hold on to his control, but she was
so hot, so wet. He wanted her as he had never wanted

a woman before. She was a vision, an angel, *his* angel.
His lips moved back to hers. He kissed her almost savagely. She returned his passion with her mouth and her
hands. He felt her quiver deep inside and knew a moment of deep satisfaction when her body contracted
around his thrusting fingers.

Katherine's thoughts spun out of control. The world
seemed to splinter into color and light. It felt so good.
His fingers were magic. He was taking her higher and
higher. She strained, wanting more. She shuddered with
pleasure and suddenly her body exploded, overwhelming
her. He shifted. His hand was gone, replaced by something bigger and stronger. Instinctively, she moved her
legs apart, wanting more, wanting him.

Iain tangled his hands in her hair. He felt the heat of
her and took a deep breath. He wanted to plunge into her,
deep inside her, feel her surround him. She moved her
legs, shifting to open for him. With a small cry, she
lifted to him. He pushed into her with one strong stroke.
He felt resistance and vaguely wondered at the sensation,
but his need was great and he had to have her. She felt
so tight, surrounding him with her heat. He held still,
deep within her, allowing her to adjust to the feel of
him. He strained with the effort to hold back. Slowly,
he began to move again.

Katherine's eyes were wide, her heart pounding. She
felt him moving deep within her. At first, there had been
pain, but now . . . now it was pain edged with a fierce
pleasure. She began to rock against him, feeling the motion, striving for a rhythm. He pulled away and she cried
out, but just as quickly he was back, deep inside. She
felt the sensations building again, stronger this time. She
met his thrusts with her open, welcoming body and the
fire began to grow again inside her.

Iain felt all control slip away as he climbed higher
and higher, taking her with him in a dance older than
time. He shattered into a million joyous pieces. He felt
her shudders and knew that she, too, had found this mag-

ical place. Tightening his arms around her, he held her, even as she held him, safe in the circle of what must surely be love.

Katherine's eyes flickered opened. She stretched, content in the warmth of the bed. Slowly she turned her head to look at the man sleeping next to her. The room was growing lighter with the hint of the coming dawn. She could make out the hard angles and planes of his face. Even in sleep, his strong features held a certain sensuality. His cheeks and chin were dark with the stubble of his beard. His long hair tangled about his shoulders, shining blue-black, soft and satiny. His arm, thrown possessively around her waist, was powerfully muscled. A scar, puckered and red, ran across his upper arm. Long healed, it was still a reminder of what must have been a painful wound. She could feel the strength and warmth of his thigh against her own. His breathing was even. He slept deeply.

She reached out to touch him, her fingers brushing gently across his cheek. He was incredible. Reluctantly, she pulled back and rolled away, untangling herself from his arms. She stood quietly by the bed, watching him sleep. She knew she should be mortified. She had given herself to a stranger. She ought to feel embarrassed or ashamed, but right now all she could feel was the heat of the magic they had created. Still, her logical mind knew that with dawn the magic would end and the beauty of last night would become tainted by reality. Better to leave now, she thought, and let the memory remain intact, a moment outside of time.

With a sigh, she drank in the sight of him, memorizing his powerful features. The word "warrior" popped into her mind. It was an apt description of the man. Yet she knew that, despite appearances, there was gentleness in his strong hands and in the firm curve of his lips. With a last quick look, she turned to go. Her foot touched the soft silk of her nightgown. She slid it over her head, and resolutely walked to her room. Crawling into bed, she closed her eyes and fell asleep.

Iain sat up, staring at the door connecting his chamber with hers. She was gone. He had pretended to sleep, but it had taken all of his willpower to keep from reaching for her as she moved away. Now, he sat in frustration, staring at the closed door. He wanted her still. He felt his manhood stir and tighten. Remembering the passion of last night, he closed his eyes, savoring the memory. He had been her first.

That was why he had pretended to sleep, allowing her to leave. He had wanted to give her time to adjust to their joining. With a groan, he realized that perhaps he had been wrong. Now was not the time to be apart. Last night had been more than a bedding; it had been a pledge. They belonged to each other as surely as if they were wed. He smiled a little at the turn of his thoughts. He had not considered himself a romantic man. Experience had left him wary and cynical. Suddenly, he knew that he must not lose what he had found last night. He could not let her go.

His mind made up, he rose from the bed and hurried to the connecting door. It swung open on quiet hinges as he strode into the chamber. The light was brighter now, the first pale rays of sunshine washing over the empty bed. He stood there, unable to move. Empty . . . it was empty. He quickly scanned the chamber. Where was she? He tried to pull open the door leading from the chamber into the passageway. It held fast. His brain finally registered the fact that the bar on the inside of the door was firmly locked in place. Frustrated and strangely alarmed, he returned to his chamber. Was it a dream then? His heart slammed painfully in his chest and he felt his body tighten in fear. Surely not. It had felt real. No—it *was* real.

He frantically pulled the bed coverings aside. In the center of the mattress he saw a small brownish stain.

Blood—it must be her blood. She *had* been a maiden. He felt a rush of triumph and an overwhelming sense of tenderness. But the feelings faded as he thought about the bolted door. There was no other way to leave the chamber, and real people didn't disappear into thin air.

With a frustrated gesture, he pushed his hair out of his face. She had to be real. He couldn't begin to believe otherwise. He didn't know where she had gone, but that no longer mattered. He would find her. He had to. In one night, with one act, she had irrevocably become his world. He sat on the bed, running his hands over the mattress, searching for an indentation, traces of her warmth, something that proved she was real. His hand stopped, closing around something small and cold. He held it up, turning it in the strengthening light. It was a stone of some kind, hanging on a small golden circle. The smoky amber crystal glimmered in a shaft of sunlight. He examined it closely. The workmanship was fine. He flicked the fine gold loop with his finger and was surprised when it opened. He smiled with recognition. An earring. Her earring. She was real.

The sunlight danced upon the counterpane as it filtered in through the bedroom window. Katherine woke groggily, turning to shut off the incessant buzzing of her travel alarm. She lay for a moment in sleepy silence. She felt stiff and a little sore and for a moment wondered why. Then, with a rush, memory flooded back. The other room. The stranger. No, she thought, hardly a stranger. She had never known anyone more intimately. She was and always would be a part of him. She had given him something she would never, could never, give again.

She marveled at the realization that she wasn't sorry. She should have been, but she wasn't. Even now, safely ensconced in her own room, she had to admit there was a rightness about it that couldn't be denied. It struck her that she was ashamed of her hasty exit from his room. She owed him and herself more than that. She got out of bed, marched resolutely to the connecting door, and before she had time to chicken out, pushed it open and walked into his room. She stopped, confused. It wasn't his room at all. It wasn't even a bedroom. It was a bathroom, and a small one at that. With a frown, she walked back into her bedroom, forcing herself to take a good look at it.

The window was deep, but the glass was plain and it was definitely not set in an arch. Against the adjacent wall, in the corner, there was a battered wingback chair and a rusty radiator. The plastered wall behind them showed no signs of ever having held a fireplace. The bed was tiny, about the same size as an American twin bed. Katherine sank to the floor, her hands absently closing into the nap of the carpet. *Carpet.* Her head whirled. She looked frantically for another door. There were only two. One she recognized immediately as the door to the hallway, as it sported the expected sheet of paper enumerating check-in and checkout times, along with various other hotel policies. The other, the one she had just opened, was small and unadorned. And it was flush to the wall, not set in an archway.

A dream. It had all been a dream. The most wonderful moment of her life was an illusion. Pain seared through her. No. *Impossible.* It had been so real. She felt bereft, as if someone she loved deeply had died. No. She curled on the floor, tears streaming down her cheeks. No, no, no. She huddled there for what seemed an eternity, until there were no more tears. A dream, all a dream. Her heart still cried no, but her mind, searching for a logical conclusion had already accepted it. There was no other explanation. It had been a dream.

Katherine sucked in a ragged breath and wiped angrily at her tears. She was behaving like a fool: There was no sense in crying over a fantasy. She stood up, automatically beginning to braid her heavy hair. She frowned, instinctively recognizing that something felt wrong. She raised both hands to her ears, checking for her earrings.

One was missing. With a sigh, she headed to the bed to look for it. As she moved to pull back the covers, her nightgown slid off her shoulder, the silky blue fabric dropping almost to her elbow.

With a mumbled curse, she reached for the recalcitrant gown, then stopped short, sinking down onto the bed, staring down at herself. She sucked in a breath and held it. Stunned, her eyes traced the line of her shoulder to the curve of her bare breast. There, on the soft peak, was a small reddish mark, a mark that surely had been left by a lover.

Chapter 1

SCOTLAND, 1467

IAIN MACKINTOSH LOOKED down into the valley. It was narrow, winding its way between rocky cliffs. At its head, almost hidden in the craggy outcrops, sat a fortress. *Duncreag*. From this distance, the stone walls looked silvery white, mere extensions of the rock surrounding them.

"So, at last we come to your holding. 'Tis a verra fine place, Iain. A home a man can be proud of." Ranald Macqueen turned away from the valley and glanced at the men behind him. "But enough looking for now. 'Tis a meal and a bed these men will be wanting. And not on the side of the hill, I'd wager."

"Aye. Let us be off."

A faint trail meandered through the broom and gorse to the valley floor. With a nudge, Iain turned his horse, Sian, toward the path and began the rocky descent. Glancing back over his shoulder, he watched as Ranald began to make his way down the steep embankment, the others following close behind. With a smile, Iain faced forward again, relaxing back into the saddle, allowing his horse to choose the best way down. In no time at all he'd be home.

Two hours later, they were deep in the trees lining the river, the path twisting and turning as they headed for Duncreag.

"Will they have buried your father, do you think?"

"Aye, they'll no' have waited. The message from Auntie Sorcha was o'er a fortnight old when I received it, and we've taken a long time to get here." Iain pulled back on the reins, waiting for his cousin.

Ranald maneuvered his horse so that they rode side by side. "So, that makes you the Mackintosh of Duncreag."

"Aye, I'll be named Laird, and you'll be my captain. What say you to that?"

The corners of Ranald's mouth lifted in a wry grin. " 'Tis a far sight better than my situation at home. Being third son leaves me fit for no' much but the priesthood, and you know well enough that is no' my way."

" 'Tis the truth. I canna see you as a priest, particularly in light of that evening in Inverness."

"You speak of the tavern wench, Morag?"

"Aye, she was a comely woman."

"With eyes for only you at first, if I remember."

"Nay, 'twas always you she was wanting. I was simply a diversion."

"You had but to crook your finger and she would have been yours. But as I recall, your mind and heart were elsewhere. With the fairies, perhaps, or the fey ones?"

"Ach, you know well enough that she was real." Iain reached automatically for the earring hanging from his left earlobe. The cairngorm felt smooth and warm against his fingers.

"I know nothing o' the sort, cousin. Only that you've given your heart to a creature of the mist. And that I've benefited greatly because of it. The fair Morag was mine only because of your preoccupation with a comely lass of your dreams." Ranald smiled at his cousin, his expression thoughtful. "But tavern wenches aside, I think 'tis time for you to consider the maids o' this world. As Laird of Duncreag, 'tis your duty to produce heirs. And to do that, cousin o' mine, you need to marry a lass made of flesh and blood."

Iain looked sharply at his cousin. "I've already met the woman who will bear my sons. If I canna find her, I willna marry. If it means the last of the Mackintoshes of Duncreag, then so be it."

Iain rode ahead. Ranald didn't know when to let well enough alone. He was a good man, but because they'd grown up together, he often thought he was in charge of Iain's life. Iain smiled at that thought. Sometimes Ranald was more like a mother hen than a warrior. Not that he'd share that thought with Ranald. Iain had fostered with his mother's brother—Ranald's father—at Corybrough, and when his mother died, Iain's father had left him there, too caught up in his grief to care about his son. So Ranald was not only his cousin—he was his closest friend.

Still, that didn't give Ranald the right to meddle where he wasn't wanted. Iain knew how daft he sounded, talking about a woman materializing out of thin air, but in his heart, he knew she was real. All he had to do was find her.

As much as he hated to admit it, Ranald was right about one thing. With his father gone, everyone at Duncreag would be pressuring him to marry. As Laird, it was his duty to provide heirs who could lead and protect the clan in the event of his death. Life in the wilds of the mountains was too precarious to take the risk of waiting overly long to produce offspring. But he couldn't imagine settling for anything less than the woman he had fallen in love with eight years ago. She was part of his soul. And even though he knew it was not completely rational, he believed in her existence as

surely as he believed in Duncreag and all that it embod-
ied.

His mind turning away from his fanciful memories,
Iain urged Sian onward, his eyes searching for the first
signs of the pathway that lead up from the river. There
were more pressing matters to deal with—his father's
death topping the list. The message from his aunt had
carried little in the way of information, only that Angus
had died and that Iain must return home at once. When
he had left six years ago, it had never occurred to him
that he'd not see his father alive again.

Spotting the trailhead, he turned Sian and wound his
way through the brush, up the steep embankment. As
they moved away from the nourishment of the river, the
trees played out into the rocky outcrops of the mountains. Above him stood the cliffs that held Duncreag.
This was not the homecoming he had envisioned, but it
still felt good to see the familiar landmarks. It had been
too long.

The rocks narrowed into a natural gorge. The path
veered upward sharply, barely wide enough for a single
horse to pass. Iain looked back at his men. They were
slowing to allow each man to pass single file between
the rocks marking the opening. From there, the pathway
wound around the stony outcrop, gradually climbing up
the mountain. The riders circled upward, following the
twists and turns, approaching the sturdy walls that pro-
tected Duncreag. Finally, coming around the last bend,
they saw the gate tower looming out of the twilight mist.
Iain raised a hand, signaling the men to halt.

"Will they be expecting us, do you think?" Reaching
Iain, Ranald reined in his horse, Beithir.

"Aye, I'll wager they've been watching for our arrival." Iain's gaze rested on the tower, waiting for some
sign of inhabitance. On the battlements, a dark figure
emerged from the gathering gloom.

"Who goes there?" a deep voice bellowed into the
evening shadows.

"Iain Mackintosh, Laird of Duncreag," Iain's answer rang out across the mist.

"And how shall I know ye?" the voice responded, echoing over the rocks as though disembodied from the figure on the tower wall.

"You'll know me, Fergus Mackintosh, because when I was but five summers you tanned my hide for walking the walls o' the battlements and scaring you near to death."

The voice, now filled with amusement, boomed out of the hovering mist again. "Raise the gate, lads, 'tis the Laird."

The great iron gateway groaned as it moved upward, leaving the yett a yawning black hole. Iain moved forward, impatient to be inside now that he was home. As he rode through the archway into the small courtyard, men of all ages and sizes gathered around him. Clansmen. Their roar of welcome was a sound of homecoming, bittersweet though it might be.

"Iain, my boy, welcome home." Fergus Mackintosh moved through the crowd, his wizened old face alight with joy. He extended a hand, and Iain clasped it warmly. " 'Tis a sorry reason to bring you home, but 'tis glad we are to be seeing you."

Iain slid off his horse and embraced the old warrior. His face was lined and his hair white with age, but he was still a big, strong man.

He spoke in a voice meant only for Iain's ears. " 'Tis time you came home. Things are no' right here. Now that you've come maybe you can avenge your puir father."

Iain met Fergus' concerned gaze. "We'll talk of it later. There is much I wish to know, but now isna the time nor the place."

Fergus gave a terse nod. "You'll be needing a place for your men to bed down."

"Aye, they've been long on the road and are looking forward to a good meal and a warm bed."

Fergus raised a hand, and a young man with fiery red hair broke away from the gathering. "Show the Laird's men where they can find a fire and fill their bellies."

"Aye, that I will." The lad hurried forward, coming to a halt when he reached Iain.

"And who might you be?" Iain asked.

The boy grinned. "You willna remember me except as a bairn. My father is Duncan Macgowen, the smith. My mother is Bride Macbain. You taught me to fish when you were a young lad and I naught but a wee bairn."

Iain clapped the young man on the shoulder, recognition dawning. "William, you've grown into a fine man."

The lad blushed a deep red, shuffling his feet in the dust of the courtyard. He raised an arm to motion Iain's men forward. "Come on, then, I'll show you the way."

Leading their horses, the men followed William across the courtyard to the outbuildings that housed the stables and workhouses of the tower. With a shy smile, a pasty-faced man with a slight limp gathered Sian and Beithir's reins and led the horses after the others.

Iain and Ranald walked with Fergus toward the steep, stone stairway that led into Duncreag.

"So, how did my father die?" Iain spoke softly, but with undeniable authority.

Mounting the stone steps, Fergus turned, looking uncomfortable. "I canna say for sure, but I'd say his death was no' natural. They found him at the bottom of a gorge. His neck was broken. They say he fell from his horse. But you and I both know he rode like the wind and knew these mountains like the back of his hand. If you ask me, there's more to it than that."

Iain stopped on the stairs, his brow furrowed. "Fergus, who is this 'they' you speak of?"

"Why, 'tis your auntie Sorcha and Alasdair Davidson."

Iain's frown deepened. "Davidson is here? Why?"

"Aye, he's here. Has been for more than a se'nnight. A guest he is, him and his sister, Ailis. And if you ask me, he's taking advantage of your auntie. She's been o'erwrought with grief, she has, and canna be expected to deal with the likes o' Davidson. He's got her convinced she canna get by without him and his sister here."

"I see." Iain spoke through clenched teeth.

"Who is Alasdair Davidson?" Ranald queried, his glance taking in his cousin's tightening countenance.

"An old acquaintance."

"No' a good one, I'll wager." Ranald looked at Iain, waiting for more.

"Aye, well certainly no' a favorite. He grew up here, more or less. His lands border ours and he fostered here with my father. I dinna really know what happened between them, but soon after I returned from my own fostering, he was sent back to Tùr nan Clach. I was happy to have him gone." Iain shrugged. "There are no open hostilities between us. He pledged loyalty first to my grandfather, Malcolm, and now to my uncle Duncan. As a member of Clan Chattan, he deserves my support. So, as neighbors and clansmen, we have a grudging truce— at best. But I tell you, I have never liked the man. And I've no liking for the fact that he's here now and was present when they found my father."

Fergus nodded in grim satisfaction at the words. He pushed open the heavy wooden door and stood to the side, allowing Iain and Ranald to pass before him. "Welcome home, my Laird." He bent his grizzled old head in faint supplication.

Iain looked at Ranald and suppressed a grin. "After you, cousin."

Iain stood in the entrance passageway to the great hall. It had changed little in six years. Beside him, lining the corridor, were two wooden screens: A gift for his mother from his father, the carvings ornate, formal. At the center of each, curled into the design, was the Mackintosh crest, and below it, the intertwined initials of his parents. He ran a finger along the wood, stopping at a place where the pattern was marred. Squinting down at the screen, he smiled at the childish carving: I. M.—Iain Mackintosh. His father had beaten him to within an inch of his life for defacing his mother's prize possession, but his mother had come to his chamber later and hugged him tight, smiling, her eyes full of tears. "You're part o' this family, too, Iain, never forget that. And it's more than happy I am to have your initials up there with your father's and mine."

"Are you going to stand here all night? I'm freezing my ballocks off here." Ranald's wry comment interrupted Iain's memories and he pulled himself back to the present.

"Come then, for unless I miss my guess, there'll be wine by the fire."

"Aye, that there is, lad." Fergus' craggy face split into a smile.

Ranald rubbed his hands together in delight. "Well then, what are we waiting for?"

Iain stepped from the passage into the great hall. He had forgotten how cavernous it was, much bigger than the one at Corybrough. On the opposite wall, was a huge fireplace crowned with an ornate plaster hood, a newer invention that was meant to guide the smoke from the hall. Above it hung an array of weaponry: A targe hung in the middle, with claymores and smaller swords surrounding it. The weapons of his ancestors.

Near the fire, along one wall, he saw that the great table on the dais was set for the evening meal. Three intricately carved chairs were centered on one side of the table—the biggest belonging to his father. No, he corrected himself, now it belonging to *him*.

He drew in a beleaguered breath, and turned to look at the rest of the room. It was as if time had frozen. There were the benches by the fire, his mother and father's chairs no less ornate than the ones at the table.

Behind the dais, in the window seats, he could see the bright colors of his mother's needlework cushions. Nothing had changed, yet everything was different.

"Iain, at last."

Iain pulled from his reverie to watch a small tired-looking woman emerge from the stairway. She hurried across the rushes, her hands extended in greeting. He frowned, then felt a rush of incredulity. The years had not been kind to his auntie Sorcha. She had aged far more than he would have expected in six years.

"Auntie Sorcha."

She threw her bony arms awkwardly around him and he suffered the embrace for a moment, and then stepped back, breaking free of her hold. Up close it was easy to see that she had been grieving. Her gray hair hung about her shoulders in thin wiry strands. Her eyes were ringed with red, standing out garishly against the pale white of her cheeks. It had never been a pretty face, but sorrow had sharpened it further, carving fine lines along a mouth that seemed to be set in a perpetual grimace.

She began wringing her hands. "I was so afraid that some harm had beset you. It seems an age since I sent the message to you at Moy. If only you could have been here when we laid him to rest. But never you mind. You're home now, and we have our new Laird at last." Her thin lips parted in a ghost of a smile. "And who've you brought with you then?" She turned narrowed eyes to Ranald.

Ranald's eyes were twinkling and he opened his arms wide. "Dinna you recognize me, Auntie Sorcha?"

She studied him, her eyes suddenly widening in recognition. "Ranald Macqueen. As I live and breath, you were just a wee lad when last I saw you." She hugged him with the same enthusiasm she had shown Iain.

" 'Tis true. But you've been away from Corybrough a long time. As I remember it, you were no' planning to make a permanent home here, only to help Uncle Angus through his grief over Auntie Moire's death."

"Aye, but Angus never fully recovered from my sister's death. I felt 'twas my duty to stay on. He needed me." She flushed slightly, stepping back, and hurriedly changed the subject. "But look at you now, a mon grown and with the look of your mother, I do believe."

"Aye, 'tis often said I favor her," Ranald said, his amused gaze meeting Iain's.

Ranald in fact was the spitting image of his father, but it was no secret that there was no love lost between Sorcha Macqueen and her brother Dougall. Iain grinned back at his cousin.

Sorcha pushed a lank strand of hair behind her ear. "How is Dougall? I've no' heard from my brother in ages. Is he still playing at being the Laird o' the manor?"

"He's fine and sends his regards," said Ranald, his eyebrows crooking upward with his amusement.

Iain bit back a laugh. Uncle Dougall had certainly sent no such greeting. In fact, he rarely mentioned his older sister at all. Dougall had always preferred Iain's mother, Moire.

"Are you planning to return to Corybrough now that Uncle Angus is gone?" Ranald asked Sorcha pointedly.

"Nay, I canna leave now. With Angus' death, there is more need than ever for my presence here." She turned to look at Iain, reaching with bony fingers to clutch at his sleeve. "Puir boy. With the death of your father you'll be needing your auntie, won't you?"

Iain opened his mouth to assure her that he could survive without her, but the sound of voices on the stairwell stopped him. Bodies materialized from the gloom of the alcove to go with the voices and Iain felt a wave of revulsion wash through him.

Alasdair Davidson was fine of bone, with the sleek look of a mountain cat. His brown hair curled tightly around his head. He held the arm of a tiny woman with hair the color of pale moonlight. She glanced nervously at the group in the center of the hall, and stopped walking. Alasdair followed her gaze, and his thin lips curved into the semblance of a smile. But there was no warmth at all in his pale blue eyes. Iain watched him tighten his grip on the woman's arm and pull her forward.

His aunt crossed to meet the pair as they made their way across the great hall. "Alasdair, there you are. Come greet Iain. He has just this minute arrived from Moy."

Iain took in Alasdair's cold unwelcoming stare and was reminded of another homecoming long ago, when they had been just boys. Sorcha placed a hand on Alasdair's arm, drawing him forward. "Iain, you remember Alasdair Davidson? He has been of great comfort to me. I've no idea what I would have done without him. He was with me when we found your father." Her voice trailed off and she glanced at Alasdair, nervously. Alasdair ignored her, his eyes still locked on Iain.

"Mackintosh." Alasdair inclined his head, then crossed the remaining distance between them. "I'm sorry about Angus." A brief flicker of emotion crested in his pale eyes, but, with a blink, it was eliminated, leaving only icy emptiness in its wake.

There was an awkward silence as Iain's gaze held Alasdair's, the two of them sizing each other up. Iain found nothing in this older Alasdair to alter his opinion of the man.

"Iain," Sorcha said, interrupting his thoughts. "I dinna believe you've met Alasdair's sister, Ailis." She ushered the girl forward. "She's been so helpful. I dinna know how I would have been able to handle everything without her."

Ailis blushed becomingly. "It was nothing."

"Ailis is quite skillful at managing a household." Alasdair took his sister's elbow, propelling her closer to Iain. "She has run Tùr nan Clach since my mother's death, first for my father and now for me."

Iain took the young woman's hand and bent his head over it, in a gesture of respect. " 'Tis a pleasure," He straightened and released her hand, turning to his cousin. "Allow me to introduce my cousin, Ranald Macqueen.

Ranald, may I present Ailis Davidson and her brother, Alasdair."

Ranald nodded briefly at Alasdair, then shifted his gaze to Ailis. " 'Tis honored I am to make your acquaintance, Ailis." Smiling, he, too, took her hand, but rather than bowing over it, raised it to his lips, lingering over her soft skin.

Ailis smiled shyly at Ranald, the hint of a dimple creasing her cheek. "The pleasure is mine." Their eyes met and held.

Iain shook his head, wondering how exactly his cousin managed to completely disarm every female he met.

With an annoyed harrumph, Alasdair stepped between the two of them, his attention focused on Ranald. "Ranald Macqueen of Corybrough?" Alasdair stroked his chin thoughtfully. "Your father is Dougall?"

"Aye, 'tis my father." Ranald spoke dismissively and turned back to Ailis. She blushed and ducked her head.

Alasdair frowned and continued to speak, ignoring Ranald's snub. "I met him once. I got the impression he is held in high esteem by those who know him."

Forced to acknowledge the compliment, Ranald pulled away from Ailis, returning his full attention to Alasdair. "He is a good man. I'm afraid he hasna mentioned you."

Alasdair shrugged. "I doubt he would remember me. I was naught but a boy."

"Well, the next time I'm at Corybrough, I'll be sure to tell him you were asking about him." Ranald's voice was clipped, bordering on rude. Alasdair narrowed his eyes, glaring at Iain's cousin.

Sorcha intervened, laying a hand on Ranald's arm. "Allow me to show you to your chamber. I'm sure you'd like to clean up a wee bit before our evening meal." She smiled up at him, but Iain could see that her grip on Ranald's arm was lethal.

"Fergus," she fixed her stare on the old warrior,

"please see that our guests are served some wine. And tell Flora we'll hold the meal for the Laird." She shifted her attention to Iain, still intent it seemed on issuing orders. "Iain, you know the way to your chamber of course. I ordered a bath brought in when I heard you'd arrived. The lasses have cleaned and aired your chamber. 'Tis ready and waiting for you." She threw a quick look at Alasdair. "You'll excuse us?"

Alasdair nodded absently.

With a wink at Ailis and a last amused glance at Iain, Ranald allowed himself to be led away.

Fergus waved at the benches in front of the fireplace, inviting them all to sit. "Have a seat. When Sorcha starts directing," he said fondly, " 'tis best to follow orders." The older man offered Ailis his arm.

Alasdair fixed Iain with his pale gaze. "Are you coming?"

Iain shook his head. He'd had enough of Alasdair and company. What he needed was the bath Sorcha had mentioned. "Nay, it seems, I, too, have my orders. I'll see you at dinner."

"Yes, by all means go and refresh yourself." Alasdair said, gesturing dismissively. "When you return, you and my sister can take time to get to know each other better." He smiled, but not even a hint of good humor reached his eyes.

"I'll look forward to it," Iain lied, wanting only to escape. "And, Davidson, I'll have a word with you later. I've several questions to ask you about my father's death." There was no mistaking the command in his voice.

Alasdair tipped his head mockingly. "Of course."

Iain spun around and walked into the work chamber, heading for stairs that led to the family's private chambers. He took the stone steps two at a time, wondering what in hell Alasdair Davidson was really up to.

• • •

Closing the door to his chamber, Iain welcomed the silence with relief. The wooden tub in front of the fireplace beckoned. He strode across the chamber and quickly disrobed. Sinking onto the small stool in the tub, he groaned appreciatively. The warm water lapped around his travel-worn body, soothing his aching muscles. He leaned back and let the pain of his homecoming surround him.

Dead. Angus Mackintosh was dead.

There had been no great bond between father and son. Angus had loved Iain's mother, Moire, with a passion that left little room for others. And when she had died— had it really been eighteen years ago?—when she had died, a part of his father had died, too. Iain had been fostering at Corybrough when it happened. He could still remember the smell of the peat fire as he sat with his uncle Dougall and heard the news. And not just a mother dead, but a little sister as well. A child his parents had so long waited for—Moire to have the daughter she yearned for, and Angus wanting only to please his beloved wife.

He'd come home immediately, but had found no comfort waiting there. His father had been sullen and silent, with little use for a young, grieving boy. It was then that Auntie Sorcha had come. Her presence had helped the household run smoothly, but nothing and no one could reach Angus in his grief. Never a warm and caring father, Angus withdrew even more from the son who reminded him so much of his beloved Moire. He had soon sent Iain back to Corybrough, and there, Iain had found solace with his grandfather Revan.

How different things might have been if Moire had lived. Iain's memories of her had faded with time, but he could still hear her laughter, a glorious bubbling sound like small bells ringing in the wind. She had been the center of their world, and without her he and his father had drifted apart. Still, Iain had loved his father. And he knew that in his own way Angus had loved him.

He clenched his fist, slamming it against his knee. Rage swelled as he considered the possibility that Angus' death had not been an accident. His mind simply could not accept the idea that his father had been thrown from his horse. In the morning he'd question Sorcha and Alasdair thoroughly. Since they'd found the body, there were questions only they could answer.

He frowned, thinking of Alasdair Davidson. It wasn't that he had any solid reason to dislike Alasdair. He'd done nothing to offend. In fact, in many ways it was just the opposite—he seemed almost fawning at times. Iain just didn't trust him. He never had, even when they were boys. Especially when they were boys. The few times Iain had come home, Alasdair had always been there, radiating resentment, as though Iain were an unwelcome intruder rather than the son of the house. Iain had been relieved when Angus had sent the boy home.

Iain shrugged and smiled ruefully to himself. Alasdair was harmless enough, no more than annoying, really. The worst threat from Alasdair was matrimonial in nature. Obviously, Alasdair thought the new Laird of Duncreag needed a wife. And, of course, he saw a perfect candidate in his sister. What was the girl's name? Iain frowned in concentration. Ah yes, Ailis. Pretty thing. A bit timid, though. He supposed that with a stretch of the imagination it was a good match, for Ailis at least. He shook his head wearily. He was not going to marry some milk-faced lass just because he needed an heir.

He brushed his hair from his face, and in so doing touched the tiny stone dangling below his ear. How he wished *she* were here to help him in his grief, to hold him. He closed his eyes, remembering the magical night he'd spent with her, here in this very room. If he married at all, it would be when she returned. *If* she returned. He grimaced. God's blood, he didn't even know her name. Relaxing in the warm water, he could almost feel her hands on his body. He felt like a madman, living in dreams. Yet the feel of her was so real, he could almost

see her. With a sudden start, he sat up and opened his
eyes. Reacting on instinct, he jumped from the tub, naked, dripping water. In one swift movement he crossed
the room and was through the archway into the connecting chamber. It was empty. Always, it was empty.
Feeling foolish and strangely let down, Iain turned to go
back to his chamber.

Ranald stood in the doorway, a puzzled expression on
his face. "What, may I ask, are you doing?"

Iain grimaced and mumbled, "I thought she was here."
He pushed past Ranald and began to towel off with a
large square of woven plaid.

"Thought who was here? Your fairy woman? Iain,
have you lost all sense?"

"I'll no' speak of it now, Ranald. What are *you* doing
here?"

Ranald wisely accepted the change of subject. "I came
to hurry you, man—I'm fair starving to death." He
clutched his belly in mock agony and grinned at Iain.

Iain pulled his long saffron shirt over his head and
wrapped his plaid tightly around his waist, belting it in
place. He pulled the remaining end over his shoulder
and fastened it with a large silver brooch. The brooch
had been a gift from his father and was shaped into the
crest of the Mackintoshes, a salient cat. He cherished it
almost as much as he did his earring. Finishing the lacings on his boots, he straightened and slapped Ranald
on the back.

"Lead on then, cousin. I would hate to lose you to
starvation." Both grinning, they left the chamber.

In the corner of the room a small flicker of light shim-
mered and, unnoticed, disappeared.

Chapter 2

KATHERINE STOOD ON the stone floor looking at the man in the wooden tub. His eyes were closed, his body tense, lines of grief etching his face. Her heart yearned to reach out to him. Crossing to the tub, she attempted to touch him, but though she was able to caress the essence of him, her hand passed right through the vision. Tears of frustration filled her eyes.

With the movement of her hand, the man sat up suddenly, his green eyes alight with guarded excitement. He leapt from the tub. Her pulse quickened as she stared at the magnificence of him. He was all hard muscle and sinewy strength. She longed for him with an emotional pain so deep it was almost physical.

He strode from the chamber into the adjoining room. He stopped, frantically searching for something, someone. As quickly as it had come, the hope faded from his eyes. Katherine tried to call out to him. But just as she struggled to find her voice, another man entered the room, not two feet from where she stood.

He was as tall as the first man, but huskier in build. His hair was a reddish brown, long and curled slightly at the ends. She felt as if she should know him, did know him, but the memory stayed just beyond her grasp.

"What, may I ask, are you doing?" the new man said to the other. His accent was sharp and she had to strain to understand. Gaelic. He was speaking Gaelic. Her mind struggled to translate.

Her warrior grimaced and mumbled, "I thought she was here."

She followed the two men to the other room.

"Thought who was here? Your fairy woman? Iain, have you lost all sense?"

Katherine froze. Iain. His name was Iain. Her heart began to beat faster as the rest of the words sunk in. They were talking about her. He remembered. He still remembered. She looked at Iain. He was toweling himself off with some sort of fabric square.

"I'll no' speak of it now."

The men continued talking, but Katherine was too overwhelmed to translate. The look of agony and pain had returned to Iain's face, and wanting to ease his sorrow, she moved toward him as he dressed. She noticed his clothes and tried to put them in context with a time, but her brain refused to concentrate on anything but Iain. As she watched, he began to wind a length of plaid material around his waist, finally fastening it with a silver brooch that was shaped like a cat. He finished lacing his boots and straightened, still talking to the other man, who he called Ranald.

It was then she noticed the small earring. Her heart leapt into her throat. Her earring—he was wearing her earring. She reached out to touch it, but her hand passed through the stone as if it had no substance.

Iain slapped Ranald on the back and they walked from the room. Katherine tried to follow, but as soon as Iain was out of sight, she saw the walls begin to shimmer and fade.

•   •   •

Katherine struggled through the mist of the dream into the warm morning sunlight. She sat up, her heart pounding, searching for remnants of the dream, of another time. But her bedroom was peacefully drenched in the daylight of the twentieth century with no wooden tub, no arched doorways, no dark warrior. A dream . . . it had only been a dream. Running a hand over her face, Katherine tried to banish the last lingering traces, to place them firmly into the realm of fantasy. But, as always, some part of her, deep in her subconscious, held tight to the memory, to him.

Iain. She remembered his name.

The dreams were definitely coming more frequently. And this one was stronger, closer to reality. Katherine tried hard to remember the others. But except for the first one, they remained foggy, always just out of reach, brief glimpses into another world, his world. She swallowed, her breath still coming in shallow gasps. Her fingers closed around the small smooth stone hanging between her breasts. The cairngorm earring. She was seldom without it. For eight years now she had worn it as some sort of secret talisman, a connection to a fantasy.

She shivered as she remembered another detail from the dream. He had been wearing the other earring, the mate. Her mate. She belonged with him. Her heart knew it, as surely as she knew her own name. Her body tightened at the thought. With a rush, she was filled with a need so strong it rocked her. She had to go to him.

But as quickly as the urge surrounded her, her rational mind laughed mockingly. Go where? To whom? That was the essence of her problem. She seemed to be forever bound to a man who didn't exist, a dream man. And most frightening of all, she loved this man, Iain. Loved him with a passion so strong and so deep that even the rational knowledge that he was merely a figment of her imagination couldn't sever the bond. Oh God, she must be crazy.

Resolutely squaring her shoulders, Katherine threw off the blankets and padded to the bathroom. She turned on the shower taps and began to shrug off her sweat-soaked nightgown as she waited for the water to heat. Turning to check the water, she caught a glimpse of herself in the mirror and was not surprised to see deep shadows underscoring the gray of her eyes. Like the others, this dream had left her exhausted. With a sigh, she stepped into the tub, welcoming the sting of the shower.

She wasn't sure how long she stood there, letting the water cleanse her, restore her. But finally, her mind found the answer it had been seeking. She stepped out of the shower, rubbing herself vigorously with an over-sized towel. Then donning her robe, she emerged from the bathroom, wholly refreshed and with a plan. A crazy plan, true, but then this whole thing was crazy, so it fit right in.

Her mind made up, she crossed to the phone. Picking up the receiver, she dialed quickly before she could talk herself into a more sensible course of action.

"Caldwell Travel." The voice on the other line was cool and professional.

"Vickie? Katherine St. Claire here. I'd like to book a flight to Edinburgh, with a connecting train to Inverness. Oh, and I'll need a rental car there. And I'd like reservations at a castle hotel. It's called Duncreag."

"You're late." Elaine Macqueen's voice was filled with tolerant laughter.

"I know." Katherine twisted to slip between two restaurant tables, smiling ruefully at her friend. "But then, I'm always late. So, at least it's not a surprise."

"True."

The restaurant was crowded. It was part of a chain, dark and decorated with what looked like antique buyers' rejects. Katherine stifled a sigh. Personally, she would have preferred somewhere with fewer people and more windows. But it was Elaine's favorite place and

Katherine was more than willing to meet her friend wherever she wanted.

"Sit down." Elaine motioned to a chair adjacent to hers. "How is the world of academia?"

Katherine gave her friend a quick hug and dropped into the chair. "Nothing to complain about. The usual freshman excuses and end-of-term restlessness. I'll be glad when I've paid my dues and can start teaching more upper-level classes." Propping her elbows on the table, she leaned forward and fixed Elaine with a mock-serious stare. "How is my favorite legal eagle? Still saving the good guys from the scum of the earth?"

Elaine rolled her eyes. "Just another day in the life of an assistant D.A. Seriously though we are working on a tough case. The trial is about to start. So, it's me and the library and late hours, I'm afraid. Since I knew you'd be late, I ordered for us. I hope you don't mind."

"Not at all. What am I having?"

"A Caesar salad, what else? Honestly, Katherine, you are too much a creature of habit."

As if on cue, a harried-looking waitress appeared. "Here you are, a Caesar and a club sandwich. Anything else?" They shook their heads almost simultaneously, and with a brief grimace passing for a smile, the woman turned to take orders at a table full of boisterous young men.

Katherine toyed with her salad. "So, tell me, how's life in the grown-up world? I've forgotten what it's like not to be surrounded by hormone-driven nineteen-year-olds."

Elaine laughed, tossing back auburn curls. "A wee bit jealous, are we?"

Katherine smiled. Elaine had lived in the U.S. for the last fifteen years, but her Scottish burr was still discernible. Katherine loved it almost as much as she loved Elaine.

"No, I like what I do, especially my research. It's just that at this time of year I get a bit overloaded. Thank goodness I'm not teaching summer sessions."

"So what are you going to do, spend three months in moldy archives somewhere digging up obscure bits of medieval social history?" Elaine rolled her eyes, then delicately began eating her sandwich with fork and knife.

"You make eating a sandwich a formal affair. It's a sandwich for a purpose, Elaine. You know, ease of eating it? And no, I am not spending the summer in a moldy library crypt. I'm taking a trip." She smiled, waiting for her friend's response.

It did not disappoint. Elaine dropped her fork and raised her hands in exaggerated surprise. "You're going somewhere? The woman whose patterns are so set she can't even find her way to a new restaurant? Surely you jest."

"Nope. As a matter of fact, I'm off to explore your old haunts."

"Well, since my haunts have been yours for the last eight years, I can only assume you mean the bonny Highlands." Although her smile was still teasing, her tawny eyes deepened to take on a slightly worried look. "You're having dreams again."

There were no secrets between them. Katherine still remembered the night when, emboldened by a few glasses of wine, she had found the courage to tell Elaine about her dream. It had been soon after they'd first met, when Katherine had just started graduate school and Elaine was in law school. Elaine hadn't laughed. She'd listened carefully, asking questions, analyzing, even then, in an attorney-like fashion, neither believing nor disbelieving, just accepting. And when the other dreams had started Katherine had shared those, too, with her friend.

"Yes, and they're getting stronger, clearer somehow." Katherine twirled her fork absently, chewing on the inside of her lip.

Elaine reached across the table and covered Katherine's fidgeting hand, fork and all. "You're going to Duncreag."

It wasn't a question, but Katherine answered anyway. "Yes. It's time I face the fact that this probably is nothing more than romantic fiction. Duncreag is just an old castle—no magic, no nothing. I need to accept once and for all that these dreams are just that: dreams. Then maybe they'll stop and I can get on with my life."

Elaine's grip on her hand tightened. "And what if they aren't just dreams? Are you ready for that?"

"What are you saying, that I might go there and be whisked off to some magical place and be reintroduced to the man of my dreams, literally?"

"I don't know. My legal mind says, no way. My Highland heritage says, why not? There are lots of things out there we don't understand, Katherine. Obviously, real or not, you have developed quite a bond with this man. So much so that he keeps you from finding someone here in the, quote, real world."

Katherine felt the color rush to her cheeks. "Don't start that again. You know I'd like a relationship. It's just that I can't find the right man."

"You can't find *him*."

"Iain." Katherine looked intently at her salad. "His name is Iain."

"What? How do you know that?"

"I heard it."

Elaine's grip tightened further, threatening to cut off the blood supply to Katherine's fingers. Katherine pulled her hand away, then rubbed it gingerly with her other hand.

"Sorry," Elaine grimaced, "I guess I don't know my own strength. I also didn't know you could hear things in the dreams."

"I haven't until now, except that first time. In the others it's always been more like watching a movie through a gauzy curtain. You know, sensations washing over me, but still kind of hazy. Last night, though, it was like the

curtain had been lifted and I could see and hear everything clearly. And, more important, I remember."

Elaine sat back in the chair, her elbows balanced on
the arms, her fingers laced together under her chin.
"What exactly do you remember?"

"Well, Iain was in a wooden bathtub in front of a
fireplace. He looked so tired, Elaine, like he was in great
pain. The grief was almost palpable. Anyway, without
boring you with all the details, he was looking for me,
I think. I mean, he must have sensed me, because he got
up and ran into the other room. The one from the first
dream."

Elaine grinned. "That must have been quite a picture."

Katherine blushed and smiled. "It was. Anyway, right
after that another man came into the room and started
talking to Iain. Ranald, his name was Ranald. The amazing thing is that I could hear them, Elaine. I could understand them. I think they were speaking Gaelic. I
studied it a little in grad school, in order to be able to
understand old manuscripts, but I definitely had trouble
translating it as spoken words."

"I'm not surprised. You and Jeff spoke it some with
your grandmother though, didn't you?"

"Yeah. She really wanted us to learn it, but that was
a long time ago."

"What else do you remember about the dream?"

"Well, when Iain got dressed"—Katherine stared intently at the lettuce on her fork, a red stain heating her
cheeks once more—"he put on a *leinechroich*. You
know, the large saffron-colored shirt the Scots wore?"

Elaine raised one delicate eyebrow. "You're dreaming
in color then?"

Katherine continued, completely ignoring Elaine's
sarcasm. "Yes, yes, in color. And he wrapped himself
in a plaid of sorts. I think they were called *feileadh mor*,
but I'm really not sure. The two were worn together, so
perhaps it had another name." She paused, trying to puzzle out the answer.

"Listen, my overeducated friend, I know you fancy yourself a medieval expert and you've the degrees to prove it, but couldn't you just stick to the good bits?"

"What?" Katherine jerked out of her reverie. "I'm sorry. Where was I?"

"He was getting dressed."

"Right. Well, this is the important part. He turned to fasten a cat brooch of some kind to his plaid, and when he did, his hair swung back and I noticed the earring. He was wearing my earring. You know, the cairngorm one I lost, the night of the first dream?" She held up her necklace, waving the stone to emphasize her point. "He remembers. Elaine, I swear it, he remembers."

Katherine closed her eyes, a wave of longing surging through her. She shook her head and opened her eyes. "Anyway, shortly after that he and this Ranald left, and I tried to follow, but I couldn't. The room just faded, and I woke up in my bed, in the twentieth century. Elaine, all I wanted was to close my eyes and be back there, with him. So I called Vickie Caldwell and made my plans. I keep trying to tell myself that I'm only going so that I can put an end to this. But I can't deny that I feel this urge to go. Something deep inside me wants to be there. I know it isn't rational, but I want so desperately for him to be real."

"I know you do. You always have. That's why you never let any other men get close to you. You've already given your heart away."

"Yeah, to a figment of my imagination. Very rational move."

Elaine pushed her plate away and leaned across the table to touch Katherine's cheek. "Look, I have no idea what you'll find when you go to Duncreag, but I think you're doing the right thing. I just wish I could be there with you. I don't like to think of you going through this all alone."

Katherine smiled. "Well actually, I won't be alone. Jeff is joining me, at least for a while."

Elaine brightened. "Good. I'll sleep better knowing he's with you." She paused, flicking at a nonexistent speck on her sleeve. "So, I take it that means he's still in London? Has he decided to marry the English girl, then? What was her name? Patience?"

Katherine's grin widened at her friend's feigned casualness. Elaine had been half in love with her brother for years. "It's Prudence. And I don't think it's serious. He didn't mention her at all when I called. But he did ask about you."

"Oh?"

"Yes. Shall I give him a message from you when I see him?"

Katherine noted with pleasure the stain that was now spreading across her friend's face.

"No, um, yes, well. . . . tell him I said hello and that we'll all get together and lift a pint when you get home."

Katherine reached for the check the waitress had just slapped down on the table. "You know, for an incredibly gifted attorney you are positively dotty when it comes to my brother."

"Let me get it." Elaine reached to pull the bill from her grasp.

"No, you always do. I may work in academia, but I'm not destitute. Let it be my treat this time." Katherine pulled the white ticket out of range, grabbing bills from her wallet with her other hand.

Accepting defeat, Elaine sat back. "When do you leave?"

"Tomorrow. No sense in postponing the inevitable."

"I suppose not. You'll call me when you're safely there?" Elaine pushed back her chair, gathered her briefcase and purse, and stood up to go.

Katherine rose, too, leaving the check and money on the corner of the table. "Sure, and if you're really good I might let you talk to my brother."

Elaine made a fist and mockingly swung at Katherine. They began threading their way through the crowded restaurant, pausing at the door. "Seriously," Elaine said, "if you need me I'll be as close as the nearest phone."

They hugged. Katherine suddenly had a sinking feeling that this could be a permanent good-bye. Shrugging it off, she joked, "I'll hold you to that pint. And I even promise to bring Jeff."

Elaine smiled. "Take care of yourself."

"I will."

Katherine watched until Elaine turned the corner. Then, taking a deep breath, she swung around in the opposite direction, walking quickly. She still had to pack.

Tomorrow, come what may, the adventure would begin.

Chapter 3

THE AFTERNOON WAS gray, the mountainside cloaked in mist. Iain stood on the cliff edge, Alasdair and Ranald at his side, and looked into the gorge below. His belly tightened as he thought of his father's fall.

"This is the place, then?" Iain looked at Alasdair, who was still staring intently at the rocks far below them.

"Aye, we found him down there." Alasdair moved to the edge and pointed at a pile of rocks and debris. "We came from the south. There." Again he pointed.

Iain looked back to the bottom of the gorge. The gorse and broom took on shadowy proportions in the misty gloom. He could almost see his father lying there, his body broken and twisted.

" 'Tis a long way to fall. I'd wish it on no man." Ranald placed a large hand on his shoulder.

"Aye, 'tis." Iain shook his head, trying to clear the vision of his fallen sire. "Tell me, Davidson, how it was you came to be a part of the search party?"

Alasdair's eyes narrowed and he walked away as if refusing to answer, but in a moment his voice came floating across the small clearing.

"I'd been summoned to Duncreag to meet with your father. In his usual manner, he had no' sent word as to why I was being called, just that I should report to Duncreag with all haste. I arrived in the morning, early, thinking to get the business, whate'er it was, o'er and done before the noontime meal. But when I arrived your father was no' there. He hadn't been seen since early in the morning the day before. It seemed odd to me that he wasna present when he himself had summoned me. So I spoke of it to Sorcha. She, too, thought it strange."

Iain met Alasdair's gaze and then turned away, again looking into the misty gorge.

Alasdair continued. "It was she who ordered the search. I felt, under the circumstances, the least I could do was stay and help."

"Ah, the helpful neighbor." Iain didn't look up, just continued to stare into the mist.

"We may no' be the best o' friends, man, but I wouldna wish this upon you or your kin. Of course I offered to help."

"What happened next?" He watched the man from the corner of his eye.

Alasdair paced along the edge of the ledge. "We split into several groups, each going in a different direction. I dinna think any of us really expected to find anything amiss. I wasna o'erworried. I assumed something had occurred that required Angus' attention. It wasna odd for him to ride out alone—Iain, you know that well. But Sorcha was so worried." He shrugged and stopped his pacing to look at the two men.

Ranald and Iain exchanged a glance, aqua eyes meeting green, before turning their attention back to Alasdair.

"How many were with you?"

"Around ten men, I'd say, and Sorcha, of course. The weather was much like this—misty and cold. We rode in the fog for most of the day. In fact, we'd finally decided to head back to Duncreag when we came to this gorge."

"And you found him." Iain eyed Alasdair intently, a muscle working in his jaw.

"Nay, no' at first. In fact we might no' have seen him at all if it hadna been for the wee beast up here. When it heard our horses it nickered a welcome. We followed the sound, and once we saw the horse we knew Angus wouldna be far." Alasdair paused, slowly drawing in a breath as if the memory pained him.

"I found him, curled around those rocks as if he were taking a nap. I canna say how long he'd been like that. But in view of the horse standing up here and the fact that his neck appeared to be broken, we decided he'd been thrown. After that it seemed best to get him back to Duncreag as quickly as possible. So we sent two men ahead to call in the others and I wrapped him in his plaid and laid him on his horse. Sorcha was no' well. She was near broken with grief. So I left your father to one of the men and rode with her."

"And you just stayed on at Duncreag," Iain remarked dryly.

"Nay, I took my leave shortly after we returned with the body. It was a day or so later that a messenger arrived at Tùr nan Clach. Your aunt was asking for me. I thought it best to come at once. I brought Ailis with me, thinking that another woman would be a comfort to her."

"I see." Iain moved away from the edge of the gorge across to where Sian waited. He pulled himself easily up into the saddle. "I want to see the bottom of the gorge."

Alasdair walked over to stand beside the horse. He looked up at Iain. "If you've no more questions, I'll go back now. I've no liking for the mist, and certainly no' in this place."

"Suit yourself." Iain turned his horse, ready to go. Ranald was already moving down the rocky slope.

"I always do."

Iain turned back to look at Alasdair through narrowed eyes, struggling to keep the disgust out of his voice. "I'll

see you back at Duncreag." The words held the ring of
a dismissal.

Alasdair gave a short mocking bow and climbed onto
his horse. Iain swung Sian back around, heading down
the narrow path leading from the promontory. The man
was vile. But right now he had more important things
to think about. Like what had happened to his father.

At the bottom of the gorge, they dismounted and Iain
strode over to the place where his father had been found.
The ground was littered with debris. It seemed Angus
had brought part of the rocky ledge with him when he
fell. Iain squatted down and studied the area, not knowing where to start.

The morning had not brought answers. He had spoken
with Sorcha just after dawn. Her tale matched Alasdair's, except that hers lacked detail. And he had spoken
with some of the other men. Their stories, too, were the
same. Still, even after talking with Alasdair, Iain was
not any clearer about what had happened.

That his father had fallen he accepted as fact. But how
had he fallen? Iain could not bring himself to believe
the story that Angus' horse had thrown him. It was not
impossible, of course, but it was highly unlikely. And
why, by the Saints, would his father have brought a
horse up here? He had climbed the rise many times with
his father, but always they had left the horses below.
The climb could be a treacherous one, and Iain had only
allowed the horses today to see if it was, in fact, as
dangerous as he had remembered. So why the horse?
There was no conceivable reason. Unless Angus had
been running from someone. Iain shook his head, trying
to see it all clearly. Something was amiss here, but what?

"Do you believe him, then?"

Iain, startled from his thoughts, looked at Ranald in
confusion. "Who?"

"Alasdair."

Iain paused to consider, rubbing a hand along the side of his jaw. "Aye, I do."

Ranald frowned, studying his cousin's face. "But you dinna believe Uncle Angus was thrown from his horse."

Iain picked up a rock and threw it across the clearing, his stomach churning. He knew his father was too skilled a horseman to be thrown from his horse—not without help anyway. "Nay, I dinna."

"Then I guess we will have to figure out what did happen."

Iain nodded, grateful for his cousin's support. He threw another rock and then rose to his feet, abandoning his search for clues; there was something more important he had to find. He began moving methodically around the clearing, his eyes scanning the ground.

"What are you looking for?" Ranald stared at the rock-strewn dirt.

Iain turned to look at his cousin. "My father's dirk."

"What?" Ranald's brows drew together in confusion.

"His dirk, 'tis missing. I asked Sorcha about it and she said he wasna wearing it when they found him. I thought it might have dropped when he fell." Iain pushed his hair out of his face with an impatient hand, his shoulders tightening with frustration.

"I'll help you look." Ranald squatted down and began to sift through a pile of fallen rock.

"Nay, 'tis good of you to offer, but I dinna believe it is here."

"You think someone took it? Maybe the man who killed him?"

As usual Ranald had read his thoughts. "I truly dinna know. But 'tis a question I'd like to see answered." Iain turned to Sian, reaching for the reins. "I've seen enough for now. Let's go. 'Tis still a good ride back to Duncreag."

Ranald nodded and swung into the saddle. "I'm right behind you."

• • •

Iain and Ranald sat with Fergus in the great hall, by the fire. They talked in lowered voices, casting glances around the empty hall from time to time.

"I tell you, Fergus, I've no call to doubt Alasdair. Have you been to the gorge?" Iain took a long drink from his pewter cup and eyed the old man over the rim.

"Aye, I went the next day. And I saw much as you did. But I still canna believe Angus Mackintosh was thrown from his horse." Fergus leaned close to the other two men, his voice lowering further. "And I'll tell you this: Your father didn't mention any meeting with Alasdair Davidson to me." He sat back with grim satisfaction, his eyes glowering below his bushy white eyebrows.

Iain slammed his tankard down on the edge of the bench. "What are you saying, old man?"

"I'm saying that I dinna believe there was a meeting. If Angus summoned him I would have known."

Iain nodded, understanding. Fergus had stood as Angus' captain for many years. There were no secrets between them. If there had been a meeting, Fergus would have known about it.

"Maybe he hadn't the time to tell you." Ranald put in, staring into the fire, obviously deep in thought.

Fergus drank deeply from his tankard and wiped the foam from his mouth with his sleeve. He sat back and pulled at his beard thoughtfully. "Perhaps." He turned to Iain. "Any luck finding the dirk?"

"Nay, Auntie Sorcha had no' seen it. And it wasna at the gorge. We looked. You're certain it wasn't on the body?"

Fergus fixed him with a fierce stare. "I told you it wasna."

"Could he have left it behind, do you think?" Ranald asked.

"Nay," Iain and Fergus answered as one.

Ranald cocked his head to one side, his brows lifted in puzzlement.

"Angus ne'er went anywhere without the dirk. It was a gift from his father. His prized possession," Fergus said, then stood and went to stir the fire. "I remember when he got it. He was so proud. Malcolm Mackintosh was a hard man. And Angus, being the youngest, was always trying to win his praise." Fergus settled back down on the bench.

"We were little more than boys at the time," he went on, "learning the ways o' men. We were out hunting. There were six of us: Angus, his brothers Duncan and Lachlan, Malcolm, my father Reginald and me. We had been out most o' the day, with little luck. Suddenly, Angus pulled back from the others. He dropped off his horse and motioned for us to stop. We were just lads and had no reason to think anyone would listen to us, but something in his movement made them stop. He cocked his head to the left, and I strained to see what he saw. There in the gathering mist was the biggest stag I'd ever seen. Angus knelt quietly, drew his bow, and strung an arrow. His shot was swift and true. The stag fell where he stood. It was magnificent."

Fergus shook his head, pulling away from his memories. "Anyway, being just a lad, he had no dirk to skin the beast. So Malcolm pulled his from its sheath and gave it to his son. It was a beautiful piece, the hilt wrought from gold. Angus took it, and when he was finished he tried to give it back. But Malcolm told him to keep it. 'You're a mon now,' he said, 'and a mon needs a dirk.' After that, I never saw Angus without it. Never."

"So you're thinking someone took it then?" Ranald asked.

"Aye." Iain ran a hand through his hair and exhaled in frustration.

Fergus laid a hand on Iain's knee. "I say ye find the mon who had the dirk and we'll have an idea, then, what happened on that ledge." With that he rose and stretched with a yawn. "I'm no' getting any younger, and I tell you an old mon needs his rest. We'll talk more on the morrow."

"Sleep well, Fergus."

Iain watched as the old man ambled across the great hall and out the doorway. He had quarters in the gate tower and slept there, probably with one eye open.

Iain turned back to the fire, certain that his desperation showed in his face. Sainted Mary, he wished that his cousin had the answers they so badly needed. He searched Ranald's face, their gazes locking. His heart sank.

"Iain, we may never know the truth of it. You have to accept that." There was compassion in Ranald's voice.

"Aye, I know. But I canna give up without at least trying to make sense of it."

"At least try and let it go until the morning then."

Iain nodded and then, with a sigh, drained the rest of his ale. He stared into the fire for a long moment, lost in reverie, the flames dancing in wild abandon. Finally, he pulled his thoughts back to the present and rose, turning to face his cousin again. "Thank you for being here, my friend. It makes it easier."

Ranald smiled. "I wouldna be anywhere else."

The room was dark. There was still a faint glow from the fireplace, but even it had conceded to the night. Iain paced restlessly, unable to sleep. Finally, with a sigh, he crossed the room, tugged open the door, and entered the adjoining chamber. He waited a moment until his eyes adjusted to the gloom of the shadow-shrouded chamber. He moved to the window and sat with his back to the wall. And waited. Waited for a dream. Waited for her.

All those years ago, she had appeared out of nowhere and irrevocably changed his life. She had filled an empty part of him that could now be filled by no other. Never since had he felt that kind of passion. Even thinking of it now, he felt his loins stir. He had not been chaste. But the couplings he had had over the past eight years had been just that: couplings, base fulfillment of a driving physical need, nothing more.

The first year afterward he had searched for her, looking for her in every woman, every face. Later, he had accepted the fact that she must have come by some magic. Something he could not understand. Yet, far from making him less determined to find her, the realization only made him more certain that he must have her, that their union had indeed been special. Somewhere deep in the recesses of his heart, he was certain she would return. And so, he guarded his heart and kept vigil through countless nights of waiting, wanting.

He leaned his head against the cold stones and closed his eyes. Perhaps tonight she would come. Perhaps tonight.

Chapter 4

"I'M GLAD I talked you into this." Katherine twisted, trying to settle more comfortably into the passenger seat of the rental car. It felt funny to be sitting on the left and not driving, like a Disneyland ride. Finally, finding a comfortable spot, she leaned back and closed her eyes.

"I was glad when you called. I needed a break from the architectural project I've been working on. You gave me a good excuse." Jeff glanced over at his sister. "I've been hearing about Duncreag since we were kids. Now I'll finally be able to put a picture with the stories."

"Stories?" She opened her eyes and looked at her brother.

"Yeah, Gram's and yours. You know, the lonely lady and the ravished virgin." Jeff darted another glance at Katherine. She wrinkled her nose in a grimace.

"Come on Kitty, you have to admit it all sounds a little hokey. First there's Gram telling us about this woman who lived in Scotland centuries ago. Forced to marry a man she didn't love and always pining for the one she did. Wearing a pair of earrings in his memory and then passing them down through the centuries.

Right. And then, right after college, Gram sends you off to Scotland, to Duncreag, in fact, and you come home spouting a tale of metamorphosing rooms and midnight lovers."

Katherine was silent, refusing to be goaded by her brother's words. They weren't covering new territory. Gram had regaled both of them with countless stories from Scotland, particularly clan legends and family history. Katherine had always loved the story about the lady and her lost love. Remembering the old story, she stared out the window absently fingering the cairngorm on its fine gold chain. She thought it was incredibly romantic that the lady in question had stayed true to her love, in her heart if not in her life. And the idea that she passed the cairngorms down to her female descendants as a tribute to him, practically under her husband's nose, appealed to her.

Jeff, on the other hand, thought it was all bunk. He also quite openly thought she was crazy to keep harboring hopes about what he called her "Fantasy Man."

She smiled at the thought of Iain, her mind turning to her summer in Scotland. It had been a dream come true, a wonderful graduation gift, first the trip from Gram and then the cairngorms. Just before she left, Gram had given her the small wood and gold box containing the earrings. Gram had smiled and said something about it being Katherine's turn.

Katherine closed her eyes, trying to recall the exact words Gram had used. She could see Gram standing at the airline gate, reaching out to brush back her granddaughter's hair and lightly touch one of the earrings. She could almost hear Gram's voice: "My darling, it's your turn now. Go and find your destiny. It waits for you in Scotland, at Duncreag." Now, the words sounded almost prophetic, but at the time they'd washed over her, simply a part of the magic surrounding the whole trip.

Scotland had indeed been waiting for her with open arms. Everyone on the tour had been so warm and friendly, welcoming her into the group. She had loved every minute of it. But most of all she had loved Duncreag. It had been so much more than she'd ever imagined. She had felt a connection there, a kinship. And then she had had the dream. Even now, so many years later, her body tingled at just the thought of it, awakening with pleasure. It was at Duncreag that she had been changed forever.

She had told Gram and Jeff about the dream, all of it. Gram had smiled and said something about Highland magic and holding on to your dreams. Jeff had laughed and asked her if she was feeling all right.

Jeff cleared his throat, interrupting her thoughts, bringing her back from her memories to the present. "Kitty, you have to admit that you *are* somewhat obsessed with Fantasy Man."

His use of her nickname took the sting out of the comment. He had called her Kitty since they were kids. It had started out as a taunt, "Kitty Kat," but had gradually become an endearment, a bond between a sister and brother who found themselves alone in the world at a very young age.

Katherine had been eight and Jeff eleven when their parents had been killed in a car wreck. Theirs had been a close family, and the loss was devastating to them both. They had lost not only their family, but their home as well. The apartment in New York had been sold and they had had to leave an entire life behind. Gram had taken them in, bringing them to her hometown in Connecticut. It hadn't been a bad place—in fact, it had been lovely, just so very different from the hustle and bustle of Manhattan. Caught deep in the memory of those painful years, Katherine pulled her braid over her shoulder and twirled the end of it absently.

"Hey, are you even listening to me?"

Katherine smiled at her brother. "Oh, yeah. I hear you loud and clear. But if you're so sure I'm a nutcase, why are you here with me?"

"Hey, I figured you could use someone with a level head on this little adventure." Jeff grinned and then looked back at the road, his expression turning serious. "Honestly, sweetheart, I'm glad you're doing this. It's time you put these dreams behind you. You need to accept them for what they are. Fantasy. You can't move forward until you do that. You've made these dreams into some kind of alternate reality, and because of that you've given your heart away to a dream lover."

"You're making me sound unstable. Besides, who says for sure it was a dream? There *was* the lost earring. I looked everywhere in that room for it and it wasn't there."

Jeff reached over with his left hand and patted Katherine's knee. "Look, Kitty, for your sake I wish it were real. But how could it have been? There was no other room connecting with yours and there weren't any other guests at the hotel except the ones in your tour group. And you've said yourself that they were all elderly or happily married, hardly the type to seduce young women."

"I wasn't that young and I wasn't seduced. It was mutual. My choice. So let's not talk about it anymore, okay?" She smiled crookedly at him, trying to soften her words.

Jeff ran a hand through his fair hair, leaving it all akimbo. "Look, Kitty, I'm not trying to make you angry. I'm just worried about you. This dream thing has been going on too long. It's not natural to give part of yourself away to a fantasy man."

Katherine twirled the end of her braid. "I can take care of myself, Jeff. I've been doing it since we were kids."

He burst into laughter. "Well that may be true enough but you have to admit you are a bit susceptible to what others want you to do."

"What do you mean?" Katherine watched her brother's eyes crinkle with amusement.

"Actually, I was thinking of you with marbles up your nose. Remember when I dared you to do it?"

"You said I wasn't talented enough to do it, but that if I did, I'd be famous. Boy, was I a sucker."

"You said it . . ." He shrugged, still laughing.

"I didn't think it was funny. It took the pediatrician an hour to get them all out. And I swear sometimes I think there's still one up there somewhere." Katherine grinned. "So, since *I* don't have a love life, why don't you tell me about yours? How's Prudence?"

"History. She was way too interested in becoming Mrs. Jeffrey St. Claire. So there's no love life. Tell me what else is new since I left. How are all those budding young minds?"

"Fine, although I was just telling Elaine that sometimes I get tired of living in a world filled only with nineteen-year-olds."

"How is Elaine?"

"She's good, up to her eyeballs in some big case. Murder and mayhem—she loves it."

"Is she seeing anyone?" Jeff asked, a bit too casually. Katherine smiled. Maybe her brother wasn't immune to her friend's charms after all.

"Oh, the usual assortment of men. I don't think anyone seriously. Why? You interested?"

Jeff answered her with a frown and slowed the car. He turned off the main road onto a narrow lane marked by a sign that read "Duncreag." "That's got to be the smallest sign I've ever seen. I know the Scots are a private bunch, but from the size of that sign I'd say they didn't want their guests to find them at all."

Katherine looked down the small road with anticipation. They had been winding along the River Findhorn, but now were moving up and away from it. The trees began to thin and suddenly, as they rounded a curve, she caught her first sight of Duncreag. She audibly sucked in her breath.

Jeff stopped the car and they sat in silence. The fortress rose out of what seemed to be solid rock, towering above them. A wall, or what was left of it, circled around and out of sight.

"Wow." Jeff turned to look at Katherine. "Kitty, are you all right?"

Katherine slowly wrenched her eyes away. "I'm fine. Really. It just surprised me. It's overwhelming, isn't it?"

There was no way to put into words what she was feeling. The sight of Duncreag made her feel joyous and terrified all at once. There was a feeling of homecoming, a sense of rightness. But there was also a sense of loss and sadness. It was overwhelming. And there was no way to describe it to Jeff, no way at all.

Jeff hit the accelerator and the car moved forward again. As they drove into a thick stand of trees, Duncreag disappeared from view. They were circling the great rocky promontory now, gradually drawing closer to the hotel.

"It must have been a real challenge to get here without a road and a car." Jeff peered out the window as he drove, looking at the steep rocky cliffs on either side.

"It was. There was a hidden cleft between some rocks. It was the only way in. You wouldn't have even seen it if you didn't know it was there." Katherine stopped. Where had that come from?

"How did you know that?" He glanced sideways in surprise, the look on his face just short of incredulous.

"I don't know. Maybe I read it in a guidebook or someone told me the last time I was here. Look, there's the gate tower. Or rather, what's left of it."

The road narrowed to pass between two broken sections of the wall. On one side, the remnants of what could have been a tower stretched up and over the road. They passed under it, into what had once been a courtyard. There was a sign that said "Car Park," the arrow pointing at the remains of the west wall.

"I guess we follow the sign." Jeff looked at Katherine,

but she hardly noticed. She was absorbed in the building in front of them. It rose four stories high, with a crenellated edge surrounding a high pointed roof.

"Are those the battlements?" She pointed, looking over at her brother.

Jeff nodded, his eyes trained on the structure before them, his architect's mind clearly itching to explore.

The tower was rectangular and obviously old. There was a second wing jutting away to the east. Katherine frowned. It didn't look right somehow, didn't mesh with her memory of the tower. "Jeff, is that a later addition?"

"I'll say, and not a very good one. It can't be older than, say, seventy-five years or so. It's modern in comparison to the older structure. The tower is definitely medieval."

"Early fifteenth century." Okay, where had that come from? She wasn't an expert at dating castles. But she knew. She definitely knew. The question was how?

Jeff's eyebrows rose inquiringly. "I thought *I* was the architect in this family."

Katherine smiled ruefully as they pulled into a parking space beside another fragment of wall. There was no way to explain something to Jeff she couldn't explain to herself. Better to change the subject. "How come it's called a tower and not a castle?"

He looked at her suspiciously to see if she was teasing him, and then apparently decided she genuinely wanted an answer. "It's semantics, really. Tower houses are, in fact, the early Scottish equivalent of a castle. Here in the Highlands there wasn't as much need to defend against a long siege. So all the outer accoutrements, like baileys and outer walls, weren't as necessary. It was much more important to have an impenetrable fortress. So, the tower house came into being. This one, like most of them, is actually a blend of styles, not counting the twentieth-century addition." He cringed. "I'd say that part was remuddling, not remodeling."

Katherine laughed and they climbed from the car,

stretching their legs and enjoying the fresh mountain air.

She took a deep breath. "Well, this is it. The moment of truth, so to speak. Shall we go in?"

Jeff grinned, reaching for her hand. "Actually, I can't wait. This place is amazing."

They walked along a stone pathway between carefully planted beds of flowers and herbs. As they made their way toward the entrance, Katherine scrutinized the eastern wall. There wasn't much left of it, and what there was almost abutted the new wing.

Without warning the view shifted, and instead of the flowers and cobbled pathway, Katherine saw smoke rising from a wooden building braced against the stone wall. Farther to the right she saw the corner of another wooden structure. It, too, was built flush to the wall. Then just as quickly as they had appeared, the buildings abruptly vanished, and she stood again in the ruined courtyard. She drew in a shaky breath and chided herself for letting her overactive imagination get the best of her again. She had come here to cure herself of these fantasies, not to have more of them.

"Hey, come over here and look at this."

Pulling herself out of her reverie, she hurried to follow Jeff to the front of the hotel.

"I don't think this was original," he said, intently examining the heavy wooden door. "The hinges are new and the wood looks to be only a few years old."

Katherine stopped beside him. "There wasn't even a door here originally. The entrance was over on the east side, and there was a steep stone staircase climbing to the second floor. The only entrance to this level was from inside the tower. The rooms down here were for storage and a place for more kinsmen to sleep."

Jeff stopped his examination of the door and instead fixed his intent gaze on Katherine. "Boy, that was some tourist guide you read. I had no idea you had any interest in medieval architecture; I thought your tastes ran more

toward medieval society. You know, what they ate and
wore and sang, stuff like that."

Katherine made a face at her brother and playfully
tapped him on the arm with a fist. "Well, where they
lived is part of all that, isn't it?" She actually had no
idea how she knew so much about Duncreag. It seemed
to be coming to her from out of nowhere, but she didn't
want to tell Jeff that. She shrugged mentally. Tower
houses were similar and she had studied them some.
Besides, she'd been here before. No telling what information she had picked up then.

"I feel like there should be a bell pull or something.
Do you think we just go in?" Jeff lifted a hesitant hand
to the imposing door.

"I guess so." She placed her hand on the door alongside Jeff's, and together they pushed. The heavy door
swung open. Inside it was cool and dark. They stepped
in and waited for their eyes to adjust to the interior
gloom as the door closed behind them.

"Well, it's glad I am to see you. I was just telling Mr.
Abernathy that perhaps we should be sending someone
down to the road to look for you."

The voice floated merrily out of the shadows. Katherine peered into the room and saw an ancient battered
desk in a corner, with a small plump woman behind it.
She moved around the desk, fairly bustling with efficiency. She had a sweater draped around her shoulders
and wore a serviceable tweed skirt. Her iron gray hair
was cut short, but it still curled with unruly abandon all
around her face, making her look a bit like an angel in
overdrive.

"You must be the St. Claires. We were thinking you'd
be here by noontime. Come in, come in. I'm Agnes Abernathy." Agnes moved closer and grasped Katherine's
hands in hers. "Welcome to Duncreag. You'll be Katherine, I'm guessing." Still holding Katherine's hands,
she turned toward Jeff. "And you'll no doubt be the

brother. Jeffrey, isn't it? Come now into the parlor with you. You'll be wanting a cup of tea."

Feeling a bit overwhelmed, Katherine shot a look at Jeff and allowed herself to be shooed down a hallway into a small parlor. The room was cozy, the peat fire burning brightly, and she sank into an overstuffed chair, suddenly grateful to be finished traveling. Jeff followed her, moving to stand by the fireplace.

"You both just sit and relax. I won't be a moment." With that Mrs. Abernathy bustled out of the room.

Jeff crossed the parlor and sat down opposite Katherine. "Well, that was something. Do you think she breathes?"

She laughed. "Probably not. Unless I miss my guess, I'd say we'll be well taken care of while we're here."

At the sound of clanking china, Katherine's mouth watered and she realized she was hungry. As if on cue, Mrs. Abernathy walked back into the room balancing a tea tray in one hand and a basket in the other. Jeff jumped up to help her.

"Thank you, young man, but I believe I can manage. If you'll just scoot those magazines to the side of the wee table there, I'll put this down and we can have a nice cuppa." She deftly placed the tray on the table and then followed it with the basket. She pulled up a third chair from the corner by the fireplace and sat down.

"Well now, how was your trip? Did you drive from Inverness? You're lucky to have had the weather hold. I expect there will be rain before the evening is over."

She turned expectantly to Jeff, whose mouth was already full of freshly buttered scone. He looked hopefully at Katherine. She smiled and reached for the cup Mrs. Abernathy was handing her.

"Thanks." She took a cautious sip of the scalding brew. "It was a lovely drive. I'm sorry we're late. We kept stopping along the way to enjoy the scenery."

Mrs. Abernathy passed a bowl of jam to Jeff. "Oh my, yes. It is pretty up here, especially this time of year.

The broom is fading a little now, but still blooming, and the rhododendrons are just hitting their full beauty. Aye, it's lovely along the river, it is. I'm glad you had the time to enjoy it."

"Mrs. Abernathy?"

She cocked her head as if to listen better.

Katherine smiled. "How did you know it was us?"

"Oh, that was easy. We weren't expecting anyone else this afternoon. And you two look so much alike it made it easy to be certain. You simply had to be the brother and sister we were waiting for."

Katherine glanced at her brother, still in the throes of scone ecstasy. She supposed they did look alike. They both had thick blond hair, although hers was a deeper gold. And she would admit that their faces were shaped similarly. But her brother was far more handsome. With his brilliant blue eyes and his tall, rugged physique, he turned heads wherever he went.

She was definitely the less showy of the two. Her eyes were a quiet gray and she tended toward jeans and tee shirts, not the kind of gear that made people stand up and notice her. Still, overall, she guessed people would identify them as siblings.

Katherine stifled a yawn and settled back into her chair. Jeff and Mrs. Abernathy were deep in conversation. She closed her eyes and let their voices wash over her.

"What brings you to Scotland, Jeffrey?"

"We grew up hearing stories about Duncreag and this area. I wanted to see the real thing." Jeff saw no point in regaling their hostess with Katherine's tall tales. He glanced at his sister. She was curled up in the chair with her eyes closed.

He turned back to Mrs. Abernathy. "Who were the original owners?" Jeff asked, sipping his tea.

"Well, let's see. A clan of Mackintoshes built the tower. Not the ones that are over at Moy Hall—they're

the heads of Clan Chattan, you know. These Mackintoshes were a lesser clan; I think a third son or something like that. Anyway, they built the tower in the early
part of the fifteenth century. But they didn't hold it long.
The builder had a son, I believe, but he died and there
were no other offspring.

She picked up her cup. "So the lands were awarded
to my family. And Duncreag has been in our hands ever
since. I'm a Dow, don't you know, from over Corrievorrie way. When my Jamie and I married, we never
dreamed we'd be living here. But life works in funny
ways, and all of my kin seem to have died out. So, I'm
the last and Duncreag has passed to me. My uncle, who
had it before me, turned it into the hotel. And I will say
Jamie and I have enjoyed being here, although it's a bit
much for the two of us to handle. However, the good
Lord didn't bless us with children, so we enjoy all the
people coming and going. Makes life less empty, if you
know what I mean." Mrs. Abernathy paused to draw a
breath and a take a sip of tea.

Jeff used the break to jump back into the conversation.
"Our grandmother was from Dalmigavie originally. She
was a Davis."

Agnes pursed her lips and frowned in concentration.
"Seems I do remember a family by that name in Dalmigavie. It's not far from Corrievorrie, you know. Hmm,
what was her name?"

"Mary. Mary Davis Higgens. She left Scotland right
after World War Two. My grandfather was a Yank sta-
tioned in England. She met him through the war effort
and wound up going back to Connecticut with him." Jeff
reached for another scone.

"Yes, a lot of the girls met young men during the war.
I wasn't old enough for that. Not that I ever had eyes
for anyone but Jamie Abernathy. Where is she now?"

"I'm afraid she's gone. She died a few years ago."

"Oh, I'm sorry."

"No, its okay. It's been awhile now. We miss her, but

we're used to her being gone. Aren't we, Kitty?"

Startled from her light sleep, Katherine blinked, trying to focus on what Jeff was saying. "What? I'm sorry, I wasn't listening."

"Obviously. I was telling Mrs. Abernathy"—Jeff gave their hostess one of his hundred-watt charm-the-women smiles and then turned back to Katherine—"that we grew up hearing stories about Duncreag from Gram. I was just telling her that we miss her still."

Katherine nodded. "Very much."

"And your grandfather? Is he dead, too?"

"Yes. He died just before I was born. Jeff, you remember him, don't you?"

"A little." Jeff wiped buttery crumbs from his chin and sat back with a contented sigh. "Mrs. Abernathy, that was delicious."

"Well, you certainly know how to make a lady feel good. But listen to me carrying on. You must be tired and ready for a wee wash. Sit right here and I'll get keys for you." She jumped to her feet, striding briskly away from them toward the desk in the other room. In minutes she was back, keys in hand.

"You're both in the tower. Katherine, you're on the second floor, and Jeffrey, you're just above her on the third. You'll remember that we start with a ground floor here. I think you Americans call the ground floor the first, so don't let it confuse you. Anyway, I put you in the room you requested, Katherine." She tilted her head, her face alight with curiosity.

"I stayed here once before and thought it would be fun to stay in the same room." Katherine looked down at her shoes, rocking back and forth in the chair.

"You were here at Duncreag? I would think with a head of hair as beautiful as yours I'd remember you. When was it you were here then?"

"Eight years ago."

"Ah, that explains it. We took over this place seven years back. You were here when my uncle still ran the place." She looked over to Jeff. "You weren't with her, then?"

Jeff stood, holding out his hand to take a key. "No, I wish I could have been." He flashed a grin at Katherine. "Seems I usually miss all the excitement. But this time I am here, and I'm really looking forward to a bit of exploring."

"Ah, then we'll work especially hard to see that you feel welcome." She handed Katherine a key and brushed her hands together as if ending the whole matter. "Now off with you, lambs. Dinner is at half seven in the great hall just above you. I'm afraid we've no lift. The stairs are in the alcove just behind you." She gathered the tea things, and before Katherine could rise from her chair, she was gone.

"I feel a little like Alice down the rabbit hole. Do you think she was surprised that I had been here before?"

Jeff swung an arm around his sister. "I doubt that anything fazes Mrs. Abernathy. Let's go up and see what the rooms are like. I'll bring our luggage up later."

"You'd best hurry or no doubt Agnes will have poor Jamie doing it. I can't wait to meet him. I'm picturing John Cleese in *Fawlty Towers*."

Katherine sat on the end of the bed and looked around the room. It was much as she remembered it. The walls were plastered and painted a pale peach. The carpet was nondescript, somewhere between cream and beige. The radiator sported a new coat of paint and the wingback chair was covered in a Laura Ashley print, a slipcover, probably. The bathroom was small but serviceable. The window perpendicular from the bed was set into the wall and contained a small window seat. The seat had a cushion covered in the same fabric as the chair. All in all it was basically as she remembered, a comfortable room. And one that bore no resemblance to the room in her dream. She sighed, a knock at the door interrupting her thoughts.

"Come in."

Jeff stumbled into the room laden with suitcases. He extracted two from under his arm and deposited them in front of the radiator. "Hey, not bad. Does it look the same?"

Katherine ran a hand along her braid, then pulled it over her shoulder. "Pretty much. A few touches here and there. But I'd say it's basically the same. How's your room?"

"Bigger than this. It's one floor up. Unfortunately, it comes with the world's shortest bed." He looked down at his long legs and then back at Katherine with a wry grin. "I doubt that I'll fit into it comfortably."

"Well, it can't be any worse than camping out in that little tent of yours. You'll adjust."

"Probably. Look, I want to get this stuff stowed away before dinner. So, shall I meet you down there in thirty minutes?"

"Sure." Katherine sat absently twirling the end of her braid.

Jeff watched her for a minute. "Hey, are you okay?" he finally asked.

"Yeah. Why?" She shot him a questioning look.

"Nothing really. It's just that you always twirl your braid when you're nervous or upset about something."

"I'm fine."

Jeff shrugged. "Do you think we need to dress for dinner here?"

Katherine dropped her braid and stretched out on the bed. "Yeah, probably a little. But you don't have to break out a tux. I'll see you in half an hour."

Jeff turned to the door, still lugging his bag. He smiled at Katherine over his shoulder. "It's going to be all right. Now that we're here those dreams of yours will soon be history."

Katherine watched the door close and then turned to look out the window. Tears filled her eyes. The problem was, she didn't want the dreams to be history. She wanted the dreams to be real.

Chapter 5

"BUT YOU'VE ONLY just arrived." Sorcha shielded her eyes with one hand as she stood in the courtyard.

Iain regarded her dispassionately. She'd been hovering ever since he'd arrived. It was both touching and annoying. "I've a need to see my land, woman. We'll be gone no more than a se'nnight, probably less. Fergus will be here to see to your protection." He bent to examine Sian's forelegs and hooves.

"And who'll be protecting you, I'd like to know?" Sorcha shifted to stand with both hands fisted on her hips.

Iain looked up at her, still holding the horse's leg. "I'm no' a wee boy, Auntie Sorcha. I can take care of myself. Besides, I'll have Ranald with me. And a man couldna ask for a better companion." Iain rose, turning to check his saddle. "Dinna fash yourself. There is little chance of harm befalling us. And if it does, I've no doubt we'll o'ercome it."

He exchanged a glance with Ranald while tightening Sian's girth. "It willna be the first time we've found ourselves forced to depend on each other, aye?"

Ranald nodded and grinned. "Aye, a little excitement is just what I'm needing. Something to stir the blood and keep me from going soft."

"Humph." Sorcha eyed them both with a mixture of exasperation and concern. "Well, you'll be needing food for the journey." With a shrug, she called to a large red-faced woman coming down the entrance steps. "Flora, see what you can find from the kitchen for the Laird. And mind that it's fresh."

The woman stopped and, like Sorcha, moved her hand to shield her eyes from the sun. She bobbed in a sort of curtsy. "I'll no' be but just a moment." She hurried back the way she had come.

Sorcha tipped her head up, squinting at Iain. "You'll be taking some of the men as well?"

"Aye, a few. But I'll leave the main body here to stand in protection of Duncreag." He paused in his preparations and eyed Sorcha curiously. What was the old woman up to now? "You sound as if you expect something to happen. Are you no' telling me all you know?"

"Nay, there's naught to tell. 'Tis only that we've just gotten you home. I hate to see you gone again." Sorcha licked her thin lips nervously. "We've only just lost your puir father. The people need time to adjust to a new laird and 'tis a hard thing to do when that Laird is off gallivanting around the countryside."

"Enough, woman. I'm the Laird and I'll go as I please and no' be mollycoddled by the likes o' you." Iain swung up into the saddle.

Sorcha trotted to his side, her bony hand clutching his arm. "Be careful. That's all I'm asking." Her gaze held Iain's for a moment.

He covered her hand with his, wishing he could read the message in her dark eyes. "Have no fear for me, Auntie."

Flora appeared at Sorcha's elbow, a large sack in

hand. "Here ye are. Oats fer yer parritch and some bread and cheese."

She reached up, handing the sack to Iain, her ruddy face growing even redder when he smiled at her. "God go with ye."

Iain nodded and urged Sian forward, watching as his men rode toward the tower gate. He turned once, looking behind him and was surprised to see Alasdair gripping Sorcha's arm, his usually unreadable face mottled with anger.

As he moved to ride back, his aunt jerked away, her shrill voice carrying across the courtyard. "I'll see you in hell, Alasdair Davidson, afore that happens."

Iain smiled, turning his horse back toward the gate. Sorcha obviously had things well in hand. He sighed. Hopefully, she'd keep watch over Alasdair until they returned. Truth be told, he didn't trust the man. But perhaps, in Sorcha, Alasdair had met his match.

"There's a wee loch a bit ahead. I'd say 'tis as good a place as any to stay the night." Iain turned in his saddle to look back at Ranald.

"Aye, I'm ready for a bit of a rest. 'Tis a large holding you have here. I thought perhaps you intended on my seeing it all in one day." Ranald pulled up to ride abreast of Iain. "Tell me, cousin, have you given any thought at all to the fair Ailis?"

Iain looked out over the rocky crag. "Nay, should I have?"

"Well, you're no' getting any younger and she is a comely thing. You can't marry a fantasy, you know. And I suspect there are worse fates than having that sweet young maid in your bed."

Iain studied Ranald's face. "Maybe I should be asking if *you've* been thinking of . . . what did you call her? 'Fair Ailis'?"

"Aye, well, a man would have to be blind no' to notice her. Her hair is so pale it's almost white. And you have to admit she is fair of face."

"True enough. But I'll no' marry her."

Ranald shrugged and let out a dramatic sigh. "Well, I promised Auntie Sorcha I'd speak to you of the matter. She seems to think that Ailis is the perfect lass to become mistress of Duncreag. I told her you had definite ideas about wedding and that I didna think Ailis was part of those plans."

Iain frowned, anger swelling inside him. "What else did you say to her?"

"Easy, cousin, I said naught of your passion for a dream woman. I think those feelings are best kept between us. I wouldna want your folk thinking their new Laird is no' quite right in the head."

Iain relaxed. "Since when do you jump to do our auntie's bidding?"

Ranald had the grace to look a bit embarrassed. "When she promises me some of Flora's fresh pastries."

"So, you can be bought for a bilberry tart. As little as that then?"

"Nay." Ranald tried his best to look offended. "I'll have you know I canna be bought for less than three o' the wee pies."

They laughed together and rode on in companionable silence. The late afternoon sun moved out from behind a cloud, illuminating the narrow gorge as they passed through it. The sunlight turned the leaves of a small stand of birch to a greenish gold. The wind whispered over the rocky ground, lifting Iain's hair with gentle fingers. The mountainsides were yellow with broom and gorse. Here and there the purple of rhododendron flowers peeked out of clusters of dark glossy leaves.

From somewhere off to the left a bird called. Iain caught a flash of red from the corner of his eye and turned to see a crossbill fly low into the trees. Off to the right, he could just see the silver of a tumble of water. As winter snows began to melt, spring always brought waterfalls to the Highlands. To his way of thinking, it symbolized new life, his life, a new beginning as Laird of Duncreag.

Without a conscious shift of thought, his mind turned to her. He would give years of his life to be able to show her his holding. He imagined her sitting here on Sian just in front of him, his arms holding her close. He shifted uncomfortably in his saddle as his body began reacting to his thoughts.

"I thought you told me your cattle were all in the high country." Ranald's voice was low and cautious.

Iain snapped out of his reverie. Ranald sat motionless. He pulled Sian to a stop, holding up a hand to warn the men behind them. "Aye, they are." He spoke quietly, all his attention focused on Ranald.

"Then what are those?" Ranald pointed in the direction of a group of trees seemingly growing out of the rocks.

Iain squinted into the sunlight. He could make out the dark reddish color of Highland cattle. Focusing intently on the small clearing beyond the trees, his eyes picked out at least five of the beasts, though at this distance, it was hard to be certain.

"Looks to be cattle, my cattle. But I've no explanation as to why they're here. Unless . . ." Iain bit off the word and gestured to Ranald to move back into the shelter of the rocks and trees. A group of men moved into the clearing. They were all on horseback and seemed intent upon the cattle.

"Reivers." Iain spit the word out in a whispered hiss. His hand closed automatically over the hilt of his claymore. He tightened his grip, feeling his muscles flex as he moved to unsheathe it.

"Nay." The single word cut through the silence, slicing through Iain's anger. Ranald grasped Iain's wrist. "No' yet." With the words, rational thought returned. Ranald relaxed his grip and Iain released the pommel of

his sword, knowing it would be foolhardy to race into
the glen without an organized assault.

With a quick gesture, Iain signaled his clansmen, and
they dismounted, moving swiftly, melting into the
deeper shadows of the mountain's rocky terrain. Iain and
Ranald followed suit, and then carefully made their way
up a steep slope to a promontory of rock that afforded
a good view of the clearing below. Cattle ambled
through the meadow, heading for the rocky gorge where
Iain and his men waited, their shaggy red-brown coats
blending with the tall grass of the meadow. Just behind
them, partially hidden by the trees, Iain could make out
the muted red and gray of a plaid.

"I count five men on horseback." Ranald spoke barely
above a whisper, his ear just inches from Iain's as they
lay on their bellies watching the small clearing below.

"Nay, there is a sixth horse o'er there in the shelter
of those trees."

"Ach, you're right. I can see the wee beastie's tail."
Ranald slid forward a few inches in an effort to try and
see more clearly. "What do you want to do then? Attack
or wait?"

Iain looked down at the group of animals and men.
The men were moving into the clearing now, oblivious
to the fact that they had an audience. They were talking
and laughing, obviously in no great hurry.

Again, he felt his anger rise. He clenched his teeth in
an effort to regain control. Frowning, he counted four
men in the clearing. Two were still in the woods, barely
in view. "We wait. The risk is greater now. They'll have
to move through the gorge. When they do, we'll attack.
With luck, the narrow enclosure and the surprise of an
attack will give us the advantage."

Iain felt rather than saw Ranald's nod of acceptance.
With eyes glued to the meadow below, the two men
quietly inched back into the heavy undergrowth.

•   •   •

Iain sat waiting atop Sian, peering into the gathering evening shadows. The rocks loomed on either side of him, glowing eerily in the late afternoon sunlight. Although the sun was still some hours from setting, the height of the canyon walls would soon block most of its light. He fingered the claymore held tightly in his right hand. He glanced across the gorge floor to the dark shape among the rocks he knew to be Ranald. In front of him, not more than a few lengths away, young William crouched low over the neck of his mount. The beast stood perfectly still, muscles taut, ready to leap into action at the slightest touch. Behind him, Iain knew the others waited for his command as well.

The cattle began to move, breaking the silence that shrouded the canyon. The reivers flanked them on both sides—two on the left and three on the right, with the sixth man bringing up the rear. They moved slowly, almost laboriously, up into the gorge.

Iain drew in a breath, waiting, as the men drew nearer. He tensed with anticipation, completely focused on the movement of the reivers. The men moved closer, unaware of the surrounding danger. Still, he waited. He could hear them now, talking among themselves. The leader, a big man with a shock of red hair, gestured wildly, and the others laughed at whatever tale he told.

Iain again looked to Ranald. His cousin, too, was crouched low over his horse. Meeting his eyes, Iain saw the question there. He silently shook his head. The men waited in absolute silence as the reivers drew ever closer.

The first man passed close to William, who shifted only slightly, pulling farther into the rocks bordering the gorge floor. Iain drew in a breath and held it, his muscles bunching, ready to spring into action. The second man moved past William. The third was just in front of Ranald. Iain fingered the pommel of his claymore, his thumb brushing against the cross-guard. The first man passed Iain. The last was just even with William.

Iain silently raised his sword and looked across the way, making eye contact with Ranald. Suddenly without warning, a sharp sound cracked through the gorge. Iain narrowed his eyes scanning the terrain, trying to locate the source of the noise. A large bird shot screaming into the air. William's horse, startled by the clamor, skittered and slid down the slight embankment where they had been hidden. Caught by surprise, William slipped to the side of the horse, hanging on by one hand and one foot as his horse, frightened further by this strange new distribution of weight, charged forward into the gorge and the milling cattle.

Chaos irrupted. The cattle stampeded, the thunder of their hooves making them sound like ten times their number. Iain fought to maintain his mount, watching as the reivers scrambled to assess the situation, raising their claymores, and trying to evade the charging animals.

It was now or never.

With a blood-curling cry, Iain signaled his men, charging forward into the dusty whirl of men and beasts. The cattle, fear reflected in their eyes, crashed forward, oblivious to anything in their path. Through the great cloud of dust, Iain saw William, still clinging to his horse's flank, twist to avoid the point of a horn. Then, in a surge of cattle, men, and dust, he disappeared from view.

A man emerged from the fray, charging in on his horse from the left. Iain reacted swiftly, swinging his claymore in a defensive counter just as his opponent reached him. Metal clanged against metal. Using his knees to twist Sian to the right, Iain swung again and this time caught the man's upper torso in a glancing blow. Bleeding and enraged, the man screamed and swung, his weapon hissing as it sliced through the air.

Iain whirled to the left, barely avoiding the blade. The motion saved his life, but caused him to lose his balance and fall from Sian. Hitting the ground shoulder-first, he quickly rolled to an upright crouch, his weapon ready.

His opponent tried to maneuver his horse and strike a
blow. Iain tensed and sprang, his claymore raised high,
slashing. The motion was enough to spook the horse and
unseat the man. He, too, recovered quickly, and rose to
stand a few feet from Iain.

They circled each other warily, and then the man
lunged. He was so close Iain could see the feral gleam
in his eyes. Iain stepped to the side and spun into the
man, thrusting quickly upward, catching him full in the
chest. Without waiting to see the man fall, he turned to
the sound of fighting behind him.

Ranald was standing on a rock, defending himself
handily against two of the reivers. Satisfied that his
cousin was holding his own, Iain grabbed Sian's reins
and pulled himself into the saddle, his claymore ready.

A scream echoed through the gorge. Iain reacted
immediately, urging Sian toward the center of the canyon. Searching for the source of the cry, he spotted William on the ground, scrambling for cover. Behind the
boy, a reiver raised his weapon, his face contorted with
blood-lust.

Iain's heart pounded as he rode forward, trying to
gauge the distance. There was no time. William froze,
terror etched on his face as he watched the claymore
descend. Iain yelled in frustration, as he pushed forward
toward the boy and his attacker.

The reiver, distracted, turned to the noise. William,
suddenly free of his fear induced paralysis, scrambled
away from the still falling blade. The edge caught his
leg, but he managed to roll free. The reiver turned his
attention back to the now injured boy. Smiling with anticipation, he again raised his great sword.

This time Iain knew he had the advantage. He rose in
his saddle and with a hefty swing, felt the blade slide
deep into the reiver's back. The man stopped instantly,
then teetered for a moment and fell to the ground, his
now useless claymore clattering beside him. Iain felt a
rush of satisfaction. That would teach the blackguard to

threaten an innocent boy. His battle-lust faded and he
reined in Sian, sheathing his bloody sword.

Sliding from the horse, he ran to William's side, just
as a grim, blood-smeared Ranald knelt beside the boy.
Iain stood guard over them, warily eyeing the shadows
of the gorge, searching for other signs of life. Everything
was eerily silent, save for the lowing of a cow in the
distance.

He could see the bodies of two of the reivers. And he
knew one other lay by the rocks, dead by his own hand.
That left three unaccounted for, as well as two of his
own men. A movement to the left drew his attention.
Roger Macbean, one of Iain's best warriors, emerged
from the quickly settling dust.

Iain raised a hand in recognition. "You are unhurt?"

"Aye, which is more than I can say about the wee
mon I ran through. He'll no doubt be dancing with the
devil tonight."

Iain nodded. Four accounted for then. "And Andrew?
Have you seen him?"

A dark shadow passed over the man's face as he nodded. "Dead."

"You'll see to his body then?" Iain asked, his throat
tight with anger and grief.

Roger ran a hand through his hair, his face drawn with
pain. "Aye, I'll wrap him in his plaid and secure him to
his horse. 'Tis sure to be a mournful homecoming. Mari
will no doubt be torn with grief."

Iain thought of the lovely young Mari. She and Andrew were newly wed. And now she was a widow. He
arched his shoulders, rubbing the back of his neck as
Roger turned and disappeared behind a small outcropping of rocks. Iain put the image of Mari and Andrew
out of his mind. He would need to deal with it, but now
was not the time.

He called to Ranald. "How is he?"

"He could be better. His leg is still bleeding something fierce and I'm certainly no healer."

"Aye, well, you're a fine sight better than me. So do what you can."

Iain turned back to scan the rocks and shadows. Finally satisfied that there was no further threat, he knelt next to Ranald at the boy's side. William lay still and pale, his leg deeply gashed. Bloodstained, the dirt around him a deep brownish red. Ranald worked to staunch the bleeding. Iain knew from his own experiences with battle injuries that William's situation was a serious one. They were a long way from Duncreag and the boy needed a healer. Even then, Iain knew that if fever set in there was little hope.

"Can he ride?"

Ranald looked up from his ministrations. "Aye, with one of us."

"Then we'll ride back as far as the wee burn. We can tend to his wound properly there and stay the night. On the morn we'll head back to Duncreag. Sorcha has a bit of the healing touch. She'll see to the lad."

Ranald nodded as he tied a strip of linen around William's leg.

The boy moaned and opened his eyes. " 'Tis my fault they saw us too soon." His voice was weak, but Iain heard it and saw the pain and remorse in his eyes. He reached over and covered William's hand with his own.

"Nay, 'twas the bird that alarmed them. You've no cause to blame yourself. Besides, it looks as though we bested them." The boy gave Iain a weak smile and slid into unconsciousness.

Ranald raised an eyebrow. Iain grimaced. " 'Twas but a small untruth, and one that may well help the lad in his healing."

"How many down?"

"Four—five if you count our own Andrew." Pain seared through him.

"So that leaves two. Do you think they rode away then?"

Roger joined the group. "Nay, they didn't ride. Their

horses are all still here. So they're on foot, I'd say, or riding a cow."

The men smiled with grim humor at the picture that made.

Ranald stood. "Have you a thought as to who the reivers were?"

Iain frowned. "Aye, by the looks of their plaids I'd say Macphersons. But I've no idea why they'd be wanting Mackintosh cattle. They've plenty o' their own. 'Tis odd."

Ranald's eyes skimmed the gorge, taking in the full extent of the carnage. "Well, whoever they are, there are considerably less of them now, I'd say."

"Aye." Iain watched Ranald absently run his hand over the torn and bloodied sleeve of his shirt. "Have you hurt your arm?"

" 'Tis no more than a scratch. I've suffered far worse and lived to tell the tale."

Iain smiled wearily at his cousin. "Aye, that you have."

Iain mounted Sian and the other men lifted the boy into his outstretched arms. He settled the boy's weight against his chest and locked his arms around him. Ranald swung into the saddle, gathered the reins of the extra horses, and began the somber procession from the gorge. Roger followed, leading Andrew's horse, the red-and-black-wrapped mound over its midsection testimony to a battle fought and won, but not without cost.

Chapter 6

Iain SAT ON a fallen tree branch, elbow on knee, chin in hand. He watched as Ranald checked William for fever. His wound, now washed and freshly bandaged, still seeped blood, but most of the flow had been successfully staunched. Iain clenched his fist reflexively, awaiting the verdict.

Ranald covered the boy with a blanket and adjusted the folded plaid under his head. He sat back on his heels, releasing a sigh of exhaustion. His steady gaze found Iain's. "He's warmer than I would like, but 'tis no' yet the fire of fever, I'll wager. I canna say it willna come. But at least for now he rests."

Iain nodded and stood, surveying the clearing. It was small, not much more than a grassy knoll set among a stand of young trees. The mountains surrounding it rose like ethereal gardians out of the fading light. Somewhere behind rocks and trees, a small burn bubbled merrily, its song joining the rustle of leaves in the wind. Small trails of the ever-present Highland mist curled in and out of the trees, creeping forward into the clearing, waiting, perhaps, for the last vestiges of sunlight to slip away.

William moaned, twisting and turning restlessly. Iain
knelt beside him and pressed a gentle hand to the boy's
flushed face. He quieted almost at once. Iain rose again
and began to pace back and forth across the small en-
campment. Roger sat a bit apart on a large rock, watching the edges of the clearing, searching for signs of
intruders.

"It wasn't your fault." Ranald's words were quiet,
meant only for Iain.

"Ach, I know. 'Tis only that I'm the Laird. Damn it,
man, I should never have let William come. He's naught
but a lad, and Andrew no' much more so." Iain ran his
fingers through his hair in frustration.

"You were no' to know we'd stumble upon reivers.
And you remember as well as I do what we were doing
at Andrew's age."

Iain thought for a moment, a flash of humor making
him smile. "Fighting Camerons."

"Aye, and relishing each and every battle. 'Tis also
true that, had we been given the opportunity to fight at
William's age, we would most certainly have done so,
and well you know it. Would you deny them the chance
then to become men?"

"If it meant Andrew would be alive and William
whole? I might."

"Iain, you said it yourself. You're *only* the Laird, no'
God Almighty."

"Aye, no' God and right now no' much of a Laird,
either." Iain tipped back his head and looked at the pink
and orange staining the evening sky. "I think I'll go for
a wash in the burn." He rose. "Tell Roger I'll be taking
the watch when I return."

Ranald raised a hand in acknowledgment and Iain
strode off toward the sound of the bubbling stream, leaving his cousin sitting by himself on the knoll.

Iain sat on a large rock and listened to the noises of the
Highlands. He trailed a hand in the water absently. The

little stream was cold and clear. He breathed deeply, letting the cool air fill his lungs and wash through his soul. Somewhere in the distance a grouse's call rang out, "Go back, go back."

Iain sighed. Go back where? He'd never really belonged anywhere. His growing years had been spent at Corybrough. The big castle had been home to the Macqueens. But even though his mother's blood gave him the right to the name, he had never felt that he truly belonged there. All he had been able to think of was returning to Duncreag. But his homecoming had been empty. Angus had been consumed with grief, unable to see the need in his own son. Iain had tried to stay. For four years he had fought to win his father's attention. But in the end, when his uncle Duncan had summoned him to Moy into service for Clan Chattan, he had jumped at the opportunity.

The next six years had brimmed with danger and excitement, the stuff of a young man's dreams. He and Ranald had enjoyed the battles and skirmishes, fighting rival clans like the Camerons, as only the young and fearless can. They had lived in the minute, enjoying everything life had to offer. But always, somewhere deep inside, he had felt empty. Yearning for something, someone to fill the void.

Now he was Laird of Duncreag. And what had he accomplished as Laird? Iain blew out his breath in disgust. He hadn't found suitable answers to the nagging questions about his father's death. He'd managed to get a man killed and another wounded. And he was wracked with longing for a woman who more than likely existed only in his head.

He leaned back on the rock, supporting himself on his elbows and closing his eyes. Unbidden, his mind circled around the memory of golden curls and warm gray eyes, of sweet breath stealing his soul with the kiss of an angel. For one brief moment in time, the emptiness had

dissolved, filled with soft touches and shivers of delight.
He had felt free.

He grimaced, shaking his head at his fancifulness.
Free, indeed. He stood quickly, annoyed at his emotions,
and crouched beside the swiftly flowing water. He
dipped a hand into the cool depths and bent to drink his
fill. And then, as if to wash away his thoughts, he
plunged his head into the stream, letting the water rush
around him.

With a great spray of water, he threw back his head,
droplets flying from his hair. Suddenly he jerked forward, nerves tingling with awareness. He froze, listening. The voices of the evening were still. He waited. The
silence deepened. He scanned the area for the source of
the change. His gaze went to the clearing on the opposite
bank. It was empty.

Or was it? There was a shimmer of movement on the
bank across the water. As he watched, the shimmer darkened and solidified until a figure emerged. It was a
woman. Iain crossed himself. She was dressed in a night
shift of brilliant green and her unbound hair fell in
golden waves around her shoulders.

Their eyes met and his breath caught in his throat,
recognition dawning. Her eyes were wide with emotion.
Her lips moved frantically in some silent message even
as she raised a hand and pointed repeatedly at something
behind him, fear washing over her features. The hairs
on the back of his neck rose. He reacted instinctively,
reaching for his dirk and whirling around, throwing the
little knife even before he had completed the turn. Still
moving, he rolled to the ground and pulled up quickly
to meet the unseen challenger.

The clearing was quiet once more. Iain slowly raised
from his crouch. A spot of color marked the place where
the assailant had fallen. Cautiously Iain approached, circling around the body. The man was lying on his side
and Iain could see his dirk sticking out of the man's
plaid, a stain of brownish crimson spreading across the

wool. There was no movement. Gingerly, using a foot, Iain turned the man onto his back. He recognized one of the reivers, the leader. With grim satisfaction, he marked five accounted for.

As his blood-lust faded, he remembered the burn. He turned sharply, almost stumbling in his haste to reach the burnside. His gaze raked the opposite shore. The small patch of meadow was empty. Iain stared at the gently waving grass, his heart pounding. Where was she? She'd been right there, warning him. He could still see the fear in her eyes. Fear for him, mixed with another emotion, one that made his body grow warm.

Almost in a panic, he waded across the stream, hurrying up the opposite bank to the place where she had stood. He knelt in the grass, pushing it aside, looking for some sign of her physical presence. He stayed there, motionless, hands pressed to his thighs as he accepted the fact that there was nothing, no one, there. She was gone.

"Iain. What's wrong with you, man? You look as if you've seen a ghost." Ranald called from the other side of the burn. He stood ready for battle, his sword drawn.

Slowly Iain rose, turning from his futile search. He shook himself from his lethargy and once again crossed the burn.

Ranald sheathed his sword. "Are you all right, then? I was coming to find you when I saw you kneeling in the grass there. Have you taken to prayer?"

"Nay." Iain raised a weary arm and gestured toward the dead man.

Ranald walked to the body, circling it as cautiously as Iain had.

"He's dead." Iain came up beside his cousin and looked down at the body dispassionately. " 'Tis one of the reivers. The leader, I think. He was trying to sneak up from behind when I was washing in the burn."

Ranald looked at Iain curiously. "So, tell me, how did

you know he was there? Have you eyes in the back of
your head, now?"

Iain stared at his boot tips, silent for a time, then
looked up at his cousin. "Nay. She was here, over there
on the bank. She warned me. Ranald, I swear by all that
is holy, she warned me."

Ranald gaped at Iain, his astonishment plain to see.
"She. You mean your fairy maid? She was there on the
grass?" He looked across the burn to the empty bank.

"Aye. I'll no' expect you to believe me. But she was
there and had she no' been, I'd be dead. I owe her my
life."

Ranald gave Iain a look of tolerant disbelief. "Ah,
well, if it's so, I only wish I had a fairy like that in love
with me. But where did she go?"

Iain grimaced. "I dinna know. When I turned back
from the reiver's body she was gone. I canna explain it.
But I did see her. I know I did."

Ranald bent to the body, busying himself with freeing
Iain's dirk. He wiped the blade on the dead man's shirt,
then straightened and offered the knife to Iain with a
flourish. "Your knife, my Laird."

Iain winced at the title, but quietly took the dirk and
replaced it in its sheath.

All signs of teasing disappeared from Ranald's face.
He reached over, placing a hand on Iain's shoulder.
"Cousin, if you say you saw her, then I believe you."
The two men stood in silence for a moment before Ran-
ald turned to the body. "Do you know this man, then?"

"Nay, save that he was there in the gorge. His colors
are Macpherson."

"The same as the others?"

"Aye." Iain crouched down beside the man and deftly
searched the body. Finding nothing save an empty sporran, he almost stood again but halted midway at the
sound of Ranald's voice.

"What's that?" Ranald asked. "There, by your foot."

Iain looked down and saw something protruding from beneath the reiver. He moved the body and picked up the small object. He rose, holding it carefully balanced on the palm of his hand. The little dagger seemed to glow in the fading light.

Ranald studied the dirk. "I've seen this before." He frowned, deep in thought. "I just canna say when."

Iain stared at the knife, turning it slowly in his hand. " 'Tis my father's dirk."

"Well, I guess that explains why I thought I recognized it. You and Fergus certainly painted a clear enough picture of it the other night." Ranald nodded at the body. "How do you suppose he came by it?"

Iain narrowed his eyes. "I've no notion, but 'tis a question I'd well like an answer to. I'd venture to guess my father didna give it to him."

Ranald bent to examine the dirk. "Is it possible, then, that the Macphersons killed your father?"

"Aye, 'tis possible. But I canna fathom the reason. One thing is for certain—this man canna tell us anything."

"I'd best be getting back to check on young William. And I imagine Roger will be ready for you to spell him."

"Ach, I'd forgotten. Tell him I'll be along in a minute."

Ranald nodded and began the short walk back to their campsite. Suddenly he looked over his shoulder, aqua eyes crinkling with mischief. "Watch out for the fairies." With that, he left Iain standing in the little clearing alone.

The sun dipped at last behind the horizon. Iain looked again to the grassy spot beyond the burn. She was close. He felt it deep inside, even if he did not truly understand it. He turned, suddenly anxious for morning, anxious to get home. He told himself his urgency was based only on the events of the day, on the Macphersons and his need to avenge his father. But he knew, also, that his haste was at least in part to gain the privacy of his chamber, to sit again through an endless night, waiting for a love his practical mind told him did not exist.

Chapter 7

KATHERINE STOOD BY a stream in a small clearing. The evening sunlight glittered off the beginning tendrils of mist, lending an ethereal quality to the clearing. The stream gurgled melodiously and the trees waved dreamily in the gentle breeze.

Sensing movement, Katherine looked toward a small group of trees. A man emerged from their shadow and stepped into the light. She caught her breath watching him walk across the meadow grass toward her. He moved with the lithe grace of an athlete, his dark hair swinging with each step, brushing his massive shoulders. His legs, free of covering save knee-high boots and a length of woolen cloth fastened around his waist, moved with leashed power. He was beautiful. Her heart cried out to his, recognizing, even before her eyes did that he was Iain.

He drew closer, and her breath felt trapped in her throat. His face was twisted with anguish. He looked tired and unkempt. Katherine longed to reach out and soothe his brow, but knew that as with the other times she could not. She clenched a fist, feeling his pain deep within her.

She watched as he sat on a large rock, his powerful hand caressing the water of the stream. Her body ached with need. She wanted more than anything to feel his hands caressing her body. He shifted, leaning his head back, eyes closed, lost in thought. She stood helpless, wanting to go to him, knowing she could not.

Iain knelt by the stream and drank deeply. Then with one swift movement he dipped his head into the rushing water. She marveled again at his strength and beauty. Her pulse quickened as she saw another face, behind Iain, a face mottled with rage. His lank red hair was matted around his head and shoulders. His mouth was twisted into an angry snarl. His large arm was raised, and he held a knife of some kind. Katherine could see it glitter in his hand as he moved.

She tried to scream but no sound emerged. Her heart pounding now, she stared at Iain, willing him to look at her, to see her. Iain swung his head out of the stream, shaking the water from his hair. Just as quickly he tensed and looked up, his entire body alert. Their eyes met, his widening in surprise. The red-haired stranger was drawing closer.

Again she tried to warn him, frantically pointing at the threat behind him. She saw the recognition dawn in his eyes even as he struggled to understand her. Her entire body began to shake as she watched the red-haired man inch forward. She opened her mouth to scream out a warning but found no breath for sound, so deep was her terror.

But Iain moved faster than his enemy, turning and throwing something, almost in one motion. She watched as gleaming metal arced through the air, unerringly finding its target. The burly man fell. Iain approached the man with practiced caution and she watched as he nudged the body with his foot. He appeared dead. She sighed with relief, feeling as though she herself had fought the battle.

She hurried to cross the stream, but already the little

meadow was beginning to fade away, like so many times before. She struggled to hold on to the image, to reach for him, but as the gray mist surrounded her, she woke into the night.

The room was black, the night air heavy with rain. She tried to calm herself by breathing slowly, in and out, in and out. Unbidden, the tears came. She reached with shaking hands to wipe them away. A profound sense of loss swept through her, as though a little of her soul had been left behind in the dream with him.

The dreams were getting stronger somehow, more powerful. This time Iain had seen her. For a moment, at least, their eyes had met. She was sure of it. He had recognized her. She shuddered, thinking of what might have happened if Iain hadn't understood her warning. But the other man was dead. Iain was safe. But safe where? In some counterworld? A world that was barred to her except through her dreams?

She pushed sweat-soaked hair off her face and neck, absently braiding it out of the way. She reached for the light by the bed, knowing that sleep was now impossible.

The lamplight's soft glow illuminated the room, casting long shadows into its corners. She slowly blew out the breath she had been holding and drew her knees up under her chin. She surveyed the room, its odd mixture of centuries evident in the furniture and architecture. The earlier shape of the window and its little seat were hidden now by plasterboard and cotton, but with a little imagination it was not hard to envision the stonework under the printed fabric and the arch under the plaster. Of course in truth it was easy for her to imagine it. After all, she'd been there. Hadn't she?

Katherine closed her eyes, embarrassed by her foolishness. What was she implying? That she had traveled through time? That she had found a doorway most said did not exist and that others would kill to find? Right.

She, Katherine Elizabeth St. Claire, had crossed through time. She flipped her haphazard braid back. Oh, how she wished it were true. And if it was true, how she wished it would happen again.

She sat motionless on the bed, her eyes closed, her head resting on her knees, waiting . . . until the pink fingers of dawn slipped through her window, the delicate beams dancing lightly across the bed.

"Good morning, sunshine." Jeff plopped down in one of the hotel restaurant's chairs and glanced around curiously. The great hall was empty, more or less. Only one or two tables in the restaurant were occupied. It obviously wasn't high season. He smiled at his sister. "I see you're still here. I thought you'd be off to visit Fantasy Man."

Katherine frowned, barely looking up from the oatmeal she was listlessly stirring.

Even in the cavernous gloom of the hall, he could see that she looked terrible. He sobered instantly. "Jeez, Kitty, I was only joking. I'm sorry. Didn't you sleep? You look like death warmed over."

She abandoned her spoon, offering Jeff a weak smile. "Thanks a lot."

He frowned at her. "Did you have one of your dreams last night?"

Katherine nodded, chewing on her lip, staring at the hunk of butter melting in the bowl of porridge.

Jeff tipped a finger under her chin, forcing her to look at him. "Come on, sweetie, tell me what happened."

"You won't believe me."

He reached for her hand, not certain he wanted to hear what she had to say. "Look, I can't promise I'll believe you—but I love you. So I'll promise to listen."

She pulled away from his touch and sniffed. "I guess I might as well tell you. Otherwise you'll just hound me until I do."

"Ah, how well she knows me." He grinned, leaning

forward, elbows on the table. "Okay, spill it."

"You won't laugh?"

He solemnly crossed his heart with one hand. "I won't laugh."

Her lips curved upward with a hint of amusement.

Jeff listened with growing astonishment as she told him about her latest dreams, one that had precipitated her trip to Scotland, and another that had happened last night. When she finished he sat in stunned silence, trying to put his whirling thoughts into some semblance of order. Finally, with a deep breath, he plunged in.

"Okay, let me see if I've got this straight. Four nights ago, in New York, you saw Fantasy Man in your dream, only he was here at Duncreag." Katherine pursed her lips at the name, but nodded. "And you could hear him and some other guy talking."

"In Gaelic."

"Right, in Gaelic. And you're pretty sure dream boy—"

"Iain."

Jeff threw his hands up in mock-apology. "Sorry. So you're pretty sure 'Iain' was aware of your presence even though he couldn't see you. How am I doing so far?"

"Fine."

"For two nights you had no dreams at all. Then last night you had a doozy. You actually appeared to dream bo . . . Iain and saved his life."

Katherine twirled her butter knife and avoided Jeff's gaze. "Put like that, it does sound a little odd."

"Odd? Kitty, it sounds certifiable."

"But it happened." She spoke slowly, enunciating each word, glaring at him.

"Okay, okay, don't get mad." Jeff raised his hands again, this time in surrender. To buy himself some time to think, he reached into a covered basket, pulled out a small cake, buttered it; and popped the whole thing in his mouth. His mouth immediately telegraphed its plea-

sure. Swallowing, he licked his fingers with relish and
reached for another. A fellow couldn't deal with time
travel on an empty stomach. "These are really good.
Have you had one?"

"Uh, uh."

"Do you know what they are?"

"Mrs. Abernathy called them bannocks," she offered
unenthusiastically.

"Well, they're great." To illustrate his point, he
popped another into his mouth and grinned.

Katherine sat back with an exaggerated sigh.

"Hey, a guy's got to eat." He shrugged apologetically.

She raised both eyebrows and he recognized the determined glint in her eyes.

So much for stalling. He pushed away the bread basket with a sigh. "All right, let's say for the sake of conversation that Iain is or was real, and that you actually
did travel back in time eight years ago. Assuming that's
true, how do you think you did it?"

Katherine sat forward, eyes narrowed in concentration. "I don't know. I read everything I could find about
time travel right after I got back from Scotland, but there
really isn't a clear consensus as to how time travel could
occur. There are all kinds of theories. Some of them are
poetic. They use catch phrases like 'ripping the fabric
of time'. Others are very scientific, along the lines of
quantum physics, which I can't even begin to understand. Then there is all the new age stuff about souls
and destiny and all that."

"So do any of these explanations fit your situation?"
He hadn't realized she was so serious about this.

"Well, it's not like there are case studies out there.
And at the time I just figured that if it was real, it was
a fluke. You know, some big cosmic accident."

"But you had other dreams, right?"

"Yeah, but they really were more like normal dreams.
I knew they were about Iain, but I could never remember
them clearly afterward. You know, like trying to remem-

ber a movie you saw a long time ago. You remember
you loved it, and maybe generally what it was about,
but the details are hazy." She paused, taking a sip of
juice. "Anyway, until these latest dreams I'd really convinced myself that whatever happened eight years ago
was only an isolated event, and that I'd probably never
really understand it."

"And now?"

"Well," she paused, meeting his gaze, "I'm beginning
to think that maybe I'm linked to Iain somehow. Certainly, Duncreag is involved. I don't know—maybe it's
a gate of some kind."

Or the Starship Enterprise. He forced himself to follow the thread of her logic. "If that's true, then why
weren't you zapped back last night?"

"I think because we both have to be present for the
gate to work."

He ran a hand through his hair in frustration. "Okay,
I'm not following you."

"I'm not sure I'm following it myself, but look at the
facts. The one time Iain and I were together, we were
in Duncreag at the same time."

"Well, technically . . ."

She frowned at him. "All right, there's the matter of
five hundred years. But in our respective centuries, assuming time passes more or less the same for each of
us, we were both here."

"At Duncreag."

"Right. Then I went home."

Jeff blew out a breath. "Yes, but you still had the
dreams."

"Well not for awhile, and when I did they were less
tangible, more dreamlike. But last night, it was almost
as if we were separated only by the thinnest of barriers.
So it seems like the closer we come to actually being
together, the stronger the link."

"Okay, then what about the dream you had right before we came here? You certainly weren't at Duncreag."

"No, but Iain was. Remember I saw the room—his room. And I'm almost certain that, except for the first time, he's never been at Duncreag when he has come to me."

"So, wait a minute. You're saying that this link you have gets stronger when one of you is in residence at Duncreag?"

"Yeah. I think the reason my dreams have been hazy is that neither Iain nor I have been at Duncreag. When he returned, the link strengthened. When I arrived here it grew even more powerful, allowing me to warn him."

Jeff sucked in a breath, the impact of his sister's words hitting him like steel on granite. "You think that if he comes back to Duncreag while you're here, you'll . . ." He stopped and looked at his sister, unable to say the words.

She nodded and finished for him. ". . . be able go back to him."

"My God. You figured all this out in New York when you dreamed that Iain was at Duncreag. That's why you decided to come back here." His head was spinning. This was way beyond anything he could clearly comprehend.

Katherine tilted her head slightly, the expression on her face answering his question.

"Kitty, if you're right, and I am not saying that I believe you are, then you could be going . . . I mean you might not be coming . . . Kitty, I might never see you again."

She gently placed her hand over his. "I honestly don't know what will happen, Jeff. I just know that I need to try. I need Iain. I need him at some level so deep inside me that existing without him hurts. He makes me whole." She held up a hand as he opened his mouth to speak. "Don't say it—I know how insane all of this sounds. But if he is real, in whatever time, I want to go to him. I need to. Even if it means leaving you."

Jeff turned his hand so that it enclosed hers. "A part

of me thinks this whole thing is hogwash. But you're basically a sane, well-grounded human being. So another part of me has to accept that it's possible that what you're saying is true." He felt tears prick at the back of his eyes, and blinked rapidly. "You know I want you to be happy. And if that happiness lies on the other side of some mystical gateway, then I'll have to accept that." Jeff tried for a grin but failed miserably. "It'll certainly be a long way to travel for Christmas."

Katherine brushed at her own tears. "Nothing has happened yet. And if I *am* living a fantasy, then we can plan for Christmas in New York."

Almost as if on cue, Mrs. Abernathy arrived at the table. "Good morning to you. I see you've finished your breakfast. I hope it was to your liking."

Jeff pulled his gaze from Katherine. "I enjoyed every bite."

Katherine laughed. "And he means it."

Mrs. Abernathy looked pleased. "Well, then, since you're finished, what do you say to a wee tour?"

Jeff's mind immediately shifted from time travel to architecture, his eyes lighting up in anticipation. "Perfect. Can we start with the battlements?"

Chapter 8

"KATHERINE WATCHED HER brother bend down to examine what looked to be several small holes in the floor of the battlement walkway.

"Hey, come over here and look at this." His voice was filled with awe.

She recognized the tone and knew she was about to learn more than she ever wanted to know about battlements. She carefully picked her way over the rough stones and dutifully bent to see the holes.

"See these?"

Katherine nodded, trying her best to look fascinated.

"They're called machicolations. They're for dropping things on your enemies."

"Boiling oil?" she asked dryly.

Jeff ignored her sarcasm and enthusiastically continued his explanation. "More likely hot water or stones. Anyway, what's cool about these is the way they're designed. See, if you look over the side of the wall . . ." In his excitement, he hung himself halfway over the retaining wall, his upper body dangling upside down in midair, demonstrating his point with dizzying effect.

". . . you can see that the battlement is actually built out over the tower."

Katherine swallowed nervously and peered cautiously over the crenellated wall. The ground below her blurred. She drew back quickly, her breath coming in gasps.

Jeff pulled himself upright. "I'm sorry, Kitty. I forgot about your fear of heights."

Katherine stepped back from the wall. "It's not a fear of heights. It's a fear of falling. Vertigo. Anyway, I'm fine as long as I stay away from the edge." She smiled and gamely tried to change the subject. "So these mach-icohickies are unique to this tower?"

Jeff needed little persuasion. "No, but tower houses of this kind were the first to extend stone battlements over the edge of the building. Pretty nifty trick. And they're called mach-i-co-la-tions."

Mrs. Abernathy poked her head around the corner of the battlement. "If you're finished up here we can go downstairs."

Katherine hurried to their hostess' side, anxious to have four tall walls and a ceiling around her again.

"Not to worry, dear, I've no liking for the battlements myself. Although you must admit the view from here is rather spectacular."

Katherine drank in the wild beauty of the Highlands. Beyond the tower itself she could see part of the river valley below and the scree-covered mountains rising on all sides. It was easy to see why Duncreag had been built on this outcropping of rock. It would have been almost impossible to attack.

"Wow, Mrs. Abernathy, this is great. I can't wait to see what you have in store for us next." Jeff reached Katherine's side just as she turned to walk down the spiral stairs leading to the battlements. "Whoa, Kitty there's no door there." He grabbed her elbow, stopping her from careening into the stone wall.

Katherine stared at the wall as if it would magically open, then shook her head and turned back to her brother and Mrs. Abernathy. "I could have sworn that's where the door was. Sorry."

An odd, contemplative look passed across Mrs. Abernathy's face. "How strange. You see, there was a door there once. It led down to the second floor. But it was closed off many years ago. Insurance dictates, you know."

Katherine felt her stomach lurch. "Was it open eight years ago, Mrs. Abernathy, when I was here before?"

The older woman smiled. "Oh no, dear, it's been closed for more like twenty. I remember it open when I was a child. But that was a very long time ago, indeed." She shooed them back around the corner to an open door. "Actually, all the old stairways in the house have either been closed off or changed. We couldn't pass a fire inspection without the new ones, you see. The inspectors allow some latitude, but not enough to leave the old ones in place."

She paused to draw a breath.

"The house used to have five staircases. There was one on the outside to let you enter the great hall and one going down to the old cellar; that'd be our lobby stairs now. Then there were two in the great hall. One of them lead to the third floor and the other lead to the Laird's quarters on the second floor. You couldn't get to the family any other way. And then there was the staircase you thought you saw. It was just to allow the Laird access to the battlements. It opened off of one of the bedrooms on the second floor."

As they descended, Mrs. Abernathy continued talking of staircases and battlements. Jeff followed close behind her, asking numerous questions. Katherine tuned them both out and tried to remember how she knew about the stairs on the second floor. Frustrated, she finally decided it must have been coincidence. She'd just been confused about the location of the door they'd used to reach the battlements.

"Come right this way, lambs. I want to show you one

of these rooms." Mrs. Abernathy walked through the small sitting room on the second floor to a wooden door set in a stone archway. She opened it with a flourish and stepped aside so that Jeff and Katherine could enter.

"We left it the way it was originally so the guests could see. There've been repairs here and there, but it's structurally much as it would have been six hundred years ago. I thought you'd enjoy seeing it, Jeff."

"*Enjoy*" was probably too mild a word. Katherine watched as Jeff stood in the middle of the room with his mouth hanging open. "Look at those beams." He pointed to the roof. "And the arch over the window." He walked to the small enclosure to examine it closer.

Katherine walked over to the huge stone and plaster fireplace. An ornate hood hung out over the flue.

"A bit much, isn't it? The plaster is a copy, but the stones are original."

Katherine jumped at the sound of Mrs. Abernathy's voice. She was entirely too edgy. She needed sleep. Or a good therapist, her rational mind taunted.

"I'm sorry, dear, I didn't mean to scare you." Mrs. Abernathy met her gaze, concern lighting her gentle eyes.

"Oh no, you didn't really. You just startled me." Katherine fingered the earring on its chain and smiled at Mrs. Abernathy.

"Is that a cairngorm I see?" Agnes reached out and lifted the earring carefully away from Katherine's chest for closer examination. "It's beautiful."

She moved forward so that Mrs. Abernathy could see it better. "Yes, it is. It's a family heirloom. My grandmother gave it to me. It's actually an earring. I lost the other one."

"Ach, don't worry, love, things have a way of turning up when you least expect them."

Katherine nodded. She saw no reason whatsoever to tell Mrs. Abernathy that the earring was likely lost somewhere in the distant past and therefore unlikely to turn up anywhere in this century.

"Now, if we can tear Jeffrey away, I'd like to show you the wee museum we have off the great hall."

Hearing his name, Jeff pulled himself away from the ashlar stone he was examining and obediently followed them from the room.

The little museum was located in what had once been the chapel. Katherine could still see the stone basin carved into the wall, and across from it, in the window, the stone seat for the priest. At the far end of the room was a counter with some odds and ends on it. Behind the counter, on a high stool, sat a rotund little man with a ruddy face that could only be described as Scottish.

"Jamie, my love, I've brought you the St. Claires. I've been showing them the tower and thought they might enjoy the museum."

Mr. Abernathy lumbered down from his perch and ambled over to them. He beamed at his wife and then extended a hand to Jeff. "Jamie Abernathy. Delighted to have you here at Duncreag."

Jeff took the offered hand. "Mr. Abernathy, it's a pleasure to meet you. I'm Jeff, and this is my sister, Katherine."

Mr. Abernathy turned and gave Katherine a portly bow. She winked and gave him a small curtsy. His laugh rolled out over the stone floor, filling the room with joy. "I see that you're a charmer, Miss St. Claire."

"No more than you, Mr. Abernathy."

"Well, love," Mrs. Abernathy interjected, "if you've quite finished with the introductions, I'll leave you with our guests and go and see what trouble Cook is up to in the kitchen." As Agnes spun to go, Jamie gave her a quick pinch on the behind. She threw him a look over her shoulder and left the three of them laughing.

Mr. Abernathy rubbed his hands together, surveying the room. "Let's see what we have here that might interest you." He gestured over to a small glass case in a corner. "There really isn't much, but Agnes likes to think of it as a museum. And if it pleases her, then it pleases me."

Katherine brushed past Jeff as she followed Mr. Abernathy, whispering, "Hardly John Cleese—more like Benny Hill."

Her brother slapped a hand across his mouth, trying desperately to turn his laughter into a coughing spell.

They caught up with Mr. Abernathy and peered over his shoulder into the case.

"There are several old family pieces here. The lady's comb dates back to the early seventeenth century. The sporran is a little older than that, late sixteenth century. The small book isn't all that old, but it's a first edition. Sir Walter Scott's. We're very proud of it. The dirk in the very back is the oldest piece we have in here."

Katherine looked at the small knife. The hilt was intricately carved in what looked like gold. Set into the gold, above the guard, was a large brownish black stone. It was uncut and looked like a crystal of some kind. The blade itself was fashioned out of some other metal and even in the case appeared very sharp. The dagger was at once lethal and beautiful, and hauntingly familiar. Katherine chewed on her lip, trying to remember where she had seen it before.

"Mr. Abernathy, how long has this museum been here?"

The Scotsman rubbed his chin. "Well now, as I remember it, Agnes started putting things in cases almost as soon as we took over the hotel."

Katherine's stomach did a little flip-flop. "So none of this was here eight years ago?"

"Oh, it was all here. Just spread about over the castle. It was Agnes' idea to put it all together for the guests."

Okay, so she could have seen it before. It was probably just displayed somewhere else in the castle. Relief mixed with disappointment flooded through her.

"That's some weapon." Jeff bent closer to the case, examining the dirk.

"Aye, it is. There was a time when a good Highlander went nowhere without his dirk. Now days we only wear them for special occasions. To impress the tourists mostly."

"Do you know who it belonged to?" Jeff asked, looking over the top of the case at Mr. Abernathy.

"No. We know it was probably in the possession of the first Laird of Duncreag. But the knife itself is older than that. So who knows how he came by it." Mr. Abernathy stepped back from the little case. "If you're interested in weapons, Jeff, let me show you the ones in the great hall."

Katherine watched the two of them walk away, deep in conversation. They were totally absorbed. Satisfied that they would not notice if she lingered, she turned for another look at the dirk. The dark stone almost seemed to glow in the late morning sunshine. Suddenly, in her mind's eye she could see Iain's strong hands turning the blade in random circles, an absentminded gesture she remembered well.

She jerked up from the case, interrupting her . . . what? Flashback? Her imagination was definitely in overdrive. First a door that wasn't there and now memories of a museum piece. What she needed was a friend. Someone who didn't think she was crazy. *Elaine.* She checked her watch and did the mental arithmetic to arrive at New York time. Assuming she'd done the calculation correctly—and she knew that was a big assumption—she ought to be able to catch Elaine before she left for work.

She dashed out into the great hall. Jeff and Mr. Abernathy were standing near the fireplace, enthusiastically examining the large collection of weaponry. Jeff held a huge sword, brandishing it this way and that with something less than grace. But what he lacked in expertise he made up for with sheer glee. He looked for all the world like a small boy on Christmas morning. Chuckling to herself, Katherine headed across the hall, satisfied that Jeff would survive her brief absence. If memory served, there was a public telephone in the lobby downstairs.

"Kitty, come here. You've got to try this." Jeff's voice rang through the large room.

"No thanks, I'd probably manage to slice off an ear or something. I'm going to the lobby to make a phone call. I'll meet you here for lunch. See you later, Mr. Abernathy."

Jamie turned, shield in hand, and waved in her general direction. Ah, weapons, Katherine mused, the universal language of men.

Elaine Macqueen hit the snooze alarm and snuggled down under her comforter with her dream for ten more minutes. She smiled sleepily and tried to remember just where she'd been when the incessant buzzing had started. Ah yes, blond hair, blue eyes . . .

The telephone rang, effectively shattering what was left of her dream. With a sigh, she gave up. Pushing riotous curls out of the way, she lunged for the phone, only to come up empty-handed. Dratted cordless phones. Now where was the darn thing? The phone rang again. She listened, trying to figure out where exactly the ring was coming from. Not an easy task, since the room was awash with, well, stuff.

She fumbled out of bed, stepping on the sharp edge of a shoe heel. Hopping and spitting out rather unlady-like phrases, she heard her answering machine pick up. Out of the corner of her eye, she caught the molded plastic edge of the elusive phone. Tossing aside a pair of jeans and a six-month-old magazine, she grabbed the receiver.

"I'm here. I'm here. Just hold on a minute. I've got to turn off this blasted machine."

Still holding the receiver, she managed to hit every button on the answering machine except the one that turned it off. She finally hit the correct button, only to be greeted by hysterical laughter.

"All right, you've had your jollies. Who is this?"

The voice on the other end was still breathless with laughter. "It's me—Katherine. What did you do, kill the machine?"

"No, I don't think so, but I'd really like to."

"You can't blame the phone, you know. It isn't like you can find anything in that room of yours."

Elaine sighed. It was the beginning of an old conversation. So she ignored it. "I'm glad you called. I was going to try you later. I assume you've arrived safely?"

Katherine filled her in on the trip down and her day at Duncreag.

"So you and Jeff have talked about your theories. What does he think?"

"That I'm crazy as a loon. And that if I'm right the implications are somewhat overwhelming. And that Christmas in medieval Scotland could be interesting."

"All that, huh?"

"And then some."

"So, how are you? I mean, really, how are you?"

"I'm fine—just a little afraid, I guess."

"Afraid that something will happen or afraid that something won't happen?"

"Both. How's your case going?"

"Well now, that's why I was going to call you. As they say, there's good news and bad news."

"I'll bite. What's the bad news?"

"The man pled guilty, so there won't be a trial. Which I suppose is good news for the man on the street, but bad news for me. I was really looking forward to trying the case."

"Elaine, you're the only person I know who would actually wish a murderer wouldn't confess. So what's the good news?"

"I'll be seeing you in the heather tomorrow afternoon."

"What?"

"I figured you and Jeff shouldn't have all the fun. So, I'm on my way to Duncreag. In fact, I leave in a few hours, so I'd better ring off and start packing." She paused. "Hey, it's okay for me to come, isn't it?"

"Absolutely. In fact, I'm feeling better just knowing you're on your way. Whatever happens, I'll be glad you're a part of it."

"Good. Hey, will you reserve a room for me? I'll take mine without a doorway to medieval Scotland, if that's okay."

"Very funny. Jeff will be glad to know reinforcements are coming."

"Reinforcements?"

"Yeah, he'll figure if he can't talk sense into me, you'll be able to. Bye."

"See you tomorrow."

Elaine hung up the phone and looked around her room, wondering how in the world she was going to find her suitcase.

Katherine sat by the phone, smiling with relief. Elaine was coming.

Jeff came bounding down the stairs. "That's a big smile. Who were you talking to?"

"Elaine."

Jeff's eyes lit with pleasure for a moment before he masked the look with studied nonchalance. "How is she?"

"You can ask her yourself. She'll be here tomorrow."

"I thought she had a big case."

"She did, but the guy confessed. So she's coming here to be with us."

"You mean to be with you."

Katherine nodded absently, thinking that in actuality Elaine was probably coming to be with Jeff, not with her. Which was exactly how she wanted it.

Chapter 9

"YOU'RE SURE THEN that they were Macphersons?"

Iain stood in the window alcove looking at the two men seated in his working chamber. Ranald sat back, his arms crossed, one booted foot resting on the table. Fergus sat forward, arms on the table, his eyes narrowed in thought, waiting for an answer to his question.

"They were wearing Macpherson colors." Iain looked at his cousin. "Ranald can verify that. We saw them often enough at Moy."

"That we did, and the sett was definitely Clan Macpherson's. But as to whether the lads wearing the plaids were Macphersons, that I canna say. Seems to me 'twould no' be impossible for a weaver to copy the Macpherson colors."

Fergus frowned at Ranald. "You're saying then that they werena Macphersons?"

Iain answered for him. "I think he's trying to say we canna know for sure. All we can say with certainty is that they were dressed like Macphersons."

"I say if they dress like Macphersons they *are* Macphersons," Fergus snorted.

"Well, there was certainly no one left to ask," Ranald added dryly.

Fergus' craggy face split into a lopsided grin. "Aye, I wish I could have been there to help you send the thieving bastards straight to hell. All of them dead but one, and I doubt that he'll have much interest in stealing Mackintosh cattle now."

" 'Tis true. He probably thought he'd met the devil himself when he saw Iain brandishing his claymore." Ranald leaned back against the wall and propped his other foot on the table.

"More than likely it was your ugly face that sent him screaming from the pass." Iain felt the corner of his mouth twitch in amusement, then drop back into a frown. He narrowed his eyes in speculation. "If they were Macphersons I canna figure out why they'd be reiving on Mackintosh lands. Our clans are at peace, united under Chattan. It doesna make sense."

Fergus pursed his lips thoughtfully. "Aye, well the call of an empty belly can sometimes be stronger than the ties of clan alliances. And those cattle would have gone a long way toward filling hungry mouths."

"True enough. If it were just the reiving, I'd be inclined to consider the matter closed. They paid dearly for their arrogance. But there's this still to be considered." Iain drew his father's dirk from its sheath and with a flick of his wrist sent the dagger slicing through the air. It landed point-down, embedded in the table. Fergus pulled it out and examined it carefully.

" 'Tis Angus'. You say you found it on the body of one of the reivers?"

"Aye, the leader, a big red-haired man. I'd never seen him before." Iain crossed to the table and straddled a chair, his arms resting on its back.

"Ah, but he seems to have known you." Ranald looked pointedly at Iain, then dropped his feet to the floor and reached to take the knife from Fergus.

Fergus looked puzzled. "I dinna ken."

"Well, the man obviously followed us after the battle, to get revenge for his clansmen, one would assume. But our lad pointedly ignores the opportunity to pick off Roger and me. We both went to the burn to wash up before Iain. Alone. And yet neither of us was attacked. Nay, the man waited until Iain was alone. And then went for him with a vengeance. I'd say 'tis no' a man with an interest only in general revenge. Add to that the fact that he carried Uncle Angus' dirk and I dinna think you can see it any other way." Ranald handed the dagger back to Iain, hilt-first.

Iain absently twirled the dirk in his hand, thinking about Ranald's conclusions. The stone on the hilt turned black as sunlight from the window passed over it.

Fergus watched them both, grim understanding illuminating his face. "You think that the reiver killed your father?"

Iain looked up, stilling the knife with one last twist. "Aye, 'tis likely. I'll never believe that he fell. So that leaves murder. And the man with the dirk seems a likely candidate. The only alternative I can see is that he stole the dagger from the body or that someone else gave it to him. And given the circumstances, those ideas seem to be wee bit far-fetched. What say you, Ranald?"

"I think 'tis possible that the man who killed Uncle Angus is dead."

Fergus sat stroking his beard thoughtfully. "Well, if what you say is true, lad, then I'd say you've avenged your father's death. He'll rest easier knowing the way of it."

Iain nodded. "Aye, but what of Andrew?"

Ranald spoke. "We left five of the reivers dead. Odds are that one of them was the man who killed Andrew. I'd say that we've avenged him as well."

"Have you had the chance to talk to Mari?" Fergus rose and walked to the fireplace to warm his backside.

"Aye." The knife in Iain's hand started to spin again.

"How did she take the news?"

Iain shrugged. "As well as can be expected. She's a strong lass. Did you know she carries Andrew's bairn?"

"Nay. But I imagine the babe will be a comfort to her. A little piece of Andrew, if you know what I mean. 'Tis a mon's duty to leave his seed to grow after he's gone."

"Is that a hint, Fergus?"

"Nay, nothing more than a bit of hindsight from an old mon."

"Fergus, surely you're no' calling yourself old." Ranald shot an amused glance at the burly man.

"Aye, lad, that I am. And if I was to be doing it o'er, I'd find myself a bonny wee lassie and set about making many fine sons."

"I presume you're trying, in your no' so subtle way, to convince me o' the importance of my choosing a bride. It seems to be on *everyone's* mind these days," Iain offered dryly, raising an eyebrow at Ranald.

Fergus looked across the table at Iain. "Aye, well, it's only right that the Laird have his Lady. Freedom may seem appealing, but there are many boons that come with taking a wife."

"The bedding being the best, o' course." Ranald arched his eyebrows mischievously while rubbing his hands together, his expression somehow simultaneously angelic and devilish.

"And am I to understand that you both see the Davidson lass as a suitable candidate?"

They grinned.

"Did someone mention Ailis?"

All three men turned at the sound of the voice. Alasdair leaned insolently against the doorframe, a sly smile leaving his handsome face cold.

"What is it you want, Alasdair?" Iain stopped spinning the dirk and with a fierce motion jabbed it into the table.

Alasdair sauntered into the chamber. "Surely you've time for a wee chat with a neighbor. In fact, 'tis providential that I find you discussing my sister. You see, 'tis Ailis I wish to talk about."

Fergus' lips twitched, but he held his laughter. "I'll be taking my leave then. Dinna see how I can be helping you with this, Iain."

"Wait, Fergus, I'll go with you." Ranald tossed a quick grin over his shoulder and hurried after him. Their laughter echoed in the great hall.

Iain groaned silently. Deserted. "Well, Alasdair, you seem to have my undivided attention. Have a seat."

Alasdair slid onto the bench Ranald had deserted, the long fingers of one hand cupped under his chin. "Your father was planning your marriage, you know."

Iain fought to control his surprise. "My father is dead." He was relieved that his voice sounded cool and reserved.

Alasdair lifted his other hand, inspecting his nails. "True enough. But I assume you would still want to honor his wishes."

"And how exactly would you come to be privy to those wishes, Alasdair?"

"Angus and I were close, more like father and son really. 'Twas his greatest wish to see our families united. We had agreed that marriage between you and my sister would be the perfect way to accomplish such an alliance. 'Tis why he called you home."

Again, Iain felt a rush of emotion and strove hard to contain it. Alasdair and his father close? He found the idea repugnant.

"Even if those were my father's wishes, Alasdair, surely you understand that the decision is mine to make."

"Of course, of course. 'Tis just that with your puir father barely in the grave I thought you'd be wanting to know of his wishes." Alasdair reached out to stroke the handle of the dagger.

Iain fought against a powerful urge to snatch the dirk from Alasdair's grasp. "I'll take them into consideration,

Alasdair, but I'll tell you now, I've no desire to wed Ailis."

Alasdair wrenched the knife from the table. "Are you implying that my sister isna good enough to become a Mackintosh?" His face was flushed with fury.

"Nay, calm yourself, Alasdair. There is nothing wrong with Ailis. You misunderstand me. I've no wish to marry at all. My feelings have nothing to do with your sister."

Alasdair slowly laid the dirk on the table, his features gradually relaxing into geniality again. "Forgive me. I have a great affection for my sister and canna stand the thought of any man rejecting her. All I ask, indeed all your father would have no doubt asked, is that you think about the proposition. Ailis would make you a good wife. She is pleasing to look at and well trained in the running of a household."

Iain picked up his father's knife and quietly put it in its sheath. "Alasdair, as I've said, I've no wish to marry at present, but I promise to consider your sister should I change my mind."

"I suppose that will have to do, for now." Alasdair pushed away from the table, straightening his plaid as he turned to go.

"Alasdair?"

He stopped, his back still to Iain. "Aye?"

"How much longer are you planning to stay at Duncreag?"

"I promised Sorcha we'd stay out the se'nnight." He shot a look at Iain over his shoulder. "Does that meet with your approval?"

"Aye, I've no cause to keep Ailis from my auntie Sorcha if she is helping her in her grief. But at week's end I'll expect you to go."

Alasdair nodded. "And you'll think on the matter of my sister?"

"I said I would."

Iain sat motionless, watching Alasdair leave, studying

the man's retreating back. There was something about
him Iain couldn't quite fathom, something deep inside
carefully hidden behind layers of courtesy and conge-
niality.

Iain slumped forward, and ran his hands through his
hair. He felt outmaneuvered. It seemed everyone was
conspiring to get him to marry Alasdair's sister. First
Fergus and Ranald, then Alasdair, and now it seemed
even his father wished it so—from the grave, no less.

Iain closed his eyes, trying to picture Ailis. But instead his mind conjured a golden-haired gray-eyed
beauty dressed in emerald green. Her lips were open in
invitation. He felt himself harden in anticipation of tasting her sweetness.

He slammed a fist down on the table. He'd not be
forced into a marriage with Ailis by his well-meaning
family. And he certainly wasn't going to let Alasdair
Davidson tell him whom to wed.

"Well, I see you survived your encounter with Alasdair."

Iain crossed the great hall to the window to where
Ranald and Ailis sat across from each other on the two
facing window seats. "I believe I'm still in one piece."

Ailis colored and bent her head to examine the tapestry she was working on.

"Ailis." Iain nodded to the top of her head and sat
down on the window seat next to Ranald.

"My Laird." She glanced over quickly and then bent
again to her work.

"I trust my cousin has been keeping you entertained?"

Again, Ailis' cheeks turned pink. She looked at Ranald and smiled timidly. "Your cousin is indeed full of
interesting tales. He has been kind enough to spend the
afternoon sharing his marvelous stories of the intrigues
at Moy. It seems to have been very exciting. I do not
doubt that you miss it a great deal."

Iain grinned at Ranald. "As it happens, things here

have been rather exciting of late and so I've had no time at all to miss being at my uncle's."

"Tell me, then, is it true that you and Ranald single-handedly rescued the Mackintosh's grandson from the clutches of the Camerons?" she asked, giving Iain a shy glance, her smile hopeful. He shifted uncomfortably.

"Aye, 'tis true. We rescued the lad. But we didna accomplish the feat by ourselves. We wouldna have managed to release the man at all if it hadna been for his betrothed. Eleanor was the one who saved him, in truth. We were naught but the muscle behind her plan."

Ailis looked at Ranald in confusion. "But I thought . . ."

Ranald looked at his feet, a reddish stain creeping across his face. Iain resisted the urge to laugh. "I've never seen you blush, cousin. 'Tis quite becoming."

Ranald shot Iain a warning look. Iain ignored it, smiling at Ailis. "You see, my cousin has a habit of embellishing his stories a wee bit, always to his benefit, of course. You may be sure that there is some truth in the tales he tells. He is no' a dishonest man. He merely sees things from a bard's point of view."

Ranald sputtered. "A bard? I am certainly no' one of those."

"You're right. I should have qualified it." Iain grinned at Ailis, who was now smiling too. "You're a warrior bard, a fighting poet. A very odd breed, I'm told. Ailis, we are indeed in the presence of a rare fellow. We should count ourselves blessed."

Iain winced as an elbow jammed into his side. Ailis' lips trembled in her struggle to contain her merriment. But she finally lost the battle, and her sweet laughter rang through the hall. Ranald threw his hands in the air with a gesture of surrender, his baritone rumble joining Ailis' melodic sweet soprano.

Gulping for air, Ailis swallowed and wiped tears from her eyes. "And to think I thought you merely a gallant fellow. I had no idea you were so . . . unique." She started to laugh again, her eyes shining as she looked at Ranald.

Iain removed his dirk, laying it beside him, then began massaging his chest. "Well, Ranald, I'm certainly living proof of your warrior side. I think you've broken a rib."

"Now who exaggerates, cousin?" Ranald asked, grimacing in good humor.

"Oh, do stop it, both of you. I cannot breathe for laughing."

Ranald immediately moved to sit beside her, his concern evident as he awkwardly patted her arm. "Are you all right then? I certainly didna mean to cause you any harm."

Ailis smiled at him. "I am fine, honestly." She reached for Iain's dirk and ran a gentle finger over the smoky stone in its hilt. "I see you found Alasdair's dirk. He will be ever so pleased. He told me just the other day that he had managed to misplace it."

Iain gave her a puzzled look, taking the dirk from her. "Nay, you're mistaken, Ailis. 'Twas my father's dirk. And now 'tis mine."

Ailis stared at the knife, her brow furrowed with concentration. "You are right, of course. Now that I think on it I am sure Alasdair's dirk is larger than this one. It was just the dark stone that fooled me." She turned to smile at Ranald, the dirk completely forgotten.

Iain slipped the knife into its scabbard and sat back, watching the two of them. Ailis was laughing softly again, and Ranald was almost fawning. Fawning. Ranald. Amazing. Well, Iain told himself, at least he could quit worrying about Ailis. She seemed quite capable of attracting a husband without any help at all from her brother. Ranald had better watch his step.

With that thought, Iain's mouth curled into a smile. He stifled the urge to laugh. "I'll be off, then. I've a need to find Auntie Sorcha and check on young William."

He might as well have been talking to the wall for all the notice the couple in the window seat gave him.

"How fares the lad?"

Sorcha looked up as Iain entered the chamber. She was kneeling at William's side, a needle in her hand.

"I'm just stitching him up. The bleeding's stopped, Saints be praised, but he's burning up. I canna promise he'll recover." Sorcha returned to her work, making neat stitches along the wound.

Iain moved to the side of the bed. The gash ran almost the length of William's leg, the skin around it an angry red. Sorcha tied off the stitches and cut them with her knife. She reached for a strip of linen covered with a poultice of some sort.

"What's that then?"

" 'Tis naught but a few herbs to help draw out the bad humors and ease the swelling." She wrapped the bandage around the leg once and tied it off with quick efficiency. "There is naught to do now but wait. Either the fever will take him or it won't."

The boy thrashed on the bed, moving his head back and forth. Sorcha immediately reached to soothe the boy pushing the damp hair back from his face. He moaned and quieted. "Have you told his parents yet?" Sorcha asked.

"Aye. I went to them almost as soon as we returned. They'll be here at nightfall. I think his mother would have come now, but I assured her it was best to let you tend to the boy first. I know they're comforted in knowing you're caring for the lad."

Sorcha blushed, embarrassed by the compliment. "A body does what she can."

Iain circled the bed to stand beside his aunt. Guilt slashed through him, almost as tangible as the poor boy's battered leg. "If I could will him to live, I would, but I fear 'tis no' within my power to do so."

"Nor is it your place. 'Tis in God's hands now." Sor-

cha awkwardly placed a hand on Iain's arm. " 'Tis sorry
I was to hear about your troubles. I know 'tis probably
a sin, but I'm ever so grateful that 'twas Andrew killed
and no' you."

Iain put an arm around her thin body and gave her a
squeeze. To his surprise, she burst into tears. "What ails
you, Auntie Sorcha?"

" 'Tis nothing." She scrubbed the tears away with the
back of her hand. "Only that I'm still missing your father." She turned then, briskly setting about wetting a
scrap of linen. Once it was sufficiently damp she laid it
across William's forehead. "Be off with you now. I've
work to do."

Iain stood for a minute longer watching as she min-
istered to the boy. As he left the chamber, he wondered,
not for the first time, just exactly what kind of relationship Sorcha had shared with his father.

Candlelight flickered, illuminating the bedchamber. Iain
paced like a caged beast, trying to assimilate the discov-
eries of the last few days. Two of his clansmen had
suffered, one dead and another hanging by a fine thread.
His father had been murdered. Of that Iain was certain.
Whether it was, in fact, at the hand of a Macpherson
was yet to be seen. Alasdair Davidson had weaseled his
way into Duncreag. And if Iain didn't watch his step
he'd soon find the bastard his brother-in-law.

And if all that wasn't enough, he had started having
visions. Granted it was a lovely vision, and more to the
point, had likely saved his life. But by the Saints, it was
still fantasy, wasn't it? Iain stopped pacing long enough
to pour himself some wine. He drank deeply, then wiped
his mouth with a linen-covered arm. He knelt down,
staring into the fire, wondering, not the first time, who
she was and why she haunted him both day and night.

He closed his eyes, trying to see her, to feel her. He
waited.

Nothing.

He sat back on his heels, angered at his vulnerability.
No, he *had* seen her—there by the stream. Bloody hell,
she had saved him. He closed his eyes again, and this
time she was there, standing by the burn, her eyes wide
with terror, her mouth moving in the effort to reach him.
Her slender hand pointing, desperately trying to warn
him, to save him. He trembled, seeing again the love in
her eyes. It had been almost tangible.

He opened his eyes to his empty chamber. Tightening
his fist around his cup, he shifted to sit cross-legged
before the fire, its flames dancing in hypnotic rhythm.
He sat in silence, letting the fire and the wine warm him.
Here, in the flickering light, nothing seemed impossible.
So he sat, sipping mulled wine and wishing for miracles.

Chapter 10

KATHERINE SAT BY the peat fire, watching her brother try to stay awake. His eyes were already half-closed. She knew from long experience that he would soon be soundly asleep. Never had she known anyone who could fall asleep faster. All through their childhood they had shared good night talks. The sessions had started as a family custom, with all four St. Claires gathering in either her or her brother's bedroom to wish each other good night and exchange last-minute words of wisdom and comfort. When their parents had died, the nightly ritual had taken on even more significance, the two children trying desperately not to let go of what had once been a family. Over the years the talks had become less frequent, but they had never stopped altogether, often taking place by telephone. But always, always, Jeff had fallen asleep in the middle of them. It was, at the same time, both exasperating and endearing.

"I'd say that unless you want to sleep in here tonight, you'd better get a move on."

Jeff sat up sleepily, rubbing a hand over his eyes. "Oh Lord, did I do it again? I'm sorry, Kitty. Did I miss anything important?"

She smiled at him fondly. "No, as a matter of fact, I wasn't talking at all. Just enjoying the quiet and being here with you. But I think we'd best be off to bed now." With that she stood, grabbed his arm, and pulled him upright. Both hands on his shoulders, she turned him to face the stairs. "Up you go. I'll see you in the morning."

"All right, I'm going." He took two steps, then stopped, turning back to face his sister. "You'll be okay? I mean dream boy. . . ." He stopped mid-sentence, looking sheepish.

"I'll be fine. Whatever happens, I'll be fine." Katherine crossed to him and gave him a hug. "Good night." Her voice held traces of laughter.

Jeff nodded and trudged dutifully up the stairs, his tousled hair making him resemble a toddler on his way to a nap.

Katherine stood and watched until he was out of sight. "I love you," she whispered.

The radiator hissed quietly in its corner as Katherine got ready for bed. She slid into the cool silk of her nightgown and then began brushing out her long hair. Freed from its confining braid, her hair tumbled over her shoulders, its golden strands shining in the harsh electric light.

After a few moments, she put down her brush and climbed into the tiny bed and snapped off the lamp. Moonlight filled the room. She tossed and turned, but sleep eluded her. Her brain whirled with thoughts of time travel and fantasy, dark lovers and medieval warriors.

Realizing that sleep was not coming, she pulled herself out of bed and walked over to the window seat. She curled up in a corner and watched as the moon threw shadows across the courtyard. As the stars moved overhead, Katherine felt her eyes grow heavy. Thinking that she ought to climb back into bed, she drifted off to sleep.

•　　•　　•

Iain jerked to with a start. How long had he been sitting here. The fire had burned down to softly glowing coals and the candles had long since gutted out. The chamber was filled with darkness, and he was cold. He stood cautiously, aware that his foot had fallen asleep. Stomping on it, he tried to ignore the vicious tingling.

Cursing the cold, he began undressing, casting his plaid into a corner. He watching as the garment settled into a heap on the floor. He reached down for the tails of his shirt, already moving toward the warmth of his bed, but stopped when he saw the shadow that marked the doorway to the adjoining chamber. His feet seemed to move of their own volition, taking him to the door.

He paused in the doorway, his heart pounding. Drawing a deep breath, he looked at the bed. Empty. He felt his gut lurch with disappointment. It was as always. She had not come. He turned to go, but halted when a flicker of green caught his eye. He spun around, his eyes focusing on the window.

The moonlight washed over the sleeping figure. She was curled in the corner of the stone seat, the emerald of her night shift almost glowing in the pale light. He took a step forward, hands shaking. The figure at the window shifted. He froze, watching as she opened her eyes and sat up, staring in sleepy confusion.

Their gazes met and held. She drew in a breath that was almost a sob. Pressing a trembling hand to her breast, she stood.

"You're here. . . ." Her words trailed off, a mere whisper.

He crossed the room, his eyes never breaking contact with hers. She moved toward him as well, slowly, like a sleepwalker. She licked her lips nervously, her hands mindlessly clenching and unclenching. Time seemed to stop. She was drawn to the green of his eyes, the only color, in all his darkness.

They met in the center of the room. She reached with trembling hands to touch him. His chest felt solid beneath her fingers. She let out the breath she had been holding. He was real.

He moved, and then his mouth was covering hers, hard and demanding. His arms closed around her. She was soft and yielding. He pulled her tighter into his embrace. Even with the passing of years, she felt right there as though he had held her through countless nights instead of just one.

She breathed his strong, spicy scent and sighed, her mouth opening. His tongue found its way home, stroking, sucking, mating with hers. The warmth spread slowly from somewhere below her stomach. It grew and spread until she ached from it. And still the kiss went on. His hands wound through her hair. He pulled her close, closer. She wanted . . . wanted to be closer still. Part of him. Yes, that was it, she wanted him to be inside her. Oh God, she'd spoken out loud. Hot color burned her cheeks.

He laughed and pulled her up into his arms, then he walked quickly through the arched doorway into the adjoining chamber. In two short steps they were at the bed. He released her, her body sliding against his hardness. He pulled the tie at her neck and pushed the gown from her body. The silken fabric caressed her as it fell in a pool of cool green at her feet.

She shivered, but not from the cold. He was wearing only a long shirt. With shaking hands, she tried to push it aside. He stepped back and with one long swift motion pulled the shirt over his head, his bronzed muscles rippling as he did so. Her breath caught in her throat. He stood before her naked, and her eyes drank in the sight of his hard, muscled body. Her hand, with a will of its own, reached out to stroke the puckered redness of the scar on his arm. Her eyes were drawn downward. She swallowed and moved a step closer.

He pulled her tightly against him, feeling the soft swelling of her breasts against his chest. Her skin burned him and he felt a tightness deep inside him growing harder. He wanted nothing more than to sheath himself deep within her. He lifted her and turned, lowering her gently to the mattress. He paused above her, drinking in the sight of her. She was beautiful. Her hair was spread like a fan beneath her. He wondered how it would feel to be wrapped with her in its silkiness. He lowered his body to hers, bracing himself so that he wouldn't crush her. He bent his head, his mouth again claiming hers.

Her body arched forward, straining to get closer. His hands were touching her everywhere. Stroking. Caressing. His hand brushed against her breasts. She shivered, and a low moan escaped from deep in her throat. She wanted him. It had been so long. Her hand stroked his back as his mouth continued to force her surrender. The warmth spreading inside her had grown red hot. She began to move against him, feeling his hardness against the warmth of her thigh. His mouth moved to the curve of her neck. She shivered with passion and turned her head to give him better access to the soft skin. But his mouth moved lower, to the vee of her breasts. His tongue brushed across her nipple, circling the tender, hardening bud. She arched upward, wanting more. The single word "Please" echoed through the still night. His mouth closed over her breast and he began to suckle. She cried out with the joy of it.

Never had he felt such passion. The longing for her was intense. Not just for release, although his body was aching for it, but for something more, something deeper, beyond the primal need of man for woman. It wasn't just woman, it was *this* woman. The need built inside him, growing in fury and pitch until it burned out of control. He moved a hand down the silkiness of her belly, caressing and stroking.

Slowly, his hand moved to the triangle of golden curls. It seemed to take forever. She held her breath, her heart pounding. He still suckled at her breast, teasing the nipple until it ached with need. His fingers stroked the softness that was her essence. Slow, smooth strokes. She

clenched, and then he found the small nub and began to
stroke it, quickly and lightly as a feather. Her legs were
shaking. Her breath came in ragged gasps as though she
had run a great distance. Just when she thought she
would explode, his fingers moved, inward, upward,
thrusting, stroking deep inside her. His mouth moved
back to hers, his tongue matching his fingers stroke for
stroke. She pushed hard against his fingers, wanting
more. Her hands reached downward, fumbling in her
need to find him. And still he thrust, pressing and stroking.

He felt her hand close around him. Her fingers moved
slowly along the length of his shaft. He moved his fingers deep inside her, feeling her wet hotness surround
him. He ached with the need to be inside her. He felt
her shudder and knew her climax was near. He moved
away briefly, placing a knee between her legs. She
gasped and opened for him, arching upward in invitation. He braced his elbows on either side of her and
looked deep into her eyes.

"You are mine. You have always been mine."

And with one long stroke, he was inside her. She was
hot and tight and he wanted her more than he had ever
wanted anything in his life. The intensity of his feelings
amazed him. He felt a deep and primal need to possess
her, not just in this moment but forever. She reached for
him, her hands tangling in his hair, a soft cry coming
from deep in her throat. The sound of it heightened his
pleasure. He smiled at her and slowly pulled away.

She writhed beneath him, trying frantically to pull him
back. She needed him more than she needed to breathe.
Just when she thought she'd scream from wanting him,
he thrust into her again, his heat searing her. They
moved together, locked in their own private rhythm. The
fire consumed her. Her thoughts whirled and feelings
more powerful than any she could remember came over
her in wave after wave. She felt like exploding, like
screaming. It was pure liquid fire. And then she felt his

fingers again on the center of her desire. As she lost all control, she wound her fingers in the smooth blackness of his hair. She arched her hips against him and felt herself splinter into tiny pieces of light.

He felt her shudders and the tightening deep within her. She cried out as he began to thrust harder and deeper. He closed his eyes, and color filled the darkness. He felt the world spin, and then felt only sensations. Sensations that built and burned until in a single moment the world exploded and he emptied his seed in spasms of pure joy.

She locked her legs around him, holding him to her, trying to bind them forever. He kissed her again, but with tenderness and gentleness. The fire had been released, leaving glowing warmth. He rolled to his side, pulling her with him, staying connected, face-to-face. Her breathing was calmer, but still coming in small gasps. Her hand stroked the skin of his cheek, feeling the roughness of his whiskers. She felt as though her heart was full enough to burst. Tears slid down her cheeks. And still she looked into his eyes, held there by emotions she'd had no idea she could feel.

He watched as tears rolled down the gentle curve of her cheek. He reached with a tender touch to wipe them away. He knew suddenly that he would never survive losing her again. She was as necessary to him as air and water. He pulled her close, tucking her head under his chin. He felt the warmth of her breath against his chest.

She sighed and snuggled into his arms. Somewhere in the back of her mind she was afraid. Afraid that tomorrow he would be only a dream. Afraid, too, of what it meant if he wasn't a dream. She pushed these thoughts back into the recesses of her subconscious mind and closed her eyes, content for the moment in the knowledge that they were together.

He felt her relax against him. Instinctively his arms tightened around her. He would hold her safely through the night. As he breathed in the sweet scent of her hair, he vowed silently to hold her not only this night, but all others as well. They were connected in a way he could not completely comprehend, but he knew that she was his, indeed had been his from that moment eight years ago when she had appeared at his bedside. This time he would not let her go.

And so, surrounded by love and still joined, they slept.

Katherine rolled to her side, curling into the warmth of the bed as she slowly drifted from sleep to wakefulness. She sighed and stretched, reveling in the feel of her body, a body that had been well loved. The thought brought instant clarity as she remembered the events of the night before.

Iain.

Her eyes flew open, searching for his face. The pillow next to hers was empty. She reached out with trembling fingers and touched the place where he had slept. *Cold.* Oh God, another dream. She sat up, the covers slipping to her waist, panic making her heart race.

"Ah, you're awake." The deep voice came from the alcove.

Katherine turned and saw that he was standing there, back to the window, smiling tenderly at her. She heaved a sigh, her relief making her feel giddy. Or maybe it was the sight of him. He was magnificent, his body hard and seasoned, the body of a warrior. Her breath caught in her throat. A tremor of desire whipped through her. They had loved long into the night, sleeping fitfully, only to awaken and love again. Yet, she found she still wanted him.

"I dinna even know your name."

Katherine blushed furiously, trying to gather her thoughts. What a loose woman he must think her to sleep with a complete stranger not once but twice. Backing into the far corner of the bed, she frantically pulled the bed covering up to her chin, gnawing on her bottom lip, unwilling to look at him, to see the condemnation she was certain was there in his eyes.

"I . . ." The words died as she felt him sit beside her, one strong hand beneath her chin, tipping her face up toward his.

"Names are no' important, *mo chridhe*—my heart. Our souls know each other. Aye, I think they have know each other for a very long time."

Embarrassment died as she looked deeply into his clear green eyes. The emotion she saw reflected there started her heart pounding again.

"My name is Katherine St. Claire." Her voice was shaking.

"Ah, Katherine," he said sighing. "I am Iain Mackintosh of Duncreag."

Even as he spoke, his lips moved closer to hers, his breath warm on her cheek.

"Iain." She whispered his name and melted into his kiss.

Sunlight poured through the window when next they awoke. Katherine could feel the warm weight of Iain's leg against her thigh. She rolled onto her back and opened her eyes. It was all pretty amazing. Here she was lying in bed with a man she really didn't know, in a castle in the middle of the Scottish Highlands, probably in the Middle Ages, and instead of being out of her mind with fear and worry, she was feeling as contented as a cat. She felt Iain shift and turned to meet his probing green gaze.

" 'Tis morning. I feared you would be gone." He ran the back of his hand along her cheek. She nuzzled into his touch, running her hand idly through the coarse hair on his chest.

"No. I'm here. But I don't know if this is real. I'm afraid it's another dream and I'll wake up and you'll be gone. If that were to happen . . ." Her voice caught. She swallowed, trying to hold back her tears. "Iain, if that were to happen, I'm not sure I could bear it."

He sat up, pulling her with him so that she rested against the broad expanse of his chest. She felt the rhythm of his breathing and let the motion sooth her.

"Hush now, mo chridhe, you must no' think of such things. This is real. We're together. And I'm no' letting anything keep us apart again."

She leaned into him, comforted by his words even if she didn't quite believe him. She closed her eyes, trying to find the courage to ask questions she wasn't completely sure she wanted answered.

"Iain?" She took a deep breath. "Are we at Duncreag?"

He rumbled his assent and tightened his arm around her.

"Okay, then, here's the twenty-four-thousand-dollar question. When are we? I mean, what year is it?"

She waited, listening to the steady beat of his heart.

" 'Tis the spring of fourteen hundred and sixty-seven."

Katherine's head swam. 1467. Oh Lord, *1467*. She was grateful that Iain's arm was around her. She thought she'd been prepared for his answer, but the reality was more frightening than she had ever imagined. She jerked around to look at him. "I'm not from here, Iain. And I've no idea how I got here."

Iain looked steadily at her, taking her trembling hands in his. "Katherine, I know naught of where you're from, and I canna say how you came to be in my home. But by the Saints, 'tis grateful I am to whatever power brought you here. And I'll no' question my good fortune too closely."

"Iain, listen to me. It's more than where I'm from." She tightened her fingers around his. "It's *when* I'm from. When I went to bed last night, it was here in Duncreag, but it was Duncreag more than five hundred years from now."

Katherine held his gaze, willing him to understand and not turn away from her in fear or disbelief.

"Well," Iain shrugged philosophically, pulling her back into his arms. "At least you're no' a fairy."

Chapter 11

JEFF TOWELED HIS hair dry, raking his fingers through it in lieu of a comb. Ah, what a beautiful day. Sunlight streamed through the open window, the sounds of birds filling the crisp morning air. Jeff drew a deep cleansing breath and pulled on his jeans. Here he was in Scotland, in the middle of an architectural wonderland. Things couldn't be any better. Well, he mentally corrected himself, there *was* the small problem of his sister and her visions from the past. But hey, on a day like today even that didn't seem so bad.

Jeff smiled at himself in the mirror as he glopped shaving cream on his face. Humming an off-key version of "Oh, What a Beautiful Mornin'," he twisted his mouth to the left and began to shave. Elaine was coming today. Jeff yelped as he nicked himself. Grabbing a towel, he dabbed ineffectually at the small cut.

The truth was he didn't know exactly what he felt for Elaine. Lust certainly. No red-blooded male could look at Elaine's voluptuous curves and not feel some degree of lust. But there was more to it than that. He had known Elaine since Katherine started graduate school. The two girls had been inseparable, which meant that Elaine had spent most holidays with the St. Claires in Connecticut.

Then he'd taken a job with a firm in New York, and the threesome had remained intact. Jeff tried to remember exactly when his feelings for Elaine had changed from those for his kid sister's tag-along friend to, well, whatever it was now. All he knew for sure was that he was looking forward to spending time with her. He wiped the remaining flecks of shaving cream from his face, giving himself a quick salute in the mirror. Fingers crossed, Elaine might actually be interested in him, too. Katherine hadn't said anything directly, but she had certainly hinted broadly enough.

Pulling on a blue polo shirt, Jeff grabbed his keys and bounded out the door, his humming changing to full-fledged singing. Well, maybe not singing exactly, since a person had to be able to carry a tune to sing, a talent he had never been blessed with. But then no one was around to hear him except Katherine, and by now she was used to his voice. Taking the stairs two at a time, he descended to Katherine's floor. He smiled at a maid and rapped three times on the door, humming again now in deference to the maid's ears.

"She's not there, sir."

Jeff swung around to look at the maid. "Excuse me?"

"I said she's not there. I was just in the room. It's empty. Maybe she's already gone down for breakfast."

Jeff felt a little niggling of worry, but promptly pushed it aside. They'd agreed to meet at ten. He looked at his watch, noting it was already fifteen after. Maybe she'd gotten tired of waiting. He thanked the girl and made his way down to the great hall.

However, save a solitary diner at a corner table, the hall was empty. No Katherine. Again, Jeff felt a tickle of concern. But the smell of sausages and eggs called to him. Katherine was probably just taking a walk somewhere. She'd dash in any minute, he assured himself, breathless and apologizing for being late, then she'd throw herself into the chair and proceed to tell him all about last night's adventures with Fantasy Man. Jeff smiled at the thought, all worry successfully banished.

A cheerful woman in a checkered apron delivered a basket of hot breads. What had Katherine called them? Bann something. He was in the process of buttering his third when the waitress brought a plate heaped with sausages and poached eggs. Jeff smiled as he dug in. Yes, this was definitely turning out to be a wonderful day.

Two hours later, after having seen neither hide nor hair of his sister, he was beginning to reassess his position. He'd looked everywhere—the gift shop, the chapel museum, the lobby, the gardens, even the battlements, though he'd known he wouldn't find her there. He'd been in her room and had discovered that her purse was still there, along with her keys and her wallet. Her watch was on the dresser with her other jewelry. In fact, the only thing he recognized as missing was the cairngorm earring she wore as a pendant. The slight concern that he had brushed aside that morning was blossoming into a bigger worry, although the absence of the necklace meant nothing, since Katherine rarely, if ever, removed it from around her neck.

Another hour passed with no sign of Katherine, and Jeff's worry was swiftly becoming full-fledged panic. What if Katherine was right about the gateway? What if she truly was linked with this Iain fellow? Jeff ran a hand through his hair and tried to think rationally. Nobody traveled through time. It simply wasn't possible.

So then where the heck was his sister? He retraced his steps, stopping to check all the rooms along the way to make sure he hadn't missed her somehow. But by the time he arrived back at Katherine's room, he still had yet to see any sign of her. He sat on the bed, feeling frustration blend with despair.

"Katherine! Where are you?"

The words seemed to echo through the room finally,

fading away to leave a silence broken only by the ticking of the travel alarm.

Elaine shoved her sunglasses onto her head and pushed the strap of her travel case back over her shoulder. With a sigh, she slammed the trunk of her rental car and bent down to pick up the suitcase at her feet. Where were bellboys when you needed them? Hey, she'd even settle for one of Katherine's medieval men. Looking at Duncreag, it was easy enough to imagine one. The tower house was certainly imposing. Its stones looked almost white in the glare of the afternoon sun. Elaine trudged over the rough cobblestones in the drive. This was not exactly the entrance she'd been planning. She had pictured it more along the lines of Jeff waiting anxiously for her to appear and then pulling her into his arms while swarms of bellhops carried her luggage away to be deposited in their suite. Elaine smiled at herself. It seemed Katherine wasn't the only one with wild dreams.

Spying the small sign with the word "Lobby" printed on it, Elaine reached for the heavy wooden door. It swung open with surprising ease. She stepped inside, then dumped her bags against the wall by the door. She surveyed the room and was pleased to see that it was indeed the lobby. There was a desk in the corner that Elaine supposed was where one checked in. Unfortunately, there didn't appear to be anyone around to facilitate the process. She crossed to the desk and idly examined a stack of postcards showing the tower at its imposing best, waiting for someone to notice she was there.

"Hello. May I help you?"

Elaine put down the cards as she turned in the direction of the voice. A ruddy-faced man in cords and a Shetland sweater was just coming out of a small hallway.

"Um, yes, please. I've only just arrived. I believe you're expecting me?"

"Well, I'm afraid I wouldn't know about that. My wife handles all the reservations. I'm Jamie Abernathy." He held out a hand.

"Elaine Macqueen."

"I'm supposed to handle the books and such, but to tell you the truth, Agnes doesn't really need my help. I think she only gives me things to do so that I'll feel useful. You wait right here and I'll go and fetch her for you."

Before he had even walked two steps, the outside door opened and what could only be described as a small whirlwind of energy burst into the room.

"Ah, Jamie love, there you are. I was out by the west wall and I noticed that the sign for the car park has come loose again. Would you mind having a look? I'd hate for it to come completely off the wall and fall onto one of the guests' cars. I'd imagine it's big enough to break a window."

The whirlwind took the form of an older woman. Her face was red with exertion and her gray hair curled every which way.

"Fine, love, I'll just go and check." Mr. Abernathy waved a hand in Elaine's direction. "I've just been chatting with our new guest." With that, he ambled off down the hallway.

Mrs. Abernathy bustled around behind the desk, a picture of enthusiasm and efficiency. "You must be Katherine and Jeffrey's friend. Elaine, isn't it?"

Elaine smiled at the use of Jeff's full name. No one called him Jeffrey. "Yes. I'm later than I expected, I'm afraid. There was a bit of a mix-up with the rental car reservation. But I'm here now. Safe and sound."

Mrs. Abernathy eyed Elaine with friendly curiosity. "You're Scottish." It was a statement, not a question.

"Half. My father is from Inverness, but my mother is American. We've lived in the States since I was a teenager."

"So you have dual citizenship then?"

"Well, yes, but I guess I think of myself as an American. Most of my family is there. And I have my law practice."

"You're an attorney? How lovely. What type of law do you practice?"

"I'm an A.D.A."

Mrs. Abernathy looked puzzled.

"Sorry, assistant district attorney. I prosecute criminals."

"Oh, my. You look far too sweet a girl to be dealing with criminal types."

Elaine smiled at the comment. It was not the first time she had heard it, and she took it, as she always did, as a compliment. "I'm a lot tougher than I look."

Mrs. Abernathy handed Elaine a registration card to fill out. "You said your father's from Inverness? Do you have other family there?"

"Not that I know of, although I do have an aunt who lives near Inverbrough. It's my understanding that at one time it was the site of a Clan Macqueen holding."

Mrs. Abernathy paused for a moment, her lips pursed in thought. "Yes, I believe you're right. Corybrough, it was called. I think there was a connection between the Corybrough Macqueens and the Mackintoshes who originally owned Duncreag. But that was before it changed hands."

"And your family owns the tower house now?"

"Yes, it's been in our family for just over five hundred years. But listen to me running on. I'm sure you're tired. Why don't you step into the parlor and I'll bring you a cup of tea."

"Thanks, but I'm really anxious to see Jeff and Katherine."

"Of course, of course. Why don't you leave your bags here and I'll have Jamie bring them up for you later."

Elaine nodded gratefully.

"I haven't seen Katherine today, but I saw Jeffrey in the second-floor parlor not half an hour ago. Just take those stairs to the great hall. Walk all the way through toward the gift shop and you'll see another set of stairs. The parlor is just off the first landing. Do you think you can find it? I'd be more than happy to show you."

"No, no, I'll be fine. I'm sure I can find my way. Could I have my room key, do you think?"

"Oh, goodness, I don't know where my head is today, to many things happening at once, I suppose. My mind isn't what it used to be, you know." She rummaged in a cubby behind her for the key. Elaine sincerely doubted that Mrs. Abernathy's mind was anything but razor sharp.

"Here you are. It's on the third floor, next to Jeffrey's. I'm sure he'll show you where it is, if indeed you need any help."

Elaine took the key and stuck it in the pocket of her jeans.

"Dinner is at half seven. I'm sure I'll see you then. Welcome to Duncreag." With that, Mrs. Abernathy was gone, in a flurry of activity.

As Elaine stood alone in the lobby, a quote from *The Wizard of Oz* popped into her head. "People come and go so quickly here." Laughing to herself, she turned to the small hallway which Mrs. Abernathy had promised her would lead her to the stairs.

She set off, softly chanting, "Follow the Yellow Brick Road, Follow the Yellow Brick Road. . . ."

Jeff stood at the parlor window watching the shadows from the low-lying clouds scuttle across the garden below. The roses were blooming, their aged canes heavy with intertwined peach and pink flowers. There was a small stone bench under a rose-covered arbor. Some white variety that made the little arch look as though it was covered with late spring snow.

Jeff glanced at his watch. Two-thirty. Surely Elaine would be here soon. Together they would decide what to do about Katherine.

"Jeff?"

Elaine. He turned and with a sigh, pulled her into his arms in a great bear hug of relief. "Thank God you're here."

Elaine pushed away, laughing. "If I'd known the greeting I'd get I would have taken an earlier flight." She looked into his face, and all hint of laughter died. "What is it? What's wrong?"

Jeff took her hands and led her to a chintz-covered sofa. They sat facing one another, hands still linked together. "Katherine is gone."

Elaine cocked her head to one side. "Gone? What do you mean?"

"Just what I said. She's nowhere to be found. I've looked everywhere. Elaine, she's just vanished."

Elaine frowned and pulled her hands away, worry knitting her brow. "Jeff, she can't have just vanished. Let's take this a step at a time. When did you last see her?"

Jeff ran a hand through his hair. "Last night. We were in here. We talked and I fell asleep in the middle as usual and Katherine sent me to bed. We agreed to meet for breakfast at ten this morning."

"Right. So then what happened?"

"I went downstairs to her room to meet her this morning and she wasn't there. I was a few minutes late, so I decided to go on to breakfast. I figured she'd be there or that she'd gone for a walk. But, she never showed up. So after breakfast, I started looking everywhere for her."

"Have you told the Abernathys she's missing yet?"

Jeff let out a groan. "No."

"Why in the world not?"

"I kept thinking I'd find her and we'd have a good laugh over what a worrywart I was. And then, well, I guess I let all of Katherine's talk get to me."

Elaine's brows shot up. "What talk?"

Jeff shifted restlessly, finally getting up and walking over to the window. He stood in silence, trying to gather his thoughts. She was going to think he was crazy.

Elaine repeated her question. "Jeff, what talk?"

He turned to face her. "How much has Katherine told you about her dreams?"

Elaine looked puzzled by the change in subject. "Um, everything, I guess. She told me about the first dream when we were in grad school. And I know she's had others since. But you don't think her disappearance has anything to do with her dreams, do you?"

"To be honest, I don't know what I think. She had another dream while she was here."

"And Iain was in it?"

He raised an eyebrow at the name. "Yeah. She says she saved the guy. Evidently there was someone sneaking up on him and Katherine saw it and willed herself to appear or something like that. She maintains that he saw her and she was able to warn him about the other guy."

"She actually communicated with him?"

"So she says. Look, the point is Katherine believes that she and this Iain character are linked somehow and that that's why she keeps having the dreams."

Elaine interrupted. "And she believes the key to this link is Duncreag."

"Got it in one. You're not a lawyer for nothing."

Elaine smiled, then sobered. "But I still don't see what all this has to do with her being missing."

"Well, I'm not exactly sure myself, but when Katherine got back from Scotland, she still had the dreams, but they weren't very clear."

Elaine's eyes widened. "Because neither of them was at Duncreag."

"Right, at least that's what she believes."

"Oh my God, then five nights ago when she dreamed she could hear them talking . . ."

Jeff finished her sentence. ". . . Iain was at Duncreag."

Elaine took a deep breath, a frown creasing her forehead. "Okay, so then Katherine arrives here at Duncreag and has another dream. Where was Iain when this attack took place?"

"In the woods somewhere, not at Duncreag."

"So what happened eight years ago happened because they were here at the same time?"

"Yeah. Katherine thinks that some sort of cosmic doorway exists between Iain's time and ours." Jeff gave her an apologetic look. "I know it sounds far-fetched."

Again Elaine cut him off with a wave of her hand. "If that's true—and I admit it's a big if—then it would follow that when they are both at Duncreag, the door would be wide open."

"And she could go to Iain again."

Elaine's eyes narrowed in thought. "Wait a minute. When Katherine went before, she was only there for a night. She woke up the next morning alone and very much in the twentieth century."

Jeff crossed the room and flopped back onto the sofa. "She has an answer for that, too. She says that she chose to leave Iain. She was embarrassed about what they had done. So she left and went back to what she thought was her own room."

"In effect, then, she came back through the door to her own time."

"Yeah. And left Duncreag the very next day, thereby giving up any other opportunity she might have had to return to Iain."

Elaine leaned forward, her body tense. "You think that's what happened to her, don't you? You think she found the door again."

Jeff nodded miserably.

"That's why you haven't told the Abernathys."

"What do I tell them? 'I seem to have misplaced my sister. I think she may have gone to visit her boyfriend in the Middle Ages.' They'd laugh me out of the room."

"Maybe, maybe not. Look, Jeff, we're in the middle of the Scottish Highlands. People here still believe in things beyond scientific explanation."

Jeff reached out and brushed a wayward strand of copper-colored hair away from Elaine's face. "What do you believe?" He held his breath almost afraid to hear her answer.

Elaine covered Jeff's hand with hers. "Truly? I believe that anything is possible, Jeff. There are so many things out there that we can't understand. I think that it's arrogant to pretend that we have all the answers."

Jeff felt the panic building inside him again at the thought of his sister trapped in another time. He stood up, feeling a need to move. He walked over to a fading tapestry hanging on the wall and touched it, feeling the frail aging threads. Turning back to Elaine, he clenched his fists in frustration. "We're talking like we actually believe Katherine found a doorway leading back in time."

"Yes, we are."

Jeff felt a shiver run down his spine. "So you're accepting that she may actually have found her way back to Iain, and that even now, she could be standing in this very room, in another century with a man who has been dead for five hundred years?" His voice rose as something between dread and panic gripped him with icy claws.

"Yes, I guess I am, at least for now. What about you?"

Jeff groaned. "I don't know. Rationally, I'm having a little trouble believing any of this is possible. But my gut tells me it's the truth. You should have seen Katherine's face when she told me about this stuff. I may not believe it, but she does. And my sister's no slouch in the brain department."

Elaine massaged her temples as she nodded her agreement. "So where does that leave us? Did Katherine say anything to you about her plans after finding the door?"

Jeff sat down again, taking her hands in his. "Yes."

"And?"

"She told me that if she could get to Iain again, she

intended to stay with him." He spoke softly, his voice edged with pain, his stomach in knots.

Tears welled in Elaine's eyes. "Then we might never see her again?"

Jeff felt his own eyes fill with tears. He suddenly couldn't find the right words. Numbly, he nodded, pulling her into his arms, seeking to comfort and be comforted.

Chapter 12

"SO YOU'RE IN charge of everyone who lives here? Isn't that an overwhelming responsibility?" Katherine sat on the bed, her arms loosely draped around her knees. She watched as Iain fastened his belt and adjusted his plaid. "Aye, 'tis a great responsibility, but also a great honor. Duncreag is my home, and these are my people. Are there no clans in your time?"

Katherine thought for a moment. "Well, there are families, and I suppose there are some that could reasonably be called clans. But most people aren't part of one, and certainly not bound to a Laird."

"Aye, but you're no' from Scotland. Surely, even in your time, there are still clans in the Highlands." He bent to tie the lacings on his boots.

"Yeah, but they're not the same. There is no need for protection, and people are more transitory, which means families are often spread out all over the place. I'm sure there are Lairdships, still, but I'd imagine they're purely symbolic."

"Humph." Iain straightened. "I canna say I would no' be interested in seeing this time of yours, but I dinna think I'd want to live there."

Katherine laughed. "Well, then I suppose you can begin to understand how I feel."

Iain crossed to the bed in two paces. He grabbed Katherine by the shoulders, his eyes fierce as they bored into hers. "What are you saying, lass?"

Katherine raised a gentle hand to his face, attempting to erase his frown. "Only that this is all strange to me and will be even more so when I leave this room." He released her shoulders.

"Then, you're no' wishing you could return?"

She leaned into him, kissing him full on the lips. "No."

His arms circled her slender body, pulling her closer. "Good. Because I've no intention of letting you go anywhere."

He shifted then, pushing her back into the blankets, his big body covering hers.

"Iain Mackintosh, 'tis time you were up and about," a voice boomed through the closed door.

Iain sat up with a groan. " 'Tis Ranald. I'd best let him in. He's no' likely to go away. And we dinna want him rousing the entire household."

"But Iain, I can't . . ." Katherine blushed and waved a hand over her current state of undress.

"Iain. I know you're in there." The door rattled.

"Patience, I'm coming."

Iain threw a smile at Katherine over his shoulder as he hurriedly rummaged through a trunk by the bed. "Here, this will have to do. Cover yourself quickly, woman. I'll no' be sharing you with the likes of Ranald." Iain shot her a half-amused, half-serious look as he waited for her to don his shirt.

Katherine pulled on the huge shirt, and with a smile for Iain, scrambled to sit in the straight chair at the end of the bed. Crossing her legs, she tried to look calmer than she felt. She was grateful that Iain was so large—the shirt hung well below her knees, and seated in the chair, it draped to cover even her legs. By twentieth-century standards she was decent. By fifteenth-century standards she was probably pushing the envelope, but this was hardly an ordinary situation.

Iain pushed back the bar and swung open the heavy door.

"God's blood, man, what are you doing in here? You'd think you had a wench . . ." Ranald burst into the chamber, then froze at the sight of Katherine. His cheeks darkened with what looked suspiciously like a blush.

Katherine smiled and casually waved a hand. "Hi."

Ranald stood with his mouth open, looking first at Katherine, then Iain, and then Katherine again. Iain grinned at Katherine. "You've flummoxed him. I dinna know that I've ever seen Ranald without words." Iain clapped Ranald on the back. "Come, cousin, I want you to meet my lady."

Still slack-jawed, Ranald allowed Iain to pull him forward. "Katherine, this seemingly dull-witted man is my cousin, Ranald Macqueen." Ranald managed to close his mouth, but just barely. Iain gave Katherine a wink and then turned to his cousin, obviously enjoying himself immensely. "Ranald, may I present Katherine St. Claire."

Ranald swallowed convulsively, his eyes glued to Katherine. "The fairy?"

Katherine bubbled with helpless laughter. Hopping up from the chair, she executed a somewhat less than perfect pirouette, ending with an exaggerated curtsy. "At your service."

Ranald sat on the bed with a thump. Iain closed the door. The three of them stared at each other in silence broken only by Katherine's occasional bursts of laughter.

Finally, looking somewhat chagrined, Ranald pulled himself together. "You're no' fey."

She shook her head. "No, mere mortal, I'm afraid. Touch me, if you like. I'm real."

Ranald reached out a hand, only to find it being pulled roughly back.

"Here now, you'll no' be touching Katherine without my leave. Take my word on it: She's definitely flesh and blood."

The look Iain leveled at Katherine made her legs turn to jelly and her face burn. She sank back into the chair, grateful for its support.

Ranald, his wits sufficiently recovered, looked at the two of them. "I think 'tis time you both quit having sport with me and explain yourselves." He eyed Katherine, hands braced on his knees. "I'd hazard a guess that you're the lass Iain has spoken of. The one I thought didna exist."

"I am." Feeling the need for hard evidence, she removed the chain from her neck and carefully handed the cairngorm to Ranald. He studied the small stone intently and then, with a look at Iain's earring, handed it back.

"Well, since you dinna seem to have arrived with pixie dust, can I ask how you did come to be here?"

Katherine replaced her necklace and looked to Iain for support. "It's kind of hard to believe."

Iain crossed his arms over his chest and shrugged. "I think 'tis best we tell him straight out."

"Tell me what?"

"Katherine is from the future."

Ranald's mouth threatened to fall open again. "Sweet Mother of God." He crossed himself. "The future."

"Remember, you're the daughter of my aunt Isobel's dearest friend. Your father has holdings in France and you grew up there."

Katherine nervously fingered the linen of her sleeve and tried to concentrate on what Iain was saying. She couldn't decide if it was comforting or alarming that he appeared to be as nervous as she was. He paced back and forth in front of a narrow window, his brows drawn together in fierce concentration. Only Ranald appeared at ease, sitting on a bench in front of a table piled with ledgers of some kind.

"Katherine, are you listening?"

She swallowed her butterflies and smiled at Iain. "Of course. I'm from France."

"Aye, that ought to explain why your Gaelic is less than perfect. 'Tis a blessing you speak French."

Well, at least in theory she did. Katherine blew out a breath. Learning to read Norman French for her dissertation was a far cry from speaking it with any fluency. But she'd had modern French in college, and between the two she ought to be able to pass muster with anyone but a native. And fortunately, according to Iain, there were none at Duncreag.

Ranald took up the tale, his voice sounding like a Scottish version of Ichobod Crane. "You've been staying at Moy visiting Isobel. It was there that you met Iain and me. Iain asked you to come and visit Duncreag."

Katherine interrupted, ready to stop the lessons and get on with the show. "I decided to come and was attacked on the way here. I managed to escape, but my guards were all killed or dispersed. My trunks were lost. I found my way here late last night. I spent the night in your guest room . . ."

Iain shook his head. "Chamber."

She suddenly had great sympathy for Eliza Doolittle. "Right, *chamber*, and you were kind enough to loan me some of your mother's things until mine are found. Which of course they can't be." Her voice rose a little with the enormity of it all.

"Dinna fash yourself about that, my love. Ranald and I will see to it." Iain slipped an arm around Katherine's shoulders and gave her a quick hug. " 'Twill be fine you'll see. Ranald has already told them that you're here. So they know of your troubles."

"And will ask questions." Katherine tried not to look as frightened as she felt.

"Perhaps a few. But I've told them your tale. And

warned them you're fatigued." Ranald spoke matter-of-
factly as if coaching time travelers was an everyday oc-
currence for him.

"What about this Alasdair fellow. You said I should
watch out for him." With nervous fingers, she smoothed
her overdress. What had Iain called it, an *arasaid*?
Whatever it was called she felt certain she'd never be
able to get into or out of the thing without help.

"There's nothing to worry about," Iain assured her.

If that was true, why had Iain and Ranald just exchanged glances? Katherine smiled, trying to appear se-
rene. The three of them had spent the better part of the
day working on a way to explain her presence at Duncreag.

She could do this.

Iain took her elbow, his voice pitched low, for her
ears only. "Dinna be afraid, I'll be by your side the
whole time."

She squared her shoulders and held tightly to his arm.
Standing beside him, she certainly felt invincible and if
that wasn't enough, Ranald flanked her on the other side.
Oh, Lord, she sounded like she was preparing herself for
battle. Next she'd be thinking about girding her loins—
whatever the hell that meant.

She blew out a breath, ignored the insane desire to
yell charge, and looked into Iain's eyes. The love she
saw reflected there calmed her fears. With him beside
her, she could do anything.

"Let's knock 'em dead, boys."

Katherine was glad of Iain's hand on her arm as he led
her out into the hall. It was amazing how little it had
changed. The tapestries looked newer and the tables
were different, but otherwise it could have been the same
hall she had eaten in . . . had it only been last night?

Serving girls moved about the tables, preparing for
the meal. The principal members of the household
seemed to be gathered by the fire. Two women—Sorcha

and Ailis, she assumed—sat together, heads bent in conversation. Two men stood with their backs to the fire, no doubt enjoying its warmth.

As they approached the group, conversation stopped. Katherine tensed involuntarily. Iain gave her arm a comforting squeeze. She drew in a breath and forced herself to relax, tipping her head up for a quick look at Iain. He looked calm, and devastatingly handsome. She darted a glance at Ranald. He winked and smiled. This was it then.

Iain released her arm and with a firm hand at her back eased her forward. "May I present Lady Katherine St. Claire. Katherine, this is my auntie Sorcha and our neighbor Ailis Davidson."

Iain's aunt rose from her seat, extending a hand. "You puir wee lamb. Such a terrible thing to have happen." Katherine took the woman's hand, not quite certain what to do with it. Before she had a chance to look to Iain for help, Sorcha had taken her other hand, and guided her to their bench. "Come and sit with us by the fire." With a sigh of pure relief, Katherine sank down onto the seat next to Ailis.

"Ranald told us you were attacked. It must have been horrible. However did you find the courage to get away?" Ailis' gaze held a mixture of fascination and awe.

Katherine shifted uncomfortably. "I really don't know. I guess I just ran."

"Ailis, I hardly think the lady wishes to relive her terror." Alasdair moved to take Katherine's hand. "May I introduce myself, since our host has failed to do so? I'm Alasdair Davidson, Ailis' brother." He bent over her hand, turning it so that his lips pressed against her palm. She felt the tip of his tongue flick against her skin. She shuddered and pulled her hand away as quickly as she could without causing offense.

Iain appeared behind Alasdair's shoulder, another man standing right behind Iain. Reinforcements. Katherine could not contain her sigh of relief and only hoped Alasdair hadn't noticed. "Katherine, may I present Fergus Mackintosh. Fergus, was my father's captain."

Fergus neatly stepped in front of Alasdair, forcing the younger man to move away from her. Katherine smiled. Score one for Iain.

"Captain Mackintosh, it is such a pleasure to meet you. Iain has spoken of you with such fondness and high regard."

Katherine smiled as Fergus, too, bent over her hand. The tips of his ears were pink, a sure sign she had pleased him. "My Lady, you are most welcome here. 'Tis sorry I am that your journey couldna have been a safer one." The old man straightened and smiled.

"Thank you. I'm sure if I had been traveling with you, I would never have been subjected to such an ordeal." Katherine gave him an illuminated smile and Fergus' ears immediately turned from pink to bright red.

"Lady Katherine, I understand your sire is from France." Alasdair drew close again and Katherine fought the urge to lean back, putting as much distance between herself and Alasdair as possible.

"Why yes, my father has a small holding there, in Gascony." She threw up a quick prayer that her history was correct and Gascony was a recognizable region in the fifteenth century.

"Ah, I've never been there, but I have always longed to travel to Paris. *On dit que c'est la plus belle ville du monde.*"

"*Elle est trés belle, en effet.* Your French is excellent, monsieur."

"Please, call me Alasdair."

His smile was insolent as he let his gaze drift over her body. She felt exposed, a shiver of dread running down her spine. This guy definitely gave her the creeps. It was all she could do to smile and nod in acceptance. "Alasdair, then."

Iain interrupted. " 'Tis time for our evening meal." He

offered Katherine his arm. "Alasdair, if you'll be kind enough to escort my aunt."

Alasdair shot Iain a venom-filled look and turned to offer a hand to Sorcha. Watching them cross the hall, heads together in deep conversation, Katherine moved closer to Iain.

"Dinna let him worry you, he is harmless enough. An annoyance—nothing more."

Katherine smiled up at Iain and wondered why his words did not ease her mind.

The meal seemed to drag on forever. Iain wanted nothing more than to have Katherine alone in his chamber. It was taking every once of self-restraint he had not to pick her up and carry her out of the hall, proprieties be damned. He marveled at how well she was playing the part they had devised. He might believe her himself if he did not know better. She had even handled Alasdair, responding to his comments in flawless French.

Iain wondered if he would have been able to do as well if their places had been reversed. He thought not. The wonders of the world she described would no doubt overwhelm a man. No, he was happiest here in his own time. He frowned, worried that Katherine would feel the same way. Could she truly be happy here? He vowed that he would do everything in his power to make it so.

He watched as she tilted her head and whispered something to Ranald, who laughed and offered her a bit of meat from his trencher. She smiled, then leaned toward him to take the morsel from his knife. Iain felt his belly knot with jealousy.

"She is lovely, isn't she?"

Iain pulled his gaze from Katherine and turned to his aunt. "Aye, that she is."

Sorcha turned her gaze to Ailis. "Ailis is also fair of face, do ye no' think?"

Iain glanced at Ailis. She was talking with Fergus, a

bright smile lighting her small face. "Aye, she is comely enough."

"Your father was entertaining thoughts of a match between the two of you."

"Aye, so Alasdair tells me. It seems my father discussed the subject of my betrothal with everyone but me."

"Ach, Iain, you know that Angus wanted nothing but the best for you, as Alasdair wants only the best for his sister. The two of you would make a good match."

"My father is dead and what Alasdair wants has naught to do with me. Whom I wed is nobody's business but my own."

"Peace, nephew. I was but making conversation, no' trying to meddle in your affairs." She looked at Katherine again, this time with speculation.

"Are you in love with her then?"

Iain looked at his aunt in surprise. He had not thought her so observant. "What makes you ask that?"

"'Tis written on your face. I may be naught but an old maid, but I know something of love." Sorcha's features twisted briefly with pain and regret.

"Do you now?"

"Aye that I do." Her face closed, bitterness warring with tears.

Perhaps Sorcha had loved his father. What a waste. Iain wondered what it would be like if Katherine had no feelings for him. He scowled at the thought and patted his aunt's hand in an awkward attempt at comfort.

She gave him a watery smile. "Be careful, Iain, there are those who willna take the news of your feelings for Katherine well."

"If you mean Alasdair, dinna fash yourself. He knows I'm no' of a mind to wed with Ailis. Katherine being here changes nothing."

Sorcha looked as though she wanted to say more, but Alasdair chose that moment to interrupt.

"Mackintosh," Alasdair said, leaning forward, "I

heard you had a little trouble with the Macphersons."

"Aye, that we did."

"And is it true that one of the blackguards killed Angus?"

Ranald answered, exchanging glances with Iain. " 'Tis true that one of the reivers carried Angus' dirk. Whether or no' he killed Angus we canna say for sure."

"But surely it seems likely?" Alasdair drank from his wine cup, eyeing Iain over the rim.

" 'Twould seem the most feasible explanation." Iain shrugged slightly, his expression purposely bland.

"Then I would offer a toast to vengeance served." Alasdair raised his cup in salute.

There was a pause and then Iain, too, raised his cup, the other men following his lead. Iain offered his wine to Katherine so that she could partake of the toast as well. She slowly sipped it, her eyes never leaving his. In all his life he could never remember wanting a woman like this. Just watching her drink from his cup made him ache with need. He pulled his gaze away and tried to pick up the thread of conversation.

Fergus was speaking. " 'Twas a good fight. But we were saddened at the loss of Andrew."

Ailis reached across Ranald, touching Katherine on the sleeve. "Andrew was killed in the battle. And another man, William, was injured. Sorcha has been seeing to his wound. She knows the healing ways."

"Ach, only a little bit, Ailis. And, in this instance, I'm afraid it may no' be enough. His fever is still high and he has yet to wake. I fear for him. But there is no more I can do."

Iain's gut roiled at the news. If William died, the fault would be his to bear. His body tensed and his fist tightened on his wine goblet. He should have done better by William. Katherine met his gaze, her eyes clouded with concern. Under the table, she gently stroked his thigh, her touch meant to comfort.

Fergus cleared his throat. " 'Tis too soon for these

long faces. He has only been home a few days. Give the lad time to heal. With Sorcha's care he'll be up and about in no time."

"God will that it be so." Ailis' words brought an echo of agreement from the others sitting at the table.

"Tell me about William's injuries. Maybe I can help." Katherine sat on the rug by the fire in Iain's bedroom. He handed her a cup filled with spiced wine and sat beside her.

"Are you a healer in your time, then?"

Katherine shook her head. "No. I've just always seemed to have a knack for it. I was always bandaging up something or someone when I was a kid. I actually studied medicine a little in college, but decided I didn't really have the dedication it takes to become a doctor. Anyway, just being from the twentieth century probably gives me the edge over any healer here. There have been quite a few advances in medicine in the last five hundred years. Not the least of them being cleanliness."

"If you think you can help William, I'll welcome anything you can do."

"William means a great deal to you, doesn't he?"

"Aye. When I came back to Duncreag from fostering, he was always underfoot. He followed me like a puppy. Always wanting to know what I was about. He was a bright lad, and learned quickly. When I left for Moy he was still but a boy. And now . . . now he may never see his manhood at all."

Katherine laid a hand on his shoulder. "Fergus was right. It's too soon to tell anything. My grandmother always told us there was no point in borrowing tomorrow's problems."

"A wise woman. I'll take you to William in the morning then."

"I'll need Sorcha's cooperation. I'm not sure she'll accept what I'll want to do."

"Dinna worry, I'll see to my aunt."

Iain drank from his cup and stared thoughtfully into the fire. "She knows about us."

"Who? Sorcha?"

"Aye. She knows that I've feelings for you."

Katherine froze, her wine halfway to her lips. "Pardon?"

Iain reached out to take her cup. "I said, Sorcha knows that I love you. She seems to think 'twas plain on my face for all to see."

"Is that bad?" She licked her lips.

He smiled at her, his eyes warm and tender. "Nay, 'tis only that I'd thought to share my feelings with you first."

"I see." Katherine's voice was soft.

Iain gently cupped her chin. "I love you, Katherine St. Claire."

She smiled tremulously, her eyes brimming with tears. "I love you, too."

Iain's look turned serious. "Aye, but do you love me enough to stay here in this time and place? Enough to be my bride?"

Katherine drew in a sharp breath and placed a trembling hand on his arm. "I've traveled a long way to find you, Iain Mackintosh. And now that I have, I've no intention of ever letting you go. But are you sure you want to marry me? I'm not of this place, and we have no way of knowing if I'll be able to stay."

"Hush, mo chridhe." He placed a finger to her lips. "You're here now and you're of my heart. That's all that matters."

"Then I would be proud to be your wife."

Iain pulled her close within the circle of his arms, his breath whispering against her ear.

"Then so shall it be."

Chapter 13

KATHERINE YAWNED SLEEPILY and opened an eye. The first pale pink rays of sunlight were filtering into the room. Morning. Actually, morning in the fifteenth century, and she was a married woman. She let the thought wash over her. Married. Well, there was the formality of a priest's blessing, but according to Iain, marriage in these times basically consisted of an agreement and a consummation. And what a consummation it had been. Katherine felt her face go hot with the memory of last night's lovemaking. It seemed that each time with him was better than the last.

On that thought, she rolled over, reaching for her husband. The bed was empty. Panic began to rise as she quickly sat up, eyes closed tightly, clutching the covers. Oh God, please don't let it have been another dream. Please let it be real. She slowly opened her eyes, holding her breath. She was still in Iain's room. Their room now. She released her breath, her heartbeat returning to normal.

She surveyed the room, looking for signs of where Iain might be. The door to the room was still barred

shut, so that eliminated his having left by that that route.
She knew he hadn't left by the door to the adjoining
chamber—a large and very heavy chest now barred the
way. Katherine smiled, remembering the ferocity with
which Iain had ordered her to stay away from the adjoining room, emphasizing the point by dragging the
huge trunk into place. Not that she had any intention of
going through that door. It would be a cold day in hell
before she ventured into that room again. She planned
to have a long and happy life here with Iain . . . if she
could find him.

There had to be another door in here somewhere. She
eased out of bed, shivering a little when the chilly morning air hit her bare skin. She eyed her dress, flung with
some abandon into a corner by the bed. No chance of
getting that thing on without help. She picked it up and
smoothed out some of the creases. Folding it and the
linen shift that went beneath it, she left them on the end
of the bed. She needed something easier to put on. Out
of the corner of her eye she saw a splash of yellow-
brown. Suppressing a smile, she walked over to the bedpost and, standing on tiptoe, retrieved Iain's shirt from
where it had been flung the night before. It had been a
wild night.

She slipped the long shirt over her head and fastened
the belt from her dress around her waist. The effect was
probably humorous, but she had no time for vanity. She
was on a quest.

She turned slowly in a circle, examining the room.
There had to be another way out. A shadow flickered in
the corner by the fireplace, revealing an arch that opened
into what looked to be a small hallway. Grinning with
triumph, Katherine set out to explore.

What she had thought to be a hallway was, in fact,
the opening to a narrow spiraling staircase. Katherine
looked up, trying to see in the gloom. There was a faint
light somewhere toward the top and a little bit more
coming from the small slits that passed for windows, but

no other illumination. With one hand firmly on the railing, she started to climb. About halfway up, she began to question the wisdom of her decision. So far there were no doors off the stairs. They seemed to wind upward to infinity. Katherine took a deep breath and continued. Sooner or later, it had to come out somewhere, didn't it? The stones were cold under her feet. She promised herself that the next time she set out to explore the tower she would consider wearing shoes. The stone steps twisted once more and then dead-ended. A small wooden door set into the wall stood half-way open.

In for the penny, in for the pound. Katherine reached out and pushed. The door squeaked open. She squinted as sunlight caught her full in the face. She ducked through the stone frame and found herself standing on the battlement. Instinctively, she took a step closer to the tower, not letting herself look at the incredibly short stone wall that separated the battlement from thin air. This must be the door Mrs. Abernathy had mentioned, the one that had been closed off. She drew in a breath. The door that she had remembered—the one that hadn't existed in the twentieth century.

Suddenly she could almost see Jeff standing at the wall, leaning over it, gleefully examining those machicohickies or whatever they were called. She felt the pricking of tears. Jeff. If only there were some way he could be with her here. Then everything would be perfect.

"I see you found the stairs."

Katherine sniffed and wiped at her eyes. She turned, smiling at her husband. "I did. When I woke up, you were gone, so I set about finding you."

"Well, you've found me, but I'm still waiting for a proper greeting, wife."

Katherine opened her arms. "If it's a proper greeting you want, you'll have to come to me. I can't come any closer to the outside wall." She gave him a small embarrassed grimace.

Iain was beside her in one step, enfolding her in his arms. He was wearing only his plaid. "What do you mean you canna?"

"Just what I said, I 'canna.' " She felt him rumble with laughter at her imitation of his speech. "It's a sort of fear of heights. Falling, really. Anyway, I'm fine as long as I stay here by the building wall."

Iain frowned down at her. "But you canna see the view from here, and I want to show you my holding." He kissed the top of her head tenderly. "Nay, I meant to say *our* holding."

"But I can't. Really. I get all panicky and hyperventilate. It's not a pretty sight."

"Katherine, trust me. You canna fall if I'm holding you. I'll go first and then you can come to me." He walked to stand by the edge of the pitifully low wall. He held out a hand. "Come here. Have faith that I will protect you."

Katherine swallowed and edged forward a step or two. She froze for a moment and then, squaring her shoulders, reached out for Iain's hand as she took the last few steps to join him. He pulled her in front of him, holding her next to his body, wrapping them in his plaid, his strong arms keeping her safe.

He leaned down to whisper in her ear, his warm breath sending shivers down her spine. "You can open your eyes now, my love."

Katherine opened one eye and then the other. The view was absolutely breathtaking. She could see far more than she had been able to from the tower wall. She leaned back into Iain, letting his warmth and strength drain her fear.

"Straight out there is *Càrn Coire na h-Easgainn*, a verra boggy place. I know that from personal experience. In the winter the snow and ice hide the bogs and if you're no' careful you fall right in. 'Tis no' a verra comfortable way to spend a winter's day."

"I can imagine."

"To its right is *Càrn Iain Duibh*. I've no notion of the true history of the name, it is literally *Càrn ic Iain Duibh*, but my father always called it Black Iain's Mountain, saying that it was named for me. When I was about seven, just before I left for Corybrough, I got it into my head to try and climb it. Well, of course I never even got near it, but by the time I gave up and returned home, I was covered with dirt from my head to my toes. Between the soil and my hair, I looked a wee bit black. And so, after that, my father always said, the mountain was named for me."

Katherine rested her head against his broad chest, enjoying their intimacy.

"And that one?"

"There?" He pointed to the southeast. She nodded. "Ah, you can just see it. 'Tis *Càrn Sgùlain*. See its basket shape?" He continued the geography lesson. "And there in front 'tis *Calpa Mòr*."

"They're beautiful. You can still see snow on some of them."

"Aye. O'er there to your left is the river that cuts the valley to Duncreag." He pointed at the sliver of water far below. Katherine swallowed and looked down. In her time it was called the River Findhorn. She remembered driving along it with Jeff. The thought of her brother made her wish again that he was here. So many wonderful things had happened to her, and it felt strange not to be able to share them with Jeff.

Iain's arms tightened around her. "What troubles you, lass?"

"Nothing really. I was just thinking of my brother, Jeff."

"You were missing him, then?"

"Um-hmm. We've always shared everything. I was wishing I could tell him about you, and how happy you make me."

Iain nuzzled her hair. "So tell me about your brother."

Katherine snuggled into Iain's warmth. "He looks a

lot like me only he's taller." She glanced up at her husband. "I'd say about your height. His hair is short, a little darker than mine. And it's usually standing every which way because he runs his hands through it all the time. He has blue eyes and he's always laughing."

"Sounds like a handsome fellow. Is he more than just fair of face?"

"Yeah. He's an incredibly talented architect. He designs all kinds of buildings, in cities all over the world."

"Your parents must be proud of him."

"My parents died when I was eight, in a car wreck. I told you about cars."

"The carts that move without horses?"

"Right. Anyway, after that my grandmother took care of us. We loved her, but it was still always Jeff and me against the world. Our own little family."

" 'Tis sad that I canna know him."

"He would have liked you."

"And I would like to have had a brother. I had a sister, but she died as a babe. My mother died giving birth to her. We never had much of a family after that."

"But surely you and your father . . ."

"Nay, my father might as well have died with my mother. His heart went with her. So there was no' much left for me."

"But you loved him."

"Aye, that I did."

Katherine stood quietly, still leaning against him, thinking of all that she had lost and all that she had gained.

"Katherine?"

"Hmm?"

"I know you miss your brother, but if you'll let me, I'll be your family now. And you will be mine."

Katherine turned in Iain's arms, pressing her lips to his, feeling the heat of his body against hers. He reached down, scooping her up into his arms, a devilish smile on his handsome face.

"Come, my love, I find I've the need to show you just how much I care."

"Well, can you do anything to help the lad?"

Iain watched as Katherine carefully examined William's leg. It was red and swollen, the edges raw. Even Iain could tell that it was not healing.

Katherine looked at him across the bed. "It's infected. I think that's what's causing his fever. Has he woken at all?"

"Only for a moment or two. And even then he was no' himself."

Katherine tenderly covered the boy again, brushing his matted hair back from his face.

"I think it needs to be drained."

"Can you do that?"

"Yes, but I'll need some help. I'm definitely not qualified to sew it up again."

"I'll send for my aunt. She can assist you. Tell me what you need."

Katherine thought for a moment, her gaze on the boy. "I'll need hot water, lots of it. And it will need to have been brought to a full boil. I'll also need clean linen to make a compress and more for a new bandage. It has to be sterile."

Iain sent her a puzzled look. Sometimes he simply could not understand her words. What a complicated place this twentieth century must be.

Katherine gave him an understanding smile. "Sorry, that means totally clean. Freshly laundered or never used would be best. And I'll need a knife that's been washed in the boiling water."

Iain nodded and pulled a dirk from the sheath at his waist. "Will this do?"

Katherine stared at the little knife. "Where did you get that?"

Iain frowned at her tone of voice. " 'Twas my father's, and his father's before him."

Katherine relaxed, giving Iain a weak smile. "I didn't mean to sound so harsh. It's just that I've seen that knife before, in my time. I was surprised, that's all."

"Well, my father would be glad to know that it survived." He carefully handed her the dirk, hilt-first, watching as she absently stroked the smoky stone at the end.

He turned to the doorway, calling to a girl standing in the outer hall. "Fiona, go and find Sorcha and send her here. Then bring some clean cloth and boiling water. And hurry."

The girl nodded and curtsied, glancing at the boy in the bed and then giving Katherine a look filled with hope. With a last look at William, she hurried away.

"I think she has a tender spot for our William," Iain said.

"Does he return her feelings, do you think?" Katherine asked.

"I truly dinna know. I suspect the lad is still a bit young to be giving his heart."

Katherine's mouth twitched with amusement. "If I recall correctly, you weren't much older than William when we first met. And I seem to remember you telling me—quite emphatically, I might add—that you knew you loved me even then."

"Aye, I did." He reached up to touch the cairngorm hanging from his ear, then grinned at the woman who had come to mean more than life to him. "But we are special, mo chridhe."

Katherine gave an unladylike snort.

Fiona returned with two pails of steaming water and a pile of cloth clutched under her arm. She placed the lot by the fireplace and turned to go.

"Try not to worry, Fiona." Katherine's voice was soft.

The girl gave Katherine a weak smile. "I'll just go and get some more water." She bobbed once and was gone.

Katherine turned to her patient. After washing the

knife in the heated water, she dried it and carefully cut away the stitches. The wound had festered, and once the stitches were gone, it began to ooze.

"How can I help?" Iain had moved to her side and was intently watching her work.

"Start by ripping these cloths into small squares and then fold them into a pad like this." She held up a square of cloth she had already folded. "We're going to dip the clean cloth into the hot water and then place it on the wound. The heat, along with a little pressure, should aid in draining it. What we want it to do is run clear." Katherine dipped the cloth in one of the pails of water and placed it on the wound, pressing slightly at the sides. William moaned, but remained still.

Iain began to tear the linen into smaller pieces, folding each and making a pile next to Katherine.

"What are you about in here?"

They both turned at the sound of a voice. Sorcha stood in the door, hands on hips, her face inscrutable.

"I said what are you about? Are you deaf then?"

Iain straightened. "Katherine has been kind enough to offer her help in aid of young William."

"Are you a healer?" Sorcha's brown eyes glared at Katherine.

Katherine looked first at Iain and then at Sorcha. "No, but I seem to have a healing way. And I've studied a little. I thought that maybe, between you and me, we could help him."

Sorcha's look softened a bit, and she came to the side of the bed. "Tell me what you're doing then."

Katherine explained in detail, trying to remember to use words that were not unique to the twentieth century. Sorcha listened intently, nodding now and then, watching as Katherine replaced one compress with another.

"It might work." Her forehead furrowed in thought, she turned to Iain. "Here, mon, let me do that." She took the linen and began to tear it.

Iain smiled at Katherine over the top of Sorcha's head.

"It looks as if the two of you have little need for me. I'll check on you later."

"See that Fiona brings more hot water," Katherine called to him without even looking up.

Iain smiled at the two women, oblivious to him now as they worked side by side to try and heal William.

"Well, that's it then. We've managed to drain the wound and clean it."

"Yeah, and William too. How long do you think it's had been since his last bath?" Katherine wrinkled her nose in disgust.

Sorcha gave her a perplexed look. "Do they bathe often where you come from? I've heard it said that people of the continent are quite interested in bathing."

Katherine smiled, rubbing her back. "Yes, well, they do say cleanliness is next to godliness, or something like that." She watched as Sorcha made neat little stitches in William's leg. They weren't exactly the best of friends, but they'd developed a grudging respect for each other in the time it had taken to attend to the wound. "We may need to repeat this whole process if it festers again."

Sorcha nodded as she tied off the stitches. "Is there something we can do for his fever?"

Katherine bit the inside of her lip, trying to think of some herb that might reduce fever. Nothing came to mind. What she wouldn't have given for a dose of penicillin. "I think maybe just keeping him cool will help. Perhaps if we keep him uncovered and bathe him from time to time in cool water?"

"Aye, that might work. I'll call for a clean bucket with cold water from the well."

"Sorcha?"

"Aye?"

"I think it would be better if the water were boiled first and then allowed to cool."

Sorcha looked as if she wanted to argue, but turned

to go with a shrug, mumbling something about people who were overly fond of bathing.

Katherine placed a hand on William's brow. It actually felt a little cooler. His breathing was slow and even. A sprinkling of freckles stood out on his nose, a contrast to his pale skin. He looked incredibly young lying there, and Katherine was moved to offer a brief prayer for his well-being as she smoothed his hair back from his face.

Hearing Sorcha returning, she stood and pushed her own hair back.

"Go now, child. I'll sit with him. You look as if you could use a wee rest. There's naught else to do now but wait."

"Will you call me when he wakes up?"

Sorcha nodded and turned to the boy on the bed.

Katherine stood in the doorway, wondering what Sorcha would make of her century. She'd probably take it all in stride. Sorcha seemed to be a woman with little room for fancy, and Katherine wondered briefly if she'd ever been in love. She didn't really seem the type to give affection easily or deeply, but she had spent all these years taking care of her sister's family. Katherine watched as Sorcha gently pressed a wet cloth to William's forehead. What was the saying? Still waters run deep? There certainly had to be some motivation behind her dedication to the Mackintoshes of Duncreag, because she certainly didn't strike Katherine as the sacrificing type. As Katherine walked from the room, she wondered what Sorcha's reaction would be when she found out Iain had made her his wife.

"But we dinna know anything about her."

Iain stood with his back to the fire in his work chamber, looking at the three astonished faces in front of him. The late afternoon sun filtered through the room's only window. Ranald look amused as well as astonished. Fergus just looked bemused, while Sorcha looked slightly angry.

"Auntie Sorcha, *I* know all that I need to know about Katherine. And I'll no' have you making her feel anything less than welcome in this house. She is my wife and by right that makes her mistress here. I'll have our folk treat her as such or they'll answer to me."

Fergus reached over to pat Sorcha's hand. "Your aunt meant nothing by her remark, Iain. We're just surprised, that's all. We've only just met the girl and now we find that the two of you have promised your lives to each other."

Sorcha refused to give in gracefully. "What about a blessing by the priest? Surely you canna truly be married without that?"

Fergus answered for Iain. "Now, Sorcha, ye know that a mon and a woman can pledge to wed without a priest. All that's really necessary to make a union official is a bedding." He looked to Iain with a bawdy smile. "And I'm quite sure our Iain saw to that. Am I no' right, lad?"

Iain grinned despite himself. "We are well and truly wed. But if it makes you feel better, Auntie Sorcha, Katherine wants the marriage blessed, too. We'll have Father Macniven do it the next time he comes to Duncreag. Until then, a bedding will have to suffice."

Sorcha nodded with grudging acceptance. " 'Tis no' that I disapprove of the girl, Iain. 'Tis just that I wish you'd told us first and then waited a proper betrothal period."

"Well, I'm telling you now, and what I'd like is a bit more enthusiasm. You're all the family I have, and I'd like to think you're at least a wee bit happy for us."

Ranald jumped out of his chair, crossed the chamber, and embraced Iain. "Congratulations, cousin. She's a bonny lass. Had I met her before you, I might have married her myself."

Fergus, too, rose extending his hand. " 'Tis glad I am if she makes you happy. Your father would be most pleased to know you are settled at last. It was his greatest wish that you would marry and produce an heir to carry on the Mackintoshes of Duncreag. My only regret is that he canna be here to meet your bride."

Iain shook the old man's hand, pulling him forward for a quick embrace. "You've been like a second father to me, Fergus. 'Tis enough that you're here."

Iain turned to look at Sorcha. "Have you no good wishes for me then, Auntie?"

A shadow passed across Sorcha's face. "I had hoped that you'd choose Ailis for your wife. I know those were also your father's wishes. But Angus is gone and I wish you only happiness. So if this girl is the one you truly love, then I say God's blessing on you both."

Iain reached for her hands, then kissed each of them in turn. "Thank you, Auntie Sorcha."

Ranald gestured to a pitcher of ale on the table. "We should drink to Iain's happiness."

Fergus poured the brew into beautifully hammered metal cups. He handed one to each of the others and raised his in salute. "To Iain and Katherine—may their lives be long and fruitful."

Ranald raised his goblet and then drank deeply. Wiping a hand across his mouth, he raised the cup again. "I would drink to your wife. May her beauty never fade and her heart be always full of love for you."

Sorcha, too, raised her cup. "I would wish that no other come between you."

Iain tilted his brow, looking at her uncertainly, but raised his goblet and drank. " 'Tis thankful I am for your good wishes. I hope that you'll all wish Katherine the same when you see her." Iain looked pointedly at Sorcha. She flushed under the intensity of his gaze. With a last swallow, he finished the ale, then placed his cup on the table. "And now, I intend to spend some time with my bride."

Katherine sat in the window of the solar. William was resting peacefully. He had opened his eyes a few hours earlier, informing them he was thirsty. Several cups of water later, he had lapsed again into deep sleep. There was certainly still cause for concern, but Katherine was beginning to feel like he had turned the proverbial corner. She sighed, rubbing her temples. She could really use two Excedrin right about now.

"Ah, I thought I might find you here."

Katherine jumped, startled by the voice, and turned to find its owner. She watched as Alasdair made his way across the room to the window. He stopped in front of her, his gaze raking over her body. She got the distinct feeling he was mentally undressing her, and shivered with discomfort.

"I've been looking for you most of the day. Where have you been keeping yourself?" He sat next to her on the small stone seat, and she edged farther into the corner.

"I've been helping Sorcha tend to William. In fact, I ought to check on him now." She made an effort to rise, but Alasdair placed a hand on her knee.

"Stay and talk to me. I'm sure that William can wait a bit. Besides, one as lovely as you shoudna be tending the sick. 'Tis a job for old women and serving girls. You, my Lady, should be pampered and"—he slowly stroked her knee—"well loved."

Katherine swallowed in revulsion. Alasdair's idea of being well loved obviously was strictly carnal in nature. She moved her knee, displacing his hand.

"I've a keep no' far from here. 'Tis no' so grand as Duncreag, but Tùr nan Clach is a sizable holding. Perhaps I could convince you to come and see it with me."

His hand was back on her knee, then on her thigh. He moved even closer until she could actually feel his breath on her cheek. "You are so beautiful, Katherine."

Katherine realized his position had her effectively pinned in the corner. The only way to escape would be to physically move him and Alasdair was not a small man. Tilting her chin in determination, she shoved hard against his chest, trying to push him away.

He laughed, one hand circling both of her wrists while the other one pulled her closer. "I think that I would like very much to make you mine."

Katherine struggled against his hold, her mind trying desperately to think of something that would make him release her. "Let go of me. What do you think you're doing?"

He brushed his lips against hers, his tongue circling her tightly clenched lips. She trembled with anger.

"Relax, little one, I only wish to taste your sweetness. Open to me." He renewed his efforts, one hand biting into her wrists as his other circled her breast. She tried to scream, but his mouth covered hers, making noise impossible. As she tried to wriggle farther away, his grip tightened and he yanked her back toward him.

"Release her."

Katherine suddenly felt herself freed. She leaned over, gulping for air, relief making her dizzy. Alasdair slid away from her, but did not vacate the seat. He gave Iain a speculative look.

"I meant no harm. I was merely attempting to sample your lovely guest's considerable charms."

Iain's face clouded with rage. "You have no right to touch her."

Katherine stood on shaky feet, recovered now enough to walk to Iain. But to do so, she realized, she would have to squeeze past Alasdair, and she found she simply couldn't bear for him to touch her again. She lifted a hand to her bruised lips and looked at her husband. She had never seen him angry, and the look on his face frightened her, even though she knew the anger was directed at Alasdair, not at her.

"Katherine, are you all right?"

She managed a nod.

Alasdair was either blind or a fool. He seemed oblivious to Iain's wrath. "I told you, Mackintosh, I meant the girl no harm. Besides, what do you care? You've no claim on her."

Iain advanced on Alasdair, his fingers wrapping around the hilt of his dirk.

"Ah, but you see, I do have a claim on her." He stepped closer to Alasdair, his voice deceptively soft. "Katherine is my wife. And I'll no' tolerate another man fondling what belongs to me."

Alasdair froze. "Your wife? And when, may I ask, did this take place?"

" 'Tis no' your affair. 'Tis enough for you to know that she is well and truly wed to me."

Alasdair stood and took a step forward. Katherine, seeing the way clear, rushed past him to Iain, throwing herself into his arms.

He hugged her fiercely, whispering in her ear, " 'Tis all right, my love, I'm here now."

Alasdair's normally handsome face was now purple with rage. "I thought you had no wish to wed. Isn't that the reason you gave when you insulted me and mine by refusing to even consider Ailis as a bride? Did you lie to me?"

"I spoke the truth, Alasdair. I had no wish to wed anyone but Katherine. I wasna certain she would come here, so I saw no reason to bring her name into it. There was no insult to Ailis. But the same canna be said of Katherine."

Katherine watched as Alasdair brought his emotions under control. It was almost like watching someone put on a mask, so completely did all emotion fade from his face.

"Ah, well, perhaps I have o'erreacted." He turned to bow to Katherine. "I apologize for any insult I may have given you. I had no idea you were Iain's woman. Surely a man can be forgiven for stealing a kiss from a beautiful lady?"

She rubbed a hand against her wrist. She knew there would be purple bruises to mark the place he had held her. She had no doubt that Alasdair had meant to do far more than steal a kiss. But she knew, too, that if she voiced her suspicions, Iain would have no choice but to fight Alasdair. These were violent times, and Iain had meant it when he said he would protect what was his. She had no desire to place him in any kind of danger. Her mind made up, she inclined her head to Alasdair. "No real harm was done."

Alasdair looked to Iain. "I beg you'll overlook my transgression. I can assure you, it will never happen again."

Iain tightened his arm around Katherine. "See that it doesn't."

With another bow, Alasdair turned to go. His face was shuttered, revealing nothing but a pleasantly blank countenance. But Katherine could have sworn that his cold eyes glittered with hatred.

Iain turned Katherine to face him. "Are you truly all right?"

"I think so. Just a bit shaken up, that's all."

Iain looked her over carefully, stopping to kiss the redness at her wrists. "If he had hurt you, I would have killed him."

"I know. But I'm okay, I promise. Let's not talk about it anymore. Just hold me." Katherine leaned against his hard body, letting his heat sink into her, renewing her strength.

Iain ran a hand possessively up and down her back. "We'll be rid of him in a day or so. I'll keep an eye on him until then. I dinna think he'll try anything again."

Katherine wanted to believe that. But she could still see Alasdair's icy blue eyes. She shivered.

"Come my love, you're cold." Iain drew her closer to the fire. She held out her hands to its warmth, relieved that they weren't shaking. Everything would be fine now. Iain would keep her safe.

"There you are. I was wondering where you'd gotten to." Iain strode into their bedroom, and impish smile on his handsome face.

"I thought it would be more peaceful here." Katherine watched as he walked over to the chest and began rummaging about.

"Evening meal at Duncreag can be a bit o'ertiring, especially when everyone is trying to talk to the new mistress of the clan." His voice was muffled, his head deep in the trunk.

"And trying to touch her. I think I have hand prints on every part of my gown." She looked down at herself with dismay.

Iain stood up, a look of triumph lighting his face. Crossing the room, he sat down next to her on the bed, his prize hidden behind his back. "I've something for you. A gift to start our life together."

"A gift. Oh, Iain, I've nothing for you."

"You have already given me the greatest gift of all." His look spoke volumes, and Katherine felt herself blush.

"Here." Iain pulled his hand from behind his back, presenting her his gift. "This was a gift from my father to my mother on the eve of their marriage. 'Tis fitting that it should now be yours."

She took it from him with shaking hands, her eyes already recognizing the intricate carving and golden bands. Her heart fluttered and then, if she hadn't known better, she'd have said it stopped. She stared at the box almost afraid to touch it. Afraid that somehow it would snap her forward in time. Break whatever enchantment held them together.

"Dinna you want it?" Iain's eyes reflected his hurt.

"Oh, yes, of course I do. I'll treasure it forever." She reached for the box, her fingers closing around it, relieved when nothing happened. It was after all, only a box. Her heart resumed it's steady rhythm. "It's just that I recognize it." She lovingly ran a hand over it.

"Nay, that canna be so." He frowned, staring first at the box and then at her. "My father had it made specially for my mother. I'd wager, there's none other like it in the world. It has the Mackintosh crest on the top. See the wee mountain cat?"

Katherine traced a finger along the lines of the cat's paw. "You don't understand. This box—your box—belonged to my grandmother, too. In my time, she gave it to me. So, in some odd sort of way, the box has come full circle."

He covered her hand with his, his gaze colliding with hers. "Then we shall treasure it all the more."

She stared into the deep green of his eyes, her own filling with tears. "Thank you."

"Open it." His voice trembled with emotion.

Katherine opened the latch with trembling fingers and lifted the lid. There inside, nestled against rich brocade, was her cairngorm earring. She lifted her head to look at Iain, her expression questioning.

He reached into the box and retrieved the small stone. "I thought it was time for the earring to return to its rightful owner. I wore it so that I would never forget you. Now that you are here with me, I've no longer a need for it."

She reached to take it from him, a jolt of excitement racing up her arm as their fingers met. She carefully threaded the fine wire holding the cairngorm through her ear. Iain reached for the gold chain around her neck and slowly drew the other earring from her bodice, allowing his hand to linger for a moment at her breast. She shivered with the stirrings of her desire. He unfastened the earring from the chain and handed it to her. She deftly slipped it into place on her other ear. Reverently, Iain pulled her to him, slowly kissing first one ear and then the other.

Katherine felt tears fill her eyes again, as she cupped his precious face in her hands. "I love you, Iain Mackintosh."

"Then show me, my love, show me."

Chapter 14

"I THINK WE should tell Mrs. Abernathy." Elaine held out her wineglass.

Jeff picked up the wine bottle, then refilled her crystal goblet, trying to weigh the merits of her suggestion.

"Thanks." She sipped the wine and leaned back in her chair, the firelight catching the copper highlights in her hair. The overstuffed armchair was almost big enough for both of them. If the situation had been any different he would have—he pushed the thought aside and focused on her words.

"Jeff, she has a right to know. After all, this is her home. Besides, as I've said before, she might know something. I mean maybe this doorway or whatever has opened before. We'll never know if we don't ask. And we can't ask unless we tell her what we think has happened to Katherine."

Jeff added some wine to his own glass and settled back on the sofa. They'd been over this and over this. Tell the Abernathy's. Don't tell the Abernathy's. They had spent the better part of the afternoon and evening arguing about how to explain Katherine's absence. He

suddenly felt incredibly tired. Maybe Elaine was right.
Maybe Mrs. Abernathy could help.

He sipped slowly, staring into the fire. "All right, I
agree."

"Finally." Elaine heaved a sigh of relief. "Shall we do
it now?"

"Now, as in *right* now?"

"No time like the present."

Jeff frowned into his glass, then brightened suddenly.
"We don't know where Mrs. Abernathy is."

Elaine rolled her eyes. "Hardly an insurmountable
problem, Jeff. We'll just go down to the lobby. If she
isn't there, I'm sure someone will know where she is."

"She might have gone to bed already."

"This is a working hotel, so I doubt she gets many
early nights. Besides, its not that late."

Accepting defeat, Jeff swallowed a mouthful of wine
and set the glass on the table. "Okay, let's get it over
with."

Elaine smiled as he reached out to pull her up. "You
won't regret it."

He casually draped an arm over her shoulder. "I already do."

"I see."

For someone who had just heard that a guest had possibly disappeared through a doorway to the past, Mrs.
Abernathy was reacting remarkably well. Jeff watched
as she fidgeted with a small silver pin shaped like a
leaping cat. She seemed to be mulling something over,
trying to make a decision. They sat and waited.

They had found her in her office. The small, cluttered
room had the comfortable, lived-in feeling of a family
den. There were photographs everywhere, on her desk,
on the mantel of the small fireplace, decorating the walls.
There was even one of a smiling Mrs. Abernathy and
what looked to be the Queen.

Elaine sat on Jeff's right, both of them facing Mrs.

Abernathy as she sat behind her desk in a big leather chair. It had taken them an hour or so to explain Katherine's disappearance and what they thought was behind it. Mrs. Abernathy had said very little throughout, just an occasional word of encouragement or nod of agreement.

Jeff sat waiting for the other shoe to fall. He glanced at Elaine, but couldn't read her expression at all. She seemed to have gone into attorney mode, all business-like, emotions played close to the vest. He, on the other hand, felt like a basket case. First and foremost he was worried because Katherine was missing, but running a close second was his concern over the fact that she seemed to have wandered into another century.

"I can't really say that I'm surprised by what you've told me."

Elaine's brow furrowed. "Are you saying you actually expected something like this?"

Mrs. Abernathy nodded. "More or less. When I first saw Katherine I suspected something might happen. But when I saw the cairngorm I knew for sure."

Jeff studied Mrs. Abernathy, trying to make sense of what she was saying. "You knew? Knew what?"

Mrs. Abernathy smiled cheerfully at Jeff. "Why, I knew that she was the lady in the legend."

Elaine leaned forward, resting an elbow on her knee. "Mrs. Abernathy, I'm not following you. What legend?"

"Why, the legend of the cairngorms, of course." She looked at Jeff. "I imagine you know the story, don't you, Jeffrey?"

Jeff felt bemused. "You mean the tale about the lady and her lost love? How do you know that story? I thought it was a family legend—*my* family." He pounded his chest with one hand in an effort to underscore the importance of his last words.

Elaine looked totally confused. Mrs. Abernathy just smiled again, as if this conversation were about everyday, mundane things rather than legends and time travel.

"Ah, well, the story was told in my family, too. I suspect that we must be related somewhere along the line."

Elaine interrupted, musing aloud. "Dow—that's what you said your maiden name was, didn't you? Your family's actually a sept of the Davidson clan." She smiled suddenly as she found the answer to the puzzle. "And Jeff's grandmother was a Davis, also a sept of the old Clan Davidson. Your ancestor, the one who first owned Duncreag, was he a Davidson?"

Mrs. Abernathy nodded. Jeff struggled to follow the strange turn the conversation had taken. "What is a sept?"

"It's a branch of a clan, usually a blood branch formed by a second or third son. They often took a name separate from the original clan to help differentiate themselves from everybody else. Sometimes the name just got anglicized, as with Davis."

"How come you know so much about this clan stuff?"

Elaine shrugged. "I am half Scottish. But more to the point, I've been interested in the clan system since I was a kid. I've studied it a lot." She turned to look at Mrs. Abernathy. "Tell me about this legend and how it relates to Katherine."

Mrs. Abernathy sat back in her chair, her elbows resting on its arms, her fingers steepled. "Shall I tell it, Jeff, or would you like to do the honors?"

Jeff threw a dazed look at both women. "By all means, be my guest."

"Well now, it was a long time ago. According to the legend, there was a young lady who was forced to marry into the Davidson family. It was not uncommon in those days for a woman to marry for something besides love. They often did it for protection or financial gain. Anyway, in this case, the lass in question had already given her heart to another. But fate had intervened, and he died. She married a Davidson, but she always remembered the first man and, according to the legend, she never loved anyone else. In his memory, it is said, she always wore a pair of cairngorm earrings. And as further tribute to him, she bequeathed them to her daughter. The cairngorms were then passed from mother to daughter down through the ages, a symbol of undying love."

Elaine looked startled. "Jeff, you know this story too?"

"Yeah, Gram told it to us a thousand times."

"So the cairngorms in the legend are the same ones that your grandmother gave Katherine?"

"Supposedly. But it's just a story." Jeff waved a hand in dismissal.

Elaine turned her attention back to Mrs. Abernathy. "You said something earlier about Katherine being the lady in the legend. What were you talking about?"

"Well, as I said, I didn't know for sure until I saw the cairngorm earring she wears around her neck. I recognized it immediately."

Jeff snapped out of his daze. "Wait a minute—how could you recognize something you've never seen?"

"Oh, but I have seen the earrings. Not the real ones, you understand, but a painting of them. My grandmother used to show us the wee picture and tell us the tale. I always thought it so romantic. And then, when I saw Katherine, well, it was like the legend coming to life."

Jeff struggled to hold on to his patience. He felt as though he was being led down the proverbial garden path. "Mrs. Abernathy, are you saying you are in possession of a painting of the lady of the legend wearing the cairngorm earrings?"

"Oh my, yes. Would you like to see it?"

Jeff wanted to jump from his chair screaming. He felt Elaine's hand on his arm, and drew in a deep breath. "Yes, please."

Mrs. Abernathy rose and walked over to the photo of her and the Queen. "Just a gag photo from a shop in London. They do it with computers. A friend gave it to me a few years back. Looks real, don't you think?"

Elaine smiled and nodded. Jeff made an inarticulate grumbling noise. Mrs. Abernathy removed the photograph from the wall, leaving a small wall safe exposed. She twisted and turned the dial, stopping every once in a while as though trying to remember the combination. Finally, she beamed at them over her shoulder. "There, open at last." She reached inside and withdrew a small object wrapped in black velvet. "Here it is. It's quite valuable, you know. It was painted sometime in the second half of the fifteenth century, by a Flemish artist. As portrait painting was still quite new, the miniature is a rare example of the early form of the art."

She sat at her desk and began to unwrap the portrait. "It's quite small, but the detail is extraordinary, and even though the woman in the painting is older, well . . . see for yourselves."

She handed the little painting to Jeff. Elaine moved to stand behind him, then stared over his shoulder. He heard her gasp, even as he let out an oath impugning some poor guy's ancestry.

The woman in the painting was beautiful. Her eyes were gray, her hair gleaming gold, drawn over her shoulder in a heavy braid. The cairngorms did indeed grace her tiny ears. The detail was so fine that he could see the filigree of the gold holding the stones. Her lips were barely tipping upward at the corners, as if she had just begun to smile. She looked demurely down at her hands, which appeared to be folded in prayer. And she looked just like his sister.

Jeff sucked in a breath, feeling like he'd been punched in the stomach. He struggled to breathe calmly. He looked again at the portrait. He couldn't shake the feeling that it was trying to tell him something, that something in the painting wasn't quite what it seemed.

"Who is this woman?" Jeff held the miniature out to Mrs. Abernathy. His hand trembled, but through sheer willpower he forced it to steady.

Mrs. Abernathy took the painting, then carefully cradled it in its velvet wrappings. "Her name was Katherine Davidson. She was the wife of the first Laird of Duncreag."

"What else do you know about her?"

"Nothing really, except that she is supposedly the lady of the legend." Mrs. Abernathy looked for a moment at the picture. "And that she looks enough like your sister to be a genetic clone."

Jeff felt Elaine put a hand on his shoulder as she came to sit on the arm of his chair. Her touch was comforting. He leaned closer to her and felt himself calm slightly. She was looking at the portrait in Mrs. Abernathy's hand, her brow furrowed.

"Mrs. Abernathy, correct me if I'm wrong." Elaine absently stroked Jeff's shoulder. "But I thought that women in the Middle Ages rarely took their husbands' surnames. Yet you called her Katherine Davidson."

Mrs. Abernathy pursed her lips, her face screwed up in thought. She relaxed suddenly, sending Jeff and Elaine a brief smile. "I honestly can't say that I know the ins and outs of medieval marriages, but I do remember my mother telling us once that Katherine, the one in the portrait, wasn't from Scotland. Perhaps that explains the use of her husband's name. I'm afraid there's really no way to know for sure."

Elaine nodded. "Do you know her husband's first name?"

"Oh, yes. His name was Alasdair. Alasdair Davidson."

"Not Iain?"

"No, it was Alasdair, and seeing that he was the first Davidson at Duncreag, there are actually documents to verify that. So I'm sure of his name."

Jeff ran a hand through his hair. "Could Iain have been a middle or second name?"

"Not that I know of. Why do you ask?"

Elaine stood up, restlessly fingering the photographs

on the mantel. "Because, Mrs. Abernathy, Iain is the name of the man in Katherine's dreams."

"Well, he must the other one, then."

"The other one?" Jeff looked puzzled.

"Why, yes. It fits, don't you see." Mrs. Abernathy smiled at Jeff as though she had satisfactorily clarified the matter for him.

"Fits?"

Elaine interrupted, "What she's saying is that Iain is the lover in the story."

Jeff blinked, trying to assimilate this new information. "But that would mean Katherine is—was—married to someone she didn't love." He stood, throwing his hands up in frustration. "This is crazy. We're talking about people that have been dead for hundreds of years."

"Yes, but Jeff, if that portrait is any indication, we're also talking about Katherine. *Our* Katherine," Elaine countered.

"Mrs. Abernathy, let me see the portrait again." He held out his hand.

She gave it to him, watching as he studied it. "What is it?"

Jeff answered without looking up. "I don't know exactly. I can't shake the feeling that there is more here that I'm seeing."

He studied the likeness of his sister, following her gaze to her hands, just visible at the bottom of the canvas. Suddenly, it hit him what was wrong. It was her pose. If she was supposed to be praying as the painting suggested, her hands were all wrong. Her hands should have been flat, palm to palm, fingertips pointed upward. Instead they were relaxed, the right one wrapped around the left, her index finger raised slightly. Jeff bent closer, studying the finger. The detail was so clear that he could see a small crescent-shaped scar on the knuckle.

He sucked in a breath. He felt vaguely sick.

"This is Katherine."

Elaine looked at him sharply. "You can say that for sure? How?"

"This scar." He pointed to it. "One summer, when we were kids, we were coming out of the grocery store when Katherine saw a dog in the back of a pickup truck. He was tied to the side with a rope and had somehow managed to get all tangled up, the result being that he wasn't able to move. Anyway, Katherine ran over to him to try and get him free, but the poor dog was so frightened that he bit her." Jeff paused, still looking at the painting. "He got her whole hand. But the major damage was to her index finger. His teeth almost severed it. Gram rushed her to the hospital and the doctors stitched it back together. She never got the feeling back in her finger, but it worked fine. The only visible sign that the whole thing ever happened was a small crescent-shaped scar."

"I know the one you mean." Elaine's face tightened. "She always used to joke that if you looked closely you could still see teeth marks." She leaned over Jeff's arm to look at the portrait.

"You're sure it's the same scar?" Mrs. Abernathy said as she too leaned forward in an effort to see the small painting.

"Positive."

Elaine looked up with a puzzled frown. "It's almost like she wanted us to see the scar. I don't know, like she wanted us to recognize her." She tucked a strand of hair behind her ear. "But at the same time, she seems to have gone to a lot of effort to make the pose seem casual."

"So that nobody else would notice anything unusual." Jeff handed the portrait back to Mrs. Abernathy.

"Exactly. You're really the only one who could recognize the scar. So that would mean it's either a heck of a coincidence or . . . ."

". . . a message for Jeffrey," Mrs. Abernathy finished for her.

"But what is she trying to tell me?" Jeff drew in a deep breath, frustration welling up inside him. "Mrs. Abernathy, why the hell didn't you show us this portrait when you first realized it resembled my sister?"

"I didn't want to be messing with the proper order of things. Remember, I had no idea Katherine was having dreams. So the time didn't seem right. I thought it might be important for her to be here. I was concerned that if I mentioned the portrait, it would have scared her into leaving."

Jeff started to pace. "My point exactly. And if she had left, she'd be safe, here in this century, instead of long dead, leaving cryptic messages for her brother."

Elaine put a hand on his arm. "Jeff, we don't know that it was a bad message. Maybe she just wanted you to know that she was all right."

"All right? How can she have been all right? She travels back to who-knows-where, or for that matter when, to find a guy named Iain, who she thinks is her only true love. She gets there and, best we can tell, finds out he's dead. And then, for some unknown reason, marries this Alasdair character and, if we're to believe legend, lives the rest of her life mourning the dead guy. I'd hardly call that 'all right.' "

"Jeff, calm down. We don't know anything for certain. Maybe she lived with Iain a long time before he died. Maybe she had a fondness for this Alasdair. All we have to base our understanding on is an old legend. And you know as well as I do that it could have been vastly distorted by time. Maybe Iain turned out to be a loser and she fell for Alasdair instead. It's all just supposition, isn't it?"

Jeff shook off her hand. "Except that my sister is, or was, stuck in medieval Scotland. And *she*"—he shot an angry look at Mrs. Abernathy—"had the means to have stopped her from going."

Mrs. Abernathy paled. Elaine grabbed Jeff's shoulders, forcing him to look at her. "You know that isn't true. Even if Mrs. Abernathy had shown Katherine the portrait, she still would have wanted to go."

Jeff sagged forward, his rage evaporating. "You're right." He turned to Mrs. Abernathy. "I'm sorry. You couldn't have done anything to stop her. I was just—"

Mrs. Abernathy lifted a hand. "You were just grieving for your sister. I understand. I do believe, Jeffrey, that things happen for a reason. So no matter how it turned out, I can't help but think that Katherine is—or should I say was, where she wanted to be."

Jeff sank into the chair, a hand covering his eyes. "I just wish I had a way of knowing for sure."

Chapter 15

"WELL, THAT'S ALL the stuff in the bathroom."
Elaine walked back into Katherine's bedroom, holding
a brown makeup bag in one hand and rubbing her back
with the other. "Have you finished with the clothes in
the wardrobe?"

Jeff sat on the bed, staring out the window, an open
wallet in his lap. "Huh? Oh, sorry, I guess I just got
sidetracked."

Elaine sat next to him, then reached over to pick up
the wallet. She looked down at a picture of Jeff and
Katherine as kids, decked out in holiday finery. "Where
was this taken?"

Jeff looked at the small photo. "I don't know, some
studio. Gram wanted a Christmas photo of her 'little
lambs.'" He touched the picture almost reverently. "I
didn't know Kathrine had a copy."

Elaine flipped through the other pictures, stopping at
one of her and Jeff soaking wet and giggling like loons.
It had been taken a few years earlier, on a trip to the
beach. It had rained the entire time. She felt tears prick
her eyes and brushed angrily at them as she handed the

wallet back to Jeff. "Here, you should keep the photos. I know she'd want you to."

"I just can't accept that she's gone, Elaine. It feels wrong to be going through her stuff like this."

"We're not 'going through it.' At least I'm not. We're just packing it up. Okay?"

Elaine studied Jeff's haggard face. They'd sat up late, trying to make some sort of sense of everything that had happened. "Did you get any sleep at all last night?"

"No. Every time I dozed off, I started dreaming that Kitty was calling for me. So I finally gave up and sat by the window waiting for the sun to come up. Pretty pathetic, huh?"

"Jeff, stop it. It's like Mrs. Abernathy said, you're grieving for Katherine. It's understandable. In fact, I'd be a lot more concerned if you weren't upset. Now come on, let's finish up in here." She stood and surveyed the belongings left in the room. There were still clothes in the small wardrobe and odds and ends on the bedside table. "You finish the clothes. I'll gather up the things by the bed."

Jeff nodded unenthusiastically, but headed for the wardrobe, suitcase in hand. Elaine turned to the table. As usual, Katherine had brought almost every piece of jewelry she owned. She was always certain that if she left even one piece behind, she'd need it once she got wherever she was going.

Elaine bit her lip, trying to stop the threatening tears, and started stuffing things into a small plastic bag. The last thing on the table was a wooden box. She picked it up, then sat down to look at it more closely. She turned it this way and that in the light, examining it. It was heavily carved, the hues of the wood blending into the intricate design, worn smooth in places with age.

At each end, the box was banded with gold. The gold, too, was embellished with carving. There was a seal of some kind on the top—a wildcat, sort of standing up. It actually looked as if the thing were dancing. It seemed familiar, but she couldn't quite place it.

"Jeff, do you recognize this?"

He turned from the wardrobe, a long filmy skirt in his hands. "Yeah, that's the box the cairngorms came in. Katherine carried her jewelry in it. I wouldn't be surprised if it's as old as the earrings."

"It's beautiful. Is this real gold?"

"As far as I know." He folded the skirt and laid it in the suitcase, then turned to reach for another garment.

Elaine looked again at the seal. "Do you know what the crest on the top is?"

Jeff came over to look at the box. "Nope. It looks like a cat, though."

"Thanks," Elaine said dryly. "I could see that for myself."

Jeff shrugged and returned to his packing.

A filigreed latch joined the lid and the base. Elaine opened the box carefully. It was wooden inside as well, the bottom still lined with traces of some sort of a rich brocade. She turned it over, marveling at the workmanship. It was a fine piece that probably belonged in a museum someplace. She stroked the underside of the box absently and then paused, her attention on the bottom. With one finger, she traced the line of some sort of carving.

"Jeff? Did you know there's something carved on the underside of this box?" She walked over to the window, and held it up to the light.

"There's something carved all over the box, Elaine."

She peered at the wood. "No, I don't mean decorations. I mean words. Jeff, there's something written on the bottom of the box."

" 'Made in China'?" Jeff said, looking over her shoulder.

"Ha-ha. Hang on a sec. Let me see if I can . . . Wait, I know. Hand me the pad of paper and pencil that're over there by Katherine's purse." She sat on the cushion in the window seat.

"Okay. Here. Now what are you going to do?"

Elaine smiled up at him as she ripped a piece of paper off the pad. "Well, I've no idea if it will work but I'm going to try and take a tracing of the carving. You know, kind of like rubbing an effigy." She demonstrated by placing the paper over the bottom of the box and rubbing the pencil across it.

"Hey, I think it might actually be working."

"Thanks so much for your confidence." Elaine triumphantly held out the piece of paper. "You read this and I'll look at the box. Between us, we ought to be able to figure out what it says." She peered at the carving, trying to make out the words. "Are you sure you've never seen this before? It seems like somebody would have noticed it."

"Well, I haven't seen it. And as far as I know, neither did Katherine. She'd have told me if she had." He studied the tracing. "Okay, here goes. It looks like the first word is 'with' and then maybe 'touching.' Do you agree?"

"Yes, and then maybe 'hearts'?"

It took them nearly an hour to decipher the writing. But finally, with some confidence, they felt they had a translation.

"Okay. Shall I read the whole thing?" Elaine's voice reflected her excitement.

Jeff smiled. "Shoot."

She read from the paper containing their final version.

> *"with touching hearts Our love entwines*
> *like Ivy on a Tree*
> *on Stony Ledge our love will soar*
> *our spirits to be set free*
> *the wind will House our joy and love*
> *and send us on our Quest*

Three bells will toll, away we'll fly
To North and south and West KO"

"It's a poem." Elaine put down the paper.

"Yeah, but not a very good one." Jeff looked at the tracing. "The last word doesn't even rhyme. In fact, it isn't even a word."

Elaine studied their writing. "If you get rid of the K and the O, it rhymes. But what do we do with them? KO isn't a word."

"Wait a minute. Let me see the box." Elaine handed it to Jeff, who peered at it through narrowed eyes. "I don't think it is an O. I think it's a D. That's it—KD." He looked at Elaine triumphantly.

"Great, KD. That makes even less sense than KO. At least KO had a vowel in it."

"Elaine, use that wonderful legal mind of yours. What comes in twos and would be fitting for the end of a poem? Or any work of art, for that matter."

"I don't know. A period?"

"Elaine." He shot her an exasperated look. "A signature. KD isn't a word, it's a set of initials. K. D."

Elaine gasped. "Katherine Davidson."

Jeff grinned like a proud parent. "Right."

"Wait a minute—you think Katherine wrote the poem?"

"I do."

"You sound really sure. Why? It's more than just the initials, isn't it?"

Jeff pinched her cheek. "You really are quick on the uptake, aren't you? Okay, first"—he held up a finger—"there is the fact that the carving appears to be as old as the box. Witness all our trouble deciphering it. That means we can feel fairly certain that the poem was written a long time ago. Second"—he held up a second finger—"there's the fact that this poem is written in English. *Modern* English. Since we've already determined that the carving is old, it means whoever wrote it had to know modern English. Quite a feat for a medieval person."

"Unless you happened to start your life in the twentieth century." Elaine grinned.

"Right. And when you add the initials K. D. to the mix, the poem simply has to be Katherine's." Jeff sat back on the window seat with a frown. "The real problem, though, is trying to decide why she wrote the thing. Somehow I don't believe she was inspired by a muse."

"Could she have been trying to send a message of some kind? Like the painting?"

"Maybe. It seems a little crazy, though. I mean, how would she have known that the box would make it to me? And why wouldn't she have noticed it herself?"

Elaine studied the box. "We can theorize all we want, but I'm not sure we can definitively answer those questions. What if we assume, for now, that she wrote the poem knowing full well you'd find the box in this room?"

"Well, if she did, then I'd say the poem is definitely a message of some kind. We just have to figure out what it's trying to tell us."

Elaine rubbed a hand wearily over her eyes. "We must have read this thing a hundred times and we still aren't any closer to understanding it. Perhaps it really is just a poem."

"No, I still think there's more to it. Maybe we're making it too hard." Jeff sat on the window seat studying the poem. "Maybe the answer is staring us in the face and we're just not seeing it." He forced himself to breathe slowly and deeply, trying valiantly to contain his frustration.

"Okay. We're assuming Katherine wrote this for you." Elaine sat on Katherine's bed, arms crossed, eyes narrowed in concentration. "Was there some sort of code you used as kids? If so, maybe she used it."

Jeff audibly blew out a breath. "The only one I can think of involved capital letters."

"You mean the capitalized letters make up the words of the message?"

"Something like that. In our case, we let the entire capitalized word be a part of the message." He looked down at the piece of paper. "There are some oddly capitalized words here. Wouldn't it be amazing if it was that simple?"

" 'A blinding glimpse of the obvious.' "

"What?"

"Nothing, just something my dad used to say." She picked up the pad and pencil from the table. "Which words are capitalized? I'll write them down if you'll read them out."

"Okay. Let's see. Our. Ivy. Tree. Stony. Ledge. House. Quest. Three. North. West."

"Well, that doesn't make much sense. Maybe if we break it down." Elaine chewed on the end of the pencil. "How about 'our ivy tree' together, then 'stony ledge house'. 'Three north west' seems to fit together, but that leaves 'quest' by itself." She paused looking at Jeff for input.

"Maybe quest is meant to tell us what we're doing. You know, going on a quest." Lord, this was like finding a needle in a haystack—a five-hundred-year-old haystack.

"Works for me. Three northwest sounds like a direction. Hey, do you think we're going after buried treasure?" Elaine quipped.

"Probably not." Their gazes met, and Jeff tried for a smile but only managed to grimace.

She shrugged apologetically and looked back at the pad. " 'Stony ledge house.' This may be over-simplifying, but Duncreag actually means 'fort of the crag' and a crag is a kind of rocky ledge. So maybe 'stony ledge house' is Duncreag?"

"Have I told you lately how grateful I am for your

Scottish heritage?" Hope blossomed suddenly in Jeff's heart. Maybe they were finally getting somewhere. "Okay, so we have a place and a direction of some sort, but no clue as to where the message actually is."

"What about 'our ivy tree'? Does it mean anything to you?"

"Maybe. I'm not sure. It might be a reference to a book. One winter Katherine was really into this author, Mary Stewart. Kitty read every book she wrote, but her favorite was *The Ivy Tree*."

"What was it about?" She cocked her head to one side, waiting for his answer.

"I never actually read it, but it had something to do with lovers who had a secret place, a hole in an ivy-covered tree, where they left messages for each other."

"So it could be a reference to a message?"

"Actually, I think it's more than that. Remember, it says 'our ivy tree'. Kitty thought it would be fun if we had a secret place for messages. But it was the middle of winter, and we didn't have an ivy-covered tree, anyway."

Elaine made a circling motion with her hand, indicating her impatience. "So? What did you do instead?"

"We decided to use Gram's fireplace. There was a loose brick, a perfect hiding place for our messages. In fact, if I remember correctly, it was the seventh brick on the left." He jumped up. "That's got to be it. There must be a message in the fireplace."

"But which fireplace?"

"Oh. I don't know." He sat again, his enthusiasm fading as quickly as it had come.

"Well, at least we know that we're on a quest, at Duncreag, for a message in a *fireplace*. And we still have the directions."

"You're right. I forgot. Three northwest." He blew out a breath. "That could mean a lot of things."

"Let's try breaking it down. Any ideas what the three could mean?"

"Maybe a room number?"

"Could be, but that would eliminate the need for the northwest." She twirled a lock of hair absently around one finger. "No, it's got to be something more. How about a floor number? The old tower is rectangular, and there's a room in each of the corners. So maybe it means third floor, the room in the northwest corner."

"It's worth a try. Let's go."

Elaine jumped to her feet. "I'm right behind you."

"Great. We're back where we started from." Jeff lay on the floor of the upstairs parlor, his feet propped up on a chair, feeling as though they'd done nothing but waste their time. Why was everything always a damned dead-end?

"I really thought we were on the right track. I can't believe there was never a fireplace in that room." Elaine sat cross-legged on the sofa, her face scrunched up in frustration.

"I should have guessed. A lot of these old places had flues so big that they actually heated the walls they ran through, eliminating the need for a fireplace in the upper rooms. Architecturally speaking, it's pretty neat."

"Yes, well, it leaves us nowhere."

"Wait, I just had a thought." He sat up, his gaze meeting hers. "We were on the third floor of a *Scottish* tower, right?"

"Right. But what's that got to do with the price of tea in China?" Elaine's eyebrow's shot up in obvious confusion.

He held up a hand. "Just bear with me. If this building was in America, that would have been the *fourth* floor. Wouldn't it?"

"I get it. An American might make the mistake of calling the ground floor the first floor."

"Which would make *this* the third floor."

Elaine gasped. "We were on the wrong floor."

"Exactly."

"So that," Elaine pointed to a wooden door, "would be the northwest room."

Jeff jumped up, excitement making his heart pound. "We were in there a couple of days ago. Mrs. Abernathy took us on a tour. I was fascinated with the beams. They're really old. Anyway, Kitty wasn't interested. She just stood by the *fireplace*."

They crossed the room, and swung open the door. Standing together they looked at the massive stone and plaster structure. "Mrs. Abernathy said the stones were original and Katherine must have remembered." His stomach was doing hand stands. "This is it, Elaine."

Walking over to the fireplace, he started counting stones. The first few tries yielded nothing but firmly embedded rock.

"It could have been repaired," Elaine offered.

Jeff ignored her, continuing to investigate the stones, a sense of urgency almost overwhelming him. He reached up to a row of masonry just even with his head. Carefully counting over seven from the left, he tried to move the corresponding stone. It wiggled. "This one's moving." He jimmied the stone from its place and carefully lowered it to the floor, his eyes drawn immediately back to the gaping black hole above him.

"Can you reach it?" Elaine's voice was breathless, barely more than a whisper.

Jeff swallowed. "I think so." Balancing himself against the wall, he rose on tiptoe and reached carefully into the hole. At first, he felt nothing but the surrounding stones. Then, way in the back, his hand closed around an object. "There's something here."

"Can you get it?"

He nodded and slowly pulled it out. It was flat and wrapped in wax-covered material, brittle and hardened with age. There was a frayed ribbon tied around it. "We should open this in the other room. The light is better there."

Elaine nodded, her eyes riveted on the package in his

hands. They walked slowly into the parlor and settled side by side on the sofa. With shaking hands, Jeff pulled the ribbon free and removed the covering.

The parchment was yellowed with age, the writing faded, but still legible.

"It's in English." Elaine leaned closer, whispering the words as though even sound might destroy the fragile paper.

Jeff nodded and read the first line. 'My dearest Jeff . . .' He looked up at Elaine, his heartbeat accelerating. "It's from Katherine."

Chapter 16

KATHERINE LEANED AGAINST the framework of the doorway, watching the boy in the bed. William sat propped against his pillows. His cheeks were flushed, two bright spots of color interrupting an otherwise pale face. A large ruddy-faced woman sat by the bedside intently trying to feed him what looked to be broth. If the woman's bright red tresses were any indication, this would certainly be Bride, William's mother. The woman, spying Katherine, beamed at her.

"Come in, come in. I was just trying to coax me boy to eat." She offered William the spoon. With a grumble of embarrassment, he pushed it away.

"I'm no' a wee babe, Ma. I can feed myself." He demonstrated his point by taking the spoon and slurping a few mouthfuls of soup. "See?"

The woman smiled at Katherine. "He's no' babe, 'tis for certain, but he'll always be his mother's child." She patted William's cheek. He grimaced and rolled his eyes. Katherine suppressed a smile. Relationships between mothers and sons were obviously pretty much the same, whatever the century.

Bride jumped from the stool and stood by it nervously, as if suddenly realizing the Queen was in the room. Katherine looked back at the door to see if someone else had entered. The doorway was empty. She turned back to Bride, trying not to show her confusion.

"Look at me sitting here babbling on while ye stand. Please, my Lady, take this seat."

"Oh, Bride, no. You sit with your son. I'm the one who's interrupting. I just stopped by to see how William's doing."

"But 'tis no' proper for me to sit while the Lady of Duncreag stands." Worry clouded her normally cheerful face.

Understanding dawned. This was all about being Iain's wife. Katherine realized there were probably a lot of things she needed to learn about proper protocol in these times. Seeing that Bride's consternation would not be lessened until she sat, Katherine gave in and took the offered seat. "Thank you, Bride."

Bride's face perked up immediately. She nodded happily as though all was again right with the world. " 'Tis happy we all are that the Laird has taken a wife. But I'm especially pleased. Ye saved my son's life, there's no doubt about it. I'll forever be in yer debt."

"I didn't do that much, really." Katherine ducked her head in embarrassment at the woman's earnest praise. She supposed that by fifteenth-century standards, William's recovery was nothing short of miraculous, but still she felt a bit of a fraud knowing that all she'd really done was thoroughly wash both the boy and the wound. "I just cleaned him up a bit."

" 'Twas more than that, and well ye know it. And now you've come for a wee visit with me boy." She beamed at them.

"Hello, William. You look much better today." Katherine laid a hand on his forehead. It was slightly warm, but nothing compared with his earlier fever. "Your fever is still down. That's good."

"I am feeling better, thanks to you." William looked up at Katherine, youthful adoration shining from his eyes.

"I'm glad I could help. But you did all the hard work. It was your own strength that saved you."

William threw his shoulders back, puffing up with pride. "The leg still pains me, but no' enough to warrant all this bed rest."

"You need to stay in bed a while longer. It's important for you to regain your full strength before you try and use that leg. I've asked Iain to have someone make you a crutch. But for the time being, I think it would be a fine idea for you to stay in bed." Katherine lifted a hand in anticipation of William's protest. "At least for the rest of today, and possibly tomorrow. You don't want to tear your stiches. Promise me."

William crossed his arms over his chest with a pout, changing with a gesture from man to boy. "All right. I'll stay abed. But only because you ask it."

Bride moved to take the bowl and spoon. " 'Tis rest ye need now. Close yer eyes. I'll be back this evening."

William turned to Katherine with a sheepish grin. "Would you stay with me? Just 'til I fall asleep?"

"William, I'm sure our Lady has more important things to do than sit with ye." Bride smiled apologetically at Katherine.

Katherine reached for William's hand. "It isn't a bother at all. I'd be glad to stay with you, William. Now close your eyes and try to rest." He beamed at her and then settled into the soft bed, his eyes drifting closed, his hand still holding hers.

Bride pushed a stray red curl back from her son's face. "Well, I must be off. There's much to do this day." She looked first at Katherine and then at her sleeping son. "May the Lord bless you. I know that I do." With that she left the room, dabbing her eyes with the corner of her apron.

Katherine sat in the quiet room, letting the morning

sunlight warm her back. She felt her eyes grow heavy, and finally, giving in to the urge to rest, leaned her head against the side of the bed. Her thoughts turned to Iain. He had left with the first morning light. Off with Ranald, handling some sort of pressing business. She struggled to remember where he was. He'd said something about cows, but she'd been too sleepy to listen properly. No matter, she thought, and smiled dreamily. She'd be with him soon enough.

"Katherine? Katherine? Where are you?"

The voice rang through the solar outside William's room. Katherine sat up, shaking off her lethargy. It wouldn't do to have William awakened. She glanced at the boy, satisfied that he was still sleeping. Not willing to have anyone disturb him, she slipped from the room, hoping to find the source of the noise before it bellowed again.

"Katherine?"

Katherine winced at the shrill sound. She recognized the voice. Sorcha. A small tingle of worry shot up her spine. Sorcha would never risk bothering William unless something was dreadfully wrong.

"There you are." Sorcha barreled into the solar from the direction of Katherine and Iain's bedroom. Her face was drawn and she was out of breath, puffing as though she'd been running. "I've been looking for you everywhere. You must come quickly."

Katherine felt her chest tighten. The thin needles of worry changed to waves of fear. "What is it, Sorcha? What's wrong?"

The woman clutched at Katherine, her bony fingers grasping the flesh of her upper arm. " 'Tis Iain—he's been hurt. You must come."

The fear turned to dread. "Where is he? What's happened?"

Sorcha drew a deep gulping breath. "He's in the glen

at the bottom of the rise. He fell and hit his head. 'Tis verra bad, and he's asking for you."

"Oh, God. I'll come at once. Is Ranald with him?"

"Aye, I think so. I've no' seen him, only had word from the wee lad sent to fetch you. Hurry, I beg you."

Lifting her skirts in both hands, Katherine followed Sorcha down the stairs. She stopped in the great hall.

Sorcha pulled her forward. "Come, now quickly. I'll show you the way."

Katherine ran behind her, panic licking through her like hot flames. Oh dear God, she prayed, please let him be okay. As they reached the main gate, Sorcha drew her off to the left. "Follow me. This way is quicker."

Sorcha led her to an opening in the wall that was little more than a hole.

"Help me with this door."

With great effort, the two women swung the heavy door open. Katherine ducked to follow Sorcha, brushing at cobwebs as she passed through the short tunnel. Once on the other side, she hesitated as Sorcha veered away from the main pathway, instead taking a route that seemed to drop straight down the mountainside.

"It only looks steep. It switches back and forth. 'Tis a much faster way than the other."

Katherine nodded and plunged after her. Rocks and tree roots jutted out of the stony path at every turn. She stumbled once, only just managing to keep her balance. The trees were getting thicker, blocking the sunlight and giving the forest floor a gloomy cast. She glanced behind her, but could no longer see Duncreag.

"Are you sure we're on the right path?"

"Aye, we're almost there," Sorcha called to Katherine over her shoulder, not pausing in her flight. "Hurry, child."

Katherine's breath was coming in gasps. She marveled at the stamina of the older woman. Obviously, living in the Highlands kept one in good physical condition. She tried not to dwell on thoughts of Iain. There was nothing she could do at the moment but get to him as quickly as possible. She spurred herself onward, ignoring the burning pain of her fatiguing muscles.

Suddenly, the trees opened and Katherine found herself in a small meadow. She searched the tall grass for signs of Iain, but the clearing appeared to be empty.

"I don't understand. Is this the place? There's nobody here."

Sorcha stepped back a pace, moving away from Katherine, her eyes scanning the trees on the far side of the meadow. "Nay, this is the place. Perhaps they are o'er there just in the trees. I think I see movement."

Katherine placed her hand over her brows, shading her eyes.

"Don't dawdle, child. Hurry."

Katherine needed no further urging. She picked up her skirts and ran toward the trees, her only thought to reach Iain.

Suddenly a huge black horse burst from the thicket, his rider also dressed in black. Together, they looked like the devil incarnate. Startled, Katherine slid to a halt, and whirled around to ask what Sorcha made of the intruder. Her stomach lurched. The clearing was empty. Sorcha was gone. Terrified now she spun around again, her mind scrambling to make sense of this latest turn of events. The rider was closing quickly. Her heart in her throat, she screamed and began to run.

Adrenaline coursed through her body, giving her energy she hadn't known she possessed. She hiked her skirts even higher, freeing more of her legs, and dashed for the safety of the woods. If she could just reach cover. She could feel the vibrations of the thundering horse behind her.

Just a few more yards. She stared at the line of trees, willing herself there. She stumbled and fell, then lurched back to her feet, oblivious to any pain the fall might have inflicted. Her mind sang a litany. "The trees, the trees, the trees . . ." Just a few more feet.

Suddenly Katherine was blinded as something thick

and heavy dropped over her head. She screamed and tore against the darkness, trying to disentangle herself from this newest threat. She struggled to see, to breathe, as she felt something solid and strong tighten about her waist, lifting her up into the air. She kicked out savagely, and was gratified to hear a grunt of pain. She tried to twist away from the binding arm. But it only tightened as it slung her over the saddle, facedown. She was so startled that she froze, her blood rushing to her head.

She struggled to control her terror, feeling the bile rise in her throat. She couldn't see a thing. The coarse material that bound her rubbed against her face, restricting her breathing. She decided it must be a sack or a cloak of some sort. Working to slow her breathing, she tried to calm down so that she could think.

Her body jostled and jerked with each movement of the horse. Her head banged against something hard, a leg. She winced and gagged at the smell of rank human flesh. She tried again to kick, to strike out at her captor, her desire for freedom overriding any caution. But the grip on her middle only tightened, threatening to completely cut off her ability to breathe. She stopped moving, realizing struggle was useless. She'd save her strength. Surely, some means of escape would present itself.

Again, her head slammed against something hard, this time the horse's flank, judging from the smell. She tried to gather her wits, but between the ride and her position she felt dizzy and more than a little nauseous. Willing herself not to vomit, Katherine fought against the blackness that threatened to overtake her. However, it was becoming more difficult with each passing second as the horse increased its gait, her neck snapping with the force of the motion, sending sharp bolts of pain shooting down her back.

She worked to focus, to keep her mind alert. She thought of Iain, picturing his strong handsome face. Where was he? She had seen no sign of anyone, save

the rider who held her now. Had he been the one to hurt
Iain? No. Her foggy mind struggled to think clearly. No.
Sorcha had mentioned a fall. Iain must simply be in
another clearing. Or perhaps he wasn't badly injured after all and was already back at Duncreag.

But where was Sorcha? Surely she had escaped. The
clearing had been empty. Even as she rejoiced at the
thought that Sorcha could be safe, a second thought
pounded into her brain. What if there was another rider?
What if Sorcha had been captured, too? Or even worse,
what if Sorcha was dead? She felt her stomach churning
again. She swallowed, trying to breathe slowly and
evenly, hoping that would ease her rising panic.

Suddenly, the horse stumbled, and Katherine was
jerked forward and then slammed back into the hard-
muscled leg of her captor. She felt the blackness edging
closer, trying to rob her of any chance for escape. She
shook her head, trying to clear it, trying to think, ignoring the searing pain in her back. She had to believe that
Iain was all right. Even with a serious injury, he'd find
a way to come for her. He'd never let her go. She just
had to hang on until Iain came.

Her heart suddenly turned to ice, an unwelcome
thought gripping her. She held her breath, as bleak reality tore through her, taking with it all her fanciful
dreams of rescue. If Sorcha was dead, Iain would have
absolutely no way to find her. No one except Sorcha had
seen her leave Duncreag. Choking back a sob, she closed
her eyes, her strength gone. With a sigh, she drifted into
the waiting arms of darkness.

"Tell me again what happened." Iain glared at his aunt,
barely containing his temper. A fury born of intense fear
writhed inside him, threatening to override his ability
to think clearly. He glanced over at Alasdair and
Ranald, sitting at the edge of the inquisition, watching
in grim silence. Fergus stood by the great hearth, his
arms crossed over his chest.

Sorcha sat hunched on the bench, her eyes clouded with fatigue. "I dinna know what else I can tell you, lad. I've been o'er the tale time and again."

"Then tell me again." Iain's roar filled the hall, a mixture of anguish and rage. Sorcha flinched, shrinking back.

"Easy, lad, there's no need to be harsh with your aunt. 'Twas no' her fault." Fergus placed a hand on Iain's shoulder. He shook it off.

"I've a need to hear it once more. Maybe there is something I missed."

She pushed a weary hand through her graying hair. "All right. Again." She drew a deep breath. "I saw Katherine leaving Duncreag by the wee gate in the west wall. And I was worried she might come to some harm. So I followed her to see that she didna get lost." Sorcha looked to Fergus for support. He nodded at her reassuringly.

"I supposed she had just gone a-wandering to enjoy the spring morning. I dinna want to disturb her, so I stayed back, out of sight. We came to the wee clearing at the bottom of the rise. She was intent upon picking wildflowers, so I sat in the shelter of the trees and watched."

"Why did you no' speak to her?"

"I told you, I had no wish to intrude."

Iain bit back a curse. What had the woman been thinking? She should never have let Katherine go off alone. He swallowed his anger, maintaining control only through sheer willpower. "Go on."

"The rider came out of nowhere. He was wearing a plaid of reds and grays with maybe a wee bit of white." She shrugged. "It all happened verra quickly. I had no time to get a closer look. I jumped up and tried to scream a warning, but my voice was lost in the noise the great beast of a horse made. By the time I was on my feet, the rider had Katherine thrown over the horse, bound in some sort of blanket or plaid."

"So you ran away and left her?" Iain bit the words out, clenching his fists, a muscle in his jaw tightening, beginning to twitch.

"Nay, lad, I came for you. There was naught I could do for your Katherine, save be captured myself. So I ran back here to get help. But you were no' here." The words hung in the air almost like an accusation.

Iain pushed his hair back, anxiety replacing his anger. "I know." His voice cracked with despair, and black, oily guilt rolled through him like a fog, threatening to consume him.

Fergus tried again to reach him. "Let your aunt get some rest now. There's naught more you can learn this night."

Iain sighed, admitting defeat. He was faced with the reality that he was no closer now to discovering who had taken his beloved wife then he had been when Sorcha had first told her tale. He inclined his head, releasing his aunt. Fergus took Sorcha's hand and pulled her up, placing an arm around her shoulders as he led her from the hall.

"What are you planning to do?" Ranald's quiet voice was filled with concern.

"I've no thought." Iain stared into the flickering gold flames of the fire.

" 'Tis the Macphersons, from the sound of it." Alasdair took a seat on the bench.

"Aye."

"If it were my wife, I'd already be in pursuit." Alasdair's voice was soft, but the criticism was clear.

Iain swung around, his fists clenched. "But 'tis no' your wife."

Alasdair held up a hand. "A pity that, but I meant no offense."

Iain threw himself into a chair, pain wracking his entire body. "I think 'tis best if we wait. There is naught to be gained from blundering around in the dark. And there might still be some word."

"Are you thinking a ransom then?" Fergus said as he strode back into the hall, coming to stand with his back to the fire.

"Aye, 'tis possible. But if we hear nothing tomorrow, we'll ride the following day."

"I'll prepare the men. I've convinced Sorcha to lie down, but I dinna think she'll sleep tonight." He squinted, fixing his dour gaze on Alasdair. "So, mon, will you be riding with us then?"

"Nay. I'd like to, but I must see to my own holding. And there is the question of Ailis' safety. We'll ride for Tùr nan Clach with the sunrise. Would it help if I left some of the men I brought with me?"

Iain studied Alasdair, considering his offer. Finally he shook his head. "Nay, 'tis best you travel with a full guard. I would no' want your sister to lack adequate protection on my account."

"Well then, if you dinna mind, I will go and seek my men. There is much to do to prepare for our departure." Alasdair stood. "I wish you luck with the Macphersons."

Iain watched as he walked away. "I'm just as glad he'll no' be coming with us. We'd have had our backs to watch as well as worrying about the Macphersons."

Fergus snorted an agreement.

"Fergus, send two men to the Macphersons' holding. Tell them to try and find out what they can without letting on why they are there."

"I'd best take my leave then. I'll wait until Alasdair finishes with his men before I send anyone—ye canna be too careful about who you trust. And while I'm at it, I'll see that Davidson's lads dinna leave with more than they came with. Good night to ye."

Ranald absently raised a hand in farewell.

Iain hunched over in his chair, arms braced on his knees, head in hands.

"We'll find her, Iain."

Iain lifted his head, feeling his anguish manifest itself in every movement. "Aye, Ranald, but in what condition will she be? She is no' used to the harshness of our time." He buried his head in his hands again. "I'm no' much of a man, am I, if I let this happen?"

"You dinna 'let' it happen, Iain—it just happened. You canna control everything, cousin. There are forces at work out there that no one can control. You, of all people, should well understand that."

"But I promised to protect her, Ranald. What kind of husband am I, if I canna even keep my promises?"

"A loving one. Katherine knows you would give your life for her. And she'll no' hold you responsible for this."

Iain sat back, slamming his fist against the arm of the chair. "I swear I will find her, and if she is no' unharmed I will avenge her, if it takes the last of my breath to do it." That said, he collapsed against the chair, feeling his rage evaporate, leaving in its place an agony soul-deep. He felt the unfamiliar prick of tears. He hadn't cried since his mother's death.

He struggled to keep his emotions in check, but a sudden vision of Katherine suffering and alone was his undoing. He looked at Ranald, tears coursing down his face. "I canna live without her. I canna."

Chapter 17

My dearest Jeff,

How I wish I could see you, talk to you. You've always been my lifeline, my pillar. I find it hard to accept sometimes that I will never see you again. It is my one hope that this letter, despite the odds, will reach you. I've tried to find ways to let you know that I am here and alive. Did you see the portrait? I thought the scar as good a message as any. I'm probably being silly—I realize the chances of you ever seeing it or this letter are slim. But it helps me to know that I tried. The subterfuge is due to the fact that my husband must never find this letter. He has no idea where I'm from and if he were to find out . . . well, I shudder at the thought. We'll leave it at that. But I've started in the middle of the story, haven't I? Let me try it from the beginning.

As you have probably guessed, I did find my way back to Iain. My Iain. Oh Jeff, he was the most wonderful man—everything I could ever

have hoped for, and there are times even now that
I think I will die from wanting him. I loved him
more than I thought it possible to love someone.
And the most wonderful miracle of all is that he
loved me too. The time I spent with him was the
best of my life. Without those days and the memories they invoke, I could not have survived all that
has happened since.

Shortly after my arrival at Duncreag, I was kidnapped. Even after all this time, I am still not completely certain what happened. I have no idea
where I was held, only that it was a ruin of some
kind. Alasdair says they were Macphersons, horrible men with a holding somewhere to the southeast of Duncreag. Iain tried to rescue me and was
killed in the attempt. I never even knew about it
until after my release. I still sometimes dream that
I am with him at the end. Holding him. Telling
him how much I love him. And after all this time,
it still hurts, the pain of his loss unrelenting.

A short time after Iain's death, Alasdair ob-
tained my release. He ransomed me and brought
me back here to Duncreag. Alasdair Davidson is,
or was, a neighbor of Iain's. His holding borders
Duncreag to the south.

My captivity was horrifying. I won't write the
details, as they are best forgotten, but they taught
me just how harsh life in the fifteenth century is
for a woman, especially a pregnant one.

Alasdair runs Duncreag now. I've never been
clear on exactly how he managed to come to control it, and I'm not sure I'd like the answers if I
had them. But it suits me to be here. Somehow, I
feel closer to Iain. Anyway, after he brought me
here, Alasdair insisted I become his wife. I have
no love for him. He is pompous and arrogant and
not always kind. But as I said, life in these times
is harsh, and marriage means security. When I

realized I was carrying Iain's child, I knew that I needed that security, no matter what the cost. So I married Alasdair—and with little effort (he is a vain man) convinced him that Iain's daughter was his.

Anna is the light of my life. Her eyes are her father's, green as an emerald. She is beautiful and sweet-natured, with just a hint of mischief now and then. She is almost eight, still a little girl, but beginning to hint of the young woman she'll become. Sometimes when I look at her, I see her father and I know that it has all been worth it. I have managed to survive here and provide a safe home for my child. And if I were given the chance to do it all again, I would. Those few precious days with Iain were better than a lifetime without him. And they gave me the opportunity to bear his child, my beautiful Anna. The rest is such a small price for knowing such joy, even briefly.

So, I guess all of this makes me the lady of the legend. Wouldn't Gram have been amazed to know that? I still have the cairngorms. Iain had the other one. The one I thought was forever lost. He found it and wore it always, to remember me and that night so long ago. He gave it back to me on the night we married. I wear them now in his memory.

Quite an exciting life I've led, traveling back centuries in time and marrying two men. Oh, Jeff, if only it had been different, if only Iain had lived. But listen to me, feeling sorry for myself. I made my bed, didn't I?

I plan to give the earrings to Anna when she's older. I'll tell her the whole story then, all about her mother's adventures. I'll tell her about her father and how much her parents loved each other. I'll tell her, too, how much her father would have loved her, had he lived. And of course, I'll tell her

*about her uncle Jeff. But for now, she is still too
young to understand. And I dare not risk Alasdair's finding out.*

*So the legend has come full circle. The earrings
will again be passed down through the genera-
tions. For whatever it's worth, you can be proud
to know you carry Mackintosh blood and not Davidson. It's odd to think that as you read this Iain,
Anna, and I will have been dead for more than
five hundred years. I pray that this letter finds you,
if for no other reason than to know that I thought
of you always.*

*Know, Jeff, how very much I love you. And
know, too, that I miss you. I did try to cross back
when Alasdair brought me here after my release.
But the door must have closed with Iain's death,
or perhaps my connection to it died with him. Anyway, whatever the reason, it seems I can never get
home again. And of course, now I'd never leave
Anna.*

*I wish you happiness and, of course, love.
Maybe things will work out (or have worked out)
for you and Elaine. She loves you, you know. And
I think perhaps you have feelings for her too. You
just have to take the time to examine them. Jeff,
please remember that life is short and chances at
happiness are fleeting. Whatever you do, take
every opportunity to live a long and happy life.
And think of me sometimes.*

    All my love,
    Kitty

Jeff lifted his head, meeting Elaine's tearful gaze. Her
tears were a physical echo of the overwhelming grief
that rocked through the depths of his soul.

"At least she had a little time with him. And it sounds
like that Alasdair fellow isn't too terrible. I mean, he did

rescue her." Elaine met his gaze, her eyes seeming to beg him for confirmation of her words.

"I don't know what to think. I have never felt so helpless in my life." Jeff carefully placed the letter on the table. It seemed frail and out of place. "I keep thinking this is a nightmare and that any minute I'll wake up. When our parents died, I swore I would take care of her, Elaine. She was just a little kid."

Elaine bit her lip, tears still glistening in her eyes. "You weren't so big yourself. And you did take care of her."

"But not now." He ran a frustrated hand through his hair, his chest tightening with agony. "Elaine, I didn't even believe her. I let her go off to God knows where without a second thought, believing that the whole thing was the plot from an episode of *Star Trek*." He stood up and walked to the window, his hands braced on the walls on either side.

"Katherine is grown up now, Jeff. And as much as she loves you, she's perfectly capable of making her own choices."

He felt her hand on his shoulder, the touch soft, timid. He turned to face her, his eyes locking with hers. "Katherine is dead, Elaine. That couldn't have been a good decision."

"But she had Iain, at least for a little while—and Anna. That's something, isn't it? A part of Iain?"

"I don't want her to have had any of it." He slammed his hand into the wall. Elaine flinched, her eyes mirroring his pain. "I want her here. In this world, in this time, with me. Damn it. I want my sister." He felt Elaine's arms close around him, and tipped his head against hers, allowing himself a moment of self pity. Then, with a concerted effort, he pushed away, firmly in control again. "I won't leave her there. I *can't* leave her there."

Elaine brushed at her tears, a spark of anger lighting her eyes. "And just what exactly is it you think you're

going to do, Jeff? Ride to her rescue? It's not like you
can go get her."

Jeff walked over to the parlor fire, the seeds of an
idea beginning to take form.

Elaine watched him, her eyes narrowed and speculative. "Jeffrey St. Claire, don't even think about it. There
is no way you can go there. Katherine tried to come
back. She said the door was closed."

"She said the door was closed for her. That doesn't
mean it wouldn't work for me." If there was even the
slightest possibility he knew he had to take the chance.

"But you don't have a link with someone from the
past." Elaine continued stubbornly. "Katherine had Iain.
There isn't anyone there for you."

"I have a link with my sister, Elaine."

"But Katherine's link was romantic." She stood with
her hands on her hips, her amber eyes flashing.

"There are all kinds of love, Elaine." He spoke quietly, his words hardly above a whisper. "I love my sister.
More than anything." Elaine flinched as if he had hit
her, but it was too late to take the words back. "And I'll
bet my life that my bond with her is as strong as anything she feels for Iain."

Elaine's face softened, the anger fleeing. She laid her
hand against his face. "Oh Jeff, it's just a different kind
of love. Katherine loves you both."

"Well, Iain is dead. And I'm not. If anyone is going
to save her it will have to be me." He spoke forcefully,
as if the words themselves would open the cosmic door
that would lead him to his sister. "I know I can do this.
All I need is a physical link."

Elaine sighed with what sounded like resignation.
"You mean like the earrings?"

"Exactly. And I'll bet dimes to doughnuts that Mrs.
Abernathy will have just what we need. I've a feeling
she knows a lot more about this than she's letting on."

He took a step toward the doorway, but Elaine
stopped him, both her hands on his shoulders, her gaze

locking on his. "Jeff, I just lost my dearest friend in the world. And now you're asking me to help you go away, too? I don't know if I can do that. What if you can't find her?" Her eyes pleaded with him. "What if you can't get back?"

He traced the line of her lips with a finger. "Don't you see, I've got to try? I could never live with myself if I just left her there. No matter what the risk. I've got to try and find her. Hell, maybe I can even get there in time to save Iain."

Elaine stepped back, jutting out her chin defiantly. "Okay, fine, but if you're going to do this, I'm coming too."

"No." He hadn't realized until just this moment how much she meant to him. He'd already lost Katherine. The idea of something happening to Elaine was more than he could bear. She glared at him, daring him to argue.

He took a deep breath, knowing she wasn't going to like what he had to say. "I don't want you to come."

"But I—"

He held up a hand, motioning her into silence. "Look, we have no idea if this door even works. But if it does . . . well, who's to say that I'll even wind up in the right place."

"But if you wind up in trouble I could help."

Jeff framed her face with his hands. "No. You'll be my anchor here. My link with this time. Don't you see, as long as *you're* here, I'll be able to find my way back."

He stared down into her eyes, watching as she digested the significance of his words.

"You're saying that—"

"That I care about you."

"Then don't go." Her hand fluttered to her throat. "I didn't mean that. I'm sorry I—"

He bent and kissed her gently on the lips, drinking her words, tasting the salt of her tears.

She pulled away, her eyes searching his. "Will you

come back to me?" Her lips trembled with emotion. "Katherine was telling the truth, Jeff. I do love you. And I can't imagine life without you in it," she nervously bit her bottom lip, watching him for some reaction, "even if we only stay friends."

He gently touched her lip with a finger. "I'll come back. There seem to be some important feelings I need to check out here remember?" He smiled and bent again to kiss her, this time drawing her close, his tongue testing the warm willingness of her mouth.

"Of course, I have no idea, but I think this might be just the thing you're looking for." Mrs. Abernathy reached into the little museum case, picked up the jeweled dirk, and reverently handed it to Jeff.

"The dagger? I'm afraid I don't understand." Jeff looked doubtfully at the knife.

Elaine watched him, trying to battle the little voice in her head that was praying the whole thing wouldn't work. She felt disloyal to Katherine, but going had been her choice and Elaine couldn't shake the feeling that Jeff's trying to follow her was only going to make things worse. She ran a tired hand over her eyes. Who was she kidding, she just didn't want him to go. With a sigh, she focused back in on the conversation.

"Well, you see," Mrs. Abernathy was explaining, "this dirk has been at Duncreag for longer than anyone can remember."

"Yes, I know all that. Mr. Abernathy told me all about it."

Mrs. Abernathy continued without acknowledging Jeff's interruption. "It's certain that it was owned at one time by Alasdair Davidson, but we know it's far older than that. And if that isn't enough, there's the wee stone in the hilt." Mrs. Abernathy leaned over Jeff's arm and pointed to the brownish stone.

Jeff frowned at her. "I'm still not following you."

Mrs. Abernathy gave him a disappointed look. "It's a

cairngorm, lad. Not as pretty as the one your sister has, but a cairngorm nevertheless."

Understanding lit Jeff's eyes. "Mrs. Abernathy you're wonderful." As if to illustrate the point, he swept her into his arms in an enveloping bear hug.

Elaine watched them both, wishing there were something she could do to stop them. She had never felt so afraid. "This isn't a bloody party, you know." She hated the way she sounded, but she couldn't seem to stop the words. "Even if you do manage to get through that door, there's still a very real possibility that you won't be able to get back."

Jeff dropped his arms, releasing Mrs. Abernathy from his embrace. They both turned to look at her, their surprise reflected on their faces. She felt like a heel. But they just didn't seem to realize what was at stake.

Mrs. Abernathy recovered first, and shot her a stern look. "Don't be so negative, my dear. If your theories are correct, then all Jeffrey needs to get him back safely is someone here to form a link with, and based on your outburst just now, I'd say your link is pretty strong. I've no worries about him getting back."

Elaine felt hot color wash across her face, not certain whether she was embarrassed more by her tirade or by the fact that Mrs. Abernathy could so easily read her feelings for Jeff. Not exactly attorney-like stealth. She sighed, still feeling the heat of Mrs. Abernathy's chastising stare. Surely a lesser mortal would melt under such scrutiny.

Just when she thought she couldn't take it any longer, Mrs. Abernathy smiled. "There's nothing to be afraid of, lamb. Nothing at all."

Jeff slid a comforting arm around her, pulling her close. "It'll be all right. I promise. You just have to have faith in me."

Faith. Now there was an easy concept. She pulled her scattered thoughts together and looked up at the man she loved. "I know, I know. I'm trying, I really am. This is just so hard." She pulled out of his embrace and took the little knife from him and held it up to the light, the cairngorm glittering ominously. Okay, now she was imagining things. "You really think this thing will work?"

Mrs. Abernathy pursed her lips. "There's no telling for sure, but I'd say if we're right in our conjectures then this wee dirk ought to do the trick. I'm afraid there can be no test flight. The only way to find out if it works will be to go."

"Well, no time like the present, I always say . . ." Jeff's smiled, but Elaine thought it looked a little forced. It was time for her to put her feelings aside. Katherine needed them. And if that meant she lost Jeff, well . . . Tears filled her eyes, and she wished suddenly that she were a braver person.

Sucking in a ragged breath and plastering on a smile, she handed Jeff the knife. "You'll need this."

Mrs. Abernathy nodded approvingly. "According to what you've told me, Katherine's visions were always at night. I suspect there is truth to the old tales of magic in the moonlight. You'll be best off trying in the wee hours o' the morning, I suspect."

"And Katherine's room seems to be the portal." Elaine met Jeff's gaze and for a moment they were the only two people in the room.

Mrs. Abernathy cleared her throat and looked at her watch pointedly. "It's getting late. You'd both best be about your business. It'll be time to go before you know it and I've the feeling there's things you need to be saying to one another."

She pulled Jeff into a motherly hug. "You take care of yourself now, Jeffrey. I wish you luck. Find our Katherine and bring her back. And if you cannot do that, then think of all you have waiting for you here and come home." She pulled back, her merry eyes twinkling with wisdom. "I've the feeling your place is in this time." With a final pat she was gone, leaving them alone.

Elaine swallowed, for the first time in her life at a loss for words. "I . . . I don't want you to go." She looked up at him, her heart pounding in her ears.

"I know." He reached out and brushed away a tear that threatened to tumble down her cheek.

"All right, then let's not waste the little time we have left talking about it." Elaine sniffed back her tears as she linked her hands with his.

He pulled her closer, their hands trapped between them. She lifted her face for his kiss, waiting for the first gentle touch of his mouth. And when it came, the sweetness of it almost undid her. She pressed closer against him, her need communicating with his. The kiss deepened, moving from gentle exploration to the bright spark of passion.

Elaine pulled her hands free, desperately running them over his back and shoulders, wanting to seal the feel of him in her memory. She kissed him with all of her emotions, with love and fear and longing and desire, all combined into one burning flame. She felt his hands on her breasts and arched against him, demanding more. As his fingers circled her nipples, she bit her lip to keep from crying out.

Wordlessly, she pulled from his embrace, pulling him toward the stairs and his bedroom. When they finally reached the landing, he swung her into his arms, his lips claiming hers as he carried her down the hall. When they reached his room, he gently released her, allowing her body to slide against his. She felt the power of his taut muscles as she slid to the floor and shivered in anticipation at the feel of his hardening desire. Her legs were rubbery and unsteady and she was grateful when his arms slid around her, holding her upright. His lips found hers again and she met his kiss fully, drinking in his essence, breathing in the crisp spicy smell of him.

With a groan, he pulled back, looking into her eyes, searching her face.

"You're sure?"

She raised a hand and ran it along the curve of his lip. Taking a deep breath, she met his gaze. Never had she been surer of anything. Slowly releasing the breath, she whispered, "I'm sure."

Smiling, he lifted her into his arms again and carried her into the room, kicking the door closed behind him.

The alarm shrieked out its message: "Get up! Get up! Get up!" Jeff sat up blearily, trying to remember what had possessed him to set his alarm for the middle of the night. He slammed a hand on top of the clock, effectively stopping the racket. Hell, according to the numbers on the luminous dial, it wasn't even the middle of the night. It was barely eleven-thirty. He yawned, then shook his head in an effort to pull himself from sleep. Someone next to him rolled over with a moan.

"Is it time?"

Elaine. Memory suddenly came flooding back—it was time for him to attempt to reach Katherine. He lay back on the bed and pulled Elaine into his arms, resting his chin on her head.

"It's time."

He turned slightly, then tipped her face to his and kissed her deeply. She whimpered and pushed closer to him, her body already responding to his. He groaned with regret. "I've got to go."

Elaine nodded and buried her face in his chest. He held her close for a moment and then, releasing her, gently slid from the bed.

She sat up, pushing wayward curls from her eyes, squinting when he turned on a lamp. She watched him dress in silence, her eyes never leaving him. After zipping his jeans, he came and sat on the edge of the bed. "I'll come back to you, Elaine. I swear it."

Unable to talk, she nodded, fighting back tears.

He pulled on a shirt and leaned across to kiss her. Standing, he pushed his feet into his shoes and reached for the dirk. He turned, and with a last long look at her walked to the door.

Chapter 18

THE BEDSPRINGS CREAKED as Jeff shifted and rolled onto his back. Propping his hands under his head, he surveyed the room. Not a damn a thing had changed. It was just as it had been three minutes earlier. This time traveling stuff wasn't exactly a proactive thing. And waiting was not one of his strong points.

He sighed, staring at the ceiling, thoughts of Elaine crowding into his mind. He smiled with the memory of the evening's activities. He flexed his body, feeling again Elaine's soft curves pressed against him. He was amazed at how content he felt. Usually, after an encounter like theirs, all he wanted to do was get as far away from whoever's bed he had tumbled into as quickly as possible. But being with Elaine had been different. In fact, all he had done since leaving her was think about curling up with her again.

He suddenly grimaced. No wonder he wasn't going anywhere. He had to think of the past, of Katherine. He closed his eyes and pictured his sister, her hair gleaming and her gray eyes shining with laughter. He tried imagining Duncreag as it must have been in its glory days.

He even tried to picture Iain, which was pretty close to impossible, considering he had absolutely no idea what the man looked like. But it was to no avail—unless wingback chairs had suddenly become the rage in the Middle Ages, he was still stuck in the twentieth century.

Frustrated, Jeff rolled to his side, wondering what he was doing wrong. Okay, maybe if he touched the knife. He rubbed the leather sheath at his side, pressing his thumb against the cairngorm. Nothing. He sat up disgruntled. What he needed was an incantation. He groaned, and amended that thought—what he needed was a miracle, with a time machine attached for good measure.

He walked to the window, looking out on the tower grounds below. There was only a sliver of moon visible, leaving most of the lawn in deep shadow. It was odd how the shadows almost made the old walls seem whole again. In fact, if he squinted just a little, it almost looked as though there were buildings of some kind straggling around the wall. If he'd truly gone back then there'd be a smith, and a stable, and a brew house. Now there was a welcome thought. But this was the twentieth century and those outbuildings were long gone. He sighed at his flight of fancy. Moonlight was an amazing thing, changing the landscape in an instant with a simple wash of pale light.

He frowned, his detail oriented mind struggling with something that was out of place, something beyond the magic of moonlight. He looked again at the lawn and the wall. One of the small buildings even seemed to have a light in it. A flickering light, just like a . . .

Jeff froze, his subconscious finally registering what was wrong with the picture. He should have been looking down on the roof of the new addition. *There was no lawn on the east side of the castle.* He deliberately blinked. The images stayed the same.

With a deep breath, he slowly turned around, surveying his surroundings. Moonlight filtered in through the open window behind him, dimly illuminating the room. It was hard to see clearly in the shadows, but he could tell that the corner the floral wingback chair had occupied was empty. His pulse quickened as he continued investigating. Just visible was the curve of a fireplace, and opposite that the shadow of the bed. He frowned. Surely it was larger than before. Slowly he stepped out of the window alcove, his shoes clicked against bare stone.

He released the breath he had been holding, then reached for the dirk. He felt the leather scabbard, but when his hand closed over what should have been the hilt, he felt nothing. The scabbard was empty. Stepping back into the alcove, he knelt and carefully searched the floor. He felt along the darker corners with his hands. But the little knife wasn't there.

He crossed to the bed, intent on finding the dirk. He quickly realized that if he had lost it there, it was irretrievable now, for this bed was obviously not the one he had been occupying only a little while ago. It was much larger and heavier, its frame ornately carved. And there was a fur of some kind covering the top. He brushed his hand across it absently, trying to acclimate himself to his new surroundings. He'd done it. Or perhaps more accurately, it had been done to him. He mentally shook himself. It didn't matter one bit how it had happened. The fact remained that he was here. He hoped. At least he could be certain that he was no longer there.

Laughing silently at his whimsy, he walked toward an archway set into the wall by the fireplace. He reached for the iron ring that served as a door pull and tried opening the door. It wouldn't budge. He tried pushing it. It swung open maybe two inches and then thudded softly into something behind it. Feeling frustrated, Jeff pulled the door closed and began searching for another exit.

He spotted a dark arch adjacent to the one he stood in. It was bigger, and now that he was growing accus-

tomed to the faint light, he could see that it was elabo-
rately decorated, obviously the main entrance to the
room. He walked to the door and was reaching to pull
it open when he suddenly stopped, realizing for the first
time the precariousness of his position. He was alone
and unarmed in a strange place. If he was where he
thought he was, he was surrounded by people who reacted with force first, discussion later. And—he frowned
at the thought—he had no idea how to discriminate between friend and foe. Great, some cavalry he was.

Well, he could hardly stay in here forever. Squaring
his shoulders, he slowly inched the massive door open.

Iain paced in front of the fire's flickering light. There
had been no word of Katherine, no order for ransom,
nothing. He had waited impatiently all day and well into
the evening, expecting a messenger from the Macphersons. There was no sign, either, of the Mackintosh men
Fergus had sent to Cluny. They should have returned by
now.

He had retired early, thinking to be well rested for his
own ride into Macpherson lands in the morning, but
sleep eluded him. Every time he closed his eyes, all he
could see was Katherine's face pleading silently for help.
And pacing did little to alleviate the worry that ate at
him.

It had been too long. If she had been captured for
ransom there should have been word by now. He shivered at the alternatives. Captives meant for ransom were
generally well treated, especially women. But if she had
been taken out of spite or revenge, or for any of a myriad
of other reasons, her fate could range anywhere from
imprisonment to rape—to death. He slammed his fist
into the wall, wincing more from his fear for Katherine
than from the pain.

A slight noise caught his attention, and he tensed, listening. The sound had come from Katherine's chamber.
He stood, body rigid, battle ready, waiting for another

sound, but all was quiet. He forced himself to relax his stance. He'd overreacted. No doubt he had heard a wee mouse. Sorcha did her best to keep them at bay, but there were always small vermin about.

He resumed his pacing. His mind returning to Katherine. His men were ready, their arms sharpened and their blood-lust soaring as they prepared to attack the Macphersons and secure the return of their new mistress to Duncreag. But Iain knew they were also relishing a chance for revenge. Revenge not only for Katherine, but for Angus and Andrew as well. He knew, if he found Katherine dead, his own need for vengeance would be unquenchable.

A soft thud sounded against the heavy chest he had pushed against the door connecting his chamber to what he had come to think of as Katherine's. It had been meant to keep her from the chamber, but now it seemed it was keeping something from him. He pivoted slowly, his head cocked, listening. Again the noise was followed by silence.

This time he was not so quick to dismiss it. Crossing to the bed, he reached for his dirk. Holding it at the ready, he stood in silence, straining to hear something more, but the night was quiet except for the occasional rustle of the wind outside the window. Iain felt some of the tension ease from his body. He moved soundlessly, on bare feet, to the door of his chamber. Still holding his dirk, he quietly opened the door, moving into the darkened corridor.

He crouched low into the shadows, his eyes searching for the source of the sound. A dark figure emerged from Katherine's chamber. It slowly moved into the passageway, taking the shape of a man as it left the deeper shadows of the doorway. Iain sprang at the figure, wrapping an arm around the man's shoulders, his other hand holding the dagger, its tip placed directly on the throbbing pulse in the man's throat.

"One move and you're sure to be a dead man."

The stranger froze, not moving a muscle, his body tensed against the pressure of Iain's knife.

"We'll just move slowly now into the solar, down the passage straight ahead. Nod if you can understand me."

The stranger stood without moving, giving no sign that he had even heard Iain speak. Finally, the man tilted his head slightly in agreement. Iain pushed him forward, relaxing his dirk hand slightly, but keeping his arm locked around the man's shoulders and chest.

Once they were through the doorway of the solar, Iain shoved the man away from him, keeping the small dagger ready in his hand. The stranger stumbled, but recovered before he fell, swinging around to face his adversary. The two men eyed each other warily.

Iain felt a strange pounding in his ears. The man before him was fair, with short golden hair and piercing blue eyes. His clothes were oddly fashioned and his shoes were like none Iain had ever seen. "Who are you?"

"You first."

The man ran a hand through his hair, leaving it standing in every direction. Iain felt the hair on his arms rising. "I'd say you're no' in a position just now to be asking questions."

"Nevertheless, I'll know your name before I give you mine."

The man's Gaelic was awkwardly phrased, as though it was not his first language. Amazement was quickly overriding Iain's concern. "I'm Iain Mackintosh of Duncreag and, unless I'm very much mistaken, I'm guessing you're Katherine's brother."

The other man visibly relaxed, but still kept his distance. "I can't understand but about half of what you say, but if I understood the reference to my sister correctly, then you've got it right, Iain. I'm Jeff St. Claire, Kitty's brother."

"Kitty?" Iain stared at Jeff, trying to fathom the significance of the name.

"Katherine. Sorry—Kitty's her nickname." Jeff sat

down in the chair by the hearth. "Is it okay if I sit? You scared the hell out of me."

He did look a little pale. Perhaps he was not used to combat. Iain sheathed his dirk and sat in the chair opposite Jeff. "Tell me how you come to be here."

"To be honest, I'm not exactly sure how I did it. I just was there one minute and here the next."

Iain nodded thoughtfully. " 'Twas much the same with Katherine."

"Is she here?" Jeff looked around the solar, obviously eager for some sign of his sister.

Iain's hand tightened around his dirk again. This time in frustration. "Nay, she is no' here."

"So I'm too late." Jeff words were low, spoken mainly to himself.

Iain strained to hear. "Too late?"

"Yeah, I'd hoped to get here before the kidnapping."

"You know about Katherine's abduction?"

Jeff frowned, meeting Iain's steady gaze. "Yeah, I do, and a few other things as well."

"Tell me what it is you know." Iain's heart leapt as a small piercing ray of hope stabbed through his despair.

Jeff rose to stand by the fire. "Some of it isn't going to make you happy."

Iain nodded, and began twirling his dirk with nervous fingers. "Continue."

"Okay, I found a letter Katherine wrote to me." Jeff frowned, his face looking bleak. "It was written several years after her kidnapping. That would be a few years from now." He paused, his gaze steady, concerned. "I know this is hard to comprehend."

"As much for you as for me, no doubt." Iain waved a hand at him. "Please go on."

"She hid it in one of the fireplaces. I think she just wanted to talk to me." Jeff's eyes were clouded with pain now—a pain Iain recognized.

"She misses you verra much."

"I miss her too." Jeff paused, running a hand through

his hair. "Anyway, in this letter, she mentions her kidnapping. She says she never really knew exactly what happened. And what little she did know, she got from someone named Alasdair Davidson. Do you know him?"

Iain stabbed his knife into the table by the chair. "Aye, I know him. His holding borders mine."

Jeff eyed the knife nervously. "I take it he isn't a friend?"

"Nay." The single word hung for a moment in the air between them.

"Okay, then what I have to tell you is definitely not going to sit well with you." Jeff gave a wry smile. "Remember no killing the messenger."

"Aye." Iain sat forward, his hands braced on his knees, ready for the worst.

"Evidently, you were, or will be, killed in an attempt to rescue Katherine from the Macphersons."

Iain growled, his voice the only outward manifestation of his anger and fear. "And Katherine?"

"Well, according to her letter, this Alasdair guy pays a ransom and obtains her freedom, then brings her back here to Duncreag." Jeff paused, his face creased with worry. "It gets worse."

"Tell me." Iain choked the words out—his fear for Katherine curling inside him like a snake, threatening to unman him.

"It seems that Alasdair manages to gain control of Duncreag after your death. And according to the letter, he insists that Katherine marry him."

"The bloody bastard, he canna keep his hands off her." Iain sprang from his chair, fear and rage banding together to form a cold fury that seethed for vengeance. "And did she marry him?" This last part was forced through gritted teeth, as Iain tried to gain control of his emotions.

"Not at first. She calls him pompous and arrogant."

"An apt description." Iain sat again, burying his face in his hands, an image of Katherine filling his mind.

"You love her very much, don't you?" Jeff sounded surprised.

Iain lifted his head, tears in his eyes. "Aye, more than I can ever express. She is my life. Without her . . ." He trailed off, burying his face in his hands again, his insides feeling as if someone were ripping his organs out one by one. But his wallowing in self pity would not be of benefit to Katherine. He drew in a deep, cleansing breath and reached deep inside, finding strength. Lifting his head, he pulled the dirk from the table and met Jeff's worried gaze with the eyes of a warrior. "Tell me the last of it."

Jeff sighed, and dropped down onto a bench, nervously clenching and unclenching his fists. "She tried to get back to me a couple of times. But the doorway, or whatever it is, wouldn't work. She couldn't leave. I think maybe she was still tied too strongly to you."

"How do you mean?"

"Well, it seems she discovered she was pregnant."

"Pregnant?" Iain stared at Jeff, his mind reeling, his hand holding the dirk so tightly, it cut into his thumb.

"Yeah."

"Mine?" The words came out little more than a whisper.

"Yours."

Iain's death grip on his father's dagger relaxed. And he absently wiped at the blood, the functioning part of his mind noting that the cut was no more than a scratch.

Jeff cleared his throat, his eyes never leaving Iain's. "Kitty was afraid for the baby. I think something really horrible must have happened to her during her captivity. She wouldn't write about it at all, but whatever it was, I get the feeling it really drove home the fact that a woman alone in these times hasn't much chance for survival. She might have risked it if she'd been alone, but when she realized she was carrying your child, she knew she had to find some way to gain protection for herself and the baby." Jeff shrugged. "Alasdair offered that security."

"So she married him."

"She did. Then she convinced him the unborn child was his."

"And the child?" *His child.* Iain held his breath, waiting.

"A daughter. Anna. Katherine described her as beautiful. She said she had the look of you, especially her eyes. Iain, you should know that Katherine felt that being with you and having your daughter were the most wonderful things that ever happened to her. She specifically wrote that even if she had known how it would all turn out, she would have done it again. She still wore the earrings, Iain, and she was planning to pass them down to Anna, along with the story of her parents' great love for each other."

Iain felt suddenly as if he had lost not one love but two. He wondered how much more pain he could bear, but he had to know. "Was there any more?"

"No." Jeff shook his head. "Just a few private words for me."

Iain's sat staring, seeing nothing, his mind blank, as if someone had reached deep inside and strangled his soul.

Jeff leaned forward. "Listen to me, Iain. These things I've told you about, they haven't happened yet. That's why I came here, to try and change it all, to help you find Katherine and to keep you alive at the same time. Can you understand that?"

Iain focused on Jeff's face, his senses reawakening one by one. Hope reborn in a sparkling instant. "Aye. You think there's still a chance to make this turn out right?"

"I do. But now I need you to tell me everything you know about the kidnapping."

Iain rose to stand by the fire. "There is no' much to tell. Of late we've been having problems with the Macphersons, and Katherine's abduction is only the latest in a string of attacks on Duncreag. It seems the Macphersons have been reiving our cattle. We caught them in the act and stopped them, but no' before they wounded one of my men and killed another. Later that same day, I was attacked."

"By a stream. Katherine warned you." Jeff looked at Iain in amazement. "I don't think, even after all of this, that I fully believed her until now."

"Aye, she saved my life. And the man I killed carried this dirk." Iain passed the dirk to Jeff, hilt first.

"Iain, I've seen this dirk before, in my time."

"Aye, Katherine mentioned that she, too, had seen it."

"But I've more than just seen it. I used it to come back here. The cairngorm . . ." He touched it reverently. "I thought it would help."

Iain smiled as he took the dagger back from Jeff. "Well, I'd say that it did. 'Twas my father's, and now 'tis mine."

Jeff frowned in confusion. "But didn't you say the Macpherson you killed had the knife?"

"Aye. No' long ago my father died. He fell from a cliff. Originally they thought it was an accident, but I believe it was the work of the man by the burn."

"The one you killed."

Iain nodded.

"And that would be how he came to have the knife."

"Aye."

"So you think all of this has culminated in Kitty's kidnapping. What specifically makes you think the Macphersons are responsible for the abduction?"

"There was a witness." Anger rose again, with the memory of Sorcha's tale.

"What?"

"My aunt was there. According to her, Katherine left Duncreag for a walk. Auntie Sorcha was worried that Katherine would get lost and so she followed her. She found her in a meadow picking flowers and sat at the edge of the woods to watch o'er her."

"Why didn't she say something to her?"

"I asked her the same question. She says she didna want to intrude. I think the truth is that she wasna sure what her reception would be. She says she'd been rather curt with Katherine o'er the tending of the boy I mentioned earlier."

"The one wounded in the fight?"

"Aye."

"So she sat watching while Katherine was kidnapped?"

"Nay, she ran when she realized what was happening. She thought it best to come and find me."

"I suppose that's sensible. But why weren't you able to intercept them?"

Guilt slammed through him, but he forced himself to meet Jeff's gaze. "I wasna here. I'd gone out to retrieve the cattle we'd scattered in the fighting."

"It wasn't your fault, Iain. You had no way of knowing this would happen."

"In my mind, I know what you speak is true, but in my heart . . ." Iain paused, his body racked with grief.

"Excuse me."

Iain turned at the sound of the voice. William stood in the doorway, leaning heavily on a crude wooden crutch, gritting his teeth in determination.

"I know I'm interrupting, but I'm certain that Sorcha has no' told you the truth of the tale."

Chapter 19

KATHERINE FLOATED TO consciousness, trying to quiet the drums pounding in her head. Where the hell was she? Memory flashed. The clearing. A man on a black horse.

Oh God.

She'd been abducted. Holding back a groan, she tried to sit up. Dizziness washed over her with the force of a tidal wave, but she fought it, pushing herself into an upright position. She flexed her leg muscles and then her arms, wincing with the motion. Nothing seemed to be broken. Except maybe her head. Gingerly she explored her scalp, but found nothing unusual. Perhaps she just wasn't meant to be an equestrian.

Ignoring the pulsing pain in her head, Katherine stood up, one of her hands flat against the wall to help maintain her balance. Her prison, if that's what it was, was a small dank room with a rather large hole in one wall. She inched her way closer to the opening, hoping for an escape route. The hole appeared to be the remains of a window. Part of an arch remained intact, the rest lost in a jumble of fallen stone and sky, open from floor to ceiling.

She reached the hole and poked her head out, knocking bits of the window loose with the motion. Debris spiraled downward, its descent dizzying. Far below, she could see jagged edges of rock reaching up for her. She teetered, frozen for a moment, and then dropped to the floor and scrambled back to the far wall, her breath coming in tortured gasps. She leaned back against the cold stone wall, grateful for its support. There would be no escape that way.

Tears threatened and her heart called out for Iain. She had no idea if he was even alive. Katherine gave herself a mental scolding. It wouldn't do to borrow problems. She had plenty of her own to worry about. She had to think positively. She *had* to get out of here.

She wasn't some weak damsel in distress. Okay, she was a *little* weak, but she wasn't about to sit by meekly waiting to see what fate had in store for her. There had to be a way out of here. She just had to find it.

She turned slowly, surveying the room again, this time with an even sharper eye. It was roughly circular in shape, its walls made out of rough hewn stone. Across from the broken window, there was a smaller undamaged version. It wasn't much more than a slit, situated high in the wall. The ceiling was wooden and had rotted away in many places. The stones of the roof were visible through several gaping holes.

There was a crude fireplace, but nothing with which to start a fire. From the looks of the debris inside the hearth, it had been used most recently as a dwelling for a rodent or bird. She shuddered at the thought of an unknown roommate. Some straw or grass had been piled against one wall. Her bed, no doubt. She kicked at it, but to her relief, nothing moved. At least it looked relatively clean. Not the Hilton, but it beat cold stones. She rubbed her back. She'd had an experience with them already and was not ready to renew the acquaintance.

Finally, she turned to examine the thick wooden door. Unfortunately, it, unlike the rest of her penthouse suite, was in excellent condition. She tried to pull it open, but wasn't surprised when it wouldn't budge.

Still, there was bound to be somebody on the other side, and with any luck, there ought to be a bathroom break surely or at least a little gruel for dinner. And for that the door would have to open. All she had to do was disable her captor, and get the hell out of Dodge.

Piece of cake.

Bolstered by false bravado, she edged her way to the broken window, averting her gaze from the actual opening. She selected a large stone from the pile of rubble and crouched by the wall next to where the door would swing open. She held the stone ready, both hands gripping it firmly. Whatever it was that brought someone through that door, she'd be ready.

Katherine jerked awake with a start. It seemed she had been huddled on the floor for hours. She sat as still as she could, listening for the sound that had pulled her from her fretful doze. She heard a voice outside the door, calling something, and then a clanking noise as something was removed from the door. She stood up, raising the stone over her head, her body tense, ready to bean whoever entered the room. The door cracked open and a wooden bowl scooted past the door as it began to swing shut again.

"Wait, please." Katherine shot out from her hiding place, leaving the rock behind. "Don't close the door. I need a chamber pot. Please." She didn't have to try too hard to sound pathetic. Her voice cracked, and even in her own ears she sounded on the verge of begging.

"Verra well, I'll bring ye one in a bit. Eat the food while it's hot."

Katherine breathed a sigh of relief. She'd have another chance. But she needed a new strategy. Obviously, the guard wasn't planning to come into the room with her. She stirred the gray slop that passed for dinner. Gruel would have been more appetizing. She forced her-

self to eat a few bites. It tasted foul, but it was warm
and that was more than she could say for the accom-
modations. The light was fading fast and tendrils of mist
were already drifting into the room through the ruined
window. She choked down a few more swallows of her
dinner, an idea forming in the back of her mind.

With some effort, she managed to move the pallet of
straw into the center of the room. Settling down, she
curled into a ball, attempting to look like a woman in
agony—which, actually, wasn't much of a stretch. She
really did hurt from head to toe. She lay on her side,
facing the door, holding the rock next to her chest, hidden by her hair and the straw.

This time she didn't have long to wait before she
heard someone remove the bar from the door. Tensing
in anticipation, she curled tighter and writhed in her best
imitation of wracking pain.

"I brung ye a pot. I'll just be leaving it by the door."

"Would you please bring it to me? I'm sick and I
don't think I can make it that far." Her voice sounded
weak and, she hoped, pitiful. She held her breath, throwing in a retching sound for good measure.

"Alright then, here 'tis." The man shuffled over to the
pallet and bent to place the pot on the floor, his back to
Katherine.

With speed fueled by desperation, she rolled to her
knees, and scrambled to her feet, slamming the stone on
the back of the guard's head before he had time to rise
again. The phrase 'dropped like a stone' came to mind
as he slumped over the pot. She dropped the rock and
dashed out the door, slamming it shut behind her. Relieved to find that the coast was clear, she rammed the
bar into place. That ought to hold him a while. Now to
get out of this hellhole.

She took a precious moment to assess her surroundings. The door opened directly out onto a staircase.
Stairs spiraled down below her and twisted up into the
ceiling. She was reminded of the game dungeons and

dragons. She was the princess locked in the tower. Only this was real.

She forced herself to take calming breaths. The most pressing question at the moment was 'up or down,' and given her history with heights, she chose down, praying that there either weren't other guards or that if there were, they'd all gone for take-out.

She took the stairs two at a time, her heart beating a cadence for her feet. Reaching a landing, she stopped. Voices echoed eerily from the stairwell, the distortion making it impossible to tell if they were above or below here. She ducked through an archway into a large room. Her eyes scanned the chamber, looking for cover. It was empty except for a few pieces of broken furniture and a dilapidated wooden screen leaning drunkenly against the wall. Panicked, she listened as the voices drew nearer. An open window beckoned mockingly, but she resisted, having already seen the view. There was no other way out.

Footsteps clattered on the stairs, the voices discernable now. She dove beneath the rickety screen, wedging her body between it, the wall and the floor, trying not to think about what she might be lying on. She held her breath, trying not to move a muscle for fear of making some small noise. The voices drew closer. There were two of them. She pressed herself farther under the screen.

"I tell ye, she has to be here somewhere. Ain't no way she could have gotten past Beag Dougall."

"Well, if I find her, the woman will wish I hadna."

Katherine prayed for invisibility as the two men walked into the room. She couldn't see them, but she recognized the threatening one's voice as that of the man she'd hit.

"Easy now, lad. I understand why ye would want to strike the wench, but ye heard the mon. No one is to harm a hair on her head."

"Ah but a mon can dream. And when we do get her,

I swear I'll tie those pretty little hands of hers so tightly behind her back, she'll be wishing she never messed with the likes o' me."

"That's all well and good, but first we have to find her."

"She's no' in here. I say we search the cellars."

The voices moved farther away, echoing again as they started down the stairs. Katherine released her breath and cautiously crawled out from under the screen, waiting until the voices faded altogether before she began to move toward the stairs. She slowly edged her way down the stone steps, hoping that her luck would hold and that 'Small' Dougall lived up to his name.

She stuck her head around the end of the stairwell, only to quickly draw it back again. The door and freedom loomed only a few feet away. But an ox of a man was standing between the stairwell and the door. If this was Beag Dougall, his mother had either been a poor judge of size or had a heck of sense of humor. He was huge—there was nothing *small* about him. Heck, this guy made a Jets linebacker look like Mickey Mouse. No way was she going to get past him.

She slid back into the safety of the stairwell. The other guards had mentioned a cellar. If they had gone down, then her only choice seemed to be to climb back up the tower. Maybe there'd be another way down from the top, like the one at Duncreag. Crossing her fingers, she bounded back up the stairs, passing the now open door of her prison, continuing up the remaining steps to a barred door at the top. Her breath coming in gasps, she used every last ounce of her remaining energy to pull the heavy bar up from its iron fittings. Once it was free, she dropped it, heedless now of making noise, knowing that time was running out.

She yanked the door open and ran out onto the battlements. They were little more than a narrow stone walkway with a knee-high wall. She swallowed her fear and began moving along the pathway, searching the wall

ahead for some kind of door. She rounded the first corner, still frantically looking for a means of escape. Behind her she heard the muffled shouts of the guards.

She sped up, rounding the next corner. Surely there
was another way down. Who would be stupid enough
to design a battlement without an emergency exit? She
rounded the final corner, only to be brought to a quick
halt. The walkway ended about ten feet from the corner
with a small stone wall. Beyond that was sky. Loads of
sky. Katherine swallowed nervously. This was definitely
not the emergency exit.

"There she is."

The two guards rounded the corner and skidded to a
stop, one of them brandishing a vicious looking little
knife. She took an involuntary step backward.

"Thought you could get away from old Mangus did
you now? I dinna take kindly to lassies who canna stay
where I put them."

The guards began to inch towards her, feral smiles
decorating their ugly faces. She stepped back again, this
time feeling the mortar of the retaining wall against her
knees.

"Come now, girl. Let old Bartus hold ye close, eh?"
They laughed and moved near enough that she could
smell their fetid breath. Beag Dougall had rounded the
corner now and was coming toward them. Three to
one—the odds were certainly not in her favor.

She shifted, trying to inch away from the advancing
men, and the wall behind her crumbled away. One minute it was there, supporting her weight and the next minute it was gone. There was a moment of weightlessness
when her heart beat out the message that she was going
to fall, then Beag Dougall's hand closed around her
wrist, yanking her back from the precipice. Her breath
coming in sobs, she looked up at her benefactor. "Ye be
safe now, mistress."

She wanted to laugh, to cry, to claw his eyes out.
Safe?

"Well now, did ye think ye'd be leaving us so soon?"
The guard she'd hit jerked her hands behind her, while
the other one tightly bound her wrists with a length of
rope. Katherine could feel the tender flesh on the underside of her wrists tearing, and she bit her lip to keep
from crying out.

The guard she'd attacked came around to face her,
putting a grimy hand under her chin. His grin was feral,
and she shuddered at his touch. His breath was rancid
as it passed across her face.

"If it werena for the promised reward, I'd forget all
about the orders to leave ye be. I'd like to feel myself
sinking into ye while I ring yer lovely neck. I'll no'
tolerate a wench like ye making a fool o' me. I will no'
forget it, either. I may be unable to touch ye now, but
ye mind me girl, he'll tire o'ye soon enough. And when
he's done, I'll still be here to finish with what's left o'
ye." He rubbed himself against her, leering into her face.
"And ye'll enjoy it, too. I'll be betting a high-and-
mighty *lady* such as yerself hasna ever had the likes of
me afore." He licked his lips and ran a hand over her
hair. She jerked her head away, but he turned it back,
holding it firmly in his grimy hand.

"I believe I need to teach you a lesson or two, girlie."
His mouth came closer, and she almost retched at the
smell of him.

"Come on, that's enough. Leave her be for now." The
other guard pulled his friend away. "Time enough for
lessons later. For now, 'tis best we get her back into her
room, afore anyone finds us here."

The first guard nodded and stepped back, allowing the
second to escort Katherine, at knifepoint, off of the battlements.

As soon as she heard the bar slide into place, Katherine collapsed on the floor of her prison, listening to
the two men laughing as they descended the stairs.

The full horror of her predicament finally hit her. She
was all alone in a ruined tower, in the middle of medi-

eval Scotland, surrounded by men with nothing but rape and murder on their minds, with no sign of help on the way. She tried to think of Iain, to believe he would find her in time. But despair was crowding out whatever hope she might still harbor. Hot tears ran down her face, dripping onto the cold stone floor.

Chapter 20

"WILLIAM, LAD, WHAT are you doing up at this hour?" Iain hurried to help the boy to the chair.

William sat carefully, stretching his leg out in front of him. "I dinna sleep so well these days," he said, eyeing Iain nervously. "My leg hurts most all the time."

"Just how much have you overheard?" Iain stood again by the fire, warming his backside, trying to hold onto his patience. After all, William was only a lad.

"Most of it. The room you've given me is only just there." William jerked his head toward the door behind him. " 'Twould be hard *no'* to hear." William shot a quick glance at Jeff. "Is he really—"

Iain cut him off impatiently. "Aye, that he is. Now what was it you said about Sorcha *no'* telling the truth?"

William stared wide-eyed at Jeff. "You're truly her brother?"

Jeff nodded absently. Iain began to pace.

"Your sister is a truly wondrous woman. She saved my leg most certainly and, most likely, my life as well." William's eyes gleamed with youthful adoration. "I'd do anything for her. And I'd *no'* purposely allow anyone to hurt her."

"I'm sure you wouldn't." Jeff smiled reassuringly at the young man. "William, you said something about Sorcha and the possibility that she was less than truthful with her version of the kidnapping. It would help if you could tell us more than just that."

"Right." William's look turned serious. "Katherine came to visit me the day she disappeared. She came to see me every morning, to make sure I was healing properly." The lovesick grin was back.

"William, what has this to do with Katherine's disappearance?" Iain stopped pacing, barely containing his frustration.

"I'm getting there, I'm getting there," murmured William, shooting a dour glance at Iain before he continued. "You see, my mother was there. She works in the kitchen. Anyway, she and Katherine talked a bit, about Katherine's marriage. Then my mother left, and I asked Katherine to stay with me until I fell asleep. She agreed. And as it happened, we both fell asleep." He shot a look at Iain, hot color washing across his face. "No' together, o' course."

"Of course," Jeff inserted, before Iain had a chance to explode.

Iain clenched his fists in an effort to contain his impatience with the boy's ramblings.

"Anyway, I suppose we would have slept the day away if it hadn't been for Sorcha's bellowing."

"Bellowing?"

"Aye, I'll wager you could hear her all o'er Duncreag. She was yelling for Katherine like there was something on fire."

Iain stepped closer and Jeff sat forward, both of them interested in the turn of the conversation. "What happened next?" they said almost simultaneously.

"Katherine sat up. She'd had her head on the side of the bed. She checked to see if I was still sleeping, and I didn't want her to worry, so I pretended I was. She hurried out of the chamber then, I guess so that Sorcha

wouldn't wake me. The next thing I know they're standing in here right outside the door to my chamber." He
ducked his head. "I couldna help but hear, I swear it."

Iain crossed his arms over his chest. " 'Tis all right,
boy, just tell us what you heard."

"Sorcha sounded odd, like she'd been running. She
told Katherine she'd been looking everywhere for her
and that Katherine had to come quickly."

"Come where?" Iain asked, impatiently wanting to get
to the crux of the story.

"I'm trying to tell you. Katherine asked the same
question. Sorcha told her that you had been hurt and that
you were asking for her."

Iain frowned. "Did she say where this was supposed
to have occurred?"

"Aye, in the glen at the bottom of the rise. I remember
that Katherine asked if Ranald was with you. Sorcha said
she didna know for sure, then something about only
speaking with the wee lad who brought the message. By
the time I managed to hobble to the door they were
gone."

"Why didna you say something about this earlier?"

William grimaced. "I had no reason to believe it was
important. I assumed no one mentioned your injury
again because whate'er it was, it was nothing compared
to Katherine's disappearance. Since I'm confined to my
chamber, I get my news secondhand. When I heard that
Sorcha had witnessed the abduction, I figured it must
have been while on their way to you. It was only tonight,
when I heard the two of you talking, that I realized Sorcha had been omitting some of the truth, if no' outright
lying."

Jeff's lips tightened into a thin angry line. "My God.
Iain, if this is true then your aunt is as good as responsible for my sister's kidnapping."

Iain felt the color drain from his face, and the little
muscle in his cheek working overtime. "Aye. But I
canna believe she would betray me so." He held up a

hand, effectively cutting off William's effort to retort. "Nay, lad, 'tis no' that I dinna believe you. 'Tis only that it pains me to have to face the truth about my aunt."

"Do you think she's allied herself with the Macphersons then?" William interjected.

" 'Twould certainly seem so. But for the life of me, I canna fathom why she would do such a thing."

Jeff sprang from his chair. "I don't give a rat's ass why she did it, I just want to know where Katherine is. Bring Sorcha to me. I'll wring the truth out of her."

"I'll go get her for you." William tried to jump to his feet, and failed miserably.

"Nay." The single word silenced them both. A black hush filled the chamber. Iain moved to stand behind William's chair, his thoughts bordering on murderous. "Believe me, my aunt,"—he spit the title out as though it were poison—"will tell us the truth. And then, she'll pay for what she's done. But I want to be prepared when we face her. And I want witnesses. Come"—Iain motioned for Jeff to follow as he started to walk from the chamber—"we'll go down to the hall. I'll have someone rouse Ranald and Fergus. Whatever we find out, I'd like them to hear it as well."

"Wait."

Iain turned at the sound of William's voice, concern for the boy replacing some of his anger.

William struggled to rise, intent on following them.

"Go back to bed, William. You need your rest. You've done well this night. There's nothing more that you can do now."

William frowned, his expression turning stubborn. "I love her too, you know."

Iain stood in silence, his hardened gaze locked on the boy not yet a man. His heart softened and he smiled. "So you do, lad. Jeff, wait. If you'll get his right arm, I'll take the left. Come then, William, we'll help you down the stairs."

William tilted his head in acceptance, a look of grim satisfaction on his face.

• • •

"I canna believe what you say is true. Sorcha has given
the whole of her marriageable years in service to this
family. I find it nigh on impossible to believe that she
would so casually betray it." Fergus drew up his shoulders in anger, suddenly resembling a fearsome warrior
far more than a wizened old man. "There must be some
mistake. Surely you misunderstood, boy."

William swallowed at the glare the old man turned on
him. "Nay, I heard it exactly as I told you."

Jeff sat in the great hall a little apart from the rest of
the group, watching. Iain had introduced him to Ranald
and Fergus as Katherine's brother. Ranald knew the situation and so was not surprised by his outlandish clothing and strange speech. Fergus supposedly knew
nothing, but he, too, accepted Jeff for what Iain said he
was. Either these people were extremely jaded and nothing much surprised them, he mused, or they were extremely loyal to their Laird. Either way, Jeff's opinion
of the fifteenth-century mind rose another notch. He
watched as Fergus digested this last declaration. Iain
gave a shrug of resignation.

"Fergus, as much as I wish to believe in Sorcha's
innocence, I also believe that William is telling the
truth."

Ranald pushed up from the bench he was sitting on.
"Well, I canna honestly say that I'm surprised. I dinna
know Auntie Sorcha all that well. She's been gone from
Corybrough for many years now. But I can tell you that
my father has little love for his sister. I've no notion of
the reason, but my father is a fair man and I'd trust his
opinions with my life."

Fergus grumbled something about stubborn Macqueens and walked over to Jeff. "What do you think?"

Jeff looked up at the man, surprised that he'd be interested in an outsider's opinion. "I think any information that might help us find my sister is worth exploring.
I don't know William, but he seems honest enough, and

I'm certain he's devoted to my sister. So I guess I have to believe he's telling the truth."

"Humph." Fergus sighed and turned to Iain. "I'll go and get her then, shall I?"

"I think it would be best." Iain's face was etched with emotions Jeff couldn't identify, but he felt for the man nevertheless.

Fergus turned his back on the lot of them, and headed for the stairs, still mumbling under his breath.

Jeff watched him go. "I'd like to know I had that kind of loyalty from someone."

Iain sat down beside him. "Aye, but misplaced loyalty can break your heart."

Suddenly the grim silence of the room was broken as a small boy rushed into the hall yelling, "Riders approaching." The boy stopped, bending at the waist, hands braced on knees, breathing heavily.

Jeff and Iain rose in tandem.

"Whose riders, boy?" Iain barked.

"They said,"—he pushed the words out between hisses of breath—"to tell you the colors are ours."

Iain reached the boy and with a pat on the shoulder sent him on his way.

"Who's he talking about? What riders?" Jeff came to a halt beside Ranald.

"Iain sent two of his clansmen to the Macphersons' holding to see if they could discover anything about Katherine's disappearance."

Jeff frowned at Iain. "Why didn't you say something about this earlier?"

"There was no opportunity to do so, what with William's announcement. Besides, I feared the men had met with some trouble, as I had expected them back yesterday. When they didna show, I assumed the worst."

"Well, they're here now. Let's go and see what they found out." Jeff made a move toward the door. Ranald stopped him with a hand on his arm.

"They'll be here presently. Have you forgotten about Auntie Sorcha?"

Jeff grimaced. In his excitement over possible news of Katherine, he had indeed forgotten about the woman. "Okay. We wait here." He went back to the fireside and dropped down on a bench beside William.

Iain followed, sitting in the big chair, his face devoid of all expression. Ranald paced in front of the fire. Silence enveloped the room, broken only by an occasional rustle as the men shifted restlessly.

Tentatively, William broke the silence. "Do you think Katherine is still alive?"

Iain's angry response died on his lips when he saw the stark fear on the boy's face. Instead he spoke with a soft, comforting voice. "Nay, lad, I dinna think she's dead. If she were, I'd feel it." He tapped his chest. "Here."

William nodded, too choked up to respond with words. Jeff, too, was moved by Iain's gentle concern for the boy.

"She's gone." Fergus' cry rang through the hall. "I canna find her anywhere."

Iain rose, his face flushed with a mixture of fear and anger. "Did you speak with her maid?"

"Aye. She has no' seen her since yesterday morning."

Ranald stood too. "Did she say anything else?"

Fergus shot him an exasperated look. "Aye. If you'll just be giving me a chance to finish." Ranald bowed in silent apology. Fergus turned to Iain and, after drawing a deep breath, continued. "Jeanette says that when Sorcha didna come down for yesterday's morning meal, she brought a tray to her chamber. When she tried to enter, the door was barred. She says that Sorcha bade her leave it outside the door. When she returned last evening, the tray was still there untouched. She knocked but there was no answer."

"Great. We've no idea when she left. Now we're no

better off than when we started." Jeff threw his hands up in frustration.

"I say we ride on the Macphersons now. 'Tis close enough to first light." Ranald's hand tightened on his sword. "We'll find Katherine, if we have to kill every Macpherson to do so."

Jeff and William chorused their agreement. Iain sat silently, lost in his own thoughts.

"I'd say that would be a great waste of time, lads." Roger Macbean strode into the hall. " 'Tis no' the Macphersons who hold your Katherine, Iain."

Iain fixed his cold green stare on the warrior. "What are you telling me?"

"She's no' there, mon. We scouted around for half a day or so and found nothing. So, on a hunch, I left Arthur to watch and paid a visit on the Macpherson myself. You'll remember my wife has kin there?"

" 'Twas quite a risk you took, Roger. But as you seem to have survived in one piece, I'll no' waste my breath telling you. What did the Macpherson have to say?"

"He denied all of it. According to him, there have been no raids on our cattle and he swears no attack on your father. In fact, he says he heard from Angus no' long before he died. Seems your father was trying to work out a possible marriage between you and a Macpherson lass. The Macpherson was considering the idea when he got the news of your father's death. Iain, he says he has no grievance with you. He hadn't even heard you'd wed Katherine. And he swore, in front of witnesses, he hadn't abducted her."

Iain studied Roger with narrowed eyes. "And you believe him?"

"Aye, I do. You should have heard him, Iain. The mon was honestly surprised at my accusations. I'd swear he knew nothing about any of it, most of all your wife's disappearance."

"Go and get some refreshment, Roger. There's food

in the kitchen, and I know you're anxious to get home to your wife."

"Aye, that I am. I'll be off then." He paused for a moment. "Iain, when you decide what to do next, I'll be ready to go with you." He headed off toward the kitchen.

"Where the hell does this leave us?" Jeff ranted angrily, feeling his blood pressure rise. "First the aunt, our key witness, turns out to be a disappearing liar, and then the chief suspect is found innocent. Where is Matlock when you need him?"

"I've no idea who this Matlock fellow is, but I've an idea who might be behind all of this," Ranald broke in.

A hush fell over the assembled group, attention shifting from Jeff to Ranald.

"I feel the fool really. I should've put it together sooner. But we were so sure it was the Macphersons."

Iain grabbed Ranald by the shoulders. "Put what together? Tell me what you think you know."

"All right. Remember when you found your father's dirk?"

"Aye."

"Do you remember me saying that I thought I recognized the wee thing?"

"I do. But I'm no' sure where you're going with this."

"You'll see. Do you also remember when Ailis saw the dirk?"

Iain's expression grew thoughtful. He released Ranald. "Aye. She thought the knife was Alasdair's."

"But then she thought she'd made a mistake. Well, she didna."

The room was totally silent, everyone hanging on Ranald's every word.

He smiled triumphantly. "I *had* seen that dirk before, but no' with Uncle Angus. And no' because of the stories you and Fergus were spinning. I saw it in Alasdair's chamber. It was the night we first arrived. Auntie Sorcha showed me to my chamber for a wash. I slipped out first to use the garderobe. And on my way back, I got a wee bit confused and ended up in the wrong chamber."

Iain smiled grimly. "Alasdair's chamber."

"Aye. And what do you suppose was lying on the bed?"

Jeff jumped in. "The dirk?"

"The dirk. I noticed it because of the stone in the hilt."

"The cairngorm." Jeff mumbled the comment to himself, but Ranald heard him.

"Is that what it is? Well, whatever, you have to admit 'tis a memorable stone. And I'll wager that Ailis saw it, too."

Iain's expression was darkening, comprehension dawning. "So when she saw the dirk that day on the window seat, she had indeed seen it with Alasdair. He'd simply misled her into believing it was his."

"Right. It never occurred to her, or to me for that matter, that Alasdair would lie about the knife being his. So she assumed she was merely mistaken."

Fergus frowned. "If Alasdair did have the knife that first night, that would mean he had it before ye found it on the dead mon by the barn."

"Aye." Iain's eyes narrowed in speculation. "I've no notion o' how Alasdair came to have that knife, but I'll wager it wasna an innocent coincidence."

"Well, he certainly seemed to have some sort of hold o'er Sorcha. I noticed it first just after Angus died. I told you I thought as much the night you arrived." Fergus said.

Iain groaned and sat down, head in hands.

Jeff crossed over to him. "What? What is it?"

Iain spoke into his hands. "Alasdair attacked Katherine."

"Attacked her? Why didn't you tell me?"

"I dinna think it was relevant. Katherine was no' hurt, just frightened a little. I got there in time. I thought 'twas only an isolated incident. One that was no' likely to let be repeated."

Jeff glared at Iain, barely containing his fury.

William spoke up softly. "I'm confused. What exactly are you saying?"

Iain sat back. "Let me see if I can explain. Someone correct me if I miss something. For whatever reason, Alasdair had my father's dirk. Both Ailis and Ranald saw it. Alasdair and Sorcha were seen together repeatedly after my father's death, and according to Fergus he appeared to have some sort of hold o'er her. Sometime after I arrived, Alasdair lost or gave up the dirk and I wound up with it, after killing what I thought was a Macpherson. Alasdair approached me about marrying his sister and I more or less turned him down. Shortly after that Katherine arrived and I married her. Alasdair tried, somewhat forcefully, to seduce her, but I stopped him. Just after that Sorcha, it appears, lured Katherine into a trap. Alasdair listened while we blamed the Macphersons and then rode for Tùr nan Clach, taking Ailis with him. Jeff arrived and we soon found out that Sorcha had vanished and that the Macphersons didna kidnap Katherine." He looked around at everyone. "Does that about cover it?"

"Yeah." Jeff gritted his teeth, trying not to yell in frustration. "So you're saying Davidson is most likely the kidnapper?"

" 'Twould seem so. Ranald?" Iain looked at his cousin.

"Aye. It seems likely. But we still dinna know why."

"I believe my wife's brother put it best." Iain looked at Jeff. "What was it you said? Something about a rodent's behind?"

"I said, I don't give a rat's ass why she did it. I was speaking of Sorcha, but I think it would apply to Alasdair as well."

Ranald eyed Jeff with something close to a grin. "You certainly have an interesting way with words. I agree with your sentiment, though. The most important thing is that we find Katherine."

Iain stood up, his action effectively ending the conversation. "We ride for Tùr nan Clach in an hour."

"Thank God." Jeff spoke more to himself than to any-one else, but Iain heard him and clasped his arm tightly.

"Together, we'll find her."

"Yeah, and then we'll make that son of a bitch pay."

Iain squeezed Jeff's arm and released it. "My senti-ments exactly."

Chapter 21

"I DON'T SEE why we have to wait. Can't we just storm the walls or something?" Jeff stood at the edge of the ridge where they had made camp, staring down at Alasdair's tower.

" 'Tis no' as easy as that, Jeff. We have to be sure Katherine is truly there, and then we must find a way to attack that will no' put her in further jeopardy. I'm learning that Alasdair is no' a man to be trifled with. If he does have Katherine, I've no doubt that he'll kill her if properly provoked," Iain stood beside him watching the dark shape of Tùr nan Clach rising out of the mist.

"Great, so we sit here and wait."

"No' necessarily—" Before he could finish the thought. Ranald and Roger appeared from behind a tumble of rock, dragging a struggling woman. Roger shoved her forward. She landed on her knees and stayed there, her head bent as if in supplication. Iain shot a questioning look over her head at Ranald.

Ranald gave the woman a gentle push. "Come now, lass, tell him what you told me."

The woman looked up, tears making white tracks

down her dirty cheeks. Iain realized she was little more than a girl, and a very frightened one at that. He squatted down, his face level with hers.

"Have you something to tell me then?"

The girl wiped a grimy hand across her face. " 'Tis no' much. Only that yer lady might be in there." She tipped her head toward the tower in the distance.

"At Tùr nan Clach?"

She nodded, her lip trembling. "I saw her meself." The girl bit her lip in earnest.

Iain placed a hand on her chin, lifting it until her eyes were level with his. "There now. I'll no' hurt you. I promise."

Her eyes widened. "But yer the Mackintosh of Duncreag. And I've heard yer an ogre of a man."

"Do I look like an ogre to you?"

She studied his face for a minute, then shook her head.

"Tell me your name."

"Anna."

Iain winced, his eyes locking with Jeff's, pain swelling inside him as he thought of his own child . . . the child that Katherine carried. He blinked slowly and turned back to the girl, his emotions once more under tight control. "So tell me, Anna, when did you last see my wife?"

She swallowed nervously, but looked him in the eyes. "I work in the kitchen. This morning I was scrubbing the floor in the hall when I saw a woman struggling with the Laird. He had her by the hair, he did. I think she was trying to scream. But he was having none of it and yanked her head back, jamming something in her mouth."

"Did you recognize the woman?"

"I canna say fer sure. He had her wrapped in something so that ye couldna see her face at all. But her hair was long and verra light."

"Do you have any idea where he was taking her?"

"Nay, but I'd say 'twas to the cellars. I saw them go down the stairs."

"What happened next?"

Anna lowered her head as if shamed. "I ran away. I was afraid. 'Tis well known that the Laird is no' a patient mon, if ye take my meaning."

"You were afraid he'd hurt you?"

The small head nodded. "If he thought I wasna minding me own business."

Iain tipped the small chin upward again. "Anna, can you tell me how many men there are at Tùr nan Clach?"

"Only a handful. Most of them ran when they heard that the terrible Laird of Duncreag was coming."

The corner of his mouth twitched at the girl's solemn statement. "And just how is it they knew I was coming?"

"I dinna know fer certain, but I heard it said that some clansmen were sent to watch the border between Duncreag and Tùr nan Clach. The word must o' come from them."

"And Alasdair? Did he go with the others?"

"Aye, as far as I know. Word was ye were coming fer vengeance. I guess he had no taste fer it."

Iain looked toward the dark tower, contemplating Anna's tale. "Roger, see that the girl is fed."

Roger placed a hand around her slender arm and carefully pulled the girl to her feet.

She turned to look at Iain shyly over her shoulder. "Yer no' a monster at all, are ye?"

" 'Tis no' that I doubt the girl, Ranald. I think *she* believes she's telling the truth. 'Tis Alasdair I dinna trust. There's naught to say this isn't a trap." Iain looked across the campfire at his cousin. The fire crackled, flames dancing, casting flickering light on the faces of the weary warriors.

"Aye, I'd sooner trust a Cameron." Fergus threw a twig into the fire, causing a spray of sparks. "What do ye intend to do then?"

Iain leaned back, stretching his booted feet toward the fire, crossing them at the ankles. "I think we'll have to try and take Tùr nan Clach. If there is even the slightest chance that Katherine is in there, I've no choice but to make an attempt to get her out."

Ranald sat forward, bracing his big hands on his knees. "And if it is a trap?"

Iain shrugged. "Can you see another way?"

Ranald shook his head.

"Wait." Jeff ran a hand through his hair absently. "Didn't the girl say that she thought Katherine was in the cellar?"

"Aye." Iain sat up. "Why do you ask?"

"Well, it seems to me that if there *is* a trap, it's been planned around our believing we can just walk into Tùr nan Clach and take what we want. The idea being that when we do that, they surprise us with the big guns." Jeff looked to Iain for confirmation.

Iain frowned in confusion. "Big guns?"

"It's just a saying. What I mean is they attack with all they've got. You with me so far?"

Iain tipped his head in affirmation. "Go on."

"Okay, so what if we use the back door and sneak in behind them. We'd be able to grab Katherine and be out of there before they knew what hit them."

Ranald rubbed his jaw thoughtfully. "It might work."

"Aye, 'tis a good plan, but there remains a problem," Iain said.

"And what might that be?" Jeff asked impatiently.

"There is no 'back door,' as you call it. As far as I know there is only one way into Tùr nan Clach, and that's right through the tower gate, where they'll no doubt be waiting for us."

Jeff looked crestfallen. "Then what are we going to do? We can't leave Katherine in there."

Iain stiffened. "I'm no' going to leave her."

Fergus cleared his throat, a faint smile breaking across

his wizened features. "It seems that there is in fact another door into Tùr nan Clach."

Iain studied his father's friend. He looked almost ghostly in the firelight, one half of his face in shadow, the other dappled with light. "What are you speaking of, old man?"

"Well, it seems that Alasdair's father had a weakness for ale. And in an attempt to keep himself supplied, he liked to have the ale as close as possible. The brew house was no' good enough for him—he wanted it right in his own cellar. The problem was the casks wouldna fit through the wee door that leads into Tùr nan Clach." He paused, eyeing his audience, then continued when he was satisfied that he had their full attention. "So he decided to have a door built right into the cellar wall. He hid it well, of course, and no one was supposed to know about it." Fergus' slight smile cracked into a full-fledged grin. "No one except me, that is."

Ranald raised a skeptical brow. "And how exactly is it that he told *you*?"

"Well now, there's the beauty of it. *He* dinna tell me. His steward did. Ambrose Mackay was friend o' mine. And this night, he was deep in his cups and started bragging about how Col had his ale rolled right into his storage chamber. Couldna wait to show it to me." Fergus laughed at the memory.

"I often came to Tùr nan Clach to visit Ambrose. Ye will no doubt remember him, Iain. He was a great bear o' a man. A good one, too. I never understood how he could stomach throwing his lot in with a man like Col Davidson." He stroked his beard thoughtfully.

"Anyway, this particular evening, Col was no' in residence. 'Twas always best to visit when he was away. So we were on our own when Ambrose offered to show me the secret door and I was more than pleased to oblige him. 'Twas years ago, now, and Ambrose is gone, God rest his soul. I'd forgotten all about it until Jeff here started talking about back doors and such."

Jeff leaned eagerly toward the old man. "Can you tell us where it is?"

"I'll do better than that, lad—I'll take you there."

"Hold on." Iain frowned. "We need to decide who will go. Fergus, you'll come, of course. And Ranald, I'll need you—"

"Wait a minute," Jeff interrupted. "If you think I'm staying here, you've got another thing coming. That's my sister in there." He stood up and crossed his arms over his chest. The dark cloaked him and he seemed less the twentieth century architect, more the medieval warrior. Iain wondered if it was just a trick of the shadows or something more.

"All right, you can come, but you'll do as I tell you."

"Fine." Jeff jerked his chin up as if to underline his agreement.

Iain smiled in grim satisfaction. It seemed he had a new warrior. Now if only they could rescue Katherine.

The ground around Tùr nan Clach was cloaked in black shadow. Iain was grateful there was no moon. Only a few stars had managed to best the misty clouds. He signalled the others, and merging into the dark, they edged closer and closer to the tower. No light shone from its windows. It stood black on black against the sky, its shape rising up out of the gloom, an evil menacing shadow.

Fergus motioned with a hand, and they followed him as he crept along the base stones. The tower sat at the top of a small rise, its back built into the heavy rocks of a cliff. Fergus paused at a corner where the building seemingly disappeared into the slope of the hill. Two trees tangled together, seeming to spring from bare rock. Their roots, too, seemed to blend together, and between their subterranean arms was a dark hollow. The indentation was slight. From where Iain stood, it looked like no more than a small dip.

Fergus approached the edge of the hollow closest to the base of Tùr nan Clach. He lifted some of the heavy tree limbs out of his way and with a wry grin stepped into the shadow and disappeared.

Iain followed behind him, ducking his head to avoid the low hanging branches, before stepping into the little hollow. He waited for his eyes to adjust to the new darkness. A whisper of movement alerted his senses and he turned toward it, his hand automatically closing around the hilt of his claymore.

"Here, 'tis just where I left it."

Iain relaxed at the sound of Fergus' voice. The old man stood right below him, his shoulders even with Iain's knees. There was a short sloping path leading down into a gaping hole in the side of the tower wall. Because of the angle, the path and entrance were not visible unless a man was standing directly under the canopy of the two trees.

Iain grinned at Fergus and stepped out of the shelter to motion Jeff and Ranald forward. When all four of them were safely under the overhanging branches, Fergus swung his arm toward the dark outline of the hole.

" 'Tis no' exactly an entrance for a king, but it'll serve well for our purposes. There is a short tunnel through the walls and then a passageway leading up a wee bit. Ye should come out into a storage chamber. 'Tis where Col kept his ale. From there you'll be on your own, as I've never been any farther. But I've no doubt ye can find your Katherine easily enough once you're inside."

Iain spoke in a voice barely above a whisper. "You'll no' be coming then?"

"Nay, lad, I'd only slow ye down. I'll stay here and keep watch."

Iain gave a terse nod and motioned for Ranald and Jeff to follow him into the pitch-black darkness of the tunnel. He moved forward cautiously, his hands skimming the walls to guide himself through the tunnel. He stopped suddenly as the sound of falling rocks echoed throughout the tunnel, the acoustics making it impossible for Iain to judge which direction it came from.

A hand on his shoulder made him jump. " 'Twas only Jeff. All's well." Ranald's voice was pitched low and soft.

Slowly, Iain began to edge forward again. The floor began to slope upward slightly and he had to duck to keep from scraping his head on the rock-hewn ceiling. They rounded a corner and Iain stopped. A few feet ahead a faint line of light cut through the darkness. The storage chamber door.

Moving quickly, he approached it, his hands searching the rough surface of the timber for a handle, his fingers finally closing on a rusty ring. Holding his breath, he pulled slowly, not knowing what would be waiting for them on the other side.

He squinted as the flicker of torchlight momentarily blinded him. He took a careful step backward into the shadow of the passageway and whispered quietly into the dark behind him.

"There's torchlight ahead. It seems we were right to assume that the tower was no' as empty as it seemed. We must go carefully now."

Stepping through the opening, his dirk drawn, he flattened himself against the wall of what did indeed appear to be a storage chamber. He quickly inspected the room for signs of life, and once he was satisfied that there was no one in the chamber, he motioned to the others, sheathing the blade.

"What next?" Jeff's voice was pitched low, but even so, Iain was afraid they would be overheard. Putting a finger to his lips, he shook his head and gestured to a small door set in the opposite wall. Jeff moved noiselessly across the chamber and slowly pulled the door open. Poking his head out, he lifted an arm in signal and slipped into the passageway.

Iain followed Ranald into the dank passageway, pulling the storage room door shut behind him. The passage

was narrow and darker than the storage chamber had
been, stretching off to Iain's left. At the far end, he could
see the spill of light from a doorway. Closer to them,
on the opposite side, he could just make out the archway
of a second door.

He signaled Ranald and Jeff to wait, then pressing
himself against the wall, crept down the passageway,
stopping just short of the door. The light streamed
through a small round window in the door, casting a
beam of color across the passageway. Dropping to his
knees, Iain crawled along the floor until he was under
the window. Easing himself upward, he peeked through
it into the chamber.

It was larger than the one they had just left, a spiral
stairway in the corner curling upward. Along one wall,
a shallow fireplace held the source of the chamber's
light. Three men sat in front of the fire around a crude
table. They were deeply occupied with a game of dice,
pausing every now and then to drink deeply from
wooden cups. A fourth man stood off to the side, sipping
from his cup, watching the antics of the others.

Keeping down, Iain retraced his steps back down the
passageway. "There're four of them, deep in their in
cups, I think." He pitched his voice as low as he could.

"What about the second door?" Even as a whisper,
Iain could hear the anxiety in Jeff's voice.

"We'll check it now."

"I'll guard your backs." Ranald growled, already
moving low and fast up the corridor, stopping just beyond the entrance to the guard's chamber.

Jeff went next, pausing outside the other door. Iain
met his gaze, nodding once, and Jeff carefully pushed
the door open. Iain crossed the passageway to join him.

They stepped cautiously into the chamber. It was
dimly lit by two sconces set into the opposite wall. The
room was long and narrow, with each end shrouded in
shadow. At first glance, the chamber appeared empty.
Iain released the breath he'd been holding, hope fading,

but Jeff shook his head, then pointed to the far end of the chamber. Iain squinted, staring into the shadows where Jeff pointed, and was rewarded with a glimpse of a small wooden door.

The top of the door was only slightly higher than his belt. Heart racing, he reached to help Jeff remove the heavy bar that held the door closed. Swinging it outward, he pushed past Jeff to duck through the low, narrow opening. A single candle burned brightly in the center of the small chamber, effectively casting the rest of the room in shadow.

"Katherine?" Iain's voice was hoarse with emotion. A small sound came from a corner of the room. He grabbed the candle, holding it high.

"Not Katherine." The voice was strained and cracked, but the words were clear. Iain felt his heart plummet into his belly, the ache that had been with him since hearing of Katherine's kidnapping reasserting itself in full.

Jeff came to stand beside him, disappointment evident on his face. The mound in the corner shifted, trying to rise. A flash of pale gold caught Iain's eye.

"Ailis?" Passing the candle to Jeff, he rushed to her side. He heard Jeff's intake of breath as the candlelight hit upon her ravished face and she shrank away as if the light hurt her eyes. A dark purple bruise spread along one delicate cheekbone and an angry red gash marred the smoothness of her forehead. Her lower lip was swollen and crusted with dried blood.

Holding her gently by the shoulders, Iain spoke slowly and soothingly. "Ailis, 'tis Iain Mackintosh." She looked at him blankly. "Listen to me: Ranald's just outside and we're going to get you away from this place." At the sound of Ranald's name, her eyes focused and recognition dawned.

"Ranald . . . is . . . here?"

"Aye, I'll take you to him. But first you must tell me where Katherine is."

She stood absolutely still, as if looking deep within herself, then with obvious effort tried to speak. "Not . . . here . . . Alasdair . . . has her." She shook her head emphatically, her voice growing stronger. "Not . . . here . . . so sorry."

" 'Tis all right, lass. This is no' your doing. Come, let me get you out of here." He started to pick her up, but Jeff intercepted him, handing over the candle before gathering Ailis into his arms.

"Better you have your arms free. Your sword hand is a hell of a lot more useful than mine."

"Be careful then, 'tis precious cargo you carry." He ducked and stepped out of the tiny cell. Crossing the room, he cautiously poked his head around the doorframe, peering into the corridor. Ranald was holding someone by the throat, his dirk pressed into the fat folds of the man's skin. With an apologetic shrug in Iain's direction, he twisted his knife and let the man slide silently to the floor.

Iain motioned for Jeff to hurry, knowing that it wouldn't be long before the dead man's companions decided to check on him. Jeff swung into the passageway, carrying his burden. Ranald paused by Iain's ear to whisper, "Katherine?"

Iain shook his head. "Ailis."

Ranald's eyes darkened with emotion. "Is she alive?"

"Aye. Come, man, we've no time now for talk."

The two of them hurried after Jeff, Iain still holding the candle using it to lead them through the tunnel. They emerged under the branches of the trees just in time to hear the echo of a shout from within the tower. It seemed the the dead man had already been discovered. With a quick word to Fergus, they ran quickly for cover, melting into the rocks and trees, becoming indistinguishable from the shadows of the night.

• • •

"How is she?" Iain looked up as his cousin moved to find a seat by the fire.

"She'll recover. What will happen to her now?"

"I've talked with Fergus and he's going to send her back to Duncreag at first light. Ewan will escort her."

"At least she'll be safe there." Ranald stared moodily into the fire. "How can a man do something like that to his own sister?"

Jeff spread some cheese on an oatcake. "I don't know, Ranald, but if he could do that to Ailis, I shudder to think about what might be happening to Kitty."

Iain growled, tossing his half-eaten oatcake into the fire.

"We'll find her," Ranald assured him.

Iain frowned at his cousin. "And just how do you propose we go about doing that?"

"Did Ailis have any information at all?" Jeff's expression held cautious hope.

"Nay, no' much," Ranald admitted. "She's still no' thinking verra clearly. She knows that Alasdair has Katherine, but doesna know where he's keeping her. Only that he laughed and said it was right under Iain's nose. Then she babbled something about mists. 'Coire a' Cheathaich,' I think she said. What about Katherine's letter? Is there something else there perhaps?"

Jeff screwed up his face in concentration. "I've told you most of it. She didn't know much of anything about her captivity. Hell, she thought she was being held by the Macphersons and that Alasdair *rescued* her from the ruin where they had her imprisoned."

Iain's head snapped up. "What did you say?"

"I said that Davidson lied about rescuing Katherine."

"Nay, I mean about the place she was held."

Jeff raised his eyebrows, his face communicating his confusion. "I said that he rescued her from a ruin. Katherine said the only thing she knew for sure about her prison was that it was a ruin of some kind. My guess is an old castle or tower or something. Why are you asking?"

Iain felt excitement surge within him. "Because there is an old ruin no' far from here, just on the border between Tùr nan Clach and Duncreag. 'Tis said to be haunted so most people avoid it. I'd forgotten all about it." Iain looked up at the two men, hope burgeoning. " 'Tis located in the misty hollow. Coire a' Cheathaich."

Chapter 22

THE COLD WENT bone-deep. It seeped into her skin and radiated inward to her very soul. She shifted, trying to find a comfortable position. With her hands tied behind her back and little to protect her from the stones that littered the floor, there was probably no such thing, but still Katherine tried. She had no idea how much time had passed. Hours? Days? There was a numbing sameness to it all. Now and then one of the guards came to loosen her bonds and let her eat and use the chamber pot.

She was amazed at how adept she was becoming at using the chamber pot while retaining some decorum. She was never allowed movement without an armed, leering audience. She wondered a bit hysterically if she could add this new expertise to her resume, picturing in her mind how it would read: spring 1467—imprisoned in medieval Scotland; mastered the art of using a chamber pot.

She felt tears threatening again, and marveled that she had any left to shed. She rolled to a sitting position and tried to tell from the small patch of sky visible through

the hole what time it was. It was gray with rain and not
forthcoming with a clue. She sighed. What she wouldn't
give for a clock. Even better, a clock radio. Anything to
help pass the time.

She tried to stretch her legs, pointing her toes, then
bending her knees. Her wrists were numb, but her ankles
stung where the ropes cut into her flesh. She winced,
almost regretting the kick that had been the reason for
the new bonds. Despite her discomfort, she smiled a little with the memory. She had caught the son of a bitch
right in the groin. Of course, it had accomplished nothing, but there was still a certain satisfaction in knowing
he would be speaking with a higher voice for the next
few days.

She scootched her way over to the wall and leaned
wearily against it. There had been no other visitors. Her
captors referred often to a "him," but never mentioned
a name. Katherine couldn't decide if she wanted to see
him or not, whoever he was. She sometimes thought it
couldn't get much worse than it already was, but then
she'd think of her lecherous rape-happy guards and
feel lucky for a reprieve, however uncomfortable it
might be.

She closed her eyes, tired just from sitting. She tried
to think of a song to sing. She'd read somewhere that
people in captivity often sang to keep from going crazy.
With her voice, Katherine figured she'd drive her captors
insane instead. It was worth a try. Taking a deep breath,
she launched into a rousingly bad rendition of Elton
John's *Benny and the Jets,* only to stop suddenly at the
sound of the bar rattling on the door.

The guard's voice filtered in from the corridor. "I
dinna know how I wound up watching o'er the likes of
her. And now I've got another one to see to. All I can
say is he'd better make it well worth all the effort."

There was a low grunt, as if someone was in pain and
then the scrape of the door as it began to open. From
Katherine's position against the wall, she could see the

edge of what looked like a skirt. She released the breath she hadn't realized she was holding. Not *him*—a woman.

The door swung all the way open and the guard stuck his head around the edge. "It seems the Laird has sent someone to keep ye company. Perhaps"—he grimaced as he spoke—"that'll keep ye from yer singing." With that, he shoved the woman into the room and slammed the door.

Katherine opened her mouth to speak, but snapped it shut with an audible click when she recognized the person standing in front of her.

She tried again, but only managed to squeak out a name. "Sorcha."

Sorcha looked uncomfortable, shifting her weight back and forth from foot to foot. "Aye, 'tis me. And well I know you're wishing I were someone else. But for now, child, it seems I'm all you've got."

"But how did you get here? Did they capture you too?"

Sorcha ducked her head, a bit of red staining her weathered cheeks. "Aye. I'm afraid I've made a real mess o'things."

"Mess of things? Sorcha, I don't understand. Where's Iain? Is he hurt?" Katherine looked at Sorcha, every ounce of her being pleading for good news.

"He's fine."

Katherine felt relief flood through her. "Is he coming?"

"Nay, lass, I dinna think so. He has no idea where you are, or even who is holding you."

Katherine swallowed back her panic. "And do you know who is responsible for this?"

"Aye."

"Tell me who."

"Alasdair."

Katherine sat in stiff silence, absorbing the new information. Alasdair. A shiver ran down her spine at the memory of his hands on her body. She shook herself, trying to concentrate on the present, and to hold her vivid imagination at bay.

"I see." She paused, studying Sorcha. The older woman's hands were bound, but unlike Katherine's they were tied in front of her, allowing more freedom of movement. Her feet were free, and she had a small bruise on her left cheek. It was just beginning to show color. Her hair was loose and tangled about her shoulders and there were bits of mud clinging to the hem of her gown.

"Sorcha, I don't understand any of this. If you were captured in the clearing with me, then where have you been all this time?"

Again, color swept across Sorcha's face. "I wasna captured in the clearing. The mad dash to find Iain was a trap."

"A trap?"

"Aye. Alasdair planned it." Sorcha looked directly into Katherine's eyes, her own full of regret. "And I . . . I carried it out."

"You? You're working with Alasdair?" Katherine looked pointedly at Sorcha's bound hands. "He certainly seems to be showing his gratitude in a funny way."

Sorcha flushed an even deeper red. " 'Tis no' his gratitude that left this." She gestured awkwardly at the purpling bruise on her cheekbone. "But I canna deny I was helping him in the beginning. At the very least, I owe ye the truth of it."

Katherine struggled to force these new facts into her tired brain. "So you pretended Iain was hurt to lure me away from Duncreag?"

Sorcha's lips parted in what might have been taken for a smile, except that her eyes reflected only pain and guilt. " 'Twas only part o' the ruse. When I left Duncreag Iain was alive and well." The smile faded. "But I canna say how he fares now. Alasdair wants him dead."

"Dead?" Katherine couldn't seem to do much more than echo Sorcha's pronouncements. She tried unsuccessfully to blow a thick strand of hair out of her face.

Sorcha knelt beside her and using her bound hands, carefully moved the hair away from Katherine's face. "There now, that's better."

Katherine watched through narrowed eyes as Sorcha settled against the wall beside her. "How did you get here, Sorcha?"

She glanced over at Katherine, her look painfully apologetic. "I lied to Iain and said that I had followed you to the clearing. I told him you were out for a walk and I was worried you'd lose your way. Then I told him the mon who took you was a Macpherson.

"It was all part of Alasdair's plan. He told me he wanted to hold you for ransom, in payment for all that he lost when Iain married you and no' Ailis. He wanted Iain to think it was the Macphersons so that he could get the ransom without incurring Iain's wrath. I should have known there was more to it."

She paused, looking out of the window, and then with a sigh continued. "I couldna stand the sight of Iain's pain." She turned her tortured gaze back to Katherine. "He loves you verra much, you know. Anyway, I stayed in my chamber most of the day, avoiding him. I was afraid he'd see the truth in my eyes. I woke up sometime during the night and realized I'd had naught to eat. So I went to the kitchen to see what I could find. The fire was out in the hall, so I thought I'd sit in the solar. The fire there is always banked. But when I reached the top o' the stairs I realized there were already people there. I could hear young William telling Iain he had o'erheard me telling you about Iain being injured. I panicked. If Iain knew I lied, he'd soon enough figure out I was a part of your abduction. So I left for Tùr nan Clach, thinking that Alasdair would want to know that Iain had discovered my part in the deception. It wasna easy. It was dark and I was on foot. Alasdair has his men carefully guarding the border between the two holdings, but I convinced them I was an ally with important news and they let me through."

She drew a deep breath, as though mentally preparing herself for her next words. "I got to Tùr nan Clach about midday and was told that Ailis and Alasdair were taking their meal in their private hall. So I set out to find them. When I reached the solar, I started to knock on the door. I could hear Alasdair talking. I canna say why I stopped, but I did. He was chastising Ailis for failing to capture Iain's attention. I heard him hit her." She winced as though feeling the blow herself. "The puir wee girl barely cried out. I pressed myself against the door, uncertain what to do. Alasdair was raving about how all his careful plans had been thwarted, how part of it at least was Ailis' fault. He hit her again, and then it was quiet. I wanted to leave, but at his next words I froze.

"He said something about all no' being lost—he'd still get what belonged to him, and he'd see Iain dead and you in his bed before he was through. I ran after that. You have to believe I never meant any harm to come to Iain, or to you for that matter."

Katherine tried to pull together her riotous thoughts. "Why didn't you go to Iain with this?"

"I wanted to. But Alasdair must have heard me. Before I could even reach the gate leading out o' Tùr nan Clach, two o' his guard caught up with me and dragged me back to Alasdair. He accused me o' betraying him and said I'd ne'er see Duncreag again."

"Did he give you that bruise?"

"Aye. And afterward told his men to bring me here." Sorcha gave Katherine a weak smile. "I dinna think he meant for us to be here together. But I had a wee talk with the big mon guarding the door and convinced him that we'd be easier to take care of if we were in the same chamber."

"Beag Dougall?"

"Is that his name? Well, he's certainly no' a *small*

man, is he? More the type to put a scare in a body, I'd say, but he really wasna all that hard to convince. He may be a giant o' a mon, but I dinna believe he's given to deep thought."

Despite everything, Katherine felt a bubble of laughter rise from her throat. She sobered quickly. "Sorcha, why did you do this? I mean why were you involved at all with a man like Alasdair?"

Sorcha leaned her head back against the wall, closing her eyes. " 'Tis a long story."

"I've got plenty of time," Katherine answered dryly.

Sorcha shrugged. " 'Tis no' a pretty tale." She sighed. "But I suppose 'tis best to start at the beginning.

"I was a young girl when I first saw Angus Mackintosh, but even then I knew he was the mon for me. I think I fell in love with him almost at first sight. He was a year older than I was, but already with the look of a mon about him. Tall and straight he was, with clear green eyes and fine thick hair, I used to dream about what it would feel like to run my fingers through it. We were all friends, we were: Angus, myself, my brother Dougall, and my younger sister Moire. We played the silly games of youths that summer. And every day I loved Angus a little bit more.

"He came the next summer, too, and the one after that, his father sending him as is our custom, to foster with my father. And as we grew older, my girlish crush grew into something more. I thought I'd surely die if I couldna have him. But Angus had other plans. He had eyes for no one but my sister Moire.

"Moire was the beautiful one. She was tiny and graceful and as good and kind as a person could be. We all loved her fiercely, but no one more than Angus. That last summer when I was but nine and ten, he asked my father for her hand. I cried for days, my puir heart broken into little pieces. But no one could begrudge Moire happiness. She was such a wee fey thing. A good wind could have carried her away.

"She went with him, o' course, to live at Duncreag. Father tried to arrange for my own marriage, but I would have none o' it—if I couldna have Angus then I wanted no one at all. The years passed and Iain was born. He was the light of their lives. I visited them a time or two, but couldn't bear it often. They were so happy, the three of them. And all I could see was what I might have had.

"They wanted other children, but it seemed Moire was no' to be so blessed. Then one winter we got the news that Angus and Moire were expecting a second child. Iain was with us then, fostering with my father and Dougall. There was much rejoicing at Corybrough and we all eagerly awaited the birth. Then came devastating news. Moire was dead, and the wee bairn with her. 'Twas a girl. They named her Suisan after my mother. She lived only a few hours longer than Moire.

"I suppose what I did next might seem a wee bit forward, but these are harsh times and you have to take happiness where you find it. So even in my grief o'er my sister's death, I recognized the chance to realize my own dreams and grabbed it with both hands. I convinced my brother that someone had to see to Angus and his kin and that that someone should be me.

"I arrived at Duncreag in the early fall to find an Angus I hardly recognized. He was still devastatingly handsome, but the light had gone out of his eyes. It seems his heart had died with his wife. But I was still young enough to believe I could change that. So I set about making Duncreag a home again. No' that there was anyone to notice. Iain returned to Corybrough and Angus was always locked away in his sorrow. Alasdair came to foster, but he had no time for me. He was too busy playing up to the Laird, coveting what would never be his." Sorcha paused for a moment to catch her breath, then continued.

"And so the years passed. I learned to hold on to any wee bit of interest Angus showed in me and told myself he would come out of it all in time. 'Twas naught but a lie, I know. But I never stopped loving him, never stopped hoping someday he'd wake up and notice me.

"Then the time came for Iain to return home. He'd been away at Moy and Angus felt it was time for him to give up his wandering ways and settle down with a wife to produce heirs for Duncreag. One morning, soon after he had sent the missive for Iain to come home, Angus asked me to go for a ride. We rode across the holding to the bottom of a ridge Angus favored. We climbed to the top and stood looking out o'er the land, o'er Duncreag. I should have guessed that there was more to his invitation than the simple desire for my company, but I was ever hopeful of gaining his love.

" 'Twas a fine day. The sun was shining through the clouds and the land took on a golden glow. Angus told me of his plans for Iain and how, with a new mistress in the offing, my service to Duncreag was ended. He spoke to me like an old faithful servant, with no trace of affection at all. I remember standing there, staring at him. I'd lost my voice. 'Have you gone daft, woman?' he said. 'You can go home to Corybrough now.' *Home*. Home was Duncreag. I tried to tell him that, and it was as if a great dam inside me broke wide open. The words kept tumbling out. I told him how much I loved him. How I'd stayed with him all these years in the hope that he'd come to love me. I even begged him to marry me, to forget Moire. That was my mistake. He looked as if I'd struck him. He'd never forget Moire, he told me. She was everything to him. There would never be another. And even if there were, it wouldna be me.

"I went a little crazy then. I've a fierce temper, and I've never been good at keeping it to myself. I ran at him. I dinna know what I thought I was going to do— beat some sense into him, I suppose. But somehow we stumbled. We'd been standing by the edge of the cliff, to better see the view. And in one short moment, all that I held dear in the world was gone. The cliffside crumbled away, and Angus fell. I can still hear his cry. I stood there, unable to believe he was gone. That I . . . that I had killed him." She paused, tears streaming down her face, her mind far away on a cliffside.

Katherine sniffed as her own eyes filled with tears. "But Sorcha, it was an accident."

She continued staring into her grief-filled past. "Aye, an accident, but if no' for my temper, Angus would be alive. Accident or no', I'm responsible for the death of the only mon I'll ever love. I finally understand a wee bit about his grief for Moire."

Katherine waited while Sorcha pulled herself together, drying her tears awkwardly with her bound hands. "I still don't see what all this has to do with Alasdair."

"Ah, but you see, there's more to the tale." She looked out the window again. "Alasdair was there that day. I still dinna understand how he came to be in that exact spot, at that moment. God's wicked sense of humor, no doubt. I couldna see the body from the ledge, so I was trying to find a way down, to find Angus, when Alasdair appeared at my elbow. He has a sneaking way about him, and it was as if he had conjured himself from mid-air. He'd seen the whole thing, he told me. And had found the body. Angus was dead, by my hand. He shuddered to think what would come of me now. But, he said, maybe he could help me. How? I asked.

"He told me he'd make it look like an accident, that no one would even know I'd been there. All I had to do was help him get Iain to marry Ailis. I have no excuse for what I did. But I was afraid and so numb with grief. He made it sound so easy, and Ailis was a nice enough lass. Iain wouldna do so badly if he were to marry her. So I agreed. Alasdair arrived at Duncreag the next morning with a story about a summons from Angus. It was easy then to arrange to search for the 'missing' Laird. We 'found' the body, and the worst of it seemed to be o'er.

"All I was to do was throw Ailis at Iain at every opportunity. I invited Ailis for a visit under the guise that I needed comforting, which was no' untrue. She came, and Iain arrived shortly thereafter. Things seemed to be proceeding as Alasdair planned—until you arrived."

"And married Iain."

Sorcha drew up her knees, lifted her arms out of the way, and then dropped them, so that they circled her legs. "Aye. I knew Iain loved ye the moment I first saw you together. And I feared for you both. Alasdair is no' a mon to anger. He came to me after he realized ye were wed, threatening me with exposure if I didna help him kidnap you. I was afraid of him, and afraid of what Iain would do if he found out. I am no' a very noble or brave woman, Katherine. I was frightened, and so I agreed to help him. It was his idea to pretend that Iain was hurt."

Katherine shifted, trying to find a comfortable position. "You said you thought he was only going to hold me for ransom."

"Aye, but his plans were far more grievous than that. He has no love for Iain and, his time spent with Angus only served to make him greedy in his desire to possess all that is Duncreag. He wants Iain to die, and has arranged things so that his death will most likely be blamed on the Macphersons."

"And me?"

"I canna say whether he wants you because you belong to Iain or if 'tis your beauty that draws him. Most likely a bit of both, but either way he does want you. I heard him tell Ailis that his plan was to trick you into believing he'd ransomed you from the Macphersons, after he's killed Iain. But now you know the whole truth. 'Tis a poor penance, but 'tis the best I can offer. I'll no' ask ye to forgive me, but perhaps at least now ye can understand the why of it a bit better."

Katherine sat in silence, letting Sorcha's story fill her mind. How dreadful it would be to love a man who had no feelings at all for you. Katherine thought about Iain and the strength of their love. It was a gift—a rare thing,

and if given the opportunity, she'd make certain she
never took it for granted. The thought of being without
him pulled her back to reality with a snap.

"Sorcha, we have to figure out how to get out of here.
Do you think you can undo my hands?" Katherine sat
forward, turning so that her back was to the older
woman. She could feel Sorcha tugging at her bonds.

" 'Tis no use, Katherine. The rope is tied too tightly."

Katherine turned back to her. "Okay, wait. Let me try
yours; maybe they're looser. Then when your hands are
free, you'll probably be able to manage mine."

Sorcha shoved her hands at Katherine's back. Katherine forced every ounce of will into making her hands
feel the ropes at Sorcha's wrists. She struggled awkwardly with the knot and almost gave up twice, but then
she felt a little give and with a small cry of triumph
pulled the rope free.

Sorcha rubbed her wrists, trying to restore circulation.
"All right, lass, let me try yours again." They maneuvered into position once more. Sorcha had barely begun
the effort when they both froze at a sound at the door.
The restraining bar rattled as it was removed.

"Quick, Sorcha, put your hands together. Maybe they
won't notice you're untied. It's our only chance."

Sorcha threw a panicked glanced at Katherine, quickly
gathered the piece of rope from the floor, and threw it
out the hole in the wall. Then she moved her hands so
that they were locked in front of her, palm to palm. She
pressed her arms into her body so that the material of
her dress covered her wrists, making it difficult to see
that she was not still bound by the rope.

Katherine sat back against the wall. She met Sorcha's
eyes and tried to give an encouraging smile. But the
sound of the voice outside made her blood run cold.

"You put them together? You imbecile, if anything
has happened, I'll hold you personally responsible."

Katherine swallowed and tried to calm her pounding

heart. Sorcha's face drained of color. Her voice was hoarse, just barely above a whisper. " 'Tis Alasdair."

The two women watched as the door slowly swung open.

Chapter 23

RIDING INTO BATTLE was definitely not as romantic as the movies would have you believe. In fact, Jeff thought as he shifted on his horse, trying to find some part of his rear end that wasn't bruised, riding wasn't all it was cracked up to be. Basically, it hurt. He watched the others riding along and felt a wave of envy at the way they casually sat their horses. These guys, he mused, gave new meaning to the term "buns of steel."

Fergus and Iain rode in the lead, their heads bent together in deep conversation. Following them, Jeff could make out Roger and several men he hadn't yet met. Ewan rode directly in front of him, having only just returned from escorting Ailis to the safety of Duncreag. The man must have ridden like the wind to have arrived in such short time, Jeff reasoned, wincing at the thought of what the ride must have felt like.

Twisting around, he saw the rest of the company trailing behind him, with Ranald bringing up the rear. Jeff studied the boy immediately behind him. The guy didn't look a day over sixteen, hardly old enough to be heading for a showdown with this Davidson fellow. But then,

Jeff reminded himself, life here was hard and kids grew up fast. For a minute, his mind flashed to a picture of some of the street gangs back in New York. Maybe things weren't really that different at home. Hard times seemed to produce hard children, in any century.

The kid gave a grimace that Jeff supposed was meant to pass for a manly smile. As he began to maneuver his way back into a forward position, he felt a breath of air pass close to his neck. Unsure of its origin, or indeed whether it was real or imagined, Jeff scanned the brush lining the path they were following. Behind him there was a muffled cry, but before he had time to turn and investigate, Ewan clutched his side and fell from his horse, directly in front of him.

Without further warning, pandemonium broke out. Arrows seemed to be flying from everywhere. Men jumped from their mounts and, using their horses for shields, scrambled for cover. Jeff sat frozen, watching the grim spectacle unfold. He felt a heavy hand jerk him from the saddle, then he fell to the ground in an undignified heap.

"Keep yer head down, mon, or ye'll likely lose it."

Jeff rose to a crouch, nodding thanks to his benefactor even as the man moved away. His heart was thudding in his chest and he assured himself it wasn't fear, just an adrenaline rush. Adrenaline rush, hell—it was more like raw terror. This was not *Braveheart*. This was the real thing. And a twentieth-century city boy, had no business being in the middle of it all. Jeff grabbed his sword and, holding it with both hands, began inching his way toward what he hoped was the shelter of a small group of trees.

The arrows had stopped flying, and the clearing was eerily quiet. A few men lay on the ground, feathered shafts protruding from various parts of their bodies. Jeff scanned the area for signs of Iain and the others or for the as-yet-unseen enemy. Everyone seemed to have disappeared. He drew a shaky breath and was wondering what he was supposed to do next when a hand shot out of the undergrowth and pulled him to his knees. He scrambled to lift his heavy claymore and locate this newest threat.

"Peace. 'Tis Ranald."

The bushes parted slightly, and Jeff found himself almost nose to nose with Iain's cousin. He quickly crawled into the slight cover the brush provided and lay on his stomach next to Ranald.

"What happened?" He whispered his words, trying to make as little noise as possible.

"Alasdair's men, no doubt. The archers were merely a first wave. There'll be others just behind them."

As if to emphasize the point, the ground suddenly rumbled and the air was filled with a cry that should have awakened the dead. Ranald moved to his feet, weapon drawn. Jeff marveled at Ranald's grace as he awkwardly tried to balance his own sword while lumbering to his feet.

"Stay back a bit, and watch your back. I've no doubt you can protect yourself in your own time, but I fear you're no' well trained for ours. I'd no' want to see you get hurt."

With that bit of wisdom, Ranald grinned and was gone, disappearing into the cloud of dust that marked the center of what was quickly turning into a full-fledged battle. Jeff stood on the edge of the fray, sword in hand, wondering what he should or could do to help. Hearing a noise to his right, he swiveled to find a man, roughly the size of Godzilla, rushing at him with an axe of some kind.

Reacting strictly on instinct, Jeff pivoted left and used both hands to swing his heavy weapon to the right. He felt resistance and pushed against it. Godzilla opened his mouth in surprise and fell to the ground, his battle-axe dropping from a lifeless hand. Jeff gingerly pulled his blade from the body. *Score one for the good guys*.

He planted his feet, sword held in front of him, and

swung left and right as he surveyed the fighting and watched for danger. Across the way, he could see Iain in fierce combat with someone. He was amazed at the effortless way Iain used his sword. He held it aloft as if it weighed no more than a feather. Jeff stood, watching in fascination. A second man emerged from the fray, his claymore pointed at Iain's back. Jeff started to yell a warning and realized that with the din from the fighting, there was no way Iain could hear him.

He rushed forward, his mind focused on reaching the attacker before he harmed Iain. As Jeff drew closer, the man swung around, his sword arm menacing.

Standing his ground, Jeff looked deep into the eyes of his opponent, trying desperately to recall movements learned in a long-ago fencing class. He sent a silent prayer to Gram and her eccentricities. He'd thought she was nuts to insist on his learning swordplay when he'd rather have been playing football or soccer with his friends. It had seemed a sissy sport at the time. However, a quick glance at the physique of the man in front of him assured him that "sissy" was not a word that applied to Scottish warriors.

Jeff saw the man's muscles tense a half-second before he moved. It was enough warning to propel his sword in an arc of defense. The two weapons met, clanging with the force of their contact. Jeff felt the power of the hit surge up his arm, shaking his body all the way to his feet. He jumped back, crouching a bit, bracing himself for the next blow. His opponent did not disappoint. With a snarl he leapt forward, his claymore raised high.

Jeff saw his opportunity and, with a quick lunge, swung the heavy sword to the left, his move resembling baseball far more than fencing. He felt the sword connect with human tissue and dodged back, swinging the claymore upward to deflect the thrust of his opponent's weapon. The warrior yelled something, obviously enraged. Blood dripped from the guy's shoulder, but the wound had not incapacitated him. Jeff steeled himself for the next assault. His arms were tiring and he felt as if he'd been fighting twenty men rather than just one.

With a roar, the man charged. Jeff swung defensively and once more felt the hard jolt of metal hitting metal. Again his attacker took the offensive. The mighty claymore swung high; Jeff actually heard it hiss by his ear. He parried another blow, but almost as quickly as he stopped it, the man was swinging again. Jeff tried to lift his weapon, but it seemed to have gained hundreds of pounds. Something wasn't right. He quickly glanced at his sword arm and realized the problem. His right bicep was bleeding and his hand was quickly losing all feeling. He had to think of something fast or he was going to wind up as buzzard bait. With an almost superhuman effort, Jeff raised his claymore in defense. He could see the other man's sword arcing down toward him. There was a ringing sound, and Jeff wondered briefly if it was the swords or his ears. The world started to spin and Jeff sank to the ground, his last conscious thought of Elaine.

"Ladies, I do hope you are enjoying my hospitality." Alasdair entered the room and bowed mockingly at the two women. His eyes traveled from the top of Katherine's head to her rope-bound feet, and Katherine could have sworn he actually licked his lips in anticipation. Feeling as though he had already violated her somehow, she involuntarily pushed back against the wall, as though it could swallow her and provide some degree of safety. His gaze shifted to Sorcha, all the lust draining away, derision taking its place.

"Sorcha, my dear, you should know by now that 'tis no' wise to cross me." He flicked a hand out and yanked up her chin. Sorcha stared defiantly back into his face, her hands twitching as she fought for control of what must have been a powerful urge to slap him. Katherine breathed with relief when it appeared she had mastered the desire. Sorcha's freedom was crucial if they were to find a means of escape.

Alasdair turned toward Katherine, keeping his hand

on Sorcha's chin. "Has she told you the whole sorry tale? I'll wager she has. No' one to keep secrets, our Sorcha. Did she tell you she killed Angus? Her one true love?"

Sorcha shifted. Katherine held her breath again. Sorcha was no match for Alasdair even with her hands untied. Katherine sent a prayer to God for Sorcha's willpower to hold.

"Ah, Sorcha, my stupid little ally. I'd no idea you had a soft spot for your new Laird as well as the old." His grip tightened on her chin. Sorcha winched in pain. "But even as we speak, Iain is most probably dead. I've left him a little surprise at Tùr nan Clach. Such irony that he'll meet his end trying to rescue his bride when in reality 'tis only my sister, the one he rejected, imprisoned there." Alasdair released Sorcha and turned his ice blue gaze back to Katherine. "It seems, my dear, that you are in need of a new husband. And I intend to remedy that situation."

"Iain isn't dead." Katherine watched him through narrowed eyes. "And even if he were, I would never willingly marry you."

Alasdair's mouth curled into a thin, narrow-lipped grimace that never reached his eyes. "Who said anything about willing? I'll have you whether you will it or no'. There's no one to stop me, my sweet. I killed Angus and, if he's no' already dead, I'll kill Iain."

Sorcha jumped to her feet and issued a soul-wrenching screech. "You killed Angus?"

Alasdair waved a hand in the air in dismissal, too consumed with Katherine to notice Sorcha's unbound hands. "Aye, with great pleasure. The man cheated me out of what was rightfully mine." For a moment his eyes glazed over with loathing, revealing the depth of his hatred. Then, taking a deep breath, he visibly pulled himself together, snapping his mask of sanity back into place.

"You see, my poor, pitiful Sorcha, when I found An-

gus at the bottom of the cliff—unconscious, but still
alive—it was the perfect opportunity for my revenge. It
was a simple matter to twist his neck and take his life."
He clenched his fists around a neck visible only to him
and jerked once in demonstration. Katherine flinched as
if he were actually holding Angus.

"Once I was sure he was dead, it was easy enough to
convince you the fall had done the deed and that you,
my dear Sorcha, were as good as a murderer." He turned
to face her, a smile of triumph playing over his lips.

Sorcha's face was twisted with blind rage. "You bastard." The words hung in the air as she flung herself at
Alasdair, her hands curled into claws, grabbing for his
throat. Alasdair laughed, deflecting her easily with one
hand. She came at him again, shrieking Gaelic curses.
With a vicious shove, he pushed her away again.

This time, however, she fell backward, teetering on
the edge of the opening in the wall. Katherine watched
in horror as she stood there, arms flapping like a fledging
bird, eyes wide with terror. The air in the room vibrated
with Alasdair's maniacal laughter and then was split by
Sorcha's cry as she toppled into the void, her scream
fading, until, abruptly, it stopped.

Katherine felt the bile rise in her throat and tried, in
vain, to push the thoughts of Sorcha's crushed body
from her mind. She leaned to one side and retched vi-
olently, emptying the pitiful contents of her stomach.
She felt the tears on her cheeks before she even realized
she was crying.

"He'll be fine, now. 'Tis no' a death wound."

Jeff tried to pull himself from the fuzzy blackness that
surrounded him.

"Saints be praised. Katherine would no' forgive me if
I let anything happen to her brother."

Iain's voice drifted to him, cutting through the blackness. With an effort, Jeff forced himself to follow the
sound of the voice. Carefully opening his eyes, his first

vision was of rain-filled clouds, crowding close to the horizon. He turned his head slightly, wincing at the pain radiating outward along his arm, and met the concerned eyes of his brother-in-law.

"Welcome back." Iain smiled, but his eyes remained serious.

"I take it we won?"

Iain's smile widened into a grin, this time extending to his eyes as well. "That we did."

Jeff gritted his teeth and pulled himself to a sitting position, wishing he had a really strong painkiller.

"What happened? I seem to have checked out before the last act."

Ranald crouched at his side, working on the linen bandage around his arm. "We bested them, but no' without loss. You fought well. I'd say you most likely saved Iain's life. I saw the man attacking, but couldna get there in time."

"Yeah, well, it was just luck. What I want to know is who saved *me*? I thought I was a goner."

"Actually, you saved yourself. When you passed out, you rolled forward and tripped the man. He fell on his own sword. No' a bad trick."

Ranald sat back, his ministrations completed. Jeff noticed others in the group sporting bandages. But overall, it looked like everyone was in pretty good shape.

"Did we lose a lot of men?"

Iain took a deep breath, a cloud of anger marring his handsome features. "Aye, eight, three of them during the archers' initial attack."

"And the bad guys?"

Iain's look shifted to one of grim satisfaction. "Fifteen dead and the rest scattered. They'll think twice about attacking the Mackintoshes again. Do you think you could ride?"

Jeff's interest in the battle quickly faded as he remembered their reason for being here in the first place.

"Sure. How much farther to this ruin of the mist or whatever?"

"Coire á Cheathaich. We're almost there. 'Tis o'er the next rise."

"And Katherine? Do you think she's still alive?" Jeff asked.

"I canna say for sure. But as I told young William, I think I'd know if she were dead." Iain stood then and gave the order for the men to mount, somebody having already gathered the horses. Ranald bent to help Jeff stand. He wobbled a bit, but soon found his balance.

"You've no need to go if you're no' up to it. Iain will see to the rescue of your sister."

Jeff took a deep breath, forcing his head to clear. His arm hurt, but not enough to stop him from trying to free Kitty. "I'll be fine. Just help me get on my horse."

Ranald nodded and aided Jeff as he swung up into the saddle. Once seated, Jeff took the reins from Ranald, holding them in his left hand. With a grimace, he signaled that he was ready, and Ranald left his side in search of his own mount.

Jeff felt a rising tide of urgency build inside him, almost as if Katherine were calling to him. He spurred his horse forward and pulled even with Iain. "I can't explain it, but I've got a strong feeling we need to hurry."

The air was suddenly split with an agonizing scream. The sound lingered, hanging in the air. The hairs on Jeff's arms rose and he felt a shudder streak down his spine. The sound was a death cry if ever he had heard one. He looked at Iain and found confirmation of his worst fears in his brother-in-law's eyes.

As one they spurred their horses, racing forward, the rest of the men following close behind.

Chapter 24

ALASDAIR ADVANCED ON Katherine, his blue
eyes glittering with desire. Sorcha's death seemed to be
acting as a stimulus, almost like an aphrodisiac of some
sort. Katherine swallowed and used the wall to brace
herself as she tried to stand. With her feet bound, running was out of the question, but she swore to herself
that he wouldn't have her without a fight.

His long fingers closed around her arms like talons,
pulling her struggling body close to his. "At last I have
you to myself." His whispered words washed over her
like slime in a cesspit. His lips brushed against her
cheek, his tongue tracing a pattern against her skin. She
fought the urge to gag. Gritting her teeth, she rammed
a shoulder into his chest. His breath whooshed out, but
his grip on her tightened. He held her locked to him
with one hand, while his other hand snaked around her
braid then yanked her head back. She stared up at him
defiantly through tear-filled eyes.

With his gaze pinned to hers, he released her hair and
leisurely reached between their bodies. Taking hold of
the neck of her gown, he effortlessly ripped it open to

her waist, baring her breasts. She felt his rough hand on
her nipple, stroking and caressing and then, with a vicious smile, twisting it, until she whimpered in pain.

But pain soon gave way to an all consuming rage, and
she leaned into him, biting his shoulder as hard as she
could. He released her instantly. The back of his hand
slammed into her cheek, sending her sprawling onto the
floor. She tried to inch away from him, but with her
hands and feet still bound, it was impossible for her to
get anywhere. Almost as soon as she started to move,
he was there, grabbing her by the hands and pulling her
up so that her back rested against his chest. His hand
again claimed her breasts, and he toyed with them, his
breath coming fast and hard against her ear. She struggled and tried again to turn and bite him.

He pushed her forward, still holding her by the rope
at her wrists, until she teetered on the edge of the crumbling window, her feet barely touching the floor. The
pain in her arms and hands was nothing compared with
the utter panic she felt facing the precipice and the dizzying drop to the ground.

"Will you end up like Sorcha, then? Smashed to bits
on the rocks? 'Tis no' a pretty way to die." In punctu-
ation of his remarks, he shifted his hold, forcing her to
look down. She bit off a scream and closed her eyes,
but not before seeing the mangled remains of Sorcha's
body far below.

Iain and Jeff led the way through the small gap that
guarded the hollow sheltering the ruined tower. Tenta-
cles of mist wound sinuously throughout the little corrie.
The old tower was in various stages of decay and dis-
integration, its outer walls reduced to rubble, having already lost the battle to water, wind, and vegetation. Jeff
watched as Iain slowed his horse and picked through the
fallen stones, his eyes on the tower.

Fifty yards or so from the entrance, he dismounted
and, with sword drawn, began to advance on foot. Noth-

ing stirred—the ruin seemed deserted. But the memory of the terror-filled cry still lingered in the minds of all the men and cautiously they, too, dismounted, then followed their Laird. Jeff slid from his horse and pulled a knife, the pain in his arm making it too difficult for him to carry the claymore he'd used before.

As Iain neared the tower, a huge man suddenly burst from the door, holding a battle-axe at the ready. He was flanked by two other men. They looked tiny in comparison to the brute in the center, but then Jeff quickly reassessed his observation, ruefully realizing that Arnold Schwarzenegger would have looked little next to the big guy. He watched as Ranald moved to Iain's side and three other Mackintosh men stepped into place behind them.

The two parties advanced toward each other as though part of an intricately choreographed ballet rather than a prelude to battle. Jeff held his breath and began inching forward, too impatient to remain stationary while the warriors decided the outcome. If Katherine was in there, he wasn't about to wait around for a secondhand report, wounded or not. Slipping the small knife into the scabbard attached to his belt, he grabbed his sword. Shaking with a mixture of pain and fury, he succeeded in raising it and with grim determination moved forward to stand behind Iain.

Evidently his efforts were enough to turn the tide, because the two little guys suddenly took off in opposite directions, leaving the massive warrior guarding the ruin on his own. Out of the corner of his eye, Jeff saw a couple of Iain's men dash after the fleeing gatekeepers.

The big man flexed the arm holding the axe, brandishing it in warning to those who might consider further advance, his eyes never leaving Iain, having correctly identified him as the leader. With an almost imperceptible nod at Ranald, who then dropped back, Iain and the others began to move forward, Iain slightly in the lead. Jeff, uncertain as to the plan, decided to follow

Ranald, who was stealthily winding his way around some fallen rubble toward the ruin. Surveying Ranald's route, Jeff realized his intent was to sneak up behind the big bruiser, who now stood a few feet in front of the tower steps. Careful to step quietly, Jeff followed Ranald, figuring that maybe he could add his help to the effort.

The giant was so intent upon the advancing Iain that he never even saw Ranald. With one strong thrust, Ranald ran the man through. He let out a roar, turning like a wounded beast on Ranald, his teeth bared in anger. But before he had time to inflict any damage, Iain's men were upon him. Jeff watched as Iain, without so much as a backward glance, leapt onto the steps that lead into the ruin, taking them two at a time.

Breathing heavily, Katherine tried to pull herself together. She struggled to banish the picture of Sorcha's broken body from her mind. She tensed as Alasdair tightened his arm around her, once again drawing her close against his body.

"You see, my dear, my hand"—he flexed it in front of her face—"has two personalities. It can be gentle,"—he caressed the smooth curve of her cheek—"or rough." Without warning, he backhanded her across the face, splitting her lip with force of the blow. "The choice"—he bent and with a delicate flick of his tongue lapped at the blood on her lower lip—"is yours."

Katherine spit at him, hitting him on the outside of an eye, grateful for a brother who had spent an entire summer teaching her to spit like a guy.

"So be it then, my beautiful witch." Alasdair hit her again, this time hard enough to make her head swim, but she didn't fall. She felt his hand gathering the fabric of her skirt but was too dazed to react. In an instant it, too, was ripped open and she stood before him dressed only in the tattered remains of her clothing. He reached for her with one hand and pulled her to him roughly by the hair, his other hand already groping a path down her belly. He bent his head, licked her breast, and forced it deep into his greedy mouth. Katherine struggled, trying to stop him. Her head connected with his and he let out a yelp of pain, then slung Katherine to the floor.

Her head cracked against the stone of the wall, her vision blurring and her ears ringing. She blinked slowly, feeling something wet trickle down her forehead, following the channel alongside her nose. She turned and wiped her face on her shoulder, leaving behind a smear of blood. With great effort she tried to hold on to consciousness, to fight. But the effort was becoming more difficult with each passing moment.

She heard Alasdair's sword fall with a clang as he released the scabbard from around his waist. With a feral smile, he sprang at her and straddled her body. In one swift motion, he used a knife to cut the ropes binding her legs. She tried to kick, but he shifted his weight, effectively pinning her. The hand with the knife moved to her throat even as he reached for the sweet soft center of her.

"Enough of our games, Katherine. 'Tis time for the joining."

She tried to think of a weapon, of something else she could do to him. But it seemed that there was nothing left. She filled her lungs to scream just as his lips descended on hers.

Iain stood in the remains of the great hall. It was empty. There was a floor below and a floor above. He hesitated, knowing that if he chose the wrong way, it could cost Katherine her life. Something slammed into the wall above him with a thud and he heard a muffled scream. With terror clawing at his innards, he tore up the stairs, his feet hardly touching the steps.

Katherine's scream still ringing in his ears, he stopped in front of a wooden door barred from the outside. With a strength born of fear, he loosened the bar and swung the door open, his claymore in hand.

He froze on the other side. Alasdair had Katherine on the floor, his knife at her throat and his legs wrapped around her nearly naked form. Rage replaced terror.

"Unhand my wife, Davidson." He spoke through clenched teeth, each word resounding through the chamber like a hammer blow.

Alasdair rolled over, pulling Katherine with him, the knife still at her throat. Slowly he rose, using her as a shield. Katherine's eyes flared with emotion at the sight of Iain, but then dulled over again with fear and pain.

"Let her go. 'Tis me you have a grievance with, no' her." Iain moved more fully into the chamber, careful to make no sudden movements.

Alasdair smiled at him, one hand holding the dagger, the other caressing Katherine. "Ah, Iain, so nice of you to join us. Although I must say your timing could have been a little better. I was just getting ready for a taste of your wife, and I'm afraid you've interrupted." He deliberately let one long finger stroke her breast, his eyes never leaving Iain's.

"You'll forgive me if I dinna let her go just now, won't you?" He slowly circled the chamber, moving as far away from Iain as he could. His eyes glittered with something close to madness.

Iain spoke in a low conversational tone. "I'd never have thought you for a man to hide behind a woman, Alasdair."

"I could take you with no trouble, Iain," Alasdair hissed, "but it seems that I'm over here and my sword is over there." He motioned to the abandoned scabbard that lay at Iain's feet.

With a kick, Iain sent it flying in Alasdair's direction. Inching down, forcing Katherine with him, Alasdair reached out for the sword. He closed his hand around the hilt and slowly stood again, keeping Katherine's body pressed to his. Holding the sword against Katherine's middle, he sheathed the dirk and then raising his sword arm, sent her flying toward the crumbled window with a shove.

Iain watched, his heart in his throat, as she hit the floor with a sickening thud and rolled to the edge of the precipice. She lay there unmoving, her eyes closed.

With a low growl, Alasdair lunged at Iain. He wrenched his thoughts from Katherine's still body, deftly dodging the blow. "A bit off your mark, Alasdair. You should have had me with that one." He moved back, taunting him, watching as Alasdair's face mottled with rage.

"Talk all you want, Iain Mackintosh, because soon everything that you have, including your whore of a wife, will be mine. I deserve it. I worked for it. Everything was perfect until Angus dismissed me in favor of you." He swung his sword again, wildly.

Iain met the thrust with his own, the two blades bouncing harmlessly off one another. He tried not to think of Katherine lying there, balanced on the edge of the gaping hole. "Of course he did. I'm his son."

They circled each other warily.

"Aye, maybe by blood, but all those years 'twas me who was really a son to him. I flattered him. I listened to his tales. I nursed him through his sorrow and his ale. I loved him." Alasdair hissed in anger. "And I killed him."

Iain froze for a split second, a rage so powerful it threatened to overwhelm him smashing into his consciousness. "You?"

He struck out at Alasdair with mindless fury. Their swords met, Alasdair easily deflecting the blow.

"Me. Your witch of an aunt did the hard part for me; all I had to do was finish the job. And everything would have worked out nicely, too, if only you hadn't been so reluctant to marry my sister."

"Did you think to gain Duncreag through my marriage?" Iain fought to control his anger.

Alasdair crooked his thin lips in a malicious smile. "Aye, after you were dead."

Iain glanced at Katherine. She still hadn't moved. He circled slowly, watching Alasdair for an opening. "Surely, you dinna think you could murder me and then claim my holding."

Alasdair tightened his hand on his claymore. "Of course no'. I wouldna have been accused of your murder."

"The Macphersons?"

Alasdair dipped his head slightly in agreement. "A brilliant plan, you have to admit. Although to pull it off I had to give up the dirk." He cast a covetous look in the direction of Iain's sheathed knife. "No matter," he said with a delicate shrug, "I'll have it again soon enough." He cast a lecherous glance at Katherine. "And your wife too. I canna wait to bury myself in her."

"I'll see you in hell first." Iain lunged at Alasdair, catching his arm with the tip of his blade.

Alasdair's fingers jerked opened reflexively and his sword fell from his nerveless hand, clattering against the stone floor. He snarled at Iain and slipped sideways toward Katherine. With a mighty roar, Iain rammed his claymore into Alasdair, the force slamming him back against the wall, leaving him impaled there, his eyes open but empty. Iain released his weapon, leaving it, and Alasdair, suspended from the stones.

Katherine moaned and started to move. Iain dropped to his knees and slowly began to crawl toward her. His throat tight with fear, he whispered, "Katherine, 'tis Iain. I've almost got you. Dinna move, lass. Dinna move."

At the sound of his voice, she struggled to sit, and in that instant he saw her eyes open, wild with fear. One leg slid over the opening, leaving her straddling the breach. His pulse racing, he reached for her, his hand closing around one slim ankle. Carefully, he inched his

way forward until he could pull her into the safety of
his arms. She whimpered as she burrowed into the
warmth of his chest. He held her close, rocking her and
murmuring soft nonsensical words of love. She was battered and bruised, filthy and bleeding, but she was alive.
And he had never loved her more.

Jeff rounded the last curve of the stairs and came out on
the small landing. With considerable effort, he raised his
sword, listening for some noise, a clue to Iain's
whereabouts. A scuffling sound came from a door halfway down the landing wall. Back to the wall, he worked
his way to the opening and sprang through it, ready for
battle. Across from the door, in dark relief against the
gray Highland sky, he saw Iain cradling his sister. Heart
in throat, he met Iain's eyes with one silent question.

"I think she's lost consciousness again, but she lives,"
Iain told him.

Jeff rushed to Iain's side, oblivious to the remains of
the man skewered against the wall. He had eyes only
for Katherine. With a gentle hand, he ran his knuckles
across her cheek, fingers smoothing her tangled hair
back, away from her face.

"Kitty? It's Jeff—can you hear me?" There was no
response. He felt her neck for a pulse and was relieved
to feel it beating a faint but regular rhythm. He tried
again. "Hey, you, the least you can do after my coming
all this way is open your eyes and say hello."

She moaned then, moving her head a little from side
to side. Iain tightened his arms protectively around her.
They heard her sigh, and both of them watched intently
as her eyes slowly fluttered open. Gray eyes, glazed with
pain and the remnants of horror, looked up at them. She
swallowed, trying to force out the words. "Alasdair?"

Jeff shifted quickly to block her vision of the body
on the wall as Iain lovingly cradled her head. "He's
dead, mo chridhe," Iain told her. "He canna harm you
anymore." She stared at him a moment and then, seem-

ingly accepting his answer, nestled closer into his arms,
turning her head slightly to look at her brother. Again
she struggled for words. "How? Why?"

Jeff smiled gently. "I couldn't let you have all the fun,
could I? Besides, I had to check out the guy you were
gonna marry. Brother's prerogative and all that."

Katherine lips twitched, a weak attempt to smile. But
almost before the motion was completed, her eyes closed
and she lapsed back into unconsciousness. Iain met
Jeff's worried gaze and said, "We must get her back to
Duncreag."

"Yeah, she's probably suffering from shock. And who
knows what else that bastard did to her."

Iain's jaw tightened. He carefully passed Katherine to
Jeff, then reached to unclasp the brooch that held his
plaid in place. Releasing it, he stood and removed his
belt, unwinding the voluminous material. He bent then
and, taking Katherine from Jeff, gently wrapped her in
its soft folds. He lifted her high into his arms, cradling
her against his massive chest.

"My sword." With a tilt of the head, he gestured toward the wall.

Jeff walked over to the dead man and yanked the claymore from the wall. The body slid down the stones to
the floor, landing in a heap. Using his good arm, Jeff
balanced the two heavy swords against his hip and followed Iain from the room, leaving Alasdair Davidson's
corpse as fodder for the beasts that called the ruin home.

The two men slowly made their way down the stairs
and out of the tower, Iain holding their precious burden.
Iain's men were gathered in the remains of the courtyard. The body of the giant was nowhere to be seen, but
the two smaller men were bound and tied onto pack-
horses. Jeff had momentary visions of doing violent
things to them. Perhaps, he reflected, there was a bit of
the barbarian in him after all.

Ranald approached Iain and Jeff, leading Sian behind

him, and eyeing the blanket-clad Katherine with concern. "Is she alive then?"

"Aye. But we've no idea what she's been through. I want her safe at Duncreag as quickly as possible."

"Fine, we're ready to leave. But Iain, there's something more you need to know." Aqua eyes met green. "The scream we heard dinna belong to Katherine. We found Sorcha's body on the rocks there." He pointed to the cliff below the rear wall of the tower.

Iain looked toward the rocky ledge and shrugged, his concern with the living now, not the dead. "So be it." He turned back to the group of men and carefully transferred his plaid-wrapped burden to Jeff, then swung into the saddle and reached down for Katherine.

Jeff looked up at Iain, his arms tightening around his sister. A fierce possessiveness shook him, a desire to hold on to his sister, to keep her safe. She shifted restlessly in his arms, calling out for Iain. He touched her face and, releasing a breath, lifted her into her husband's waiting arms.

Mounting his horse, he felt the throbbing in his arm and realized with a rush just how tired he was. A nice hot shower and a long sleep would probably go a long way toward a cure. Realizing that the former was most likely impossible, Jeff decided that he'd have to settle for the latter. And after that he'd see to Katherine. With a tired flick at the reins, he motioned his horse forward and followed Iain back to Duncreag.

Chapter 25

IAIN STIRRED THE last glowing embers of the fire.
The moon had set long ago, leaving the chamber clothed
in deep shadows. He replaced the poker and returned to
the chair by the bed. Katherine shifted, groaning in her
sleep. Her hands curled around the blankets, looking
pale and fragile. Her hair spilled across the pillow, and
even in the dark of the night, he could see the golden
strands. He reached out to smooth her brow. Heat radiated outward from her sleeping form, the fever that pro-
duced it still raging within her. It had been a se'nnight
since they had returned to Duncreag. Seven long days
and nights. Iain leaned against the side of the bed, bracing his elbows on the mattress, his hands threaded into
his hair. Katherine was locked in a battle for her life,
and there was nothing here to help her, nothing in this
world.

A moan from Katherine brought him to his feet. They
were beginning again, the nightmares. He sat on the
edge of the bed, taking her hand in his, worry creasing
his brow. Katherine's arm shot out of the covers, reaching above her head, frantically grasping for something.

Her cries grew in intensity, almost becoming screams. Her eyes opened wide, an unseen terror mirrored in their gray depths. He pulled her into his arms, trying to calm her spastic motions.

"I'm here, my love. You're safe. Nothing can harm you." He pulled her back against him, stroking her hair and repeating his reassurances until she calmed and was still again. He held her a moment longer, inhaling the sweet smell of her. Then, reluctantly, he let her go, settling her back onto the pillows, resuming his place at the side of her bed.

Two different dreams tormented her. They had come both day and night without fail since her rescue, one or the other, sometimes both in quick succession. This one was the easiest to deal with. He was fairly sure of its source. The captive guardsmen had told of Katherine's attempt to escape and her brush with death on the crumbling battlements of the ruin. The ordeal would have scarred anyone, but for someone with an acute fear of falling it would have no doubt been even more horrifying. It was certainly no surprise that it haunted her dreams. At least during these dreams Katherine would let him hold her until it passed. Together, Iain believed, they could conquer it.

Iain drew a deep breath, pain filling his heart. It was the other dream that frightened him. He wished that, just for a moment, he could find his way into her head and see what she saw. Then perhaps he would know how to vanquish her fears. That it was Alasdair from whom she shrank night after night he had no doubt. But his mind ran rampant with thoughts of what it was she was remembering when she screamed for him to let her go. And unlike the other dream, he could not reach her. If he touched her at all, she shrank away, her terror-filled eyes looking at him but seeing something else. He was a man of action with nothing to do. How could he protect her against demons that lived inside her head?

He reached out to stroke the soft curve of her face and felt the smooth contour of her cheek. Never had he felt so helpless. So alone. During the day others came to sit with her, to be with her, to be with him. Jeff, William, Ailis, and Ranald all came. Even Fergus roused himself from his grief over Sorcha's death to sit with Katherine. But no matter what words of encouragement they offered, Iain still felt afraid, unable to help the person he loved most in the world.

Rubbing a hand along his bearded jaw, he leaned wearily back in the chair, his eyes never leaving her face. Silently he kept his vigil, watching over her as she slept.

Jeff stood in the doorway, watching as Ailis spooned broth into Katherine's open mouth. She ate like an obedient child, but her eyes remained blank and glassy. Only when the dreams came did they lose their vacant stare, and then only to be replaced by mindless terror.

"She seems a bit better today. Stronger. I think the broth is doing her a world of good," Ailis said, smiling timidly at Jeff. Her own bruises were just beginning to fade.

Jeff wondered briefly what terrors she had endured at her brother's hand, but knew better than to ask. "She does seem stronger." He moved into the room and sat opposite Ailis on the side of Katherine's bed.

"I brushed her hair. She seemed to like that. It is so beautiful." Ailis set the bowl of broth beside the bed and pushed a strand of her own hair behind an ear.

"What are you going to do? Have you decided?" Jeff watched as she thought about it, chewing on her upper lip.

"When Katherine is better I'll return to Tùr nan Clach. Alasdair . . ." She paused as though considering her next words, then took a deep breath and continued. "Alasdair and my father both abused our holding and its people. I think I would like to try and set their ill deeds to right."

"Sounds like a difficult task—"

"—for a woman?" Ailis interrupted, smiling slightly. The small change lit up her elfin face.

"No—at least, not *just* for a woman. Undoing Alasdair's wrongs would be a hard task for anyone." His gaze fixed on Katherine.

Ailis reached across to touch his hand. "I'm sorry. I didn't mean to remind you of my brother and what he did. It was thoughtless of me."

He gave her hand a pat. "It's all right. I think it's brave of you to try to take it all on by yourself. Is there no one to help you? Ranald perhaps?" He had seen the two of them together and knew there was something between them.

She colored becomingly and looked down, intent suddenly on studying her hand. "No, I think this is something I need to do on my own. For a lot of reasons." She smiled at him again, this time more fully exposing a small dimple in her cheek. "I'll just go now and give you some time with your sister."

Jeff turned his attention back to Katherine as Ailis left the room. She lay back against her pillows, eyes open, seeing nothing.

"Kitty, can you hear me?" Jeff waited patiently, watching for some response, any response. Katherine continued to stare off absently into space. He reached for her hand and drew it into the warmth of his own.

"Damn it, Kitty, I know you're in there somewhere. I don't know if you can hear me, but if you can, I'm here and I'm not giving up on you. Remember when we were little, after Mom and Dad died? It was always the two of us against the world. Kitty and Jeff. Well, it still is. All you have to do is let me know you're there. Let me help. Please."

He reached out to brush her hair away from her face, "I know what happened was awful, and I know you don't want to face it. But I can help, I know I can. You just have to find your way out of wherever it is you are. Kitty, I miss you so much, please come back to me, to all of us."

He smiled at her and squeezed her hand. "You were right about Elaine. I do have feelings—very strong feelings—for her. I was just afraid to admit I had them, even to myself. I think we started something, though, right before I came here. So you have to get well, so that I can go home to her and finish what we started. Then you can dance at our wedding."

Saying that, he drew a rapid breath, realizing what it was he could do to help her. He bent and kissed her forehead and with a last glance went to find Iain.

"No." Iain glared at his wife's brother over his worktable. "I'll no' even consider it. Katherine is my wife and she belongs here with me."

Jeff leaned across the table, his body braced on his hands. "You have to at least consider it. She's not getting better, Iain." He pushed back and crossed his arms over his chest, watching as Iain used both hands to push his hair out of his face. There were dark circles under his eyes and his grief-ravished face was cloaked in the dark stubble of his half-grown beard.

"The fever is gone," Iain said stubbornly. "And the dreams dinna seem to come as often."

"True, but she never speaks and barely responds to outside stimuli. Hell, Iain, she's almost catatonic."

"Speak words I can understand." Iain slammed his hand on the table, obviously frustrated at more than Jeff's use of twentieth-century verbiage.

Jeff sighed and ran a hand through his hair. "We've been over this before. Katherine seems to have withdrawn into a world of her own. It's not unheard of for a person to react like that when something unspeakably horrible happens to her."

"You're saying she's mad."

"No, I'm saying she has found a safe place, away from all that has happened to her."

"Away from me." Iain sat heavily on a chair, grief radiating from his face.

"From me, too. Listen, Iain, she's been through a lot. We know she almost fell from the battlements and we are pretty certain she must have witnessed Sorcha's death. Add to that whatever Alasdair did to her . . ." Jeff let his words trail off, leaving the rest unsaid.

"We dinna know that he violated her." The tiny muscle in Iain's cheek was working overtime, and he clenched and unclenched the fist resting on the arm of the chair.

"No, we don't. But we sure as hell know he did something. You just have to watch her in the middle of one of her nightmares to know that. Iain, she needs help."

"Do you think I dinna know that, man? I'm trying to do all that I can. I dinna sleep. I barely eat. I hardly ever leave her side."

"Iain, I am not questioning your dedication to my sister. I know that you love her. But it isn't enough. She needs professional help. And the only way she can get that is in my time. You've got to let her go."

"I canna. Surely with time she'll recover. She knows that I love her. Sometimes she responds to my voice." Iain spoke with desperation.

"Iain, she simply needs more than either of us can give her."

"What about the babe?"

"We've been over that too. We don't even know that there is a baby.

"But Katherine's letter . . ."

"Doesn't exist anymore. We changed everything, remember?"

"How can I no'. In changing things, we seem to have made everything worse. At least before, Katherine lived."

"Yes, but you died and she spent her life with Alasdair. Is that truly what you want for her?"

"No, but I dinna want her to be . . . What was your word?" He paused, searching for the unfamiliar word. "Catatonic, either. At least before, she was well and was able to bear our daughter."

"Well, if Anna does exist, the best thing for her is a good medical environment, and that still means letting me take Kitty home."

Ian buried his face in his hands, muffling his words, but Jeff understood them.

"Take her then."

Katherine tried to see through the blinding fog. It surrounded her, blanketing both sound and sight. She tried to remember how she had come to be here. But her memory, like her world, seemed to be shrouded with the mist. She walked aimlessly, trying to find some way to escape the grayness, but there seemed to be no doors or windows in her fog-filled world. She knew there were boundaries, though. Great gaping precipices waiting to swallow her if she took a wrong step and fell. The mere thought was enough to send her heart racing, and she drew deep breaths, trying to calm herself. Inexplicably tired, she sank to the ground and let the cool grayness swirl around her. She dozed, feeling the nothingness seep into her very being.

Suddenly she awakened, her heart pounding. Something was out there. Something terrifying. She tried to peer into the swirling clouds, but could see nothing. She knew *he* was out there, waiting for her. Confused, she tried to remember who *he* was. But her mind remained closed, a blank. She ran blindly into the mist. Cold blue eyes, imagined or real, seemed to leer at her out of the fog. She screamed, trying to find a way out, a way to escape the eyes.

Somewhere in the distance, she could see white shining against all the gray like a beacon. She ran toward it, feeling hot breath on her back. As she drew closer, the white began to take on shape. It was a door, a great shining door. With a sob of relief, she threw herself at it, feeling it give against the weight of her body. A garden . . . it was a garden. The white door extended into walls, encircling her, keeping *him* out and keeping her safe. After all the gray, the bright colors of the garden almost hurt her eyes. She drank deeply from a little pond, feeling her pulse returning to normal.

She sat on a bench in the center of the garden and relaxed for the first time since finding herself in the mist. She felt the heat of the sun, although she could not see it. The sky, if it was indeed sky, was white like the wall and the door. In fact, the garden was like a painting she'd once seen somewhere, bright colors surrounded by the white of the canvas it was painted on.

At least she was safe here. *He* couldn't reach her here. Somehow, she was sure of it. And there were no ledges, no sudden drops waiting to swallow her. Yes, she was safe here.

Then she heard a voice. She cocked her head, listening. It was calling something. Katherine, it said. Katherine. With sudden surety, she knew that her name was Katherine. Someone was calling her. She walked through the flowers to the white door.

The voice seemed closer now. A deep voice. Even as her head struggled to put a name and a face to it, her soul responded to it with a familiar joyous longing. She fought the urge to fling wide the door and run to the voice. Her fear of *him* was too great. She knew she mustn't leave her sanctuary. Not even for the voice. She heard it again and felt it wrap around her, soft and velvety, full of love. Her longing became almost physical, but it still wasn't strong enough to conquer her fear of *him*. With sad resolve, she returned to the bench, forcing her mind to shut out the precious voice. She closed her eyes, letting her mind drift, knowing that as long as she stayed here, within the white walls, she was safe.

One last time, she let the voice echo through her head, its timbre engraving itself on her heart. She felt moisture and, in confusion, touched the single drop of water on her cheek. Puzzled, she touched it with her tongue. Salty. Losing interest, she turned her attention to the beautiful garden. Her sanctuary, her home.

Iain sat in the big bed, holding Katherine's fragile form close against his body. She neither responded nor struggled. He buried his face in her hair, trying desperately to memorize the feel of it. He had spent most of the day holding her, watching her, willing her to open her eyes and smile at him. But there was nothing, no change at all.

He tried to tell himself that they had been lucky to have had any time at all. But somehow the words rang hollow. Lucky how? If Katherine had never come, she would still be whole. And yet, had she not come, he would have remained forever empty, never having been touched by her gentle spirit and sweet enthusiasm for life. He closed his eyes, picturing her laughing up at him, flushed from their lovemaking. And in that moment, he knew he would never be the same again, that she had touched some part of him so deep and true that even now she had left a part of herself to live on here in this time with him. No matter the pain, it had been well worth it.

He sat holding her until the last rays of sunlight faded from the bedchamber. Katherine slept, her face relaxed, safe for the moment from the dreams that tormented her. He watched as her chest rose and fell with each breath. Life. Katherine still had life. And if there was a way, in her time, for her to recover from all that had happened here, then he knew he must let her go. It was the only way.

He bent and kissed her still lips, remembering other

times when those lips had parted in eager anticipation of a taste of him. He pulled away. The memories would have to last his lifetime. He knew, now, why a part of his father had died with his mother. Just as he carried a part of Katherine, so, too, would she take a part of him with her when she left. She might never remember him, but he would be with her nevertheless. Always.

He swung her into his arms one last time, then carried her over the threshold into the chamber where it had all begun. Jeff was already there waiting for him. Carefully, he laid Katherine on the bed and covered her gently with a blanket. Caressing her face with a loving hand, he leaned down for a last kiss.

"I'll love you forever. Never doubt that. And know that if I canna be with you in life, I will find a way to be with you in your dreams."

Without looking at Jeff, he straightened, walked through the door, and closed it softly behind him. Only then did he allow his emotions to take control. Helpless now before the agonizing waves of grief that engulfed him, he sank to the floor, his great body shaking with the force of his pain.

Jeff lay on the bed, pulling his sister's limp body into his arms. He held her close, and he closed his eyes tightly, turning his thoughts to Elaine and twentieth-century Duncreag. He thought of modern medicine, of hospitals and psychiatrists, of all the things they could do to help Katherine. He concentrated until his head ached. Nothing happened.

Darkness invaded completely as the moon set, leaving only faint starlight to illuminate the room. He thought of hamburgers and Disney World, of Gram's house in Connecticut and baseball games. He thought of Katherine, happy and whole. And still nothing happened.

The room grew cold, the embers of the fire long dead. Katherine moaned and shivered. He wrapped her more tightly in his arms, gritting his teeth in his determination to return to his own time. And still the room mocked him with its sameness.

He shifted, trying to keep Katherine warm, and in doing so felt the cold smoothness of her earrings against his skin. The cairngorms. She was still wearing the cairngorms. Suddenly, he was sure that if he removed this last link to Iain, she would at last be free and he would be able to get them home. Carefully, he removed the small earrings and laid them on the table by the bed. Then once more wrapping his arms around his sister, he concentrated on going home.

The first pale streaks of dawn sent small fingers of pink light in through the chamber window. The light danced along the stone floor, bending to flit across the table. Its pink glow reflected in the smooth darkness of the two small stones lying discarded on the table. It moved on then to dance across the wide expanse of the empty bed. Morning, arriving in all its splendor.

Chapter 26

KATHERINE WALKED ALONG East 86th Street, inhaling the crisp fall air. The weather was still warm, but early in the morning there was a subtle difference to the air, a hint of the winter ahead. Sounds of the city stirring filled the street. Katherine passed a shopkeeper sweeping the sidewalk in front of a fashionable boutique. Farther along, a man in front of a small grocery hosed down the area by his door. This was Katherine's favorite time of day. She stopped at a bakery and bought a cup of coffee and a bagel still warm from the oven. Eating and sipping, she continued to walk along, enjoying the vibrancy of the city.

She marveled at the fact that it had only been a little over two months since she had been released from the hospital. Even her doctor had been surprised at her rapid recovery. She had been in a near-catatonic state for about a month, brought about by the trauma of a kidnapping. *Kidnapping*. Katherine still had trouble believing something so life-changing had happened to her without her having even the slightest memory of it.

She slowed down to admire the fresh flowers at a

sidewalk stand, their colors riotous against the pristine white of the cart. Something familiar tugged at her memory and then slipped away. Katherine sighed and walked on. It was always like that—a little hint of a lost memory and then nothing. Dr. Saunders had patiently explained more than once that her memory of the kidnapping might never come back, that the mind had a way of shutting out things simply too painful to handle. Still, Katherine couldn't shake the idea that there was something else, something good, that she was shutting out with the bad.

She walked on, stopping when she reached a small bookshop. Twisting her wrist to look at her watch, she noted that she'd arrived early. The shop wasn't due to open for a couple more hours, but she was meeting Mrs. Pettigrew, the owner, at eight. She sat on the step in the doorway to wait, finishing the last of her bagel and watching the people passing by. A large man in a dark business suit stopped to ask her the time. He pushed back his dark hair, revealing startling green eyes. She watched as he left, feeling unsettled. Again, there was the nagging feeling that she was forgetting something important.

All she knew about the kidnapping, and the events immediately preceding it, came from Jeff. She'd gone to Scotland on vacation. That in and of itself was not like her at all, but evidently, she'd been there before. Just after college, according her brother. She remembered college and graduate school, but the summer in between was just one big blank, exactly just like her most recent summer.

Methodically, her mind flipped through the facts. She'd gone on vacation, only to be kidnapped by some deranged madman. She'd been held hostage in some old castle for several days before being rescued by her brother and the Scottish equivalent of the FBI. Her captor had been killed. She'd withdrawn into some sort of autistic-like state, only to awake a month later with no memory of any of it. Katherine sighed, thinking, not for the first time, that her story sounded too crazy to be true.

She spotted Mrs. Pettigrew winding her way among the growing throng of morning commuters and swallowed the last of her coffee, grateful for the reprieve from her thoughts.

"Katherine, how lovely to see you." The woman gave Katherine a quick hug, then pulled back to look her over carefully. "I heard about your ghastly experience. You're fine now?"

"Yeah. Right as rain, except I've lost an entire week of my life." Katherine grinned ruefully. "Of course, if Jeff tells it right, it wasn't exactly the best week of my life anyway."

"Well, at least you're safely back home." Mrs. Pettigrew was one of those women who seemed ageless, somewhere between fifty and infinity. She was reed-thin and her dark hair was pulled into a sweeping chignon. She favored bright colors and always wore a number of bangles that tinkled musically when she moved.

Katherine had discovered the little shop in grad school and had found a kindred spirit in Mrs. Pettigrew. They shared a great love for all things medieval, and over the years Katherine had come to depend on Mrs. Pettigrew's "finds" for her research.

Mrs. Pettigrew turned the key in the lock and after opening the door immediately crossed to the far wall and the flashing red light that marked the security system. Katherine followed her, blinking a little to adjust to the dimness of the store after the bright September sunshine.

The shop always reminded Katherine of something straight out of Dickens. It was dark and smelled of leather, furniture polish, and old paper. The walls were lined with shelves that disappeared upward into the shadows of the ceiling. Two huge, rolling ladders graced the walls, allowing the adventurous access to the topmost shelves and the treasures they hid from view. Because of her crippling fear of heights, Katherine had

never actually been up the ladders, but she liked the look
they added to the place.

"There we are. The alarm is safely disarmed. I live in
fear of accidentally setting the thing off. I only got it
because Walter insisted I have it. You know, for the
nights I work late."

Walter was Mrs. Pettigrew's husband. Katherine had
never met him, but over the years had formed a mental
picture of him based on Mrs. Pettigrew's comments.

"Come on back to the office. I'll get some coffee going. I've got your book back there."

"Great." Katherine followed her through the shop into
a small back office crammed from ceiling to floor with
more books. She sat in a side chair by a rickety-looking
desk and watched as Mrs. Pettigrew measured out coffee.

"You'll have some?"

Katherine nodded agreeably, thinking that a little caffeine high wouldn't hurt her. Finally finished with the
coffee machine, Mrs. Pettigrew sat behind her desk, her
bracelets tinkling merrily. She opened a drawer and
pulled out a small bound manuscript and reached across
the desk to hand it to Katherine.

"What did I tell you. Perfect condition. When I saw
it, I thought of you immediately."

Katherine flipped through it, careful not to tear the
pages. "It's wonderful. I've been trying to get my hands
on a copy of this guy's work for over a year now." The
book was a study of early medieval Norman agricultural
practices, written sometime during the eighteenth century by a Scot. Probably not destined to be a best-seller,
but Katherine was delighted with it.

"I've never heard of this Colin Mackintosh fellow before. Is he well known?"

Katherine looked up from her perusal of the book.
"No. I don't think so, except maybe in university circles.
He was a noted medieval historian of his time. What
makes him important to me is that he was one of the

few historians who wrote more about social customs than political history."

"I see. Well, when I located this work, the seller also mentioned having another book by the same author, so I bought it, too, on the off chance that you would be interested."

"Really? As far as I know there were only three—one on architecture, one on the practices of the church, and this one on agriculture. Is the second volume the treatise on architecture or the church?"

Mrs. Pettigrew handed Katherine a cup of freshly brewed coffee, obviously enjoying herself immensely. Her eyes twinkled as she smiled at Katherine, then answered her question with a single word. "Neither."

Katherine felt excitement begin to rise deep within her. "Neither?"

Intrigued, Katherine took the cup and sipped absently, thinking about the book's possibilities and almost scalding her mouth in the process. Putting the coffee on the desk between them, she reached for the leather-bound book Mrs. Pettigrew held out to her. Carefully opening the flyleaf, she read the title:

The Mackintoshes of Duncreag.
A brief history
by Colin Mackintosh.
1784.

Katherine felt her heart accelerate with something more than academic curiosity. Why did the name Duncreag sound so familiar? She shrugged mentally, turning the page. A large sketch of a clan crest filled the next page. It was vaguely familiar. There was the requisite drawing of a belt surrounding the emblem, which in this case resembled a mountain cat of some sort. The cat was standing on its hind legs, its front paws extended in front of it. It was turned sideways like an Egyptian figure with its head facing the reader, a small object dangling from its paw. Katherine bent closer. It looked like jewelry of some kind. Maybe an earring or something; it was hard to tell. There was a motto printed around the outside of the belt.

"The past, present, and future shall always be intertwined."

An alarm bell began to sound deep in her mind. Katherine read the entry below the crest, a sense of urgency growing stronger inside her with each passing second. The caption identified the crest as belonging to a sept of the great Clan Chattan, the Mackintoshes of Duncreag. The emblem was similar to that of the Mackintoshes of Moy, with the exception of the addition of the small earring. Katherine's breathing increased and her head began to pound. The modification was made, according to the book, sometime in the late fifteenth century by the second Laird of the clan, Iain Mackintosh. *Iain*. At the name, Katherine felt a strange surge of powerful longing. She focused her mind on the next line of the text. The clan badge was changed at that time too: The cairngorm, a gem native to the Scottish Highlands, had replaced the traditional red whortleberry. Katherine dropped the book from sweating palms, her hand reaching reflexively for her earlobe. Bits of memory swirled in her head, trying to break free of the bonds that had held them silent for three long months.

"Katherine, are you all right?" Mrs. Pettigrew had come around the desk and now looped her arm around Katherine. "You look pale. Here, drink this." She handed Katherine a glass of water.

Katherine gulped down the water, then smiled weakly at her friend. "I'm fine, really, just a little wave of dizziness. Probably just a combination of too much caffeine and the excitement of your find." She swallowed, trying to gather her fragmented thoughts. She needed to be alone. The memories were pounding at her now. And she knew it was just a matter of time before they exploded into her brain. "I still get a little tired, I'm afraid.

The books are marvelous. Both of them. Tell me what I owe you."

Still looking concerned, Mrs. Pettigrew sat back behind her desk and handed Katherine an invoice. "The old geezer wanted quite a bit more, but I held out and he finally gave in."

Katherine quickly wrote a check and handed it to Mrs. Pettigrew. "This should cover it." Rising, she swayed a little, but found her balance and picked up the two books. "I think I'll just head home now."

"Yes. I'm sure a little rest will do you a world of good."

They walked back through the store. Mrs. Pettigrew unlocked the door and Katherine stepped outside, squinting into the morning sunlight.

"Thanks again for the books."

"Oh, it's my pleasure. I so enjoy the challenge of finding them. I'll give you a call if I come across anything else."

Katherine smiled and waved, already walking away, her mind working feverishly to put her thoughts into some kind of rational order.

Two hours later, Katherine sat in her apartment in stunned silence, clutching the little manuscript. Her hand rubbed over the page with the crest as though she was trying to absorb it.

He hadn't forgotten.

The book listed him as the second Laird of Duncreag. The book said that little was known about him. He had married, but she died young and there were no children. The Lairdship had passed to a cousin. The change in the clan motto and crest were credited to him—to Iain. The author could find no documentation, but legend had it that the changes were made as a memorial to his wife, Katherine. Iain Mackintosh had never loved another.

Memories washed over her in great waves, threatening

to overbalance her tenuous hold on reality. She drew in a great cleansing breath and, with a shaking hand, automatically reached to smooth her braid, surprised to find it wasn't there. They had cut her hair in the hospital. It had simply been too much trouble for the attendants. It reached just below her shoulders now. She tucked the errant strands behind her ears and carefully placed the book on the counter.

She remembered everything. The cairngorm earrings. Her trips to Duncreag. The kidnapping.

Iain.

With a rush of emotion, she felt tears trembling on her lashes. Feeling almost weak from the release, she let the tears fall, her first good cry since waking to find a part of her life missing. No, not simply a part of her life—a part of her soul, her husband. Iain.

Her first reaction was anger. Anger at Jeff for bringing her back. Anger at Iain for letting her go. She wondered who knew the entire truth. Jeff certainly; he had been lying to her from the minute she'd awakened. Elaine? How much did she know? Surely most, if not all of it, since she and Jeff were thick as thieves these days.

Did her doctor know? Katherine quickly decided he didn't. He was, after all, a man of science. In his mind, time travel would be deemed the stuff of fantasy, a grand delusion of those a little out of touch with reality. No, Jeff would never risk sharing their secret with a doctor.

Katherine felt her anger abate. She knew Jeff almost as well as herself, and she had no doubt that he had done what he thought was best for her. He would never intentionally harm her. And Iain . . . well, she simply had to believe that he, too, had acted with her best interests at heart. But the fact remained that she had a husband she loved with all her heart, alive and presumably well, living in another century. And she was perfectly healthy now. There was absolutely no reason she could think of to stay here. It was time to go home.

She cringed as the thought that had been hovering at the back of her mind since her memory had returned finally forced its way into the forefront.

What if she couldn't get back?

Katherine angrily pushed the thought aside. *Impossible*. She had fought her way back to reality bit by agonizing bit. She had survived the horror of Alasdair Davidson's assault and Sorcha's death. Traveling back to the fifteenth century again should be a piece of cake in comparison.

She squared her shoulders resolutely. She would get back to her husband. She needed him. He needed her. Her eyes widened with another thought. She carefully massaged her abdomen, feeling its smooth curve. Was there a slight swelling? She had assumed that her cycle was screwed up because of all that she'd been through. But what if there was another explanation? Suddenly, the urge to reach Iain became almost unbearable. She saw him in her mind's eye, tall and strong. Her warrior. She could see the deep green of his eyes and feel the caress of his strong hands.

She opened the phone book and then, armed with the number of a transatlantic airline, dialed. She sent up a small prayer asking for quick service. It seemed someone had heard her—the operator answered on the first ring.

"Hello? . . . Yes, I need to book a flight to Scotland. . . . Right. As soon as possible." She listened as the woman rambled on about connections and departure times. She absently gave credit card information when it was requested and then told the operator she'd be paying cash. After a few minutes, the flight arranged satisfactorily, she hung up.

Dashing around her apartment, giddy with excitement, she started throwing things into her suitcase. Not sure of exactly what to take, or even if she could take it, she crammed pretty much everything she came across into her suitcase. Clothes, medicine, soaps and perfumes,

matches, toothpaste, shampoo, and even a tinsel-
wrapped box of Russell Stover chocolates she'd gotten
while in the hospital. Finally, satisfied that she had
everything she could possibly want, she closed her suitcase.

She picked up the phone to call Jeff, only to replace
the receiver without dialing. He'd only try to persuade
her to stay here. Maybe even take drastic measures and
have her committed or something. No, she couldn't tell
him. At least not until she was sure he couldn't stop her.
She picked up the oval frame by her bed, looking at the
picture it held. She and Jeff, together at his college graduation. The two St. Claires, out to take on the world.
She pushed the frame into a pocket of her suitcase. And
with tears in her eyes, sat down to write her brother a
letter . . . to say good-bye.

Chapter 27

"YOU SIMPLY CANNA go on like this. You dinna eat. You dinna sleep." Ranald shot a frustrated glance at his cousin.

Iain hoisted a large stone onto the wall they were working to shore up, then began tilting it to find the right fit. "I eat."

"No' enough that anyone would notice." Ranald put a hand on Iain's shoulder, forcing him to turn and face him. "Look, Iain, 'tis no' that I'm trying to get you to forget Katherine. I know you canna do that. I'm only asking that you come out of the dark place where you are and resume some form o' your life."

Iain grunted as he bent for another stone.

"God's blood, man, you're as stubborn as your father ever was," Ranald said while helping to steady the rock as Iain jimmied it into place.

Satisfied that the stone was properly situated, Iain dropped to the ground and leaned back against the wall, one knee bent, his hand resting on it. The autumn sun peeked out of the ever-present clouds, momentarily turning the landscape to gold, the gold of Katherine's hair.

Iain blinked, trying to pull his thoughts back to the present.

"I try, Ranald. But I see her everywhere. I hurt." He touched his chest. "Here." He continued to survey the countryside. The air was much colder now. In a fortnight or so the leaves would begin to change. Winter was coming.

Ranald sat beside his cousin, idly chewing on a brown blade of grass. "I dinna pretend to comprehend what you're going through. But I think you must accept the fact that she isna coming back. 'Tis almost a full season since she left."

"You're telling me naught I havena been telling myself. And still every night before I close my eyes and every morning at first light I go into that blasted chamber looking for her."

"Perhaps 'twould have been better if she hadna come at all." Ranald spoke the words hesitantly.

"Nay." Iain's answer was strong and steady. "A few days with Katherine was worth a lifetime with some other woman." With a groan, he pushed himself up. "Come now, I want to finish this wall before the day's end."

Ranald flicked the grass stalk away and rose to help his cousin.

Iain Mackintosh, Laird of Duncreag, stood on his battlement surveying his kingdom. Stars twinkled in the black velvet sky. The silvery moon illuminated the grounds of the tower, casting shifting patterns of shadows upon the earth.

He pulled the blanket closer around his body, finding comfort in its warmth, the rough fabric against his bare skin. He hadn't gone into the adjoining chamber tonight. He'd come up here instead. It was a small step, but an important one. Even now, though, the desire to check, to see if just maybe . . . He shook his head. He was a man, not a lovesick lad. Ranald was right. Now was indeed the time to let go, to move on.

Iain relaxed his tightly clenched fist, slowly opening his fingers. He looked at the little earrings glimmering in the pale light, then closed his eyes, remembering them lying discarded on the table by the bed. Even knowing that Jeff must have removed them from her ears, finding them there, like that, had felt like a betrayal. Without them surely she would not be able to return to him. His fingers closed around them again. He dropped the blanket, letting it fall to the stone floor. Standing naked on the parapet, he raised his hand over his shoulder, muscles contracting in preparation for throwing them over the wall and into the night, and thus forever severing the tie between them.

"Don't."

The single word seemed to ring through the night. Iain froze, his hand suspended above his shoulder, his heart racing at the sound of the beloved voice.

"Iain, those are my earrings and I'll thank you not to throw them over the wall."

He turned slowly, afraid to look, afraid not to look. The arm holding the earrings dropped to his side as he pivoted around. At first the shadows hid her, and seeing nothing he felt his heart plummet into his belly. But then a slight movement caught his eyes and his gaze shifted to a shadowed figure standing close to the tower wall.

With a slow, almost hesitant step, she moved into the moonlight. The moon silvered her hair. It was shorter than he remembered, flowing freely over her shoulders. She looked like an angel. He grimaced at the thought and found himself fervently offering a prayer that she was not.

She smiled then, the curve of her lips at once tender and shy. He took a step toward her, wanting only to touch her, to hold her, to feel for himself that she was real. His hand opened, the earrings dropping to the ground, forgotten.

"I'm . . ."

"You're . . ."

". . . home." They finished the last word together. And
with a soft tinkle of laughter, she catapulted herself into
his arms.

He breathed the sweet scent of her, glorying in the
feel of her body against his. He tightened his embrace,
lowering his head for a taste of her lips. Gently he traced
her mouth with his tongue. Then pulled his head back
to look into the soft gray of her eyes. The love he saw
there made him catch his breath. With shaking fingers,
he traced the curve of her cheek. She reached up to cover
his hand with hers, a smile playing at the corners of her
mouth as she looked deep into his eyes.

"I won't break." She moved his hand from her face
and with a slow graceful motion laid it on her breast,
never for a moment breaking eye contact. He felt her
nipple harden beneath his hand and his own body responding to the feel of her by tightening, hardening.

Katherine licked her lips, feeling the familiar heat begin to build deep inside her. She reveled in the strong,
smooth hardness of his naked body and rejoiced over
the fact that this man belonged to her. She looked into
the green pools of his eyes, seeing her love reflected and
returned in their crystal depths. She rubbed against his
hand, feeling his heat seep into her very soul, robbing
her of breath. With a trembling hand, she stroked the
rough hairs on his face, marveling at the texture of the
dark beard against her pale fingers. Sliding her hand upward, she entwined her fingers in the silky black strands
of his hair, her eyes lost in his. He was her entire world.
Slowly, ever so slowly, he bent his head to kiss her.

Iain tasted the sweet surrender in her kiss and felt
himself coming undone. The fire that he had so carefully
kept banked sprang into full flame, searing him with its
power. Drawing her closer, he gently massaged her
breast. She arched against him, a low moan slipping

from her lips. He captured it, feeling the movement of
her breath as she opened her mouth to him, tongues
meeting, exploring, remembering. He deepened the kiss,
drawing her into him, until it was hard to tell where one
of them began and the other ended.

Katherine ran her hand along the muscles of his back,
feeling his tightly leashed power. Urgency, spurred on
by the pain of their separation and the power of their
reunion, filled her. She leaned back against the steely
strength of his arms, feeling his lips move along the
smooth column of her throat. She called his name over
and over, unable to get enough of the feel of him, unable
to believe that at last they were together. She moaned
as his mouth found her breast, the heat of his tongue
finding her even through the material of her blouse. He
reached to pull her up into his arms, but with a touch of
her hand she motioned him to stop.

"No, I want you here. Now."

Smiling at her, his teeth a ghostly white in the black
of his beard, Iain reached for the blanket he had discarded earlier. She took his hand and drew him down
with her. Kneeling, they faced each other, their eyes doing what their hands longed to. He touched the cool silk
of her blouse, his fingers halting in confusion when they
reached the strange fastenings holding it closed.

Laughing, Katherine slowly pulled each button free,
allowing the material to fall open and reveal the creamy
satin of her breasts. Sucking in a breath, Iain bent to
taste her, his lips closing gently around her nipple. Pushing her blouse from her body, he ran his hand along her
rib cage, caressing her skin with the warmth of his hard,
callused fingers. She threw back her head, offering herself and delighting in the feel of his mouth as it greedily
devoured first one breast and then the other.

With fumbling hands, they worked together to remove
the last of her clothing, both anxious to feel the heat of
their bodies pressed together. Naked at last, she lay back

on the blanket, her glorious hair a glimmer of gold in the moonlight. Iain caught his breath as the full power of his love for this woman crested inside him. Carefully, bracing his weight on his elbows, he lowered himself to her. Their lips met and the heat inside him spiraled upward, its curling warmth threatening to blow him apart. His hand slid up her thigh until it rested at the apex of her desire. With one long finger, he parted the satiny folds and pushed deep into the hot pulsing heart of her. She writhed beneath him, her tongue pushing into his mouth, mimicking the rhythm of his finger. With hot wet kisses, he moved from her mouth, trailing down her shoulder. He paused for a taste of her breasts, laving each nipple until it stretched tight, pressing hard against his tongue.

Katherine felt his lips leave her breasts and move lower, his tongue exploring the depth of her belly button. She cried out when he removed his fingers, leaving her empty and hungry for more. His lips moved farther down, his kisses teasing her, his hands gently pushing her legs apart. She felt the whisper of his beard against the delicate skin of her inner thighs. Then suddenly, she arched against him as his tongue unerringly dipped into the sweet soft center of her. She was on fire, her body melting with the heat of it. Her hips began to undulate against him as he consumed her. Her hands reached down, tangling in his hair, begging him for more. Her head rocked back and forth, her eyes closed as ecstasy surrounded her, lifting her up to unimaginable heights. With one last flick and thrust, she felt her body come apart.

Iain felt her spasms begin and heard her cry his name. His tasting of her had built his own desires to a fever pitch, and he pulled himself up until he was poised over her. She opened her eyes and parted her lips in a slow sensuous smile, opening her legs in silent invitation. Eyes locked with hers, he caught her lips with his and entered her with one smooth stroke. The feel of her sheath tightening around him almost sent him over the edge. Trying to hold on to his control, he slowly began moving inside her. Still not breaking eye contact, he lowered his body. He felt her begin to rock against him, her body dancing with his, offering him everything. Accepting her gift, he lifted her hips and plunged deeper, losing himself in the heat of her. Locked in a rhythm of building passion, he met her unwavering gaze, willing her to feel how much he loved her. How much he needed her. With a quivering whimper, she arched against him, her eyes closing as she surrendered to her release. The sight of her face, radiating the joy of her climax, was all that he needed. Closing his own eyes, his body moving deeply into hers, he exploded with sensation and, reaching for her hand, allowed the fire to consume him.

Gently, as though falling through cotton, Katherine came back to earth. She felt the steady thump of Iain's heart against her skin and nestled closer into the warmth of him, her breathing lifting the long black hair falling onto her shoulders. With a groan, he rolled over, pulling her with him so that she lay cradled on top of him.

"Welcome home, lass. I swear, one day you'll no doubt be the death of me. I wasna certain you were coming back."

His voice was light, but Katherine could see the shadow of pain in his eyes. She smiled as she smoothed his hair back from his face. There would be time for explanations later, but not now. Now, she wanted nothing more than to be with him, to let him know how very much she loved him.

"I could never leave you, not of my own free will. You should have known I'd find my way back to you."

"But you didna have the earrings."

"I didn't need them. All I needed was my love for you."

"Aye. And my love for you."

Katherine rejoiced both at his words and at the hard evidence of his desire pressed against her. His arms tightened around her and his lips found hers. She opened her mouth to his, breathing in his essence, capturing his soul.

The stars were fading when Katherine opened her eyes. The air was crisp, bordering on downright cold. She glanced at Iain. His eyes were closed, his arm thrown over her possessively, even in sleep. She smiled and, shifting slightly, reached to pull the blanket more snugly around them.

"Ouch." Katherine frowned, shifting uncomfortably as something sharp dug into her hip. Iain sprang to his feet, awake in an instant.

"What is it? Are you all right?"

Katherine smiled at her warrior husband. "I'm fine. Something just poked me from under the blanket."

Iain relaxed immediately. With a mischievous grin, he bowed from the waist. "Allow me to assist you, my love." With exaggerated caution, he lifted the corner of the blanket while motioning Katherine to move away. Trying to control her laughter, she scooted to the opposite edge as he explored the area where she had been sleeping. With a flourish of triumph, he rose, offering Katherine the offending object on the palm of his hand.

" 'Tis only your jewel, my Lady."

Still stifling giggles, Katherine peered into his hand, her throat tightening at the sight of the cairngorm earring.

Handing it to her, he began to search for its mate. "It seems that upon seeing you, I completely forgot about the earrings."

Katherine turned the stone in her hand, wondering if it truly had played a part in bringing them together.

"I must have dropped them when I felt other things rising." He located the other one and dropped down beside her, a lustful grin lighting his handsome face. "Will you wear them?"

"No." Katherine surprised herself as well as Iain with the strength of her answer. She dipped her head, embarrassed. "What I mean is that I won't wear both of them. I'll feel better if you have one and I have the other." She bit her lip and raised her eyes to Iain's.

"I understand, *mo chridhe*." He looped the earring through his ear. The smoky stone swung jauntily from his lobe. " 'Tis a symbol of our love."

She smiled at him, fastening her own earring, grateful for his understanding. He reached out to touch hers, his finger trailing down her neck, and coming to rest on her shoulder.

"Perhaps someday we can give them to our daughter," he said quietly.

Again, Katherine saw a brief shadow of pain flicker across his eyes, and wondered at its cause. Involuntarily her hand went to her abdomen. It was still flat, but somehow, suddenly, she felt sure that what she had suspected in New York was true.

"Would you like to be a father then?"

"If you are the mother, I can think of no greater honor."

Katherine reached out to take his hand, then placed it on her stomach. "Well, I can't be sure, of course, but I think you might be a father before the winter is out." She scanned his face, searching for a sign that the news truly pleased him.

His large hand almost covered her belly. He stroked it in awe, the smile on his face radiating his joy. She felt her own happiness welling up inside, and her eyes filled with tears. After everything that had happened, she was finally where she belonged.

Iain gathered her to him, wrapping them both in the blanket. "I predict 'twill be a lass. And I think we should call her Anna."

"And if it's a boy?"

Iain rested his chin on the top of her head. "It willna be. I have it on good authority."

Katherine opened her mouth to question him and then closed it, her mind jumping quickly to her own answer. *Jeff.*

Iain must have felt the movement, because his arms tightened around her. "And if we have a wee lad, after our Anna, I think we should name him Jeffrey."

Katherine leaned back against the solid warmth of her husband and together they watched the sun rise, spreading its golden rays across Duncreag.

Epilogue

ELAINE MACQUEEN ST. CLAIRE Mackintosh, lady of the manor and wife of the thirtieth Laird of Duncreag, sat back on her heels examining the ancient rosebush she had just transplanted. Patting the soil at its base, she smiled lovingly at it.

"There, my wee one, that ought to hold you in good stead for another hundred years or so."

Pushing a wayward curl behind her ear, she rose, brushing the dirt from her jeans. Removing her gloves, she stepped back to admire the view. The newly planted rosebush stretched its gnarled canes up toward Duncreag. The tower stood majestic against the azure of the spring sky. It gleamed white in the sunlight, its full former glory reflected in its painstaking restoration. Elaine felt a swell of pride at the magnificent sight of the place she called home.

"Mama, Mama, where are you?"

Elaine held a hand to her eyes, smiling as she watched her two young sons running full tilt into the garden. Behind them came her daughter, her tiny legs pumping with the effort to keep up with her older brothers.

"There you are. We have something to show you." Andrew grabbed her hand, tugging on it, trying to pull her toward the tower.

"It's really cool, Mom. You've got to come. We waited to open it until we could do it with you and Dad." Ethan was almost dancing with enthusiasm, which said a lot considering he was almost twelve and currently into acting cool.

Elaine smiled at her oldest son. "What is it you've found?" Her mother's eye sought out her daughter while listening to her sons. She saw a tiny figure helping Mr. Abernathy plant some beans. Satisfied her smallest was safe for the time being, she returned her undivided attention to her sons.

"We're not telling. Right, Ethan?" Andy looked at his older brother for confirmation.

"Right. You'll just have to come see for yourself."

Laughing, Elaine bent to pick up her trowel. "All right, I'll come. Just let me put away my gardening tools."

Already halfway out of the garden, the boys turned to yell back at her. "We'll go and get Dad. Meet us in the great hall." Then they dashed away, with her daughter hot in pursuit again. She sighed, marveling at their energy.

"Well, Jamie, I guess I'm calling it a day." She walked over to Mr. Abernathy, watching as he efficiently planted the beans. She thought, not for the first time, how lucky they were to have him and Agnes to watch over them. She gathered a few more tools and walked toward the small shed against the wall. "Are you coming to see this mysterious unveiling?"

His eyes twinkling with delight, he leaned on his shovel. "Wouldn't miss it for the world. I'll just finish this row and then I'll be in."

Elaine nodded at him and set off across the garden. She rounded the corner and started up the steps leading to the front door, then paused at the top of the stairs, absently stroking the silver cat she wore pinned to her shirt and looking out across the lands of Duncreag. It was a wild and beautiful place. She never ceased to be grateful that it was theirs.

Walking into the great hall, she laid her gloves on an entry table and crossed over to the leather sofa in front of the fireplace. The children were gathered around something on the coffee table. Elaine sank onto the sofa, glad to be off her feet.

"Can I see it yet?"

The boys chimed the word "no" almost together. "We have to wait for Dad and the Abernathys."

As if on cue, Agnes Abernathy appeared, the perfect picture of a Scottish lady in her plaid skirt and sensible shoes. Her merry eyes danced as she came to sit beside Elaine.

"So it's a mystery we're to be seeing, is it?"

Elaine gave her an answering smile, then turned as her husband appeared in the doorway of his study. He stretched, his white shirt pulling tight across the broad expanse of his shoulders. She felt her body warm at the sight of him. After three children, he still had the power to make her heart skip a beat.

"Hello, darling. Did you finish the new plans?"

Jeff pushed a hand through his already rumpled hair. "Almost. I stopped for the moment to see what my mischievous offspring have unearthed."

At the sound of his voice, Andy ran to him and pulled him closer to the table. Sitting on the other side of Elaine, he dropped an arm around her shoulder. "So, tell us, what is it you've found?"

"Not yet, Mr. Abernathy isn't here. We want this to happen with the whole family present."

"I'm here, lad, I'm here. So let's get on with the unveiling."

Mr. Abernathy perched on the arm of the sofa nearest his wife.

With exaggerated movements, the boys raised a cloth-covered object and then, sure that they held everyone's undivided attention, jerked the cloth away.

"Ta-da! We found it in the wall of the fireplace upstairs."

Rushing over his brother's words in his excitement, Ethan added, "Yeah, there was a loose stone and we pried it out. Just like you did when you were a kid, Dad."

Elaine reached for Jeff's hand and leaned forward to better see what the boys held. It was a wooden box banded with gold. She recognized the Mackintosh crest on the top.

"Here, Mom, you do the honors." Ethan held the box out to her.

Exchanging a look with Jeff, she took the box, her hands shaking a little. Almost with a will of their own, her fingers turned the box so that she could examine the bottom. It was smooth and unmarked. Frowning, she turned it back so that the crest faced up.

"Come on, Mom, open it." Andy danced frantically in front of her, anxious to see what was inside.

"It may be empty, boys, so don't be disappointed," Jeff cautioned. He leaned over Elaine's arm, as excited as the boys to see what was inside.

"I'm sure there will be a treasure. Why else would it have been hidden behind the stone in the fireplace?" Mrs. Abernathy said, smiling reassuringly at the boys and then turning her attention back to the box in Elaine's hands.

Carefully, Elaine opened it. Inside was a small piece of brocade fabric wrapped around something. She lifted it out and slowly drew back the edges. Nestled inside were two small earrings, their smoky stones twinkling in the lamplight.

"The cairngorms." Elaine barely breathed the words as she lifted the earrings for everyone to see.

"Treasure," whispered Andrew.

"Aw, it's just jewelry," said Ethan, his nose wrinkling in boyish disgust.

"Pretty. Pretty." Jeff's small daughter reached out with a cautious finger to touch the stones dangling from her mother's fingers. "Whose earrings are they, Papa?"

Jeff's eyes met Elaine's, and they exchanged a smile.

"Why, Kitty, I believe when you're old enough they should belong to you."

Mrs. Abernathy leaned back against her husband's arm, a satisfied smile playing at the corners of her mouth as she watched the Mackintosh family.

"Everything in its time, I always say. Everything in its time."

TIME PASSAGES